Phase Walker

LYNNE GRYPHON

First published 2014

Gryphon Technology Pty Ltd
P.O. Box 1615, Macquarie Centre
NSW 2113 Australia

1st Edition

Copyright © 2014 Lynne Gryphon

www.lynnegryphon.com

ISBN: 1-5005-6899-6
ISBN-13: 978-1-5005-6899-3

Chapter 1

The Awakening

A huge sign hung above the door, 'The Brisbane Chocolate Coffee House'. The smell of chocolate and roasted coffee hung in the air, as a small queue formed for the mid-morning rush. The coffee shop was small but still had several sets of tables and chairs. Lots of young people from the local university sat chatting and drinking coffee on the chilly morning.

A young woman with a name badge printed in gold labelled 'Sarah' poured coffee from a machine. She had long blond hair and a slight tan, which was common in Brisbane. As she placed three hot coffees onto a tray, the casual observer would think that she wore a pretty ring on her index finger, but on closer inspection it would be revealed as a strange tattoo of small symbols in blue that only looked like a ring.

Sarah reached over then took her order pad and placed it in her black apron pocket. She then took the tray of coffees she was preparing over to a rowdy table. This was unusual for this time in the morning, as university classes should have been already in progress.

As she approached a friendly familiar smile beamed in her direction, an attractive man with short brown hair looked through his blue eyes and said, "Miss Sarah can you settle a debate, who should be doing home improvements, professionals or amateurs such as Jason here?"

Jason, a really tall attractive young man with an elfish look about him and darker brown hair, looked up then held his hands up, "Hey William watch who you are calling amateur, I'll have you know I helped my father on a lot of renovations so I know what I am doing."

Sarah placed three coffees on the table, the first in front of a beautiful dark haired girl she knew from her business studies night class, her name was Madison. Madison flicked her dark hair and picked up the coffee then spoke in a matter of fact tone, "Jason you have the money to hire people. Why do you insist on fixing up the apartment yourself? Not to mention the extra time it's going to take out of your studying."

William's jaw was square and there was stubble on his chin which he was rubbing while a boyish grin was on his face, knowing Madison could also see Jason's self-renovations as a time wasting exercise. Sarah leaned over William with a coffee in hand. William, sitting back, was taking in her curvaceous body and tiny waist; he then crossed his large muscled arms.

Sarah then reached over and placed the final coffee onto the table and sighed, wishing she was also sitting at the table and not being the one serving.

She pulled out her notepad and tallied up three coffees, mentally working out the price to be eleven dollars and eleven cents. She ripped off the paper bill and placed it on the table, uncertain if she wrote the right amount – it felt strange. She smiled, her green eyes bright, then looked up and said, "If you can afford the renovations I would outsource it myself if I could," then walked back to the coffee machine thinking how she never noticed three coffees equals one, one, one, one, how odd.

Belinda, an older lady with red flowing hair, was taking orders at the cash register and the order slips were backing up. Sarah picked up an order slip; it had eleven hot chocolates written on it. A tingling sensation was going through her body. She placed both her hands on her knee's to steady herself then stood on tippy toe looking over the top of the coffee machine. To her shock and surprise eleven primary school children sat at three tables pushed together. She then glanced over to William, who was staring back; it was awkward so she hid behind the coffee machine. Sarah's hands started to shake as she counted out eleven chocolate mugs. She then turned the knob on the coffee machine to the chocolate setting it was instinct for her because she had done it a million times, but today she decided to look down and study the dial. There were numbers one to twelve, the dial was set to eleven.

Belinda served the last customer in the queue and looked over at Sarah who was supposed to be making up the orders. Except she wasn't – Sarah was visibly shaking and staring at the coffee machine like it was a venomous snake about to strike.

Belinda moved over to Sarah, "Are you okay?"

Sarah looked up, her face looked upset but still attractive, "I think I better go home, I really don't feel well today I think I'm coming down with something."

Belinda seeing her shake nodded in agreement, "Go home Sarah I will cover this shift, get some rest and ring me tomorrow."

Sarah took off her black apron and placed it on the bench; Belinda jumped in front of the coffee machine and started to prepare the hot chocolates.

Sarah was wearing a black pencil skirt and a black polo shirt with the Chocolate Coffee House logo embroidered in red neatly above the pocket. To head to the exit she had to pass William's table. Sarah pondered a strategy to walk out without William noticing and came up blank, still shaking defeated she put her head down embarrassed and walked quickly past William's table to the glass door exit, her face glowed red but once outside she headed to her bus stop.

William caught sight of her leaving past his table in a rush, stood and said, "I'll go see what happened."

Madison replied sounding jealous, "Why would you chase

after the coffee girl, William," then sipped her coffee.

Jason grinned and replied, "Go, don't listen to Maddy, that girl is hot."

Madison rolled her eyes and picked up a sugar stick from the centre table.

William rushed to the glass door and then followed Sarah, who was walking in a straight line to the bus stop.

Sarah felt really unwell and was watching the taxies on the street drive by as she walked to the bus stop thinking they might be quicker to get home. She spotted one with the light off, meaning it was unoccupied, then cringed as a wave of tingling washed through her body – her eyes scanned the taxi ID number, one, one, one, one. She looked like she was going to faint. William started to run from behind and arrived just in time to catch her as she swayed.

Sarah looked relieved that she hadn't fallen to the ground, then shocked that William was holding her. "I'm sorry; I don't feel well I need to go home and get some rest."

William, actually looking worried, then said, "I'll take you home, my car's actually just around the corner."

Sarah, really unwell, agreed with a nod as she couldn't imagine sitting on the bus and getting jerked around every time it stopped and she really did not want to take an expensive taxi. Sarah smiled weakly and for some reason started to rub her tattoo around her finger. She stood on her own, leaning away from William and crossed her arms, just because it made her feel right.

William smiled and pulled some keys from his pocket, "It's this way, not far."

Sarah walked close beside him and followed around the corner. They walked past several parked cars along the street. William pressed the button on his keys and a shiny silver sports car's lights flicked on and made a beep.

Sarah didn't think much of cars so didn't recognise its brand, but a little horse on a shield was on the bonnet. She got in then thought, embarrassed, her apartment was not clean – last she remembered there were books scattered across her dining table.

The car had the new car smell, the seats were leather and the dash had an impressive array of gadgets and lights. William got in and said, "Ok, where to?"

Sarah, while clicking her seat belt on, said, "Unit eleven, eleven Clearview way," cringing as she even thought of her own address with ones.

William tapped the address into his GPS and started the car.

Sarah was still feeling what can only be described as tingling. She looked over to William, his strong tanned arms reaching down to the gear box and wheel, "Thanks so much for helping me out like this, I don't randomly get into anyone's car you know."

William smiled "I know, because I'm not anyone."

Cheeky bugger, Sarah thought, as she felt like her breakfast was going to come up.

It was a short drive before William's GPS announced 'destination complete'. He pulled up to a row of tall apartment blocks, one of which was Sarah's, Sarah had a one bedroom apartment – it wasn't far to the university and this street was popular for students.

William got out of his car and opened Sarah's car door. Sarah took her seat belt off and got out. William offered his hand, but Sarah felt awkward and smiled then stepped out herself and swiftly crossed her arms. William walked with Sarah to the foyer of her building.

Sarah then stopped and looked William in the eye, he looked genuinely concerned, "Thank you for the ride home, I'm really not feeling well."

Nervous she grabbed her long blond hair and twirled it into a pony tail then released it.

William took out a card from his wallet and gave it to Sarah and said, "This in my number, phone me to let me know when you're better."

He smiled and waved, then walked out of the foyer towards his car.

Sarah looked at the card, it read 'William Remiel, Entrepreneur'. She then went on to look at the phone number it ended with one, one, one, one. No surprise this time, she expected the new number torment as it tingled down her body after reading the last one. She then went up to the lift and pressed the button to her apartment on the fourth floor.

She opened the door to her apartment, it was a mess but she was tired and felt funny inside from the prolonged tingling feeling. She walked to her bedroom which was surprisingly well kept and tidy. There was a double bed with one side against the wall. Her bed covers were brightly coloured, there was a side table with a digital alarm clock on top, a closed window on the other wall and a dressing table with neatly placed girly figurines.

Sarah rolled onto her bed fully dressed – she couldn't even be bothered to take off her shoes. She looked over to the digital alarm clock; it read eleven, eleven she rolled over to the wall closing her eyes. She felt like something was pushing her toward the wall; annoyed by the feeling she rolled closer her knee and arm now touching the wall. The tingling in her body felt more intense and stronger than before. She opened her eyes as she rolled straight through the wall. She fell, but not very far and landed with a thud.

The tingling stopped. Sarah stood up and looked around, this was not her bedroom.

The area had a low lying mist and smelt like burnt coal, and she was warm. She was standing on a hill made out of large grey boulders. Looking down the small hill she could see a dry ravine. On the other side of the ravine she could see what looked like a flat concrete platform that led off to what looked like a concrete structure; the mists were thicker and darker in that direction.

Disbelieving it was real and thinking it was only a dream, Sarah decided to explore. She stepped down the grey hill it was misty and she could not see her steps, she accidentally missed her footing, she fell a little and scrapped her knee. This was not like any dream she had had before. The thought scared her and her heart started to pound. Walking further down the rocky grey ravine, she saw no movement, however the occasional shimmer of heat coming off the rocks drew her eye. The boulders gave off dark shadows but there was no clear sun to cast them.

She continued through the ravine to the other side. There she could make out a dark figure through the mist. An intense feeling of fear and dread filled Sarah. The air was still but her hair whipped about her face without wind. The figure was tall and had unusually large feet. The closer she got to the figure the more defined details she could see.

The dark figure had what looked like a long tail, which shocked Sarah as she watched it move. Getting closer she could see hooved black feet. The skin of the creature was dark blue, and it had white horns and a snarl on its face. It was standing side on, so she could only see one arm, which looked every bit human except blue. The creature did not seem to notice her and stared off at a different direction. Her adrenaline started to pump as primal fear kick in, but still she was drawn to the figure, further up the ravine she went until she stepped onto the platform. It wasn't concrete but one huge piece of flat stone. The figure, now noticing Sarah, turned to face her; in its other hand, that was previously hidden, was grasped a flaming sword. It stepped in her direction. The sword was black and on fire it had a decorative hilt of skulls and bones.

Sarah felt that the creature radiated evil as it got closer; if she felt fear before it was nothing compared to the utter darkness of dread she was feeling now. She held her hand to her face to flick the hair from her eyes and noticed her finger tattoo glowing. She stared at her tattoo; the creature scraped its hooves on the stone ground, its face every bit human, except the horns and glowing blue eyes. She noticed it wore thick leather pieces of armour.

It walked in her direction, closing the distance to Sarah, then stopped in a thicker part of the mist. It raised its sword in a threatening manner.

Instinct took hold of Sarah and she raised her hand, and to her surprise a sword materialised. The sword had two winged creatures on the hilt and a blue gem embedded on one side. The sword was a silver metal colour and it made a low level hum, like a vibration.

Sarah at that moment thought, fuck it, it's my dream it seems, and then rushed forward swinging the sword at the creature. Its blue glowing eyes went wide in shock. As sword hit sword, a clanging could be heard. Her sword always humming, it was odd but reassuring.

Sarah thought shit that was easy, and felt very confident that her purpose in this dream was to defeat the monster, the creature that snarled in front of her at that very moment. So she did what any hero would do, she jumped right back in and tried to defeat the creature.

It spoke a guttural language, deep and husky. It snarled again and rushed forward, knocking Sarah down the ravine.

Sarah felt the fall and scraping of her legs hitting the boulders. The creature stood at the edge of the platform looking down the ravine. Sarah felt not fear but pissed off. She stood up again and rushed forward.

The creature baiting, waved its sword. She wacked and thwacked, her sword always humming after each clank and the creature not receiving any wound but stepping back into the structure.

Sarah fought as it took several steps back.

It's baiting me to move inside the structure, perhaps another waits inside for me so I better not follow, she thought.

It came out again trying to bait her back. Sarah decided to retreat so she went back down the bolder ravine up the hill with the sword and then she was wide awake in her room in bed lying down. She did not recall an awaking, just the battle, then passing through the wall, then here on her bed. She stared at the wall and touched it. The wall was warm. She checked the time, it was eleven, eleven impossible she thought, then pulled the covers up and slowly went to sleep.

- Chapter 2 -

Wuzzle

Sarah opened her eyes. She lay in bed but her legs hurt; she poked them out of bed and felt her legs with a hand along her jeans, "ouch," there were bruises all along to her knees. She was still wearing her shoes and grey dust was caked on the bottom of them to her ankles. Sarah felt like crap and looked at the alarm clock, good I have time to get dressed for work, she thought, then went and had a shower.

Sarah took off her shoes before getting into the shower, watching the grey dust crumble to the ground. She jumped into the shower and began to think as the warm waters washed away dirt. She started to plot the events of yesterday through her head and was not convinced it was a dream, looking down once more at the bruises on her knees. She no longer felt tingles or sick so got dressed and headed for work.

The morning routine at the Coffee House was plain and boring; she no longer saw ones, and strangely enough three cups of coffee added up to eleven dollars and ten cents. Belinda badgered her about looking a lot better. It was around lunch time that William came in alone, without his entourage. He smiled at Sarah as she severed tea and cakes to another table.

William sat at a table with his laptop and started tapping keys; he paused to place several university text books out of his bag onto the table.

Sarah walked up to William, "Thank you for the ride

yesterday, I really wasn't feeling myself."

William looked up from the computer screen, "You're welcome, I didn't get a call so I thought you were still sick."

Sarah blushed and the tingling returned, "So sorry, I meant to phone, got caught up in the morning routine, I have uni tonight and an assignment as well, how are your studies going?"

William turned his laptop around and a word document popped up. Sarah looked at the screen and the time read eleven, eleven, the tingling started again, but she didn't feel sick. Perhaps she was getting used to the sensation.

Sarah spoke "Your laptop has the wrong time set."

"Oh daylight savings in Sydney, I like to keep it in sync as father is working there at the moment, so I guess its ten eleven in Brisbane," William said.

Sarah smiled relieved, but still feeling the tingling sensation, "What can I get for you then, William Remiel?"

William smiles, his blue eyes lighting up at his full name being spoken, "Oh, so you did read my card, then good – means you were thinking of me. I'll have the pancakes with a side of Sarah."

Sarah looked up and laughed, "Might I suggest ice cream?"

William smirked and was leaning back in his chair, "Sounds good to me."

Sarah wrote on her order note pad, and walked into the kitchen. Belinda was there, trying to tie the rubbish up while talking on the phone. Sarah placed the order on the kitchen board and then shooed Belinda out while taking the rubbish.

The kitchen was small and tidy and James was on kitchen duty. He clanged the pots and took the order off the board. Sarah dragged the rubbish out of the kitchen, paused to stop and opened the back door, then started dragging it down a few stairs.

It happened – she felt tingling again, it was very strong; she looked around and glanced at her finger tattoo, the one she'd had since birth. She was told it was a birthmark but it always looked more like a tattoo to her. The symbols started to glow. Then she saw movement over at the huge metal box, the kitchen skip, used to dump the rubbish from the cafe.

A large bear-like creature was throwing trash into the air and eating old leftovers from within the skip. The creature was brown and covered in fur, it had large eyes and did not even notice Sarah – or chose to ignore her. It stood on its hind legs, very tall, probably about seven foot she guessed, and had a small little tail; it looked hungry. Strangely enough Sarah did not feel fear, like the blue creature she had encountered the previous day, more a sense of curiosity, so she didn't scream or even move, she just merely watched for some time, even laughing when the bear creature found an old milk carton, lifted it and poured old smelly milk all over its face.

She felt the tingling even stronger and then the back wall behind the skip glowed momentarily and a little girl came through what looked like a crack. The glowing stopped then closed behind her. She had lovely long brown hair and beautiful green blue eyes. She wore a pretty light pink dress and had matching ribbons in her hair. Sarah thought she looked like one of those little pageant girls, then panicked because she thought the large bear might think the girl was food.

Sarah dropped her rubbish bag and came rushing down the stairs screaming, "Little girl, stop, don't move, there is a bear!"

The bear did not turn to the small child but to Sarah, it bared its long fangs and hundreds of long thin teeth.

"Fuck!" Sarah screamed.

The little girl spoke "Wuzzle, calm down, we have phase company."

The giant fanged bear did not back away but merely closed it mouth.

The little girl spoke again, "Hello, I am Miss Caitlin, nice to meet you; we just came for a snack for Wuzzle."

She waved at Wuzzle and the giant toothed bear returned

to the skip and started to eat rubbish.

Caitlin, who looked to be a child of seven or eight, beamed a smile, "What's your name?"

Sarah bent down to the little girl and looked her in the eyes, "I'm Sarah. Where are your parents?"

Caitlin giggled turned her back and walked to the skip, Wuzzle let out a huge burp. Caitlin giggled again and Wuzzle picked Caitlin up and put her on his back. Wuzzle walked on two legs to the phase that was opening on the wall. Caitlin waved her hand from seven feet in the air, perched on Wuzzle's shoulder like a bird.

She flashed a little impish grin, "See you soon, fellow Phase Walker."

Wuzzle walked through the phase and it closed shut.

Sarah stood in the back alley for some time before she collected her thoughts, her finger tattoo was no longer glowing and the tingling sensation was gone. She picked up the trash on the step then threw it into the skip and ran back up the stairs into the kitchen to check out William's pancakes.

James had finished flipping the pancakes and was actually just sifting icing sugar on top.

Sarah swung by, grabbed the plate and said, "Thanks James."

She walked straight to William's table and placed the pancakes down. When she leaned over she caught a smell of William's heavy cologne.

William beamed a smile, "Well isn't this lovely and I'm not talking about the pancakes."

Sarah actually blushed, "So what are you working on?"

William spooned a piece of pancake into his mouth, "A business plan actually."

Sarah, surprised, then asked, "Do you like the pancakes?"

William looked up admiring Sarah's body, "Lovely, totally lovely."

Belinda spoke up, "Sarah I need you."

Sarah walked briskly back to the coffee machine and started to fill orders. Occasionally she would glance at

William and then her watch. As much as she would have liked too, she was not planning on spending time with William today but was planning on going back down the alley to look around to see if she missed anything and to steady her sanity; only thirty more minutes till her afternoon tea break.

Finally it was time for Sarah's break – she poured herself a take away coffee with the extra kick she liked, then holding the plastic coffee cup, headed back through the kitchen, stopping only to wave at James who was busy stirring something in a pot, then opened the door back out to the alley.

Slowly Sarah stepped down the stairs and toward the skip. It stunk like vomit and every vile flavour mixed up, then she looked down and noticed it, a humongous pile of Wuzzle dung. Eww, is all that Sarah could think of.

Sarah then felt a tingling and a pull toward the wall behind the skip, she looked down at her finger that was glowing as she held the plastic coffee cup which was warm, then she watched the wall as a glowing phase opened up. Sarah stepped backwards expecting something to come through but it didn't, so she waited for some time watching the glowing phase; eventually curiosity got the better of her so she stepped through herself.

Sarah, passing through the glowing phase, was starting to get used to the tingling that was occurring in her body; if she concentrated she could control the feeling, and concentrating, was what she was doing.

On the other side of the phase Sarah looked around and saw she was in a green forest. It was thick and dense, filled with vegetation, odd looking because every tree or plant ended in a curl. She turned to see where she had emerged from and behind her was a very thick trunk of a tree with markings carved in unusual patterns. There was a heavy flowery smell in the air. Sarah then sipped her coffee, it was reassuring and gave her a buzz.

The forest had a little trail that led off in one direction, it was warm and the air felt thick and humid. Sarah was thinking she didn't want to venture too far as she was on her break from work, then she started down the trail. Her senses were heightened and every little sound startled Sarah – a bizarre purple bug running along a curled leaf making a skittering noise; the crunch of her own steps on the ground as she walked through broken leaves; even the rumbling of her own belly made her jump.

Gawking at every leaf and every plant Sarah pressed on down the trail. She could hear the sound of running water and splashes. As she got closer she could hear a hum, it was familiar to her, then she could hear scrapes and more splashes. Walking further down the trail she could see a clearing and small pond of water. Then off to the side of the pond a strange large mound shaped building. The building was brown; looked made of mud and covered in green moss and it had a largish wooden door. Sarah took another sip of her coffee, warm and refreshing; nope, not dreaming, Sarah thought.

Off in the distance next to the pond she could see Wuzzle with a tiny dot she assumed was Caitlin on its shoulder, and a purple creature, larger even than Wuzzle.

Wuzzle threw something at the large purple creature, then to her surprise a man sized creature leaped out of the still pond and squirted a jet of water also at the creature and dove back into the still pond with a splash.

Sarah sensed Wuzzle and Caitlin were in trouble so she pushed forward towards what was looking like a fight. It was some distance, so she started jogging along beside the pond. The pond had strange insects buzzing in circles around lily like flowers that bobbed and floated.

She made it to the large mound structure and stopped to catch her breath. She could see a small wooden table and chairs outside and a cooking fire with strange meat roasting on a rack, its smell was sickly sweet. She gulped down the last of her coffee and placed her plastic coffee cup on the table. She looked down at her tattoo, it was glowing again; she wondered what made it do that.

She looked up and could make out what was going on in more detail now; Caitlin was off Wuzzle standing beside him and throwing a silvery boomerang at the purple creature. It looked just like the demoniac monster that she battled earlier except purple and meaner. It had black hooved feet, purple skin and wore decadent silvery armour. It had a shield and a large jagged sword made from a coppery material. Intense feelings of fear overcame Sarah again, dread and loathing pressing heavily upon her. She pressed forward wishing she had a weapon again; she held that thought and the same weapon as last time materialised in her right hand.

It gave a familiar hum in her hand. It was not heavy and felt well balanced. With each step she took she studied the purple demon.

Its horns were longer than the other and black.

Its eyes glowed yellow and oddly enough its human-like features may have been considered attractive.

She was close enough to identify it as male, he had black long hair to his waist that was tired up in several silvery skull clamps which formed a warrior's hair tail.

His arms were muscled and toned and his body was also attractive, like a buff beach babe.

Too bad about the whole evil thing Sarah thought as it projected fear at her, then sighed as she rushed the final distance forward.

She gasped as the strange water creature surfaced again; the humanoid appeared a man when looking at its face and arms but had a fish's tail and jet black skin that shimmered from the reflection off the water. It smiled at seeing Sarah and squirted a jet of strong water at the purple demon.

As soon as Sarah was close the demon spoke a guttural language of harsh sounding tones and dropped its sword. It raised its arm up into the air and symbols glowed along its purple skin. Then darkness fell down, completely engulfing the entire area like a curtain had been let down. The only things to be seen were those that were glowing: Caitlin's boomerang, Sarah's sword and the demon's tattoos all over its body.

A wave of dread and loathing washed over Sarah. She heard the demon scrape its hoofs on the grass and dirt, she saw the glowing tattoos lunge at the ground where Caitlin's boomerang was. The tattooed claw grabbed something near the ground and jerked it into the air; the glowing boomerang followed. Caitlin screamed as she dangled upside down with the boomerang in her hand.

Wuzzle made a primal howl and a large snarling form lunged for the demon in rage, obscuring the tattooed form. At that moment Sarah knew what had to be done; she also jumped forward towards the demon with her sword held over head.

Wuzzle then did something unpredictable – the large bear's silhouette disappeared only to land with a thud on top of the demon, with sheer body weight as its weapon. The boomerang dropped to the ground and rolled free. There was a splash as the water creature leaped up to see what happened and not being able to see through the darkness drove down into the water again. Then Sarah, with the demon momentarily pinned down in the darkness, glowing, smashed her sword down on its neck, slicing its head off with a single stroke. The demon's tattooed head bounced with the force of the sword and rolled. The demons tattoos stopped glowing, as did the boomerang and sword. It went completely dark.

- Chapter 3 -

Plastic Coffee Cup

Gas shot up into the air between two rocky crops and then settled as mist that lay low over the boulders. The air was strangely warm and thick outside, even though no visible sun could be seen. There were no trees or vegetation outside, only stone and rock covered in mist. No life or movement was around because for that you had to go underground. This was the plane of Nevid where the race known as Delvin ruled.

The Delvin were a mystical warrior race that controlled the magic of flame and fire. They had been corrupted by chaos magic centuries ago on a grand scale affecting the entire population in their vain quest to terraform their plane. The people of Delvin were once humanoid, but their refined features were now dark and demonic, twisted by chaos. Their flesh turned many colours their feet turned hoofed and their heads sprouted horns or spikes, their bodies had grown tails, their minds had become evil twisted soaked in chaos magic with only thoughts of power and greed. But worst of all was their eyes, windows into their souls they glowed with the sheer power of chaos magic. Their very being was a conductor for chaos and evil and they projected fear and every negative emotions through their very existence. The Delvin were nothing more than servants of chaos twisted into its form.

One such Delvin was the leader of a supposed council that ruled Nevid. His leadership had been gained through lies, deception and betrayal, like all good Delvin. This Delvin was unusual as he had the capacity to hold more chaos magic then any known Delvin. He was the strongest, the smartest and the most powerful, or so he thought. He also had a rare tint to his skin, that of blood red, his horns were huge and black reaching high and adding another foot to his seven foot body height. He was covered in tattoos created by evil chaos magic, binding parts of his soul and body to unknown demon gods. His eyes glowed yellow and he wore deep blue robes of office, enchanted with many magical abilities. He had charms hanging from his belt and several magical pendants hung around his neck. He was a cruel master and a torturer. His name was Morack, and Morack was in his laboratory.

The laboratory was deep in an underground cave system guarded by his magic and lesser Delvin that Morack controlled.

Morack shouted orders to a half-Delvin creature, "Get my glass of spectra moss now, Alastor!"

Alastor moaned, he was of human height, very attractive with a square jaw and light jewel sky blue eyes. He had whitish blond hair that was long down to his waist and strapped back with black leather strips into a warrior's tail. He had small black horns protruding from his head and a tail with a black tip. He had a warrior's body, buff and shapely, but was wearing rags that smelt and barely covered his tanned flesh. Magical tattoos of chaos magic and something else marked one arm, a tiny symbol of light magic that went unnoticed.

Alastor looked down at the ground as he walked up to a well-stocked shelf where there were many strange things in jars lined up and neatly stacked with labels in magical script. He took the jar labelled 'spectric', looked around and saw the master looking into the vision pool. The vision pool was a large bowl made of rock, filled with vile liquid. Alastor placed the jar onto the stone bench next to the pool. Morack snarled, took the jar and ripped off the leather lid then tossed some of its contents into the pool. Morack stared into the pool waters for some time until it was calm but still nothing happened.

He picked up the jar and read the label then smashed the glass on the ground. He walked up to Alastor and raised his hand, several tattoos glowed on Alastor's arm and he fell to the ground shaking in pain.

Morack stepped over Alastor's twitching body and selected the right jar, 'spectric moss', opened the lid and poured some if its contents into the vision pool, stirred it and then gazed at the vision that started to unfold.

His brother Zarack was standing next to a pond, a little Phase Walker and its pet was nearby. Good, Morack thought, I will acquire the essence I need soon. Watching further, Morack laughed as the pet threw a rock at his brother, he watched it bounce off his armour. Then the little one activated the phase power, Morack stared more intently trying to appraise how much essence he would get out of her. Zarack was then covered in water from a nearby water creature, Morack burst out in laughter again looking at his brother's surprised face. Another Phase Walker appeared, and then there was sudden darkness. Morack had seen this trick before, a favourite of his brother's, the next would be a grab hold and bag for the Phase Walker, because he needed them alive to extract the essence.

Scratching his head Morack watched the Phase Walker's pet growl and jump into the darkness, Morack laughed then looked concerned as the second Phase Walker began to charge in with a sword. Morack grabbed hold of the vision pool bowel tightly as he watched his brother's head rolling out of the darkness. He screamed and knocked the bowl over then saw the twitching Alastor on the ground and kicked him in the stomach with his hooved foot and marched out of the laboratory.

Alastor lay on the ground until he stopped twitching and the tattoos stopped glowing. He groaned in pain but it wasn't the physical pain, it was the pain of what he had become. Corrupted by experiments in dark magic he was subjected to and then turned into a slave by the ruler of Nevid, Morack. He stopped groaning and laughed as he knew that Morack's brother had done something wrong again, judging from Morack's outburst – good, I hope he didn't get another Phase Walker, he thought.

Alastor stood up and started to tidy the laboratory, picking up glass pieces and aligning everything that had been moved out of place. He stood for some time, remembering his twin sister – it had been at least five cycles since he had seen her pretty white silvery wings. He touched his own back to check that his had not grown back; he sometimes felt phantom movement like they were still there.

Morack walked through several caves and tunnels, passing his minions and guards, snarling and pushing them out of the way. He marched into an extra-large cave, its ceiling was domed with stained glass. There were pictures of himself and Delvin bowing in reverence, pictures of torture and death. A large pentagram marked the floor with glowing symbols all around. There was a roaring fire along one wall, unnatural and caused by powerful magic. There was a large stone throne, ornate and decadent. There were several rows of stone benches along one side of the throne opposite the wall of flame. Two Delvin guards were inside the throne room, he boomed his voice in his guttural language, "Form the council, summon them now!"

Morack tapped his stone throne with his clawed red hand and cracked his neck a few times; he was not happy, if a Delvin could ever be; it seemed that torture, pain and death would be the only things that make Delvin happy. He was not happy because he had lost his best tool and needed to enlist a new one. He had the perfect hold on his brother as they were from the same clutch of eggs; too bad all the others from his clutch are dead as they would be easy to control. The thought of this further enraged Morack who wanted revenge; those Phase Walkers would be caught shortly and he would be extracting their essence slowly.

There was a scraping on the ground as several Delvin

entered the throne room, each bowing before the Overlord, then sitting along the stone benches; none spoke. When they had all arrived Morack roared his guttural language snarling, "I want all your best hunters to assemble tomorrow, I need two Phase Walkers brought in alive, and it is an urgent matter. I will display them on a vision stone tomorrow. Now get out!"

The throne room emptied of Delvin as they left to do Morack's bidding. Morack was alone with his thoughts and plotted the torture of the Phase Walkers, committing their faces to his memory, a small squishy pink one and the funny looking blond one. He was even thinking to capture that water creature and feast on its flesh, then another thought entered his mind – a nice rug made from the tiny pink one's pet.

The darkness was receding slowly, and Sarah was coming to the full realisation of what she had done. She had never killed anything before, not even a spider or a mouse. She began to shake and the sword dematerialised. Catlin stood up; there was a tear in her eye, she wiped it away. Wuzzle sat up shifting his weight off the Delvin and walked over to Caitlin ever so slowly. There was a flapping noise and shouts of, "Help, over here!"

Sarah turned her eyes over to the noise. It was at the ponds edge, the black water creature had flipped itself out of the water, perhaps it did this in a panic trying to help. Studying the creature's details further, it had a surprisingly human face, arms and a tail, reminiscent of the Earth myths of mermaids and mermen, he was midnight black and his scales shimmered in the approaching light.

Sarah spoke aloud, "Caitlin are you ok? Your friend over there needs help I take it, he needs to be in the water right?"

Caitlin looked at Sarah from behind Wuzzle, "Yes, Martin needs help. Wuzzle, can you carefully lift him back into the pond?"

Sarah figured it was more of a command than a question because Wuzzle started to walk to the strange humanoid water creature who was flipping on the land, struggling to edge its tail back into the water.

Caitlin ran closer to the creature, so Sarah followed, "Martin are you hurt?"

Martin closed his eyes and did not respond, his face was attractive for a black fish man Sarah thought. Wuzzle leaned down with his huge clawed paws and threw Martin into the water; he landed with a small splash. Caitlin sat along the pond shore line and watched for movement, Sarah sat down beside her and Wuzzle just hovered behind them standing. Sarah thought of images of bears eating fish in the wild on Earth and quickly dismissed it, trying to take in the situation.

They both sat there in silence for some time, and then Martin popped up his head from the water and smiled, "Sorry Miss Caitlin, I threw myself out of the water in a panic, I'm glad that the Delvin is dead. I saw its head roll on by."

Sarah cringed again at what she had done. She looked over at the shimmering black fish man and smiled, "Glad you're ok, you are very brave to have leapt out of the water to save Caitlin, and I take it you cannot survive on land?"

Martin dove into the water again.

Sarah was thinking his disappearance into the water was rude, if you don't want to talk to me about it then tell me, don't swim away. She turned to look at Caitlin then heard a splash again.

Martin resurfaced, "That is correct Phase Walker; I cannot be out of water for too long, I am a Poseidon, my people live under the water, it's not the air breathing that is the problem it's my skin drying out."

Caitlin spoke, "I suppose introductions are in order Sarah, Martin, Martin, Sarah."

Sarah responded, "Nice to meet you Martin," then looked down at her watch, "Sorry I have to go, my work break is way over, can you take me back to the tree?"

Caitlin, surprised, stood, "The phase to your plane is back

there, but please we must talk, there is much to say."

Sarah stood and dusted off herself, "I know, I know, but I am late, there is much to know because, trust me, I am very new at this, I mean what the fuck is a Phase Walker?"

Sarah started to walk back around the pond.

Caitlin started to follow and shouted, "Wait, come back please."

Sarah realising this was a real reality, walked faster, "Seriously I need to go, we will talk tomorrow, I have the day off," then she kept walking back along the forest trail not looking back.

Caitlin walked back to the pond and sat chatting to Martin, "So do you think the Delvin will return to our plane Martin?"

Martin pushed his head out of the water higher and spoke in a concerned tone, "I do think so Miss Caitlin, you might have to go into hiding, they know where you are."

Caitlin sat looking into the pond staring at a water lily, her thoughts racing, deciding where to go next, she knew a few planes, she had friends on a Celestial plane of the sun though she had not seen them in a while, Shandra and Alastor, she was much younger then. She also thought of the plane called Telswan, she had merely been there once but was certain not many Phase Walkers visited there. But whatever plan she came up with the first thing she needed to do was talk to the elders in her tribe.

Caitlin waved at Martin, "I need to go, much to do. You should be okay Martin, just stay with your people underwater and don't surface for a few weeks just to be safe, they're only after Phase Walkers. Thank you my friend."

Martin waved, "Take care little Miss Caitlin I want to see you grown into a lovely women someday."

Caitlin walked up to Wuzzle and her pretty pink dress revealed a label, Pumpkin Patch. Wuzzle reached down and put Caitlin on his shoulder.

She whispered into Wuzzle's ear, "To the elders, please."

Wuzzle started to walk toward the structure, then walked

past several wooden chairs and a table with an empty plastic coffee cup, then reached down and grabbed the meat that was cooking over the fire. Caitlin clapped her hands and the fire went out. Wuzzle happily started to munch down on the meat as it headed down another trail deep into the thick forest.

Sarah power walked to the thick tree trunk, symbols clearly marked it as a phase point. Sarah didn't really know what to do so she stood for a time thinking, she started to feel the tingling again and a crack of light was starting to open, funny she thought she didn't remember light last time, just a little bit of crackling energy. The light grew brighter and it opened and she stepped through. The light was blinding and bright, she was through the phase and realised she was staring into a garbage trucks lights. She recognised the truck as the one that comes to empty the Cafe skip once a week. She hid behind the skip hoping the emptying part was done. She was right, as it drove back down the alley. It was dark, shit, Sarah thought. She checked her watch and saw it was eight o'clock. Fuck, Belinda might fire me; I wonder what William thought, fuck. I better go home and tell Belinda how sorry I am and think up an emergency why I left. Sarah headed home back down the alley thinking oh and a university lecture tonight too, I'm so dead. Strangely enough she didn't think more on the phase or the strange events of the day, perhaps she accepted it.

Wuzzle was happy munching down on his freshly cooked meat and they were almost upon the village. The path to the village was thick and dense with overgrown forest. The village contained over thirty large mounds and each with two doors, a large door and a smaller door. All the mounds had vegetation on top: some had moss, some had pretty flowers or various pretty grasses.

There were people walking around doing chores for the

day, dressed in homespun tunics and breeches, but occasionally something looked out of place, such as a young women tending her garden, she was wearing a white chemise typical of this regions style of clothing but what stood out was that she was also wearing a pair of blue designer acid wash jeans.

There were also a row of old television sets along another mound house, which were broken and used as a stands for flowers.

As Wuzzle walked deeper into the village, approaching the common market, a hum was heard. This hum was of activity, there were sentient animals everywhere helping with the day's trade. Huge bears like Wuzzle were common, a white one was sweeping the ground around a cart filled with colourful fruit while a huge bird with a large pointed beak was tending a herb garden.

Caitlin's people were known as the Fas, a reclusive tribe of people that lived hidden away from the main population of her plane known as Kelstone. The Fas only leave their village to trade and only if they were in dire need. Every member of the tribe of Fas was bonded to a companion animal or two. This was their way of life and also this gave them an ability to age slowly, but Caitlin was special as she was the Fas's only Phase Walker and that was why she was allowed to live on the outskirts of the village, so she could walk into the phase without bringing attention. Although Caitlin was young, only twenty cycles, she was treated almost on the level of an elder because of her Phase Walker ability and her ability to acquire things from other planes, which fascinated her entire tribe.

Wuzzle kept his pace walking through the market heading to the elder's hall. It was the biggest mound in the village so it could not be missed. The doors were swung wide open and something was in session, the timing was good Caitlin thought as the elders really only held a meeting or two a week.

Caitlin spoke softly to Wuzzle, he lifted her down and

they both walked side by side into the hall. The room was vast, bigger on the inside because it was also dug into the ground and steps went down to the main room. Several elders sat on long backed wooden chairs around a round table that was decorated in many magical symbols. These symbols were of nature magic, wards to keep evil away and to bring animals into harmony. On the plane of Kelstone those that used nature magic were known as druids. There were two other bear like creatures standing around looking bored, a winged horse and several smaller animals moving around; these were the bonded animals of the council members.

Caitlin stood and watched for some time. There was a large fireplace at the far end and a few people preparing food for the council – it looked like spiced tea and some bread. There were six elders seated and two empty ornate high backed wooden chairs. The village chief sat with his head leaning into his hands. He was a plump grey headed man and had many chains around his neck. Two elders, Marco and Realon, were throwing their hands in the air. Marco looked to be about twenty five but his real age was around fifty and he wore traditional elder robes. Realon was about sixty and still looked twenty five, she had had more experience as an elder as she had been the youngest member ever to join. Those two were always at odds, but it was more in a flirtatious manner then an outright argument. Realon was wearing something Caitlin had brought back from Earth – a Winnie the Pooh t-shirt – and a traditional Fas skirt of many layers. Caitlin smiled because she was proud of that find, she liked the earth bears, even though they were smaller they reminded her of the Arktos on Kelstone like her Wuzzle.

Arktos were loyal animals, they can grow up to ten feet tall and all Fas buildings were built to that height to accommodate them as was Fas tradition. Arktos were usually solitary animals and even prefer a bond with a Kelstoning than to be with their own kind. The Fas village was just one of many that bonded with Arktos. They were sentient, alert and understood the common language although most could not speak it. They could wave their pawed hands in a rough sign language, which was taught to them when they bonded and impressed on their Kelstoning. Catilin's Wuzzle was different because he was bonded to a Phase Walker.

It was more common to bond with an Arktos on your bonding day than any other animal. The bonding day tradition happened when you were around five cycles old. A call would go out into the forest using nature magic and one or two animals would respond to the call and present themselves in the summoning ceremony; an Arktos would normally always come. Arktos may look cuddly but they were formidable foes, especially if they were bonded to a companion that was in danger. They were very loyal, and devoted their life to the wellbeing of their companion. They would leave their bonded once a cycle to see their mate or pack.

Caitlin looked up as both Marco and Realon sat back down on their seats. The chief looked up at Caitlin and motioned her to take a seat. Spiced tea was served and bread was placed on the table.

The chief, looking less bored, moved his head off his hands, "What brings you to the round table Caitlin of Eliwise, Phase Walker of Fas?"

Caitlin sat straight in her high back chair, all eyes around the table were looking at her as she flicked a dainty brown curl from her face and beamed, "Sorry to interrupt a council session but I was attacked today by a Delvin, he was very nasty and I was almost taken. If it wasn't for the help of another Phase Walker, I would not be here. Also the Delvin was killed; I fear more are on their way."

There were gasps at the table and both Realon and Marco sat forward on their chairs.

The Chief had greying hair and had seen many things, he was over five hundred cycles old. He looked at Caitlin through blue eyes and thought for a time then responded, "I'm sorry Caitlin but you need to leave the village for the safety of the people. I cannot hide a Phase Walker. I wish I knew the magic but the phase is not in the realm of nature, but what I can do is hide our people no living creature can see through our veil."

"This has actually come at a time when the village needs to stop expanding our trade," – both Marco and Realon gave death stares – "I think it will do the village some good to have some alone time and reflect on our traditions. Two years would be enough for that, into the veil, and then we will reassess the situation."

Caitlin, before they knew she was a Phase Walker, had been in the veil, she even had been shown the nature magic to help cast it.

"I understand Chief elder, I will leave as soon as the veil is cast."

The Chief spoke, "The veil will be cast now, I will not have them find our village," as he waved both his hands at the council elders.

There was a scrapping of chairs and all elder council members started for the door. Caitlin sat for a little time as the village bell was being rung to gather the Fas into the square.

The Chief, looking at Caitlin continued, "Now Caitlin, tell me more about this other Phase Walker that helped you?"

Caitlin sat on the edge of her chair, excited to tell the tale. She had only met a handful of Phase Walkers and it was great news that she found another.

"Her name is Sarah, she is from the plane called Earth, where I have been going a lot lately. I like it there. I don't think she knows what she is, I probably should tell her. I'm not sure what phase abilities she has but she produced a weapon in battle, a sword actually, and she came through the phase here alone."

"I'm going back to Earth to talk to her, and then I will go visit my other phase friends Alastor and Shandra in the Celestial plane. After that I will explore the new plane I was talking about, Lorvisa; I haven't spent much time there."

"Then I will seek out the village, it should be two years

by then."

Caitlin then changed her tone and spoke softly to the Chief elder, "Can I borrow the Raznik crystal in case I get into trouble out there?"

The Chief sat and listened and considered, "The Raznik had changed since last you used it Caitlin, but for the better, and I'm not sure the village should be without it."

Caitlin asked, "How has it changed?"

The Chief proudly spoke, "It now has the ability to heal."

Caitlin beamed her blue green eyes, "Then I need it more than anyone in the village, you have people who can cast healing magic but I cannot heal anything; I'm a Phase Walker, I don't get that ability and my nature magic is limited."

"It's rough out there on different planes, anything can happen and two years is a long time."

The Chief looked at Caitlin's tiny body, she was young, too young to be a Phase Walker he thought, then responded, "Okay, but don't make me regret giving it to you, it needs to be returned in two years, it's on loan only."

Caitlin's eyes widened. She loved the Raznik – she had used it before, it sped up time for a short period making her go fast, really fast – it was fun. If she made a mistake and ran too fast and hurt herself she could now heal. Too many fun thoughts raced through her head.

The Chief stood up and walked to the back of the room; Caitlin followed, so did Wuzzle. He walked up to a plain brown chest and opened it up with a wave of his hands, then reached inside and shuffled about several scrolls. He pulled out the Raznik, wrapped in a brown cloth and tied in a leather cord. Slowly the chief unravelled the gem, it was green and glowed softly. It was in the shape of a triangle and was very small in the Chief's palm and was strangely lit.

The Chief handed the gem to Caitlin, "Take this then and go help the others cast the veil. Good luck Caitlin, I will see you in two years' time."

Caitlin took the gem and slipped it into a zipped front pocket on her dress, then hugged the Chief, like a small child hugs a parent. She stood back and waved, then walked with a bounce in her step to the small gathering in the village square.

The village square was lined with strange crystals; Caitlin smirked as she was the one who had acquired them. They were not magical, just purely decorative – she had bought them at a two dollar shop on Earth where they were called plastic garden gems. She had bought several large boxes of them as she knew everyone in the village would think they were pretty.

Caitlin would guess that all the druids of Fas had come to the call of the bell. At least fifty, she guessed. She waited with Wuzzle for some time before the Chief made an appearance.

He stood on the village speaking stone and intoned in a formal manner, "Once more, people of Fas, we need to cast the veil down in great haste. The Delvin have discovered we have a Phase Walker and it won't be long before they come here looking."

He paused and waved Caitlin to come to the speaking stone. Caitlin walked up and told Wuzzle to stay. She stood beside the chief and looked so pink and tiny.

He continued, "The veil will be raised for two years then we will bring it down again, Caitlin will be travelling to other planes in this time and will return then. Please start the veil now, each moment counts. The village's safety needs to be assured."

The small crowd of druids started to form a circle. The folk of Fas wore odd clothes, local Kelstoning medieval garb mixed with out-worldly pieces.

They all linked hands and there was a strong vibration in the air; their bonded animals were outside the circle, still and quiet. Caitlin joined the circle, a pink clear hue began to materialise around the parameter of the village starting from the ground, the circle started to chant and the pink clear hue started to rise. It was a slow process but it was the beginning of the veil, when complete it would stay until it was removed. Caitlin was feeling tired, it had been a long day, but kept chanting with the others as she looked up into the sky and watched it get blotted out by the large pink dome that was slowly closing. The chanting got faster, louder and it was then complete. The circle was broken and the Fas returned to their homes. The veil was complete, the village was now hidden.

Wuzzle lifted the child Caitlin onto his shoulder and carried her to the perimeter of the veil. Caitlin was too tired to search out her friends to say goodbye and she knew she had to leave quickly so she did.

The veil on the inside of the village looked like a pink hue; Caitlin moved her hand and chanted words and a small spilt started to occur from the ground up. She made it big enough for Wuzzle to get through and they walked to the other side of the veil. Turning back to look at the veil she could no longer see the village, it was forest, but the crack she made was visible like a strange pink thread, hovering. She started to chant again watching the veil close like the zipper on her pocket. Thinking of pockets, she checked hers to reassure herself the Raznik was still there.

Wuzzle then plodded along the trail back down past the dwelling and to the tree trunk that was the phase point to Earth, while Caitlin napped on his shoulder.

Sarah awoke in her apartment. She'd had the best night sleep ever and felt great, until she started to pour her morning coffee and realised she had to have excuses for the rest of yesterday. She dressed for work and caught the morning bus in.

Belinda was just opening up the Coffee House and Sarah chimed in, "I'm sorry about yesterday Belinda, I was very ill and had to leave straight away, I was going to call you but then feel asleep I was that sick."

Belinda looked her up and down then continued to push open the door then said, "Fine, don't do it again unless I see a doctor's certificate."

Sarah replied, "Certainly Belinda, sorry again."

Belinda started to turn on the machines and lights, "Right then, let's get this happening."

Sarah fell into the morning routine at work filling coffee cups and table service; it was uneventful until William showed up again. He sat down at his usual table then waited for Sarah to come over and take his order. William smiled, Sarah's heart almost melted William was so attractive, his smile gave off confidence, "I missed you yesterday, what happened?"

Sarah's heart began to race and she replied, "I'm sorry William, I was unwell again unfortunately. How are you?"

William stretched back in the chair, "Well I'm great but this girl I've been trying to get to know keeps avoiding me."

Sarah spoke fast, "Oh no William don't think that, I really have been unwell, I would like to get to know you too."

William sat forward in his chair and played with a silver salt shaker that was on the table, "Really, well maybe we need to fix that problem, how about dinner tomorrow night, give me your number and I will phone you?"

Sarah blushed at his forwardness, "Sure sounds like fun," then took a serviette from the table and scribbled her mobile number, giving it to William.

William folded it and put in his pocket then said, "I guess I better order something for lunch."

Sarah took his order then waited in the kitchen and ordered lunch for herself too. She picked up both plates when the kitchen completed the orders and sat down at his table for her lunch break. William looked surprised.

William grinned, his green eyes beamed at her, "So I have the pleasure of your company for lunch, the day has just got even better."

Sarah laughed, "You're good for my ego."

They enjoyed lunch, laughed and chatted for half an hour. Sarah then picked up both plates and stood, "Back to work unfortunately, I will see you tomorrow," then headed for the kitchen.

Sarah entered the kitchen and heard a knock at the alley

door; she opened it thinking to let a delivery person in. A giant bear standing on two legs and an extremely cute little girl stood in designer clothes on the step.

"Fuck!" Sarah shouted and slammed the door. Sarah stood for a time looking at the closed door before she heard knocking again. Sarah opened the door and stepped outside; it was crowded, everyone standing at the top of the stairwell. Being this close to Wuzzle, Sarah could smell pine and the sea, it was very pleasant; she had expected him to smell like a shaggy wet dog, after all he was standing in the garbage skip previously.

Sarah, trying to take it all in, looked down to Caitlin, "Why are you guys here?"

Caitlin didn't smile but looked at Sarah, "We really need to talk now Sarah, it can't wait and I need to sleep, I'm very tired."

Sarah just closed her eyes for a moment then opened them again but the giant bear was still there.

"Okay come to my house, I need to talk to my boss to leave early again."

Sarah was going through scenarios of how she can explain being sick to her boss and walked inside, leaving Caitlin and Wuzzle on the step.

- Chapter 4 -

Hunters and Hiders

Morack was sitting straight-backed on his throne, his horns evilly pointing to the stained glassed roof; it was cold, the fire was not roaring along the wall. Alastor lay at his feet, battered and bruised. There were five Delvin standing before him, the hunters he had asked for; he had hoped he would get more but it was the skill not the quantity, he thought.

Two blue, a grey, a black and a purple; at least he had a selection he thought. They all came with their own equipment, arrows, swords, maces and spell components. More like a rag tag group of adventurers then hunters he thought again, but he was going to make them his minions and brief them on his bidding.

Morack screeched, "Alastor, get me my chalice."

He kicked his hoofed foot at Alastor on the ground under his throne.

Alastor moaned but didn't want more pain so got up from the cold hard floor and went to fetch the chalice that was on a stone table off to the side. He returned with the cup and Morack grabbed it, then Alastor backed away to the wall and watched.

Morack pulled a tiny jewelled dagger from his boot and slashed his red skinned arm. Blood trickled out and filled the cup. He stood and chanted his horrible language, the blood boiled and turned black inside the chalice, and the fresh taint of chaos magic could be detected in the air.

Morack spoke to the hunters before him, "Everyone drink this. It is an enchantment to help me communicate with you, and noncompliance is death, of course."

Morack was always blunt.

The five demonoid creatures look at Morack defiantly, one came forward and Morack shoved the chalice into his purple clawed hand. The purple Delvin then gulped from the chalice and passed it to the Delvin next to him. The black Delvin received the chalice then passed it on to the grey which grunted and stepped back from the cup leaving the black holding it.

Morack demanded, "Drink it!"

The grey Delvin was bigger than the others and more buffed, he was young and held a mace, his armour was leather and he had miniature skulls hanging from his belt; he turned and started to run for the throne room exit.

Morack stood and screamed, "Nicoruffknee."

A blue electrical bolt shot out of his hand and went straight through the grey's back and out of his chest.

Alastor looked away in horror as he saw the poor Delvin still attempting to run with a gaping hole in his chest.

Then the blue bolt of energy bounced off the stone wall in the throne room, changed direction and came straight for the grey's head. It was a most unpleasant sight as its body hit the ground with a thud; the grey's head was a bloody mash of pulp.

The remaining two blue Delvin shuffled their hoofs on the ground. One carrying a bow and a bolt of arrows, the other a sword. Both drunk from the chalice then stood waiting.

Morack cringed at thinning his numbers but it had to be done, they had to be loyal. Morack, with a blank look spoke, "So I have four, well that has to be enough. I'm going to send you all through a phase called Kelstone to hunt down the valuable Phase Walkers. Bring them to me alive so I can extract their essence. Follow me to the laboratory now."

Morack stood and walked down caverns that led to his laboratory, then he went down a flight of stairs to what looked like a dungeon and unlocked a large wooden door. Morack then swung the door open and inside was a large room with several magical symbols glowing yellow on the ground; it was also damp and cold. A beautiful Celestial woman was in a cage along the back wall. She had black hair and light green eyes. Her wings were white and one was bloody and torn. She stood staring at Morack from her cage.

The four Delvin came into the room followed by Alastor, who bowed his head in shame once he looked at Keyness trapped in the cage. She was a fellow Phase Walker like Alastor, from the Celestial plane, and was everything that he once was. Alastor had been transformed in one of Morack's cruel experiments, turned into a half demon physically, but his mind and soul remained a Celestial. Remembering, Alastor touched a small black horn on his head that poked out of blond white hair and felt the movement of his tail; he arched his back, a movement natural to one with wings, and realised they were no longer there.

Morack once had an idea to enslave all Phase Walkers by turning them into Delvin, until through his research he found out about something more horrifying, extraction. Morack's new line of experiments on Phase Walkers were to extract their essence and consume their power for himself.

In the centre of the room there was a wooden machine, it had leather straps attached to a chair, a large thin pipe that went from the chair to a desk and ended in a glass jar under the pipe.

Morack walked up the cage and clapped his hands and the cage door opened. Morack spoke firmly, "Come and sit in the chair Keyness, I wouldn't want your other wing to break."

Keyness knew that if she didn't do as Morack demanded she would lose the other wing, she knew the chair hurt but it was temporary and she was almost recovered from the last time. She leaped out of the cage onto the ground and then strode gracefully over to the chair and sat down. Morack stared in Alastor's direction.

Alastor quickly walked to the chair, scraping his hooves

on the ground and strapped Keyness down using the strong leather strips, he whispered into Keyness's ear, "I'm sorry. I'm so sorry."

Keyness looked ahead and spoke slowly, "I do not blame. Your apology is accepted."

Alastor's heart sunk, rage and torment filled his mind as he stepped away from the chair. He went through various scenarios of how to break Keyness free and imagined pounding Morack's head into the ground, then hung his head low in knowing what was to come next.

Morack came forward and started chanting. The symbols on the stone floor glowed brighter and a magical energy grew above Keyness's head. She sat on the chair, back straight, and focussed on the wall.

The chanting stopped and Morack motioned his hand down. A green ball of energy from the roof above the chair dropped on Keyness, and she screamed in pain all the while staring at the wall. Blue liquid collected in the pipes and then trickled into the jar.

Morack held the jar and put his clawed index finger into the liquid.

Then he screeched, "Hunters, come in here."

He walked up the hunters standing in the laboratory and rubbed the liquid on their faces.

Morack actually grinned, pleased with himself then spoke, "Congratulations my hunters, you are all temporary Phase Walkers. You have about six months before the effects fade."

The Delvin looked pleased that they had gained a temporary power.

Morack waved to Alastor and continued up the stairs. Keyness lay still slumped in the chair, Alastor carefully undid the leather straps on the chair, he felt so much guilt and rage it was difficult to stay on task. He gently lifted Keyness's body from the chair and carried her to the cage. Alastor slowly put her limp body down inside the steel prison, moved her hair from her face and kissed her on the head. He closed the cage and it locked with a click. He sat on the floor in front of the cage and stared at Keyness through his light blue eyes, thinking and plotting for a way to get free.

Morack was back in his throne room, there was a stone vision pool next to his throne, and he was stirring his clawed finger through it.

The four hunters looked relaxed. Morack spoke abruptly getting their attention, "Come look into the pool."

Alert, the hunters moved forward and looked.

In the vision pool the faces of little Miss Caitlin and Sarah appeared, frozen from the scene at the pond, just before they battled Zarack.

The black Delvin hunter laughed, "This little one should be easy and the other a female, it shouldn't take us long," finishing his words with a snarled lip.

Morack grinned, "This is what I wanted to hear."

Morack spoke in a grunt, "Come, let no time be wasted, I will lead you to the Kelstone phase."

The hunters, still peering into the pool, looked up and moved away when the mention of the phase was spoken. The black Delvin's face looked blank.

Wuzzle was in the dumpster again eating the trash, this time a mouldy loaf of bread. Caitlin sat on the back steps of the Chocolate Coffee House watching the alley entrance. Sarah opened the cafe back door slowly and peered out. Almost expecting the scene before her not to exist; it did, so she came out the door and to the steps, then sat next to Caitlin and spoke, "Okay I've got the afternoon off but how do we get Wuzzle back to my apartment?"

Caitlin smiled, "The phase, of course."

Sarah spoke, puzzled, "I thought that the phase was only used to gain entry to different planes, not within the same plane?"

Caitlin stood up, "Of course we can phase within the same plane, how do you think I get around all the shops. Shopping is fun, the one thing I really love about Earth."

Caitlin moved deeper down the alley to where Wuzzle was in the skip eating trash.

Caitlin waved, "Watch this Sarah."

Pointing at the Chocolate Coffee House wall near the stairs, Caitlin had a concentrated look on her face and moved her arms around, no words or chanting, and then a phase started to open.

Sarah, wide eyed, "Wow I thought you needed phase points like the one back there" – pointing to the back alley wall where she went through to Caitlin's plane last time.

Caitlin looked up, "Yes you need phase points, special places in the phase, to go to other planes, but within the same plane you can open the phase anywhere in that plane as long as you have been to that destination before."

"So Sarah, that's where we need you. Please link with me and complete the phase. Concentrate on the destination as you know it."

Sarah looked down at her watch it was eleven, eleven, "Okay, I need to ask you about the ones as well."

Caitlin took Sarah's hand, "The one symbol is a Phase Walkers linking ability, it is how you know there is another Phase Walker around you get the prompts which are ones, I'll explain later, let's go."

Sarah's tattoo around her finger glowed as she concentrated on the entrance to her apartment and she felt a tingling sensation all over her body, strangely she didn't feel ill.

Caitlin let go of Sarah's hand, "There it's done, let's go."

Caitlin went over to Wuzzle and he started to follow her from the skip. She walked through the open phase, which was a white glowing light projected on the alley wall (looking closer it was a bright tunnel), and Wuzzle followed her. Sarah stood in the alleyway for some time studying the phase and then walked straight through.

Wuzzle and Caitlin were waiting, standing at the entrance to her apartment, Sarah walked briskly to join them.

They all walked inside the foyer, Wuzzle only just getting through the door without having to bend down. Sarah pressed the lift to go up and they all waited. The lift door opened and one of Sarah's neighbours came out, Mrs Letting, a middle aged woman that lived alone amongst the university students because the apartments were cheap. She gasped at the sight of Wuzzle, who had his mouth shut so looked like a cuddly giant bear standing on its legs.

Sarah spoke quickly, "University mascot, we just came back from a game, go team!"

Sarah shook her fist in the air to emphasise it.

Mrs Letting walked out of the lift and didn't look back.

Wuzzle, Caitlin and Sarah got inside the lift. Wuzzle had to bow his head down a little. The lift's maximum capacity was twenty people so they would be right, Sarah thought, and pressed her level on the lift's buttons.

The lift door opened and Sarah led them to her apartment. Caitlin sat on one lounge and Wuzzle stood for a time then sat on Sarah's other lounge with a boof, Wuzzle's fur scattered all over the lounge; Sarah cringed.

Sarah pulled up a dinning chair to her lounge room coffee table then looked at Caitlin, who was so small and tiny like a little china doll. She closed her eyes a few times struggling to keep them open.

Sarah asked, "So what did you have to tell me that was so urgent I had to leave work?"

Caitlin's eyes fluttered open, "You're in danger, well we both are, the Delvin are on their way looking for us now, since we killed one. The one that attacked me wanted me alive, I don't know why but he called me Phase Walker, he knew what I was."

"I know the Delvin leader is Morack and he's collecting Phase Walkers. I can't be sure if they know about you Sarah, so I came here to warn you and to stay a while, as I cannot return to my people."

"You see being a Phase Walker gives off residual magic that is unique and can be identified by those who know where to look, it's like a signal beacon that identifies us–"

Sarah interrupted, "What do you mean us, do I give off a beacon? How did I become a Phase Walker? What are the ones I keep seeing? What is the tingling and how can a little girl know so much? Oh and what exactly is a Wuzzle?"

Sarah pointed her finger to the creature on her lounge.

Caitlin sat at the end of her seat, "I'll answer all your questions without games, you seem like a relatively new Phase Walker. Let me see, well, yes Sarah, you give off residual Phase Walker energy, you are a Phase Walker, you don't get to choose it, you just become it."

"The universe only picks a handful of beings to become Phase Walkers, it's unknown how this occurs or why but if you manifest the ability you have been chosen. Upon a Phase Walker's body a birth mark will appear, this identifies the phase magic for that being. I don't know any Phase Walkers on your plane Earth, you are the first I have encountered. On my plane I am the only one. But what I do know is the location of another two Phase Walkers on the Celestial plane, twins actually, brother and sister. But I'll tell you about them later."

Sarah spoke up, "The ones, I saw them a lot and got a tingling?"

Caitlin said, "Not much else into it Sarah, the ones or uno, they are just symbols that identify another Phase Walker is nearby, you will be prompted by them to get your attention. It's how we know each other. If you saw them earlier it was probably because I was nearby in your alley."

Sarah looked over at Wuzzle who was actually sleeping on her lounge.

Caitlin continued, "The tingling you feel is your gift, the phase, its energy being activated in your body. I may be little yes, I am young among my tribe the Fas, but to you I seem childlike. I am 20 years old in your time. So I'm probably the same age as you, I do not age as fast as humans is all, but being this small has its advantages."

Caitlin paused then smiled at Wuzzle, "Well Wuzzle is my

protector, my animal companion; it's a tradition on my plane, not just my tribe, to bond with an animal. Wuzzle can walk through the planes only because he is bonded to me; he is not a Phase Walker."

"Now, I was thinking to stay on Earth for a while then visit my friends in the Celestial plane. Thanks again for saving me from the Delvin. You can join me in the Celestial plane if you would like to be introduced to that plane. You have to be shown the plane before you can enter it unless you learn it through natural instinct, which is rare."

"I only know of a half dozen or so planes. The latest I have not explored very much, my friends in the Celestial plane have shown me how to reach it, perhaps you should come and pick up that plane too. Phase Walkers should know as many planes as they can."

Sarah shuffled in her seat "Well that's a lot to take in. So who is Morack? What's a Delvin and tell me more about Nevid?"

Caitlin put her feet up on the lounge then tucked them close and made herself into a little ball, making her look even more tiny; she yawned, "I know you have many questions, there still is a lot more to know about, I'm so tired. I'll answer this then I need to have a nap sorry Sarah."

"Morack is the leader of the Delvin from what I know. He killed an entire council of his people and proclaimed himself the ruler of Nevid. He is an evil warlock tyrant that can cast chaos magic."

"The Delvin are a demonic race who were corrupted by chaos magic centuries ago. They live in a plane of gas, smoke and stone; almost nothing lives on the surface but underground in caves is where things grow and the main population thrives. My friend Shandra has explored there a little each time a major battle has occurred, and has warned me not to go there, the Delvin are very much a waring race and they turn aggressive very easily."

"I must sleep Sarah, I will speak more when I awake."

Caitlin closed her eyes.

Sarah walked back to her cupboard and took two blankets out, she threw one on Wuzzle and neatly tucked the other around Caitlin, then she went into the kitchen to pour herself some coffee, and a thought came to into Sarah's mind: when she first went through the phase was Nevid the plane she went into? Going by Caitlin's description it sounded so.

- Chapter 5 -

Pizza

Deep underwater it was clear and light because large bubbles with little lights inside lit the nearby surroundings. Looking closer there were water filled domes nestled on the floor, deep at the bottom of the pond (that linked to a vast ocean). Inside the domes there were structures and creatures swimming around. This was where the Persidion lived, this was Martin's village.

Martin was at the market, his silvery black skin shimmered under the lights of the vendors. There were tables made out of large shells and they were neatly lined up in rows. Hawkers shouted their wares. Martin came across a lovely girl, her body was grey and she was covered in black spots, her tail was pretty and she had long white hair and clear blue eyes. She lifted up some large fresh clams. Martin nodded and signalled with his hand that he wanted to buy some, a tradition used in the markets. The aquatic girl shoved several clams into a basket made of green reeds woven together. Martin handed over some shiny coins. The coins had pictures of the current Persidion queen and little magic symbols of the royal vault.

The girl smiled and thanked him for his purchase and Martin put the basket of clams around his strong shoulders and moved on. He could see pink bubbles strapped to a display bench, little snails on leaves put into finely woven reed cages and flowers in bunches swaying in the water. He had purchased what he needed for a meal, his wife and children were waiting, so he jetted his tail and swum past the hustle and bustle of the village. He headed to a nearby large shell like structure; it had a door and window much like a little house. Martin knocked on the front door.

A very pretty woman with a green body and tail answered the door; she had yellowish long hair in braids and wore a sling across her body. Inside the sling a small baby Persidion slept.

A little boy, thirteen cycles, with black with green stripes flipped his tail and shot up to the roof when he saw Martin, "Dad!" he said.

"Hello little Jas, I hope you have been good for your mother," Martin sat on a chair that was made from woven green grass; it was a living plant affixed into the ground.

Jas replied, "Of cause father, I'm always good," and bounced in the water currents.

Martin placed the bag of clams onto the stone table.

A phase point on Kelstone opened; four large Delvin stepped through a large tree trunk with phase symbols glowing. They looked mean and pumped for a fight. They murmured their guttural language to each other and scraped there hooved feet along a trail that lead out to a pond. In military type moves they searched the area, fanning out, walking toward the large moss covered mound. A blue Delvin with a scar on his eye and white hair, carrying a sword, kicked down the wooden front door to the moss covered mount with a thud. Inside pretty flowers were arranged on a large wooden table and pink things lined the room. The room smelt sweet and a bed lay in the corner; it was modern and not from this plane but the stupid blue Delvin did not notice. The bed was next to a neat display of playing cards that were stacked on a shelf.

Another blue demon came into the moss covered mound structure he was larger and heftier than the first, and had a jet black warrior's tail down his neck. He walked up to the table and knocked over the flowers, revealing underneath a wooden chest, but it was locked. The black haired blue demon then smashed the wooden chest by punching it with his large blue hand; it flung open and threw blankets and dolls everywhere. In frustration he then knocked over the shelf and the cards came tumbling down. Both demons left the room in a mess and walked outside. The black Delvin was smashing small wooden tables and chairs outside, making a plastic polystyrene coffee cup drop to the ground, while the purple stood for some time studying the surroundings, raising his bow and arrow on the ready.

The purple Delvin spoke, "Reednak come here, this place is no good, it's empty."

Reednak, the blue Delvin with a scar and white hair, cracked his neck from side to side and responded while walking out of the structure, "Grimlock, I have a scent," and waved a little pink blanket that was taken from Caitlin's bed.

The black Delvin came forward, opened up a leather pouch and sprinkled dust over the blanket, "Metaroon". The blanket's scent was heightened and chaos magic hung in the air.

"Good, Grimlock," Canya the purple Delvin replied, while putting an arrow in his quiver.

All four Delvin started to walk towards the Fas village along a trail into a dense thick forest. They doubled back a few times and lost the scent, so they could not progress, it was a dead end. They walked back to the pond and there was a faint scent along the edge of the pond.

Canya, with dark purple skin, demanded attention, "Maybe the Phase Walkers are under water."

Grimlock replied, "I will do a water breath spell."

Grimlock was very attractive even for a Delvin, he had red long hair, was very buff, and had red glowing eyes contrasting to his jet black skin. His horns were red, a rare colour for Delvin and curled around his head rather than pointing straight up. He wore thin robes that were black and he waved his arms and chanted then several tattoos on his arms glowed purple.

He then pointed his hands at each of the Delvin, a thin veil of blue like a bubble went over their faces and popped.

All the Delvin jumped into the water at once followed by a series of large splashes as they dived down into the water. Underwater there was a lot of activity, little eels, small fish and plants moved with the currents, all of which swam fleeing the Delvin in fear as the Delvin's natural ability was to project negative emotions, the most powerful and primal of which was fear. Some strange green shiny walking fish even leapt out of the pond and ran into the forest.

The Delvin swum deeper further into the pond until it was black and then until light could be seen on the pond floor. They swam toward the light.

Grimlock motioned and they watched the village for a time from a distance then they spread out. Canya went around the back and the two blue swam to the front of the village where a gathering was taking place of fish people.

Grimlock waved his hands and chanted guttural words that could not be heard underwater; all his tattoos glowed blue this time and a ball of red flame shot into the village market.

From the back and front of the village all the Delvin rushed in, crushing shell structures and murdering Persidion as they fled in fear. Both the blue Delvin were systematically searching for the Phase Walkers, stopping on occasion to hack Persidion tails off.

Martin was dishing out clams into shell bowls when he looked out the window of his house and saw Persidion folk and small sea life rushing by, swimming in all directions. He felt fear and panic, then dropped a bowl of clams that floated slowly to the floor. Martin knew this feeling as he had felt it when little Miss Caitlin who lives by the pond was battling the demonoid creature.

Martin panicked and saw his wife, baby and child standing in the corner cowering down. A blue demonoid with white hair burst the door open and raised his sword. In a swift movement it chopped off Martin's scaly arm followed by his head.

His wife and children screamed, the blue Delvin pushed forward and struck the wife and babe down in another stroke. Jas shot out of the house as fast as a child could, his black and green stripes swimming for his life, compelled by fear.

All was still in Martin's dwelling save the demonoid. The Delvin left and approached the next dwelling, until he heard Nica call his name.

He responded, "I'm done, they're not here."

Reednak looked around and watched the last of the Persidion folk flee, "This is no fun, they do not fight back and no Phase Walkers are here."

Grimlock made his way to the Delvin hunters holding a bag of gems, "This is maybe not a Phase Walker but look, magical ianoids; they are good to help us fight."

The purple Delvin, Canya, approached, "We didn't come for pretty stones; I do not want to anger Morack, we need to find the Phase Walkers."

The Delvin spent some more time going through the village until it was still and lifeless then surfaced from the pond.

All four Delvin demonoids stood and plotted for a time before being interrupted by a booming voice, "Where are my Phase Walkers?"

Grimlock boldly spoke while holding a small blanket he had in a bag, "They are not on this plane my Lord Morack, but we have a scent."

Morack screamed, "Fools, come back through the phase at once and bring me that scent."

Morack stomped his hooves around the throne room then walked to the wall. He then stretched out his hand and scraped his claws around the stone wall, leaving deep scratch marks in the solid stone. He continued around the walls and through the fire that was roaring magically on the side wall and his red skin did not catch fire.

The Delvin left the pond and walked to the trail that led home via the phase.

The iPhone on Sarah's bedside table rung, Sarah awoke and looked at the time; it was eleven, eleven in the morning. Screw you ones, Sarah thought as she answered the phone, "Hello."

A deep male voice answered, "Hi Sarah, this is William, and how are you pretty lady?"

Sarah's mood changed, "Oh, hi William, I'm great. So what are we doing tonight?"

William laughed, "Straight down to details, I was thinking on coming to pick you up around six tonight and then on to the Lyric Theatre to see Wicked."

Sarah was really happy and replied, "Wow really that's so awesome of you, I really wanted to see Wicked, that's just made my day. Did I mention how awesome you are?"

William laughed again louder this time, "I'm glad someone thinks I'm awesome, I'll see you tonight, I have a uni class at eleven thirty in a few minutes."

Sarah's heart sunk at hearing the time and responded "See you tonight at six, bye."

She jumped out of bed "fuckety, fuck, fuck" she said as she walked around her room getting her clothes ready for work. She was late again, half the day was gone. Then her iPhone rung again, she dropped her work clothes onto her bed and leaped for the phone thinking it maybe William again.

Sarah answered, "Hello."

Belinda responded firmly "Sarah where are you? You didn't ring in sick, you left early yesterday, this is just not professional."

Sarah spoke panicked, "I'm so sorry I will be there as soon as I can."

Belinda spoke with a very formal tone, "Don't bother Sarah, your fired."

Sarah spoke again with feelings of dread, "Are you allowed to do that on the phone?"

Belinda spoke again, "I don't know, are you allowed to have multi sick days off with no doctor's certificate and answer the phone perky when you're supposed to be at work? I'm sorry Sarah I need someone who is going to be here to work."

Sarah replied softly, "I'm sorry I understand, bye."

Sarah hung the phone up and sat on the end of her bed.

Crap she thought, but decided to enjoy her date tonight, so she got dressed in blue jeans and a t-shirt then started to go through the cupboard working out what to wear tonight to Wicked.

There was a knock on Sarah's bedroom door, which frightened her, then a more insistent knock. She picked up a pillow, having nothing else, walked up to the door and hesitantly opened it a crack, not knowing what to expect.

Cute little Miss Caitlin was in the doorway and said, "I was wondering when you were going to get up."

Sarah had actually forgot that Caitlin and Wuzzle were in her house, then it all came rushing back.

Sarah responded, "I will be out in a moment, give me a few."

Caitlin walked back to the lounge and picked up the remote control and flicked TV channels.

Sarah came into the lounge room and Wuzzle was seated on the lounge watching TV with Caitlin.

Sarah sat on the lounge next to Caitlin and said, "So I've just been fired from my job, not good."

Caitlin flicked a channel and responded, "Why do you need a job?"

Sarah looked shocked at Caitlin, "Well to earn money to buy things, how have you been buying things?"

Caitlin smiled, "Yes I do buy things and that's one thing I love about Earth, shopping but I don't need a job, I can take my own money."

Sarah wide eyed asked, "Well how do you 'take' money?"

Caitlin started chanting and a tattoo on Caitlin's arm of what looked like a bear glowed with symbols and she held her hand out and a chunk of Australian hundred dollar notes were in her hand, materialising from nowhere.

Sarah shocked spoke quickly, "Okay, how did you do that?"

Caitlin looking a little embarrassed, "Um, well I took it from somewhere else, I used my phase ability to open a small phase rift on a teller machine, reached in and took a handful of notes, just remember an ATM location, it can be anywhere on this plane and then just use the phase to reach in and take it, I took this from a Sydney ATM so they won't know or miss it; high crime rate there."

Sarah frowning, "That's stealing."

Caitlin responded in a matter of fact tone, "Well not really, I only take from ATM machines, it gives other people money if they have a card, why not me."

Sarah thought for a moment, well the money in ATM machines are insured, "Well it can't be too bad, I guess the money is insured. So you're shouting pizza for lunch then, I can order in home delivery. After lunch you can show me exactly how you did that?"

Sarah pointed at the wad of cash in Caitlin's tiny hand.

Caitlin gave a girly smile, "Sure Sarah, as a Phase Walker you will find you're too busy jumping through phases into planes to worry about generating wealth. This ability can be used in any plane and anything."

"If you didn't want to order pizza you could just take it out of a pizza oven, same principle, but it might be hot," Caitlin giggled.

Sarah looked perplexed, "I'm not sure how moral that is, I can probably go as far as taking the money from a machine but not steal from someone else."

Caitlin sat up straight on the lounge, "I realise this is new to you, but just never take more then you need and it will be all fine."

Sarah pondered for a while, then got up and picked up

her phone to order in some pizza. Sarah looked at Caitlin, "How many pizzas for Wuzzle?"

Caitlin looked thoughtful, "Probably ten, he needs to go on a diet, he had fifteen earlier."

Sarah ordered eleven pizzas and cringed when she realised more ones. Then went back to talk to Caitlin, "So can you tell me more about the Celestial plane?"

Caitlin smiled, thrilled she had access to another Phase Walker, "Well the Celestial plane was shown to me by Alastor and Shandra – they are twins. They came through to my plane about five years ago."

"I haven't seen them since but I know how to reach them. They showed me the way to their plane. The celestial plane got its name because it was created in a disastrous accident; the people, once humanoid like us, were rained on by pure light magic in the great sun storm hundreds of years ago."

"The populous of the Celestial plane were warped with pure magic, it changed their bodies from within and physically, wings grew and flight became part of their society, their eyes turned lighter, more colourful and their inner being was able to control the light waves of magical energy. There were also others that got transformed into other things of light magic, but still to this day they are still discovering them and they are rare."

"Their world was magically created, natural things like trees and plants grew no longer, nothing was organic. The trees they have now are not like the ones on Earth or my planet, they are more perfect and decadent, each leaf will be the same and perfect in size, this is the result of magical creation. Every living thing changed in the great sun storm, so many things will surprise you. I spent about six months in the Celestial plane."

Sarah put her feet up on the coffee table, while relaxing on her lounge room chair, "So who are the twins, they're Phase Walkers?"

Caitlin perked up, "Yes, they are Phase Walkers. You would like Alastor, funny and chirpy he has blond hair like yours except maybe a little more whitish, his flesh is tanned and eyes are blue, he has lovely white fluffy feathered wings, oh and so does Shandra, his twin sister. She is kind and caring they did a lot of things for me when I was visiting on their plane, this is why I want to go back and spend time with them until my village returns."

Sarah flicked her blond hair behind her ear, "Your village returns?"

Caitlin sat back in the lounge, "I thought I mentioned it, my village is under the veil for two years, they have private matters to attend too and they didn't want to get caught up in Phase Walker business. But we should be safe here as I have not seen any Delvin in this plane before."

The doorbell buzzed from down in the lobby and Sarah answered her intercom, "Hello."

The speaker on the wall responded, "Pizza."

Sarah replied, "Okay, send it up," then buzzed her security button, allowing the pizza guy to use the lift.

The pizza arrived and Caitlin paid the pizza guy one hundred and eleven dollars. The pizza guy tried to peek inside but didn't see Wuzzle, then spoke, "So you guys having a party? I thought a big delivery came earlier?"

Sarah replied, "No party, just me and my daughter, we are having a pizza day."

The pizza delivery guy looked at little Caitlin who smiled, "Mummy, I'm hungry for pizza."

The pizza delivery guy replied, "Kids, they eat a lot, eh?"

Sarah took the pizzas from the delivery guy and put them on the coffee table, then slammed the door shut. Both Caitlin and Sarah laughed loudly. Wuzzle picked up a pizza and ate it whole, square box and all.

Sarah asked Caitlin, "Could I have some money to get my nails and hair done, might as well not waste it, I have a date tonight."

Caitlin, glad to help, handed Sarah the money and continued to eat a slice of pizza.

Sarah, holding a slice of pizza in one hand and a lot of

hundred dollar notes in the other spoke, "Okay, well you guys relax while I get my hair and nails done, I'll be back in an hour or two."

Caitlin, licking her fingers, "That's fine, have a good time. I want to rest and think things through."

- Chapter 6 -

Lady of Light

Morack stomped through the throne room, his hooves scratching the surface of the stone ground; the room smelt of burnt flesh and sulphur. He was holding a pink blanket, which he waved around, then boomed at the top of his voice, "Where are they?"

Alastor was standing with his back against the wall, watching, hoping Morack did not notice him. A white blond tuft of hair moved over his left eye, and he smoothed it away so he could study the four Delvin. The purple looked agitated and stroked his bow with his clawed hand. The two blue had their eyes transfixed on Morack deeply taking in his words. The black had heavily been using chaos magic from what Alastor could tell because its skin still had blue symbols glowing faintly. Alastor was glad that Morack only had a small pink blanket and not a Phase Walker.

Alastor shifted his hooves, careful not to make a noise, and then wondered why a Phase Walker would have something like that in the first place. Only a child would have something so small and dainty, then he gasped as he knew a child Phase Walker who had a liking for pink. Frozen in worry, Alastor dared not to move.

Alastor touched his black horns, they felt like a shell from the ocean, as a reminder of what had happened to him. In the centre of the throne room he saw a ripple that distorted it, followed by a hum. Alastor knew what was to come, a phase was opening, as he had seen many times before, within this phase a green humanoid creature stepped out, it had four arms and silvery bright wings, and was female.

She stood about six feet tall and looked regal. She wore navy blue finery and a light blue tabard that had a golden triangle symbol, her face was humanoid and beautiful, it was green with dark green spots on her cheeks. Her hair was long blond and plaited in many braids, two long antenna stood regal from her forehead. Before anyone could react she turned and cast ice over the four Delvin hunters and then stared at Morack, who raised his arm above his head about to cast a spell.

"Don't you dare strike at a Lady of Illumination! Morack, demon of the Delvin, I bring a message: stay out of our plane or there will be war coming to Delvin like you have never seen."

Morack growled in contempt, "The Lorvisa do not frighten me, the Delvin will go where they please, Phase Walker. Give the Lady of Light this message…"

He threw a lightning bolt at the bug like creature. The Lady of Illumination stepped to the side and walked back through the phase and it snapped shut.

Grimlock was melting the ice around his feet with chaos magic.

Morack walked back to his throne holding the blanket.

Alastor slinked away unnoticed.

Sarah, feeling fantastical about herself, had a skip in her step, her beautiful blond hair had a bounce and her nails were painted pink, she usually wasn't that girly but spending time with Miss Caitlin inspired her to pink. Sarah opened the door to her apartment, it was late afternoon and Wuzzle was on the floor spread out on his back, eyes closed, snoozing. Caitlin sat watching a documentary on lions.

Sarah, happy, smiled, "I'm going out tonight but will be back tomorrow."

Caitlin not looking back, shushed Sarah.

Okay then, Sarah thought and went and got changed for her date to Wicked. After looking through several outfits she decided to go back to basics for a first date, the little black dress and an oriental silk blue jacket, going for the Firefly Kaylee look but without the overalls. Sarah laughed to herself.

Sarah emerged from the bedroom. Wuzzle was still sleeping, but Caitlin looked up, "You look nice Sarah, one more thing I was thinking about it, you probably need to know more about the Delvin, please sit down."

Sarah sat down on the lounge next to Caitlin who smiled like a lion.

Caitlin spoke, "The Delvin are a race of evil beings that only think of power, wealth and status, they were created by chaos magic. I don't know why but they are hunting Phase Walkers, which means we are both in danger. So I think its best that you come with me to the Celestial plane like I said before, probably sooner than later."

Sarah's iPhone rung and the name William flashed on the display and she spoke quickly, "Sorry Caitlin, I was listening, but I really need to take this call."

Caitlin looked disappointed as she knew her words were more important, she carefully composed them to say to Sarah all afternoon. Sarah walked into her bedroom and closed the door, answering the phone, "Hi William."

William voice was smooth and happy, "Hi Sarah, I'm a little early, downstairs now."

"Okay, coming down," Sarah then ended the call.

She walked out of her bedroom, and then closed the door. She stopped and waved at Caitlin, "Back late tonight, we will talk more in the morning."

Caitlin had a little frown on her forehead and picked up the remote control of the television.

Sarah walked out of the foyer to her building and saw William's car, then jetted towards it.

William looked very attractive and clean shaven, the

stubble was gone, he wore a black leather jacket and smiled as Sarah caught his eye, "You look great, the show starts later but I thought I would get in a little early to get a park."

Sarah smiled back and tossed her blond hair, something she never does and cringed when she caught herself doing it, and got into the car.

They arrived and as William parked the car there were bursts of laughter coming from within. They walked into the theatre holding hands to watch Wicked.

The Lady of Light was considered to be the most beautiful being on Lorvisa. She was the ruler and deity of the populace, revered throughout her plane and fanatically protected by all of her known kin.

The Lady of Light lived on a large island known as the Illuminoid where she held court known as the Illumination. Members of her court hold rank and title with the secondary title of Illumination.

It was a day where the court was fuller then normal and a session was in motion.

The court room itself was under a large glass dome. Inside the dome birds flew and trees touched the glass. There was a lot of strange vegetation and flora around the outside circle of the Illuminoid. Stranger bugs glowed pink and blue as they flew about the flowers. There were many, if not hundreds, of white stone benches in lines in front of a large reflective throne made out of silvery mirrors. The first twenty or so front benches were all full of creatures sitting in neat rows. Giant caterpillar like beasts carried buckets of water. One such caterpillar shuffled over to another creature seated on the bench. This creature had blue skin, four arms with hands, not legs, and a shiny shell, it had a shocking humanoid head, its face was blue and feelers protruded from its head. The large caterpillar, after exchanging words, stood back and threw the bucket of water onto the blue skinned beast, the humanoid head enlarged its jaw and swallowed all the water while it floated in mid-air. Other creatures on the benches consisted of spiderlike people, bird like people and worm like people to name a few.

They all sat still and watched. Then the most beautiful creature on the planet made its entrance, the Lady of Light. A massive seven foot tall butterflied humanoid entered, she had fair pale pink toned skin and white blond hair to her waist, her face was human, her eyes sparkled brown while butterfly antenna poked through her hair. She wore a long flowing blue dress; she had four thin arms and hands and stood on two legs. What was most breathtaking was her wings, they were huge and reflective like mirrors. She moved her wings backward and forward, fluttering. She sang a musical cord and sat in her throne. The light was blinding and bright, this was the Lady of Light.

There was a small platform a little distance in front of the Lady of Light, it was heart shaped and green. A rift in the phase opened and a blue crackling light appeared, a smaller green butterfly humanoid came through the phase and onto the platform. The phase closed behind her. She had four arms and two legs, her wings were silvery, and she wore navy finery with a blue tabard and the symbol of Illumination, a large triangle, on the front. She bowed before the Lady of Light, her wings spread out.

The Lady of Light watched intently, sat still on her throne and raised one arm and spoke, "Lady of Illumination, how goes your mission, please report."

The Lady of Illumination stood and looked directly into the Lady of Light's eyes, "Your eminence, the message was delivered to the Delvin leader Morack, his response was that the Delvin will do as they please and their Phase Walkers will continue to enter our plane, then he attacked by throwing a ball of lightening at me and I phased back here to report."

The Lady of Light stood then spoke, her brown eyes looked somewhat coppery from the light reflecting off her wings and throne, "The Delvin will no longer have access to our plane, they steal our Phase Walkers and violate our lands, all Delvin must be destroyed."

Her voiced echoed around the plane of Lorvisa like sonar, except on a grand scale, each living creature felt her voice vibrate them, each living creature on Lorvisa obeyed the will of the Lady of Light. This was how powerful she was, she did not only control her people but the plants and creatures as well. She was the ruler and her word was law. But with great power there is great responsibility, the Lady of Light was a noble and just ruler, everything was for the good of the people.

The Lady of Light then sat on her throne and looked up, "Thank you, Lady of Illumination."

The Lady of Illumination left the platform and walked back to the benches and sat. Two creatures with spider legs walked up to the platform, they were small, only four feet high and had heads like human children except their flesh was brown and a little fury. They were both very attractive, if spider-like people could be attractive. They had six furry legs, one was a boy, the other a girl. The girl spider had little bands of pretty blue flowers around her feet. Both spider children bowed their front legs.

The girl spoke, "Greetings Lady of Light, I am to present myself to you, I am Anita and I am a new Phase Walker."

The crowd cheered and clapped, some stomped their feet.

The little boy also spoke, "I am Leto and I am also a new Phase Walker."

There was a second applause and cheering.

The Lady of Light smiled, then spoke and her voice had a melody, "Thank you for presenting yourself to the court. I would ask if you wish to train and become a Lady and Lord of Illumination or seek a different path?"

Anita formally spoke, "My Lady of Light I wish to travel and explore the phases, I feel my destiny is out-worldly."

The Lady of Light beamed a smile, "May your travels be safe and you always return to Lorvisa, Phase Walker. Thank you again for presenting yourself to the court."

Leto smiled and cute little dimples showed up on his

cheeks, "Your Eminence, I wish to train to become a Lord of Illumination and help the land and people of Lorvisa."

The crowd on the benches cheered and clapped. A worm carrying a tabard of Illumination and a sword came forward then bowed in front of the young spiderling and presented the items.

Leto put the tabard over his head and held the sword in the air.

The crowd went wild, cheered louder and then clapped faster than before. Even Anita was smiling and clapping, knowing her decision did not bring her such glory but that was okay by her, for she chose another path.

The two children left the platform and all was quiet.

The Lady of Light stood and announced, "Are there any more who wish to seek audience with the court?"

There was stillness and the eyes of the crowd looked around.

The Lady of Light smiled and continued, "May your day be happy and you achieve your goals today, the court of Illumination is closed."

She bowed her head and clapped her hands, and with that a bright light radiated from within her and she disappeared.

The benches started to empty, some flew with wings to the top of the dome where there was an open window. The others walked, crawled or hobbled away, clearing the court.

- Chapter 7 -

Stockings

It was around eleven and William's car pulled up outside Sarah's foyer to her apartment. Sarah smiled and spoke, "Thank you so much for taking me to Wicked, I so enjoyed it and the singing was perfect. The green Ferris wheel afterwards was also fantastical."

Sarah stopped talking and lent over to give William a kiss goodbye. It was an awkward first kiss, like William wasn't expecting it so he kind of moved a little to the side, which Sarah thought for a moment he was pulling away, but nevertheless it was passionate and lasted quite some time.

Sarah sat up, unclipped her seat belt and smiled, "Thanks for a good night, talk to you soon, goodbye."

She then opened the car door stepped out and closed it then waved, William smiled back, "I'll phone you in the morning."

Sarah walked to the foyer, entered and went up the lift to her apartment; she was tired and had had a long day, not only physically but emotionally. She saw Caitlin curled up in a ball next to Wuzzle on the floor, it was cute.

Sarah went to her room, kicked off her high heels and put her handbag on the ground; she took out her iPhone and lay in bed holding it. She rolled over to one side of her bed and rolled all the way through the wall. She landed with a thud and had the faintest tingling feeling knowing she passed through a phase. She looked at her iPhone which was still in her hand, the time read eleven, eleven.

Then Sarah looked around, she had been here before, there was mist and stone everywhere, a sulphur smell was in the air, there was a stone flat platform off into the distance and a large structure. Looking down at her feet Sarah was surprised she hadn't noticed it first, but Caitlin and Wuzzle were sound asleep on the ground. She put her phone into her pocket and quickly awoke Caitlin by pushing her gently.

Wuzzle growled as he awoke first and Caitlin awoke slowly and looked up at Sarah with curiosity in her eyes, "Where are we Sarah?"

Sarah spoke, "I don't know, I came home from my date and rolled into the wall next to my bed again, I assume I went through a phase. The time is eleven, eleven when I checked."

Caitlin stood up, "Indeed we passed through a phase. I think I recognise this place, we must have linked if you saw ones and you brought me through – it's a proximity thing, we need to watch that now we are together, it's easy to do that."

Wuzzle stood up; Caitlin put her hands out waving, "I feel a phase point just there behind you Sarah. It's a new phase point for me, I haven't felt this one before and I know a few. I need to confirm what plane we are on. Do you know Sarah? How did you learn this phase point?"

Sarah looked at Caitlin and took in the questions, "Well I don't know this plane but I have been here, once before I met you Caitlin, before I knew about Phase Walkers. I fought a Delvin here, like the one on your plane, and it fled. I do not know how I came here or where here is?"

Caitlin looked around at the rocky crop; little stone mounds were all over with a thin veil of mist. She peered over to see a tiny platform off into the distance.

"Well we should at least try and work out what plane this is. Seeing Delvin here is no surprise lately they seem to be on all planes these days, probably hunting Phase Walkers as there is a phase point just there."

Wuzzle reached down and picked Caitlin up and placed her on his shoulder, she wore a purple dress with little flowers and zip front pocket, like the pink dress. She carried something in her pocket and she rubbed it to check it was still there, "Okay follow me."

Sarah looked down at her feet, she was not wearing shoes and was bare foot; it was worse, she was wearing thin tanned stockings, "I don't think I can walk very far, I don't have shoes."

Wuzzle walked off toward a ravine, nothing to be seen except rock and varying shades of grey and mist, occasionally some heat would shimmer off a group of rocks. Sarah followed a little behind and they went down the ravine, Sarah was taking every step slowly trying not to rip a hole in her stockings but the rocks kept catching them, little tears and snags started to appear at the bottom of her feet, then they all stood on the large platform made of stone.

There was an open entrance to a stone structure. Wuzzle moved on and they entered the stone entrance moving further in a winding passage and it seemed to lead down. The ground was rock but covered in moss. Occasionally Sarah slid on the moss and caught herself holding onto the stone wall. At this point her tanned stocking were trashed so she removed them and dropped them to the ground; she was now barefoot.

The twisting stone passageway ended in a door. It was wooden and had a symbol that Caitlin did not recognise. A half-moon with an arrow in the middle. Wuzzle pushed open the door with his paw the door swung inward freely. They entered the room, it was stone, crude chairs and a table were against a wall. A little open chest was in the middle of the room and a burnt out fire pit with what looked like old cooking equipment tossed in a mess to the side. Metal pokers, a pan and hooks, and a metal fork laid twisted in a mattered cloth. Sarah went and looked at the pan, she picked it up and looked at the handle; it looked plastic she turned it over and there was a label on the back it said IKEA.

Sarah shouted, "Fuck."

"What is it?" Wuzzle walked over to Sarah quickly, Caitlin spoke again, "What happened, what's wrong?"

Sarah looked up, "The pan, it's from Earth, it's from a home store, look at its markings."

She pointed to the IKEA label and further read to herself "stainless steel do not scrub contains a non-stick coating".

Caitlin said, "This isn't Earth I can feel the difference, probably a Phase Walker left it there, this place is different I don't feel at ease. Strangely I actually have several of these exact pans back at my house, they must be popular."

Caitlin had a puzzled expression on her face.

Sarah's phone rung, it broke the tension that was building, Sarah answered, "Seriously, I get reception."

A voice spoke, "Hello."

Sarah, surprised, replied, "Hello, who is this?"

The voice answered, "Sarah, it's me Mary, your assignment buddy. How's your research going? We need to get together and finish by the end of the week."

Sarah shifted her feet while Caitlin was staring intently at her, "I will meet you Thursday lunch at the library, can I talk to you tonight after our lecture?"

Mary replied, "Okay, talk to you tonight, oh I also took spare notes for you."

Wuzzle started down another tunnel, Caitlin was still on his shoulder. Sarah slipped her phone into her pocket and walked fast to catch them, her bare feet now very sore. They were in a large room underground, moss covered the stone and mushrooms of different colours sprouted up between the rocks. There were several doors.

Sarah slipped on a stone and hurt her bare foot; it cut her toe and it started to bleed. Sarah started to moan so Wuzzle started for her direction, Caitlin looked down, "Are you okay Sarah?"

Sarah stood awkwardly on one foot, "No, I should not have walked down here without no shoes."

Wuzzle lent down and picked Sarah up with his large paw and with one arm, then sat Sarah on his shoulder. This felt so wrong Sarah thought, looking around in a panic, hoping that no one saw her.

Caitlin giggled, "Wuzzle doesn't mind carrying you too Sarah. We need to find out where we are."

Wuzzle, carrying little Caitlin on one shoulder and Sarah, who was grabbing his fur with a death grip, on the other shoulder, walked like a beast of burden down to the middle door. This door was locked. Caitlin clapped her hands and Wuzzle pushed the door again, it opened. Sarah felt the tingling of the phase when Caitlin clapped.

Sarah's phone rang again, it rung out three times before Sarah could get it out of her pocket, the ring tone was loud. Caitlin frowned. Sarah answered, "Hello."

A warm male voice responded, "It's William, how are you, lovely? It's lunch and I'm at the Chocolate Coffee House, where are you?"

Sarah, holding Wuzzle's fur in one hand and the phone in the other, spoke, "I meant to tell you about that William, I no longer work there, I decided to use my spare time studying."

"Really, I thought you were a starving university student."

Sarah, holding onto fur, "I am, I am, it's only for a little while till I catch up and I will get another job."

William replied, "Oh well, I guess I will buy my lunch elsewhere, no one makes better coffee than you Sarah."

A Delvin burst through the door, it was blue and snarled, it had sharp teeth; it was the same one that Sarah battled in her last visit.

Sarah, wide eyed, spoke fast, "I got to go, talk to you soon, bye," and hung up.

Then she struggled to put the phone into her jacket pocket.

(Meanwhile, William thought, that was strange, then hung his phone up and walked out of the Coffee House.)

Wuzzle, under Caitlin's orders, ran out of the room, up the tunnel and out of the structure. Sarah was hanging on tightly, bouncing with Wuzzle's every step; Caitlin was having no trouble and didn't even hang on. The stone walls streaked by in blurs, Wuzzle was moving exceptionally fast.

Sarah felt a sense of dread and fear come at her in waves, then she could hear the loud scraping foots steps of hooves on stone. Wuzzle ran down the ravine and back to the phase point all three entered the phase and landed on Sarah's bed. The bed sagged with all the weight until Wuzzle got off and stood. Sarah lay on her bed from where she rolled off Wuzzle's shoulder, Caitlin was still perched on Wuzzle's other shoulder. Unbelievable Sarah thought and almost giggled but just smirked.

Caitlin peered down at Sarah on the bed, "I don't know where that was but we need to go back and find out, it was strangely familiar, maybe leave your mobile at home next time."

Sarah looked up, "So sorry, it's not like we went in prepared, it was an accident," then looked down at her cut toe; the bleeding had stopped.

"I didn't realise my phone would work on another plane, damn my mobile phone company is fantastic!" Sarah said.

Caitlin replied "The phone must be linked to you, when a Phase Walker goes to another plane they are kind of still on their own plane and it kind of goes around you, it's very complicated but I can understand how it probably would work. Only objects that are not living can go through the phase, other people and even plants cannot pass unless they're Phase Walkers."

Sarah looked at the time, "How can it be night already, surely we were only in the phase an hour at most."

"Sometimes time moves differently it depends on what plane you're in, actually that's a good point, it may be a clue to where we went."

Sarah sat up in her bed, "I need to get ready for university, I have to meet someone beforehand about an assignment, excuse me."

The blue Delvin stopped at the end of the stone platform and looked down the ravine, mist came to his knees and he stood for some time. He then returned back inside, walking down the tunnel, his hoofed foot stood on something and it stuck clinging to the bottom of his foot. The Delvin stopped and flexed a huge muscled arm and reached down to picked up a pair of tan colour stockings with holes as he kept walking down to the underdark.

Morack's throne room was deep underground, it was empty and fire roared along one wall. When the blue Delvin entered the smell of burnt flesh was in the air and the blue Delvin stood then waited. Time passed and it waited more, there was movement then Alastor came into the throne room. The half breed was small and tiny, a disgrace to the Delvin kind, the blue Delvin knew it was Morack's toy, one of his experiments, but wanted it dead.

The blue Delvin simply pointed at Alastor. Alastor frowned, it was one thing taking crap from Morack but from one of his under-grunts, Alastor wasn't having it so he walked over to the blue Delvin.

Alastor gave a grin as he approached the blue Delvin who looked mean, his horns were black and curled upwards.

"What do you want?" Alastor's voice was deep.

The blue Delvin spoke with a grunt, "I am Gravnee, I am the watcher, give this to Morack, I found it in the entrance when I chased intruders from the upper entrance."

He shoved the pair of stockings into Alastor's arms.

Alastor asked, thinking this Delvin must be stupid, "Who were the intruders?"

Gravnee spoke in a grinding voice, "A strange large hairy creature with big teeth, carrying two non Delvins on his shoulders, one big, one small."

Alastor raised an eyebrow thinking it sounded like a phasewalker he once knew, "Rather odd, I will tell Morack, just curious why you are telling me?"

Gravnee responded laughing, "You are Morack's pet, now be a good pet and go tell Morack, I'm going back to do my watcher job."

Alastor cringed at hearing that and plotted in his mind

how to free Keyness and in that moment put the stockings into his ragged pocket and walked away back down to the laboratory.

In the laboratory Alastor was alone as Morack had gone somewhere into the phase, he sat on the stone floor placing his hand through the tan nylon stocking, strangely the same colour of his skin. He used a little bit of light magic to try and work out who it belonged to, the magic was slippery. He got a flash and a blond haired beauty danced in his mind, he picked up that she was a Phase Walker but her kind was unknown to him. He knew that Morack would love to get his hands on more Phase Walkers, so Alastor clicked his fingers and a small weak flicker of light magic hovered in his hand burning a blue flame and he set the stockings on fire to hide the evidence.

Sarah returned from university, she had a pile of notes and it was late. Caitlin had ordered in pizza again for dinner, Wuzzle was busy munching down on one, including the box.

Caitlin spoke, "Sarah, I think we should go into the phase tonight, this time prepare and work out that phase point we went to last time. I've been thinking, strangely enough that cooking pan I picked up looked like it was mine. I took several from a huge house shop called IKEA. I just can't shake the feeling it is mine."

"I should have used the phase to work it out but was distracted, this time I will. Come sit down have some pizza and then we will enter the phase."

Sarah joined Wuzzle and Caitlin on the lounge then started to eat cheese pizza. All three sat in silence eating for some time until all the pizza was gone. At least she didn't have to worry about filling up the trash Sarah thought while watching Wuzzle eat the last empty pizza box. Though she did think she needed to invest in a good vacuum cleaner as Wuzzle's fur was everywhere on her lounge. Picking up a few of his hairs she tossed them on the floor.

Sarah sat forward on her chair, "Okay I'm ready but let me get changed first."

Caitlin lay back and turned on the television, "Okay."

Sarah got dressed in blue jeans and a frilly white shirt, and wore red sneakers she used for jogging. Sarah put on makeup and freshened up with scented musk perfume. She opened her bedroom door and called, "Caitlin, I'm ready now, let's go; I'm leaving my phone."

Sarah placed her phone on the bedside table.

Caitlin stood up and entered Sarah's room, Wuzzle followed. Caitlin just waved her hand and the phase point near Sarah's bed opened. Sarah was amazed that each time a phase opened it was slightly different but still the same. This time a silvery line appeared, it hovered for some time before it opened and you could see blurry things inside. All three stood on her bed the springs sagged and made a noise then they all walked through the phase.

Sarah stepped through and barely felt the tingling, she must be getting used to this, she thought. Caitlin, following, stepped through, "Okay, let's go, we have our phase weapons if we get into trouble."

All three went down the ravine past the platform and into the structure entrance. It was still and quiet, they walked down the tunnel and into the large room again, the cooking equipment still lay untouched where they left it last time.

Caitlin picked the IKEA pan up again and used the phase; it had residual energy from Earth and her plane. She thought for a while and recalled she gave some pans like this to Martin to use as a racket in an underwater game known as shells.

Very confused, she reached out and felt the phase in this plane, it felt wrong and twisted, then she even felt fear when touching the phase for a short time.

Caitlin was waving the pan, "Okay, we need to go further into this place, it has got me puzzled."

Sarah just replied, "Okay, I'm following you."

Caitlin walked into another the room, the door lock was broken previously, it led to another large room and several more doors. She was really frustrated, then she felt for the phase.

Alastor heard the scrapping of hoofs and footsteps echoing away as the hunters left the hall and he walked back to the throne room in the hope Morack was not back.

Sarah looked around as Caitlin studied the doors, several large shapes appeared to be coming their way, hooves scraped on stone and the guttural language of the Delvin was heard.

Caitlin, Sarah and Wuzzle ran to a door, opened it and closed the door. They were in a small room, there were two beds made out of straw and mushrooms grew in the corner in a neat square pattern as if they were cultivated to grow that way.

The voices grew louder, "Morack says we have to find these Phase Walkers, Morack needs more essence so we need to step up our search, Grimlock, we need to find this unknown phase where they are hiding."

Within the room, hiding, Caitlin was shocked she hadn't pick this up before. It rung in her mind they were on Nevid, the homeland of the Delvin, those twisted by chaos magic, no wonder the phase felt wrong.

There was more talking another voice and more footsteps, "Hey you there, what are you doing?"

Caitlin froze like in a child's game, Sarah did not move an inch trying to work out if the voice was talking to them and Wuzzle just looked up from where he was sitting. All three didn't move and were still as can be.

A loud voice boomed back, "I am the watcher, I guard this entrance for Morack, have you seen Morack's pet?"

All three in the room, frozen, then had the realisation that the voice was not talking to them. Caitlin placed her index finger to her lip and looked at Sarah.

Grimlock, a black Delvin with flaming red hair and horns replied, "No. Do not tell Morack we have returned yet. Why do you ask about the half-breed Celestial, Alastor, for?"

Caitlin's ear picked up, Alastor was the name of her friend in the Celestial plane. What's the chances, she thought, I guess he's not a half-breed so it's not him, we have to get out of here as soon as it clears.

All three waited for a time until the voices faded and words could no longer be heard. Sarah decided to count the mushrooms because she was getting bored.

Caitlin finally spoke, breaking the silence and ending Sarah's mushroom counting, "Sarah we need to get out of here now, hold my hand we are linking and phasing to the phase point."

Sarah held Caitlin's hand she thought of ones and Caitlin chose the destination the other side of the ravine next to the phase point. They walked through the phase rift, it shimmered silver, in the small room, they arrived at their destination. Caitlin quickly opened the phase point to Earth and they all walked through the phase into Sarah's bedroom onto her bed. The springs crunched this time as Wuzzle stepped on them.

Sarah thought she better change the room around.

Caitlin got off the bed and spoke, "I know where the plane goes to Sarah, I don't know how you found it but it goes to Nevid. Where the Delvin are, they are hunting Phase Walkers. I realised that the pan in the first room was from IKEA I think it's the pan I gave to Martin."

"I need to talk to him. I'm also worried about my friend Alastor, it may be nothing but after visiting Martin I want to fast track that trip to the Celestial plane."

Sarah looked confused, "I have university two nights a week and I've started dating, I'm not sure I have the time to do all this Caitlin and I'm also tired."

Caitlin looked indignant, "Sarah you are a Phase Walker, you don't get a choice unless you don't want to live. You are hunted, they want to kill us, you killed one of their Delvin, and they will not stop. People you love will get hurt, including yourself, if we don't go on the run and work this out. Anyway sleep now and we will talk more in the morning and set plans in motion."

Sarah looked down to meet Caitlin's eyes, "You know I find it really odd taking orders from a little kid, you look like you're seven years old."

Caitlin looked up, "I'm actually twenty two of your Earth years, hopefully you don't think what I say is an order rather than very good advice. Good night Sarah."

Caitlin followed Wuzzle into the lounge room.

Sarah closed her bedroom door, got into her bed, picked some of Wuzzle's fur off her pillow and went to sleep.

- Chapter 8 -

Everybody Eats

Leto proudly walked out of the Illumination court wearing his new tabard, his six legs marching in every step. He had his sword tucked into his belt. His sister Anita was still smiling, she couldn't wait for adventures. They both headed back to their colony to retell all that happened in court. It was a two day walk so they both walked with a skip in their step.

Outside the domed court was thick vegetation, but there were neat little trails in all directions and those that knew the way had an easy travel to their destination. A few fellow court goers came by and personally congratulated them.

Anita, really excited with it all chatted constantly, and was very proud of her brother Leto, "So let's go, can't wait to get back to the colony and tell everyone, will you leave us for Illumination training?"

Leto spoke in a regal tone, "Yes, I need to report in for training I will be gone for a year or two I guess, I need to take the Illumination oaths, I'm not a Lord yet."

Anita replied, "I miss you already."

Leto raised a furry spider arm and placed it on his sister, "And I you sister, but there is a greater good and that is what I want to serve, to keep our lands, people free and safe. I cannot wait to take the vow."

Anita, a little worried at the enormity of Leto's decision, said, "You are the most noble, selfless person I know, I am so proud to call you brother."

They walked until the afternoon through many trails lined with vegetation, then decided to make camp for the night. Anita found a nice tree, the dirt underneath was warm and loose. She began to use all her feet to dig a hole at the base of the tree. Leto followed her to the tree and stared at the ground next to where Anita was digging.

Anita looked up "What is it Leto? Why are you not making a burrow for the night?"

Leto looked at Anita kicking up dirt, "I don't want to get my new tabard dirty and I don't want to take it off. It was given to me by the Lady of Light."

Anita replied, "Ah-ha well that's up to you. I'll be safe and warm underground. If you want to turn into some strange surface creature that's your problem."

With that said Anita snuggled into a hole in the ground. She moved dirt over herself and burrowed deeper into the earth until she could no longer be seen. Leto stood under the tree, crouched all six legs then closed his eyes.

It was dark and still in the forest, but a large white larva creature shuffled along, it was fluffy and thin, oh so thin. It moved to a bush with many plush leaves, reached its mouth forward and chewed with its large mouth filled with pointy white teeth and spat out the leaves. It did not appear to satisfy its hunger.

It moaned and shuffled on further into the forest, oh so hungry, it's only primal thought. There were mushrooms at the base of a tree, it moved forward, its body arching, then stretched its mouth forward once more and chowed down on the mushrooms. Its body twitched and the white worm creature moaned again, the chewed mushrooms then landed in a heap on the ground. The pain increased in the creature and so did the moaning.

It moved on further down a trail and up a little hill, there was another trail it followed for some time before it saw a brown thing hunched over at the base of a tree.

The white worm creature moved to the brown thing, thinking it would be tasty, opened its mouth extra wide and swallowed Leto head first. Leto's sword fell to the ground with a thud, his lovely tabard with a golden triangle crumbled with every bite in the large worm's mouth. Leto made no noise, it was silent and still. His legs convulsed outside the worm's mouth until the creature consumed Leto. A large bump was in the worms belly it looked odd and protruded to one side. A strange energy surrounded the worm, it glowed. The creature stopped its moaning and moved on in search of more of what it just ate.

The night turned to morning and Anita burrowed to the surface, she looked around and could not find Leto. That was odd she thought, her six legs scuttled along the base of the tree. She found Leto's sword, it was shiny, she knew Leto would be around because she was sure he would not leave it unattended. So she waited and she waited. Morning turned to midday and then she thought maybe something very important happened and he left. She was determined to make her way back to the colony and let them know everything that had happened. Carrying the sword she headed off on a trail deep into the forest.

Caitlin awoke in the morning and left the apartment. Wuzzle was awake and watching TV. Sarah woke up, Wuzzle was alone and she asked, "Where is Caitlin?"

Wuzzle stared at her and pointed to the front door.

Sarah didn't understand and went back to her bedroom and started to get ready for the morning. No work so she guessed the day was free and she could wear comfortable clothes. She then walked back into the lounge room wearing tracksuit pants and a sports t-shirt.

Caitlin opened the front door with no key apparently; she came in with four massive bags of McDonald's breakfast take away. It looked comical, a little girl with large bags coming in. Sarah wondered why the attendants served her so much food without asking where an adult was.

Caitlin gave three bags to Wuzzle who started to chow down on a bacon burger in one gulp.

Sarah picked up an OJ and started to eat a hash brown, "Thanks for breakfast Caitlin, very thoughtful."

Caitlin replied, "No problem, I wanted us to have a large breakfast before we head off."

Sarah, almost spitting up her mouthful of OJ, "Well I need to talk to you about that?"

Caitlin looked up while unwrapping a burger, "About what?"

Sarah put the OJ down on the table, "Well I'll go with you on the condition that I still go to university two nights a week and see my new boyfriend. I guess its early days for that but William I must see once a week for a date."

Caitlin, aghast, "Sarah it would mean we would be always walking through the phase never on one plane for long before returning here."

Sarah spoke, "Well it doesn't have to mean all of us, I could come back, do my thing, then meet you up again in whatever phase you're in, isn't that what Phase Walkers do, move around?"

Caitlin sighed, "I guess we can try, if that's what we have to do to keep you safe."

Sarah smiled, "Well we have two days then before uni, so where are we going?"

Caitlin munched on a hash brown and put it down, "I want to go home and talk to Martin, I want to find out if any Delvin came back and if he still has those two IKEA pan's I gave him to rest my mind at ease. Martin is my best friend, he saved my life when I was but a toddler, I fell into the pond. Plus I miss him and our daily chats."

"Once we are done then that afternoon we can phase to the Celestial plane and visit my friends, they will give us a nice place to sleep. Stay a day and I will teach you more Phase Walker things, and then I guess you can go to university while

I spend time with my friends and you meet me back in the Celestial plane, sounds like a plan?"

Sarah, taking it all in, responded, "Sure, but I need to take a few things."

Caitlin finished off her hash brown, "Okay, we leave after breakfast."

Sarah went back into her room then took a perfume, her mobile, two sets of clothes and some breath mints and shoved it into a backpack. Then she walked out to join Caitlin for some more breakfast.

Wuzzle gave a huge burp.

Sarah laughed, "I take it he's finished."

Caitlin packed away several wrappers inside a brown Macca's bag then walked over to Wuzzle and handed him the bag, Wuzzle grabbed it with his huge clawed paws and ate the rubbish.

"The phase point to my world Kelstone is back in the alley where you used to work Sarah. It seems the phase point here is only connected to the Delvin plane."

Sarah shrugged, feeling that perhaps she created the phase point in her bedroom, "That's fine, I'm ready," then picked up her backpack and put it on her shoulder.

"Sarah, think of the ones, I need a link."

Caitlin then opened an intra-phase to the alley from the kitchen table, it appeared along the kitchen wall as a silvery slither, then an opening.

Wuzzle stood and Caitlin held his clawed furry hand, they walked through the phase, straight through the kitchen wall. Sarah followed behind then it snapped shut.

All three stood in the alley behind the Chocolate Coffee House. Sarah thought this is exactly as she remembered it, Caitlin opened a phase on the wall behind the skip that was her plane's phase point.

Then without talking to one another they all entered the phase into the plane of Kelstone.

They were in a forest, it was thick, with a trail leading out to the pond. From a distance everything looked the same, all the trees still ended with a curl. Caitlin walked with a fast step to her house, Wuzzle actually trailed behind her for a change, trying to keep up.

Caitlin came to her house, the door was gone, she looked inside, all her pretty pink things were scattered around and furniture was over turned. Wuzzle came behind her and started to clean up, picking pillows from the ground and piling books from the floor onto a shelf.

Sarah walked in last then looked around, "Crap, you have been robbed. Delvin you think?"

Caitlin frowned, "Probably, I can't be sure, but what I can be sure of is nothing appears to be stolen so they were looking for something."

Caitlin touched her front pocket, making sure her prize was still there.

Sarah walked further in and started to help clean up as well.

Caitlin's little house was starting to look how she left it then she smiled, "Wuzzle can you get the door, a neat trick I need to show you Sarah."

Wuzzle walked outside and fetched the large wooden seven foot door and stood before the entrance.

"Just hold it there," Caitlin directed, then moved her hand around the door; Sarah felt the phase power and the tingling was strong. The door was repairing itself and attaching to the wall.

Sarah wide eyed, "Wow, that was cool, I could actually see the phase being used when you did that Caitlin."

"Good, you're understanding how it works. Okay, let's go and summon Martin, we can come clean the rest of this mess another time."

Caitlin went to her shelf and took a large sea shell, it was curled to one side and bright yellow.

Caitlin walked outside her house and waited, Sarah was the last to leave and shut the door behind, impressed at how well it mended.

All three walked to the pond, it was still and the water

looked refreshing. Caitlin briefly looked back at her house and cringed when she saw the outdoor furniture smashed. Caitlin then lifted the yellow shell to her mouth and blew inside the shell. A little vibrating hum was made. They waited for a time; Caitlin was scanning the water looking for movement. She decided to blow the shell again and raised it to her mouth. Then a little movement could be seen in the water. The water lilies moved, dancing in the pond.

Jas poked his head above the water; his little cheeky face, usually smiling, was void of expression, his black and green scales reflected off the water.

Caitlin, trying to read his expression, spoke, "Jas, how are you, where is Martin? I need to speak to him."

Jas's bottom lip trembled and he spoke, "The village was attacked by demon creatures."

Caitlin spoke fast, "Is everyone ok?"

Jas's face was wretched in pain, "Many of my people were slaughtered, father, mother and my baby sister dead, I am alone and broken."

Caitlin fell to the ground along the pond bank, her head dizzy and trying to take in what was said, a tear trickled down her tiny cheek. She spoke in a soft tone, looking up from the ground, "Martin is dead, and your family is gone?"

Imaginary tiny daggers were being pushed into her body.

Caitlin saw Jas in the water, his face stern and still, then spoke, "I'm so sorry for your loss Jas, if there is anything I can do please let me know."

"How many demons did this? Also did they take anything or say what they were looking for?"

Jas bobbed in the water, "Well, there is something you can do."

Jas's face looked mean and his eyes were scary, "I want to avenge my family and kill the demons that have done this to my village."

"There were four demons, two blue, one black and one purple. They took the village's magical ianoid stones, among many other things."

Caitlin stopped crying and started to feel enraged, she sat fully upright. Sarah stood listening and taking it all in, shocked that Martin was killed and his family. Wuzzle, well he stood looking at the ground like a sad teddy bear with a frown.

"Jas I'm going to try and make things right. I don't know how, but I am going to find a way and put a plan together. Your father was a noble Persidion, always there to help others, a good friend to me. I will come back when I can little Jas, know that your family loved you very much and be strong."

Jas looked blankly, not really knowing what to say, waved and leaped down deep into the water until he could see the floor of the pond.

Jas sat and thought of how noble his father was and thought a lot of good that did him. He had a plan and if he had to kill the demons by himself, he would. Jas was going to be two legs and walk outside the pond; he knew some of his people had become two legs before. Snarling, Jas swam back to his village.

There was a rustle in the forest around the large tree which was the phase point to Kelstone.

A large fat white worm wriggled and moved down the trail deeper into the forest.

Caitlin took the shell under her arm and moved back toward her dwelling, she looked at Wuzzle who now saw the outdoor table and chairs a mess. He walked up to them and started to tidy up but the chairs remained broken.

Sarah followed and then laughed, she knew it was inappropriate but she just couldn't get the Teddy Bears' Picnic song out of her head when she watched Wuzzle move the chairs around the table.

Caitlin frowned, "What's so funny?"

Sarah responded, "So sorry, just an Earth song going through my head."

Caitlin then motioned Wuzzle back to her, "Let's go to the Celestial plane, it's not safe here. We need to work out what's going on."

Sarah replied, "Okay."

Caitlin, Sarah and Wuzzle were walking back to the phase point along the trail when they saw movement in the bush.

Caitlin, annoyed, walked to the bush ready to kill, feeling for the phase, "Who is in there?"

A small frightened voice replied, "It's me, Mixy, I'm scared and lost, I can't find my clutch, I also feel different."

Caitlin, trying to sound sympathetic, replied, "Please come out, I will see if I can help you."

A huge white fluffy worm poked its huge head out of the bush. It had large eyes and a huge mouth, very frightening, Sarah thought.

The worm spoke, but its mouth did not move, "I'm here, and do you know the way back to my clutch. I think I ate something wrong because I feel so different."

Sarah, shocked she understood what the worm said, spoke, "What did you eat? How do you feel different?"

The worm rolled and spoke, "I ate a brown thing, it was tasty, then I felt tingling, lots of tingling, it makes me feel sick."

Caitlin did not know this creature though her people specialised in the animals of Kelstone and even share special bonds with them. Caitlin used some of the phase on the worm to see if she could get a clue to this creature.

The worm's eyes widened and it looked scared.

Caitlin felt the phase reaching out to her linking. The worm was a Phase Walker.

Caitlin was puzzled, "It's okay, you seem to be a Phase Walker."

The worm Mixy looked worried, "What's a Phase Walker? I want to go home."

Caitlin looked at the huge thick tree trunk with markings,

almost expecting it to open with several Delvin rushing through or more white worms. Trying to deal with the situation, Caitlin centred herself, "Mixy there is a lot to explain it seems, I keep meeting new Phase Walkers, Sarah is one too."

Sarah stepped forward and smiled, "Hi I'm Sarah, this is Caitlin and Wuzzle," pointing to all in turn.

Caitlin looked to be very tiny compared to Wuzzle and the large white worm.

"Standing right here is dangerous, we are right next to a phase point, there are bad creatures called the Delvin that just slaughtered a village of aquatic people called Persidion, they are hunting Phase Walkers like us and I really want to get out of this area."

"I'm sure you have lots of questions but we must go. Please link with us and follow us through the phase, there we can be safe and talk more."

Mixy replied, "Okay, please take me somewhere safe, how I link?"

"It's okay Mixy, I will help you link."

Sarah walked up to the giant fluffy white worm, trying not to look at its mouth, and put her hands on it, the phase linked to hers and she linked back to Caitlin. Caitlin felt the phase then made a door, she used different symbols that Sarah had not seen before, but Sarah tried to remember them. The phase on the tree trunk opened and everyone walked through the phase except Mixy.

Mixy was scared she looked around realising she was alone and then shuffled quickly into the phase.

The phase closed behind them, they were in a thin forest, the trees were silver and the leaves were perfectly shaped. The ground was green and fresh, the grass was low. There were pretty flying bugs with colourful wings dancing around a bush. The air felt fresh and the scent of pine was strong.

Caitlin felt safe; she was tired but knew she had to go to Remiel House and sort out her thoughts.

"Okay, my friend's estate is not far, it's called Remiel

House, they are friendly and will give us rooms and food."

Mixy cheered, "Food, I need food, I am very hungry."

Caitlin smiled then said, "Phase Walkers usually don't need anything. I have much to teach you Mixy and you too Sarah. I don't know how I became the teacher because it wasn't long ago that I was learning the lessons of being a Phase Walker myself. My friends Shandra and Alastor know more than me about being a Phase Walker."

Caitlin started to walk out of the forest and along a stone cobbled path, each stone was perfect and aligned neatly, the perfection of the road was eerie.

Caitlin began to speak as she walked, "We are in the Celestial plane, magic on this plane is good and pure. As are the things and people here. Though nothing on this plan is natural, unfortunately everything you see has been created by magic, even the trees, nothing naturally grows here, it was made by the Celestial people."

"See look at this leaf," Caitlin said, while pointing at a tree.

"Each one is perfectly shaped and the green is an even colour, no imperfections."

Sarah, studying the leaves on the tree, "So everyone is magical on this plane?"

"Pretty much it's the way of life for people here, but Phase Walkers, like on every plane, are rare," Caitlin replied.

After a time following the path, Sarah stopped and looked around her surroundings; it was getting dark but a large building was in view from the distance. It had a stone grey bridge and lights shone blue along the top. The bridge was not huge nor the water underneath deep at all, she could see the pebbles on the bottom from the distance and wondered if the phase enhanced her view.

Walking toward the building the grass was strange; it looked too well manicured, and too freshly mowed. A grand building came into view, this was Remiel House. Sarah, amazed, studied its details. It had a huge doorway and arches covered in decorative silvery lattice work; it appeared to be three storeys high and had many rectangle windows and a large round window on each level with detailed stained glass, which a bright light shone through.

There was a little bit of a hill to the entrance but everyone walked on, Mixy the worm surprisingly kept pace and took the hill in its stride.

Caitlin walked up to the door and knocked several times. Moments later a guy answered the door, really hot looking, Sarah thought.

He had tanned skin and stood about six feet tall, his eyes had a strange light blue hue to them, somehow unnatural, he had huge muscled arms and brown long hair to his shoulders, he somehow looked too perfect, like he had been digitally photoshopped, Sarah thought.

Caitlin looked up, "Ethan, hello, how are you, I come for a visit and brought friends."

Ethan smiled warmly, "Greetings Miss Caitlin of Kelstone, please be welcome and bring your friends inside."

Ethan opened the door wider and took a little step back then stretched his silvery wings wide.

Sarah opened her mouth in awe and shock.

Caitlin and Wuzzle entered into the entry and Sarah followed with Mixy crawling behind.

Ethan had a warm voice, "My sister is here, Shandra, but Alastor is not, he has been missing for some time I'm afraid, for several years."

Caitlin responded quickly, "What do you mean he's missing?"

Ethan's smile turned to sadness, "Alastor, being a Phase Walker, we believed he went into a phase and never returned, I hope one day he does return to Remiel House. Please come sit and have some tea by the fireplace."

Caitlin was not taking all this bad news well as tears welled up in her eyes.

Ethan motioned them to the next room and a small blue glowing orb the size of soccer ball with a face beamed to Ethan and spoke in a humming voice, "Shall I make them tea

Ethan?"

Ethan looked at the blue orb, "Yes, please, and can you tell my sister we have guests, also can you prepare lodgings for our guests?"

The blue orb replied, "Certainly Ethan."

Sarah raised an eyebrow wondering what type of creature or being that was.

The next room was vast, it had several plush lounges and a roaring fireplace with blue flames if indeed it was fire. There was a huge wooden table in the centre of the room and it appeared there were freshly cut flowers in vases around the room, giving it a perfumed scent.

Ethan closed his wings, they neatly sat along his back, Sarah tried not to stare.

Caitlin sat on a lounge, it was red and plush, Wuzzle stood behind her, Mixy started to chew on the flowers in a pretty vase. Sarah sat on the lounge opposite Caitlin, it was soft and comfortable Ethan sat next to Sarah, a little too close Sarah thought even though another person could sit between them, his wings imaginarily touching her.

Ethan gave a sad smile, "Alastor just set off one morning like he did most days and never returned. I do feel that foul play was at hand. Shandra has been searching for him ever since, you can imagine as his twin it's much more distressing for her then me, it pains me even further to see her pain daily as I deal with my own."

The orb returned but it had hands and was holding a large wooden tray, on the tray was tea and large mugs, which it passed out to everyone except Mixy. It came back and brought out a large wooden bucket filled with sweet smelling water and placed it in front of Mixy who gleefully drunk its contents by sticking her head into the bucket.

Everyone was sipping their tea from a mug including Wuzzle, which made Sarah giggle seeing a giant teddy bear drinking from a mug. The teddy bears picnic theme song played in her mind once more.

Shandra walked into the room and beamed a smile, she

was radiate. Sarah had not seen such a beautiful women before except in fashion magazines, she was stunning, she had long golden hair to her waist and bright golden wings which were spread out in a large fan. She wore a white dress with blue patterns that glowed in its fabric and her eyes were also the same strange glowing blue as Ethan's.

Shandra spoke and opened her arms, "Caitlin, oh how I have missed you."

Caitlin, who had shared all that wisdom with Sarah, looked like a small child; she got off the lounge and ran into Shandra's arms like a child to a parent.

Sarah was also very aware of the closeness to Ethan on the lounge; she was excited and uncomfortable at the same time.

Shandra spoke with an ethereal voice, "Ethan has told you of Alastor?"

Caitlin stepping back, "Yes, I'm so sad for your news. I also have much to tell you both about."

Shandra waved both arms to the lounges, Caitlin walked back to where she was sitting and Shandra sat between Sarah and Ethan. Now this is really uncomfortable Sarah thought.

Mixy looked up and spoke, "Hello, I am Mixy, thank you for the tea, yum, yum."

Shandra giggled, "I feel the phase from all of you."

Caitlin smiling, "Yes, let me introduce Sarah and Mixy, they're new Phase Walkers, I was hoping you can help me teach them like you did for me."

Shandra smiled, "Pleased to meet you Sarah and Mixy, I will do my best to show you what I know."

Caitlin then continued, she recapped what happened, how she met Sarah, what happened to Martin, how her village was in the veil for two years and with extreme detail all the Delvin activity and what she had heard about Alastor on the Nevid plane.

Ethan gripped the chair and then sat forward listening to every word about Alastor.

Shandra's reaction surprised Sarah, she sat back in the

chair stretched one arm out over Ethan, resting it on the back of the lounge and tapped her hand looking agitated at Caitlin and looking away several times. It was strange because she was most attentive when Caitlin was talking about how she met Sarah. Sarah didn't really like the pretty women, it was an inkling she felt deep inside.

There was silence for some time until the great white worm lifted its head to the roof and burped.

Sarah was shocked, Caitlin laughed, then the rest joined in laughing except Wuzzle who was sipping his tea. Sarah imagined she saw a smirk on the giant teddy bear.

Shandra spoke, her tone was serious, "Well I'm not sure the Delvin have our Alastor, I'm sure he's in the phase somewhere safe exploring and lost track of time."

Ethan shot her a glance, "Sister, if even there is the remote chance that Alastor has been caught by the Delvin we have to investigate, those creatures are monsters."

Shandra stood, "Okay I will go, I need to think on all what was said, I will return to my chamber. Thank you again for joining us here Caitlin and friends."

Shandra left for the door and disappeared.

Ethan spoke warmly, "You must excuse my sister, she really hasn't been herself since Alastor left and she hasn't been sleeping, many nightmares. Yanni, Yanni."

A blue orb appeared again.

Ethan continued, "Please show out guests to the visitor room's and make them comfortable, please excuse me I need to speak to my sister. Please enjoy Remiel House, home of my ancestors."

The blue orb hummed and blue ghostly arms materialised and made hand signals pointing in the direction to some rooms.

- Chapter 9 -

Phase Training

Her white wings bent, her jet black hair tossed to the side, Keyness was strapped to the chair yet again; Alastor was not in the laboratory. Morack scraped his hooves on the ground as he adjusted the last leather strap on the chair. Keyness was not frightened but resolute, she stared at the wall looking regal. Morack started his machine and cast the required spell above Keyness's head. The energy went through her body but this time it didn't stop, it went on and on. Morack watched, ignoring the Celestial's convulsions of pain, waiting for the final drop of essence. Time went on until Keyness was still and the glass jar was almost full. Keyness's face was gaunt, her eyes closed and head fallen to the side lifeless. Morack picked up the jar and headed for his throne room.

There were many Delvin in Morack's throne room, an army one would say, hooves, horns and tails filled the room. A fire roared on the along the side of the room and the demon's shadows cast on the walls flickered in an evil dance. Alastor lay on the ground at Morack's feet like a dog.

Morack screeched his guttural voice, "Silence, my hunters have lost the trail to the Phase Walkers I seek, so I need a bigger army to hunt them down, these are the Phase Walkers that killed my brother Zarack, so in order to catch a Phase Walker we need to make all of you Phase Walkers."

"This is just the start, once we catch these Phase Walkers I can make more of our people Phase Walkers then we can take over the other planes and rule, I will give you more power, wealth and glory. The time of the Delvin is now."

Roars were heard throughout the throne room, they echoed with the underlying sound of the flames roaring. Alastor looked up and saw all the demons and stared at the wall, unfortunately there many shadows cast where he was staring with horns and tails flickering into his view.

Morack stood forward kicking Alastor with his hoofed foot and spoke again, "Come brothers, bring glory to the brood mother and our kind."

Morack held up a full brimmed jar of blue essence. Alastor watched in shock and outrage as he knew that was Keyness, he wanted to run to her and leave the throne room, and the urge was so strong that he did.

Alastor stood up and ran back through the tunnels into the laboratory. Morack glanced at Alastor and smiled, then started to indoctrinate his new Phase Walkers, smearing the blue essence on the demons faces with delight.

Alastor heaved as he ran smashing into the locked laboratory door. It was magically sealed, he screamed with pure agony and lay slumped at the door thinking with a clarity he had not had since he was taken by Morack years ago. He was going to get out of here and stop Morack's army.

Sarah woke, she was in Remiel House, her room was neat and small, and it had a fireplace to the side, with unnatural blue flames burning. It was pleasantly warming. She lay on a comfortable double bed, the ceiling had stars and moons painted daintily, very pretty. There was a wash basin and a large red cushioned chair to the side, it was morning. Sarah got some fresh clothes from her backpack, a pretty blue rockabilly dress with white polka dots. She slipped on her shoes then walked outside to the main room. She saw a hive of activity; Mixy was munching on something that looked like hay or wheat. Wuzzle was receiving something from a large blue hand apparition. The room was wooden panelled with a huge wooden table in the centre, Sarah guessed about eight per side could sit at the table. Ethan sat at the head of the table drinking clear liquid from a glass.

Sarah walked in and said, "Good morning."

Ethan responded, "And to you Sarah," he beamed a smile and took another sip.

Ethan then continued, "Once Caitlin gets back we will discuss what we can do today."

Sarah beamed a smile at this perfect man creature, "Sure."

A blue orb approached Sarah, it just hung in the air floating.

Ethan looked up, "Just let Yanni know what you want to eat."

Sarah, looking puzzled, then spoke to the blue light, "I'll have eggs and bacon please."

Yanni spoke in singing voice, "Right away Miss Sarah."

The blue light hovered for some time then two blue arms protruded from it and a wooden tray materialised with bacon and eggs on a plate, complete with a knife, fork, salt and pepper.

Sarah accepted the breakfast and sat at the table near Ethan's end, "So how did Yanni know what I wanted exactly, I can't imagine you have café style cooked eggs and bacon here much?"

Sarah moved the eggs over and examined them more, "You know what, it looks like it's been cooked in the Chocolate Coffee House if I wasn't mistaken. Even their pepper and salt shakers are the same."

Ethan grinned, revealing a dimple in his cheek, "Yanni probably read your mind and took the image you had of what you wanted and magically recreated it for you. It's how Yanni works."

Sarah, puzzled, asked, "What exactly is a Yanni?"

Ethan spoke while watching Yanni leave the room, "Yanni is an interdimensional being, kind of like, a Phase Walker. After the magical rain came to my plane centuries ago beings like Yanni appeared, they latch themselves to large families and started to serve them, always asking us what we want and how can they help."

"We never intended Yanni to be like a servant or perhaps a mother to us, it's just how it evolved. Yanni is only happy when doing something for us or others, so we let Yanni do things for us; I guess we have become dependent on Yanni to a degree."

Sarah put her fork down, clearing her mouth of bacon, "So how is Yanni interdimensional?"

Ethan replied, "Well I'm not a Phase Walker, but Yanni sometimes appears to my brother or sister in other planes and wants to help, we still don't know how Yanni does it. We wanted Yanni to find Alastor but Yanni could not."

Shandra walked in, "Enough of Yanni, we have more important things to talk to about."

Ethan, surprised, replied, "Indeed sister."

Shandra continued while sitting at the table, "I suggest we train the new Phase Walkers before we attempt to find Alastor. All Caitlin said was she didn't know exactly where he was or even if it was our Alastor."

"I would rather have confidence that the new Phase Walkers can help if we get into any trouble than go crashing into the Delvin plane not ready."

Yanni hovered over to Shandra, who spoke, "I'll have fruit and honey mead."

Yanni's hands materialised and a wooden tray appeared with a bowl of fresh strange fruit and a thin ornate glass of honey coloured fluid. Shandra reached over and took the items then ignored Yanni. Shandra stood briefly then left the table unnoticed.

Yanni disappeared and materialised into a stone room in Remiel House, it tried to phase out, blinking and a red light blocked its attempts, it seemed to be a beam that went all the way around Yanni, constricting it.

Caitlin was outside Remiel House, the grounds near the

estate were beautiful, the gardens were neatly manicured and the flowers were all at full bloom. Caitlin knew they were created by magic and unnatural but that did not spoil it. She walked up to a white gazebo, it was pretty and looked relaxing. As she stood inside the gazebo moved, she looked around and did not see the ground move outside, just the gazebo, then all of a sudden a piece of white wood ripped from the structure and almost hit her in the face. She stared at the gazebo and thought, was I just attacked by a gazebo?

The wooden structure moved under her feet. Caitlin leaped out onto the grass and watched the dreaded gazebo move in a menacing way. Still confused, staring at the gazebo, slowly backing away, not losing eye contact with it, she reached into her boot and took out a small dagger. Then to her own surprise, as it lurched again, she threw her knife to attack the gazebo. Its reaction frightened her, it started to splinter wood from its rails.

Unknown to Caitlin a figure watched from the roof of Remiel House, it had golden wings and weaved chaos magic, a purple stone flicked in the light then the figure was gone.

Caitlin ran back to Remiel House through the main doors and into the main room where everyone was seated.

Yanni felt Caitlin enter the main room and materialised from the stone room in front of her.

Caitlin was breathless as her little feet had just run inside. Yanni was almost on top of her little body. Caitlin waved Yanni away, "Not now."

Yanni moved away and started to pick up straw from the ground that Mixy had dropped everywhere.

Sarah and Ethan both looked surprised by Caitlin; Shandra walked in then sat back at the table and continued to unwrap the skin from a purple fruit, her entrance was unnoticed.

Sarah, concerned, "What happened? Caitlin are you ok?"

Caitlin shook her head, "I was just attacked by the gazebo?"

Ethan surprised, "What, the one outside in the garden?"

Ethan stood, "Let's go outside and see it."

Sarah stood, as well as Ethan, and they walked out the front door to the garden gazebo. Sarah followed with Caitlin a few steps behind and Wuzzle a few steps behind Caitlin.

The wooden Gazebo was still and a little dagger was sticking out of a wooden panel. Ethan pulled the dagger free and walked back toward Caitlin. He passed it to Caitlin hilt first then laughed and said, "Let's go back inside, whatever it was is not there now, Shandra has plans on teaching you all how to use your phase ability."

Shandra walked outside also with Mixy trailing behind, then spoke, "Since we are all outside I think we should all have a lesson. Let me first tell you a little about myself, I am the daughter of a Phase Walker and all my father's knowledge has been passed on to me. I want to teach you some basic survival skills, I have been to well over sixteen planes and I'm still discovering more."

Ethan looked up in awe of his sister, "Well this sounds like Phase Walker business so I might go back inside, enjoy your lesson."

Sarah waved and Caitlin said, "Goodbye."

Ethan gave a funny wave and headed back to Remiel House. Sarah watched him fold his feathery silver wings on his back, it looked strange she thought.

Mixy, the large white worm, spoke, "Excuse me Shandra, I have only recently become aware of my singleness away from the clutch, I know I can move to other places but why do I have this gift?"

Shandra, taken aback by Mixy's intelligent question, pondered then responded, "The universe picks those rare beings to be Phase Walkers to right the balance in the planes and to bring harmony to one's plane. It's a responsibility we all have."

Mixy, confused, "But I don't know my plane, only my clutch."

Shandra gave a warm smile, probably the first time Sarah thought she looked friendly, "It's okay Mixy, we will help you find your clutch and your plane."

Mixy hummed, "I'm happy to hear that, I really need to get back to my clutch."

Shandra with a very regal tone spoke, "Okay, now let's get on with the first lesson. If you are in danger there is a trick you can use I call it the double phase. You open a phase to two known planes in the same spot you walk through both and even a Phase Walker does not know which plane you walked into and they do not know which phase to follow."

"This is handy if you want to cover your tracks or if you think you are being watched. If indeed these Delvin are Phase Walkers this trick is good to lose them."

"The next lesson is your phase weapon, I want you all to materialise it now."

Sarah materialised her weapon first, it was a sword, the shaft was long and silvery and a blue gem was on the side. Caitlin made hers appear, it was a boomerang, silvery and small almost not like a weapon at all but more so a small child's toy. Mixy looked confused then a lasso appeared about her, it was silvery and simply looked like a loop on the end of a rope, not really threatening either. All three Phase Walkers were glowing with symbols to some degree, Sarah's finger tattoo, Caitlin's arms and to everyone's surprise Mixy's entire body glowed blue like a large glow worm. No symbol or tattoo, just the entire body.

Shandra was a little taken back and summed up the might of everyone's weapon, she materialised a large trident, it was not silvery, it was black and obsidian, it reflected Shandra's image like a black mirror.

Shandra continued, "Well done, great to see everyone has their phase weapon, we can get into more details about our phase weapons in the next few weeks."

Caitlin glared at Shandra and spoke loudly, "Shandra we don't have a few weeks, I think we should go tomorrow and look for Alastor. The longer we leave it the more danger he may be in. I know they're hunting Phase Walkers, they killed Martin's village. These vile horrible creatures need to be stopped at all costs, there is no end to their evil. I do not want this to happen to other innocents because our training took too long."

Shandra looked annoyed she was interrupted and continued, "Caitlin, tomorrow would be too soon, I haven't gone through the Anchor with them yet, I know you know of it. I can only imagine they have many questions as well."

Sarah, dematerialising her sword, "What's the Anchor?"

Shandra jumped in looking pleased that the subject was changed and spoke, "An Anchor is each Phase Walker's individual plane of existence, only they can enter and leave. Not even another Phase Walker can go into someone else's Anchor. It's a safe spot you can open and phase too. You can use your Anchor at any time or place, it does not require a phase point like between planes phase travel. The Phase Walker's Anchor is usually a very small plane of existence, sometimes just a room or a small island, it's a Phase Walker's sanctuary. If you like I can help you find you're Anchor through various exercises I can show you."

Caitlin, annoyed, spoke fast, 'Show them today Shandra because tomorrow we will be going to Nevid."

Sarah thought Caitlin looked more like small child talking back to a parent, but Caitlin was her friend and she was not going to leave her side now even though she thought training more would give her more confidence with the phase. She always did well at on job training anyways so thought tomorrow would not be a problem.

Shandra cringed at Caitlin's pronunciation of Nevid then spoke, "Fine than, lets continue the lessons, we will each find our Anchor, everyone focus on stillness and open a phase."

There was a large ripple in the air, it looked unstable, it was clearly coming from Mixy. Shandra looked up and spoke urgently, "Stop please, that phase is unstable."

Mixy opened her large worm eyes and the phase disappeared.

Shandra looked at Caitlin, "I think we have had enough for today, we clearly need time Caitlin, we have been out here all afternoon, I suggest we go inside."

Shandra started to walk back to Remiel House.

Sarah caught up to Caitlin and said, "I know this might be a bad time but I have a uni lecture tonight and William's in this class."

Caitlin looked frustrated and spoke, "Fine, but be here early in the morning because we are leaving for Nevid."

Wuzzle faithfully walked behind Caitlin and Mixy, following everyone a few steps behind, deep in thought.

Ethan was preparing supper sitting by the unnatural blue fireplace and waving his hands at Yanni, giving it instructions. Yanni hummed and was busy finishing setting the table. Ethan's large wings were extended, relaxing. His warm eyes followed Sarah's as she entered with everyone else, "So how was Phase Walker lessons?"

Sarah replied awkwardly, "Great, but I have to jet and go to university; I don't want to be late."

Ethan raised an eyebrow at hearing Sarah was going to leave his company, "Oh will you be coming back? I was under the impression you were staying at Remiel House a few months."

Sarah had warmness in her eyes, "Oh I probably am but I still must attend my university lessons as well, I will be back later tonight."

Ethan smiled, "Well, I will await your return."

Caitlin sat at the table and started to eat lovely soup that was set out in a wooden bowl. She thought to herself, she loved her dear friend Shandra but she questioned her commitment in finding her brother, she didn't seem like the old Shandra she spent time with years back. She was different. Caitlin spooned another mouthful of soup into her mouth.

Wuzzle was worried about Caitlin, a frown was on his bearish face, he found a giant bowl of soup in front of him, looked at it and thought to himself, Wuzzle has food now, Wuzzle is going to eat.

Mixy also had the same soup in a bucket; Mixy didn't

think anything except, eat now, yum. All three sat in silence eating supper. Shandra sat in the other chair next to the fireplace which was next to Ethan.

Shandra spoke softly, "I'm not really hungry brother," her perfect beauty was reflected in the blue flames.

"I don't think they are ready to find our brother, they're nothing but youngling's when it comes to being a Phase Walker."

Ethan, to Shandra's surprise, argued, "Dear sister, if our brother is in danger I really think you should go as soon as you can, he is our brother and he may need your help."

Shandra closed her eyes deep in thought for a time.

Sarah walked back upstairs to her room, she put some perfume on to freshen up, then created an intra-phase opening that went to the phase point. Then she activated the phase point and walked straight through like an old pro, she didn't feel sick and was only remotely aware of tingling, it's amazing how she can adapt to any situation she thought, standing in the alley behind the skip. It was depressing she couldn't get away from her old job, half her luck, she thought. She opened an intra-phase rift to her apartment and walked into to foyer. She needed to get her books and study bag for uni tonight, then headed for the bus there.

Caitlin returned to her room saying good night to Ethan and Shandra, even hugging Shandra. Mixy went to her straw bed and Wuzzle followed Caitlin.

Shandra studied them until the room was clear, then she spoke to Ethan, "It must be nice to have someone eternally following you and your every command, and would even die for you, that is loyalty. Wuzzle is a noble creature."

Ethan smiled a boyish grin, "Do I detect jealously sister, well you have Yanni, it will do as you ask and help when you are in danger, if it can reach you. I do wonder why it has not helped our brother, maybe he doesn't need help."

Shandra cringed and stood, "I want an early night, we are going into the Delvin phase tomorrow, it seems."

Ethan waved his hand to his sister and stared into the fire, he folded his wings and held his knee to his chest.

Shandra's room was mostly white, but everything in it was ornate, she had a large wooden white bed with carvings of flowers all over the poster poles, a canopy was over the poster bed, it was purple lilac. Shandra closed the large wooden door behind her with a thud, then walked over to a chest of draws caved in the same manner of the bed. She opened a drawer and pulled out a brown cloth, she unwrapped what was inside and a small purple gem was revealed. She took the gem into the palm of her hand then walked over to the wash basin which was on her bedside table and filled it with fresh water.

She stood back and looked at her reflection in the still water then took the gem from within her palm into her fingers and swirled the gem around in the water. She added a little phase and watched as the water crackled blue and a vision was shown. Morack was in his throne room, there were many Delvin all shouting and cheering. Morack sat on his throne, two Delvin presented a chest of objects to Morack who hurled it across the room. The Delvin cheered again and Morack stood from his throne. The vision cleared and the basin was still. Shandra held the purple stone tightly and thought, what are you doing Morack, raising an army, all that power is going to waste. She returned the gem to her drawer and made preparations for tomorrow before she went to sleep.

Sarah was sitting next to William in the back of the lecture hall while the instructor was talking about business finance and book keeping. There were many students in the lecture room, some writing on notebooks and others not even listening. Sarah thought it was boring. William was wearing a black collared shirt and black jeans and he had grown a stubble on his chin. Sarah thought it was cute. William typed some notes in his laptop. Sarah was holding her phone, it was on record, it was how she kept notes on her classes, writing everything down was so old fashioned she thought, but she carried a notebook and pen just in case the battery went flat in her phone.

William spoke between the lecturer's pauses, "So want to go out for a drink tonight, happy hour at the Manga bar?"

Sarah, excited, replied, "Okay but I can't be too late ok; I have a lot to do tomorrow."

William smiled, "Did I mention how cute you look in that dress."

Sarah was still wearing the blue rockabilly dress with white dots.

Sarah blushed and the lecturer seemed to of raised his voice and was looking in their direction but continued to rant on about what forms to fill in to apply for a tax break.

The class went on for an hour and Sarah was drained trying to take in all what was taught. The students all picked up their things and started to leave, Sarah spoke softly to William, "This subject isn't that interesting but the company got me through."

She smiled at William and stopped recording on her phone.

William packed up his laptop and reached down to hold Sarah's hand, "Let me help you up."

"Thanks William, let's go to the Manga bar, it sounds like fun."

The Manga bar was small, it had various figurines along the wall, all from comics and cartoons. The bar was packed with university students. Happy hour was tonight and William bought a round of drinks.

William and Sarah stood at a high table with a row of empty glasses in front of them. It was crowded and there wasn't much room to move. Music played in the background and people played computer games along the walls.

Sarah drunk a few drinks, she was relaxed and started to prattle to William, "You know I wasn't really sick, the phase made me sick."

William tipsy but not drunk replied, "What phase, do you smoke it?"

Sarah prattled on again, "Oh you don't smoke it, but it gives a tingling feeling every time you use it. I've used the phase a fair bit now so I don't really feel the tingling sensation anymore."

Sarah slurred her words and repeated, "I think I got too used to it."

William, worried, "A- ha, well maybe you should stop using phase, it doesn't really sound good for you."

Sarah considered with a perplexed face and put her drink down, "You know what, I don't really want to use the phase now I think about it. Something inside me calls and urges me to use the phase it's kind of weird that way."

William put his drink down, "Well I think we better sober up then."

Sarah holding the table she was standing at, "Yeah I have important stuff to do tomorrow."

William ginned, "So want to come back to my place?"

Sarah burst out laughing, "I'm sorry, but that's a really tacky line."

William laughed, "It wasn't a line, I was genuinely asking?"

Sarah looked him in the eye, "I enjoy your company and we should go out on a date again, but seriously I have a big day tomorrow, I really shouldn't have come here, I probably should go."

William smiled, his cheeks had dimples, "Ok, Sarah I will put you in a cab home."

Sarah smiled reached over and kissed William. William accepted it although it was a little slobbering. William held her hand and led Sarah outside to the taxi ranks. He put Sarah in the first available taxi along with her university bag. He then told the taxi driver her address and payed him some money.

The taxi driver didn't speak and accepted the money then looked over at Sarah stretched out on the front seat of his cab. The cab driver drove off and William waved to Sarah, who did not notice because she was passed out. The cab did not drive off to the direction of Sarah's apartment, but off to a secluded park. Sarah, oblivious, snoozed.

The taxi driver had black hair and smelt like heavy cologne. He drove off the road and into the park. The trees were thick with leaves and it was very dark. He stopped the taxi, got out and opened the passenger door, he took Sarah's backpack and pulled out her things. Notebooks and pens scattered onto the ground amongst the leaves and dirt. He found her wallet. He opened her wallet and it had over seven hundred dollars in hundred dollar bills, nice, he thought and slipped the money into his cheap red checked shirt pocket.

The taxi driver's face was misshapen, there were burn marks across the side of head, he must have had really bad ache as a child because there were scars on his cheeks. He had dark brown eyes and his skin was tanned and red. His nose was bulbous and eyebrows were thick and met in the middle.

After helping himself to Sarah's belonging's he decided to help himself to Sarah. He got back into the taxi, closed and locked all the doors.

Sarah lay sprawled over the front seat she was wearing her pretty blue polka dot dress. The taxi driver touched Sarah's leg. She moved a little and he reached up her skirt. Sarah sat upright in a daze and looked at the taxi driver. He slapped her across the face. She screamed and reached for the phase then tried to open the front car door, it was locked. The taxi driver raised his fat brown hand again. Sarah materialised her sword and pointed it at the taxi driver's throat.

She screamed, "Opened the damn doors now!"

The taxi driver, too shocked for words, did as he was told.

Sarah then screamed at the taxi driver again, "Get out!"

The taxi driver did and backed away to a nearby tree, the dry leaves on the ground crunching at his every step.

She screamed again while stepping outside the car, "You filthy scum."

She grabbed her bag and shoved her things inside, picking up leaves and dirt from the ground as well, then scratched the front of his car with her sword. It peeled paint on the orange cab and made a pattern.

The taxi driver pleaded, "Please stop this is not my car."

So Sarah played naughts and crossed with the sword along the entire bonnet of his car then stood on the bonnet, swaying, and scratched a happy face on his roof. The scratching noise was loud as paint peeled off. The taxi driver sat in horror at the base of the tree.

Sarah got off the bonnet and walked into the forest. She opened a phase point to the alley of the Chocolate Coffee House and stepped through.

The taxi driver touched his pocket realising he still had the money then jumped inside his taxi and took off at a fast pace.

Sarah stepped into the alley and thought to herself, you know what, I do not want to stop using the phase. She staggered to the skip, opened the phase point to the Celestial plane and stepped through swaggering her bag. She still had her sword and she dematerialised it. She then opened the intra-phase to Remiel House and stepped through.

It was dark, the lights to the house were strange candles burning a blue frame. She pushed open the door and Yanni appeared, it hovered for a small time then left. Sarah walked through the main room. Ethan was sitting by the fireplace, he looked up at Sarah. Sarah burst into tears. Ethan stood looking regal as his wings spread a little, "Is everything okay, how was university?"

Sarah walked to Ethan and fell over on the ground. Ethan bent down and helped her up then with a soft voice spoke, "I think you should get some rest, you have a big day tomorrow."

Sarah just nodded and Ethan led her to her room holding her arm and then closed her door shut.

Sarah collapsed onto the bed and fell asleep.

Ethan returned to the fireplace and sat wondering why Sarah had cried.

- Chapter 10 -

Brood Mother

Morack was alone in his throne room, the only noise was the sound of the flames burning along one wall. His army of Delvin Phase Walkers had gone into the phase looking for the Phase Walkers that killed his brother.

Alastor was outside the laboratory sitting near its door, he was very angry and upset, he hoped that Keyness was okay. Realising he could not get inside he walked back to the throne room. Morack ignored him and continued his train of thought.

Alastor saw the jar of Keyness's essence on the floor next to Morack's throne. Alastor had not been able to feel the phase since the change when Morack experimented on him and warped him with foul magic to be part Delvin. Alastor moved his tail when thinking of the change, he tried to contain his rage. He walked up to the jar and took it, then he placed his large finger into the jar and smeared the contents all over his face and licked his finger.

Morack stood and screamed, seeing Alastor in the corner of his eye. Alastor, feeling the tingling, the phase, then did what any Phase Walker was taught to do when in danger: open a phase to your Anchor and jump through. The phase snapped shut behind him and the empty jar crashed to the ground splintering glass shards.

Alastor was alone in his Anchor, for him it was a house, a small cottage with ornate furniture and fruit trees outside.

Alastor picked some fruit and went inside, it was exactly how he remembered it, it had been so long since he felt the phase, the thrill was intense and so was his anger. Alastor sat in a cushioned chair, ate the fruit and thought of a plan.

He was going to free Keyness and then return home. There he and his sister could help the Phase Walkers Morack was chasing. Perhaps even put a plan together to end Morack for good. Alastor liked that thought and smiled.

Morack screeched at the top of his voice at Alastor's disappearance into the phase, like a child whose toy was lost. Morack smashed over the vision bowl and summoned some Delvin waiting to seek audience with him into the room.

Two Delvin entered the room one bowed low. Morack grunted, "Well, what is it?"

The Delvin that was bowing low was orange in colour with black spots, he stood up and looked Morack in the eye, "The brood mother is sick and needs help."

Morack was caught by surprise and replied, "Tell me exactly how she is sick, I did not even know she had awakened."

The orange Delvin continued, "My name is Grendne, I am one of the many keepers of the brood mother, she awoke yesterday. She is moaning in pain and cannot lay her clutch."

Morack flicked his robes out with his massive arms and tilted his head; his horns looked very menacing, then spoke, "Fine, take me to the brood mother."

Grendne walked outside Morack's lair, Morack marched behind him and they went deep into the stone plains until they came across a hole in the rocky ground, they both started to descend into the ground steeply through a stone tunnel.

The tunnel going down was lit by red single flames every few feet; the ground went from slopping down to stairs. The tunnel started to widen then got larger until they were in a vast cave, the walls were lit by flame and a foul stink was in the air. The brood mother lay on straw, she was twice the size of Morack. Her horns were long and tall, her breasts were uncovered and she wore only a loose ragged skirt. Her skin was dark blue and she moaned a screeching sound. She saw Morack and her eyes transfixed upon him.

Morack inquired, "Brood mother, you are awake I see, what ails you? Are you going to lay another clutch?"

The brood mother's eyes glowed red and she spoke in a grinding guttural voice, "They came and poisoned me, they offered me food, I was so hungry I do not know how I was awoken, it's not time to lay a clutch of eggs. I should be in slumber."

Morack spoke, "Who are they? Who came, brood mother?"

The brood mother spoke, clutching herself in pain, "The winged ones, bright and shiny, they wore robes and there was a golden triangle. They offered me food, I took it, I was hungry. Morack find me the Raznik, heal me."

Morack cringed, "The Raznik has not been in our possession for over a century brood mother. But I will find a way to heal you. I do not recall it had that ability."

The brood mother replied, "It does now, I feel it."

Morack bowed to the brood mother and walked back to his throne room, he was very angry that the Lady of Light struck at the brood mother. He had been sure that messenger was just playing with him and it had not been a real warning. Morack then did something that even surprised himself, he started to grind his teeth and growl. He needed to avenge his brother, heal the brood mother and send a storm into Lorvisa and bring the Lady of Light to her knees.

The Lady of Light was in her Chapter house. Unlike her court, which was an open space, the Chapter house was huge with many rooms and was totally organic, it was a living building. Many plants entwined around each other to form a large hall. There were live flowers around the doorway and a thick rectangle of grass formed the hallway carpet. Inside large mushrooms formed seats and a throne was at the back of the room, smaller than the Illumination court but still decadent, ornate and shiny. A few Lords and Ladies of Illumination were seated in the hall chatting softly. More seemed to come through the open doors as if a gathering was taking place. The Lords and Ladies of Illumination wore their blue tabards with a golden triangle. The whispering stopped when the Lady of Light materialised in front of the throne.

The Lady of Light was beautiful, her wings shined. Her long hair moved as she walked down the stairs from the throne to the mushrooms. There was complete silence as the Lady of Light was going to speak and her words were joy, "Greetings my Lords and Ladies of Illumination, I thank you for your work in the Nevid plane, the only way to stop evil was to stop them at the core, cutting off their existence, breeding. It's a little harsh I know but I cannot lose another one of you. You are all so precious to me. Please report, Illumination leader."

A rather odd looking spideroid fellow, who was grey and had six legs, approached the Lady of Light. He bowed low and started to speak, "My Lady of Light, oh how you radiate, we arrived on Nevid and found the brood mother, it was very easy, she was for the most part unguarded. Even though she brings life to the Delvin she is not highly treasured or regarded so it was simply a matter of offering the brood mother poisoned food."

The spideroid stood straight and continued, "The brood mother will not live long once our poisons have set into her body and the breeding cycle of the Delvin will be no more. This is the first step you ordered, it's complete and we will begin our march on Nevid soon to cleanse it of its scourge."

The Lady of Light walked forward to the spideroid and touched his head, it glowed green and she spoke, "Thank you very much and for your service I shall reward you."

The spideroid creature was happy, fulfilment and joy was in his mind, total completeness. This feeling he never wanted to stop and to feel like this forever, the spideroid bowed then left the hall.

Outside the hall the spideroid stumbled then trembled. It fell on its back, its six legs wiggling in the air from convulsions. The grey spideroid laid there for some time then righted himself quickly, looking left and right then quickly scuttling along while fixing his sword and tabard into place.

The Lady of Light was happy so she began to sing, the plants swayed and all the Lords and Ladies of Illumination stood transfixed, feeling the Lady of Light's love and retuning devotion.

Sarah awoke to a warm room, her bed was comfortable even though she slept on top of the covers. She recalled the events of the night almost feeling sick from what could have happened. She emptied out her backpack, leaves and dirt were also within, she cringed then went into her chest of draws and got dressed in blue jeans and a white t-shirt. Rather generic, she thought, but she wanted to feel plain. She felt a tingling, then pulled out her green shirt and camo pants from the chest of drawers. She quickly changed, it was just a strange feeling that green would be more useful.

Everyone was gathered in the main room. Ethan at the chair by the fire like he hadn't moved from last night. Wuzzle and Mixy eating, which seemed to be their usual activity, Sarah thought. Little Caitlin was in a pretty pink dress and Shandra looked like a super model, well if models had golden wings. Sarah was approached by Yanni, Sarah looked at the blue glowing ball, studying the magic within. She stared for some time and could see a red band around its middle, crackling, it felt wrong somehow. Sarah spoke, "I'll have cheese on toast, please."

Yanni reached out with a wooden tray, its blue arms glowing; on the tray were two pieces of toast with cheese.

"There you go Miss Sarah," Yanni intoned in a music voice.

Sarah accepted the tray and sat at the table.

Caitlin smiled, "I hope you slept well Sarah, how was university?"

Sarah answered, "I seem to be up to date on study for the moment," her face was neutral and expressionless.

Caitlin didn't know what to think of her response so changed the subject, "Okay, well we are going to Nevid after breakfast. We will try and find out if Alastor is there, and if there are any Phase Walkers we can help. So who's in?"

Sarah spoke first "Okay, I will help you Caitlin but there are more monsters on Earth."

Caitlin looked worried, "What do you mean Sarah?"

Sarah put her cheese toast down, "Human stuff, don't worry, I'm for finding Alastor."

Mixy, looking larger, answered, "I'll help if you help me find my clutch afterwards, I want to go home, need my clutch, food here is good though," then put her head down and started to eat again.

Ethan watched the conversation and sat waiting for his younger sister's response.

Caitlin watched Shandra, puzzled.

Shandra stood and brushed her hands down her white dress, straightening it even though it didn't require straightening, feeling she must speak, "Of course I will help you Caitlin, I want to find my brother Alastor so much, I'll pack a few things and be ready."

Caitlin put a hand next to her pocket and felt the Raznik, "Okay, well I'm ready, I assume you are too Sarah."

Sarah looked up holding the last piece of cheese on toast, "Yes after I eat this, so ready."

Ethan smiled, happy that everyone was going to try and find his brother, Remiel House was not the same without him.

Shandra walked into her room and closed the door. She went to her drawers and took the purple gem, it glowed at her evilly; she placed it in an ornate leather pouch with magical symbols embroidered in gold thread and tied the pouch to her golden braided belt. Then she rejoined the main room.

Caitlin, surprised, spoke, "That was quick, okay, let's link and phase to Nevid."

Caitlin felt Mixy link first, it was primal, almost aggressive, Sarah linked, then Shandra, then she opened a phase to the phase point.

Sarah waved to Ethan, "See you soon," then walked through the phase.

Shandra smiled and took long strides into the phase, Mixy followed, Caitlin, then Wuzzle was last.

Ethan watched the phase snap shut, silvery electricity hung in the air a small time before it dissipated, he then stared into the blue flames and thought of Alastor.

They were in the Celestial plane, at the phase point not far from Remiel House, getting ready to enter Nevid. The Remiel phase point was a white shiny large stone as big as Caitlin with gold painted symbols etched all over it, obviously Celestial made. A combination of symbols opened planes. Caitlin, linked to the others, selected the right symbols and opened the phase to the Nevid plane. It started as a silvery thread and spread to a blurry opening, but just as it opened a purple crackling light occurred and a thread appeared right next to the already open phase to the left. The phase opened, they all stood back and waited. Everyone was puzzled at two phases opened at the same phase point.

A black Delvin walked through the purple phase, his hair was bright red to his waist, tied with black leather strips, his horns were twisted and red also. He wore lose black robes and snarled. A grey Delvin also entered from the phase. He had blue spots and looked young because his horns were very white and small.

Shandra stood behind a tree and did not move, watching and touching her leather pouch.

Caitlin summoned her phase weapon, a dainty boomerang and stood her ground. Sarah, watching Caitlin, also summoned her weapon, a large silvery sword with a blue gem, and stood next to Caitlin. Mixy looked confused and crawled past Caitlin and Sarah up to the black Delvin in robes. Sarah panicked and spoke loudly, "Mixy, come back."

The black Delvin's tattoos started to glow purple and Mixy squealed because she felt the fear projected from the Delvin wash over her. The huge white fluffy worm dove behind a nearby tree, perfectly shaped leaves floated on the wind she created from her movement.

Caitlin jumped forward, brave and resolute, holding out her weapon, feeling the fear, then blocking it from her mind as she had felt it before. She was small and alone, the Delvin was not even surprised he saw the tiny weapon. He snarled and threw the spell he created for Mixy on to Caitlin. A golden web surrounded Caitlin. Wuzzle stepped forward and punched the black Delvin in the face. He recoiled in shock.

The grey Delvin spoke in a guttural voice, "Grimlock, you ok?"

Grimlock the black Delvin shook his head and knew instantly he had found one of the Phase Walkers Morack wanted. Sarah jumped out with her sword swinging, unaffected by the fear. Grimlock smiled and stepped backwards through the phase. The grey Delvin scrambled for the phase and ran through.

Both the phases closed.

Shandra came out of her hiding spot, "Wait, we should not go to Nevid now, they know we are coming."

Caitlin stood for a few moments with her boomerang cutting a hole in the web then she stepped out and dematerialised her weapon, Sarah also dematerialised her weapon.

Caitlin alarmed, "Usually Delvin fight to the end. Why did they leave? I'm worried they're going back to bring more. How many phase points are there on the Celestial plane Shandra?"

Shandra raised an eye brow and spoke, "Hundreds if not thousands of phase points, we use this one because it's close to Remiel House."

"Well, what are the chances they found this one, someone showed them the way," Caitlin said.

Shandra, almost taking it personal, spoke, "I don't know, bad luck?"

Caitlin asked, "Shandra how do you seal a phase point?"

Shandra stared at Caitlin and pondered, "Well in theory if we all link and all focus we could probably do it, never tried. Phase Walkers usually walk the phase and want more phase points, not to close them."

Sarah worried, "Let's try to seal it."

Caitlin took over, it was rather odd getting orders from a little girl, "Okay, let's all link."

Sarah's ring tattoo glowed, Mixy glowed, Caitlin's tattoos glowed and Shandra's dress glowed; Caitlin tried to seal the phase point.

The phase point was glowing green all around the stone and what could be seen were rainbows of colours clashing and the phase was slowly sealing. The threads of colour latching onto one another, knitting in a strange pattern. The phase point stone smashed into tiny pieces, almost powdery.

Caitlin fell to the ground with a thud, Shandra fell gracefully as if her feathers cushioned the fall, Sarah fell near some bushes and Mixy was already on the ground but instead of looking round and fluffy it was as if something had flattened her to the ground. They all lay for some time unconscious except for Wuzzle who shed a little tear down his huge brown fury face. He watched as Caitlin lay still for a time and picked up her little body. Then he started to walk back to Remiel House each step very heavy, his bond to Caitlin was very weak.

Ethan was weaving celestial magic in the front room, he was creating an ornate drinking glass, the patterns swirled and collided, he was deep in concentration. Wuzzle walked into the house with a heavy step holding Caitlin's little body in his huge clawed hands, Ethan stopped instantly, the drinking glass dropped to the ground and Yanni caught it before it broke, then he stood before Wuzzle.

Wuzzle spoke in a deep calming voice, "Caitlin tried to close a phase point and she is injured, I don't know what to do, she does not wake."

Ethan was shocked that Wuzzle could speak as he had only used hand gestures in his previous stays at Remiel House.

Ethan looked at Caitlin and felt a pulse, "Where are the others? Come lay her in her room."

Wuzzle spoke again, "They are still at the phase point, I apologise for not trying to carry more, Mixy is so big. I figured to come and tell you."

Ethan in a sympathetic voice said, "That's okay, I know the way to the phase point, I have seen Alastor and Shandra go there, I will go bring them back, Yanni is very strong."

Wuzzle walked into Caitlin's room and put her gently onto her bed, he laid her face down for some reason and the stone in Caitlin's front pocket, the Raznik, activated. It glowed green and then resonated all through her body. Caitlin stirred then woke up, sitting on the bed. She had a massive head ache. Wuzzle came close and bowed down on one knee, feeling his bond to Caitlin strengthen.

Wuzzle spoke softly like he always did to Caitlin, "I was scared, I thought you were fading the link between us was so thin I could barely feel it."

Caitlin hugged Wuzzle and smiled sitting up on the edge of the bed, "Well I'm back and almost better than ever, what happened?"

Wuzzle started to explain what happened in a soft tone.

Ethan walked outside through the front door of Remiel House and took to the air, his silver feathered wings out spread casting a shadow outside and Yanni floated in the air, following. Ethan was headed to the phase point outside Remiel House, when he arrived he looked down from the sky, scanning, looking for his sister and friends.

First he saw Mixy, it was very easy to spot a large flat white worm, Mixy was still. Then he saw Shandra sprawled out on the ground. Yanni started to materialise a huge carpet, it was ornate and had tassels.

Ethan spoke to Yanni, "I will pick them up, they are fragile."

The carpet landed near the bodies and Yanni floated overhead.

Ethan first went to his sister, looked at her and felt her life force, smiled and placed her on the carpet. It was hard to find Sarah, he panicked scanning the ground, then he saw Sarah, her clothes blended in with the ground and bush she was near, making her camouflaged, clever, Ethan thought.

Then he walked to Sarah, she also had a life force, and put her on the carpet. There was a strange beep coming from Sarah's pocket. Ethan put his hand inside and pulled out her iPhone.

There was a text message, it read, "Party at Emma's house Sat night will pick up 5"; Ethan did not understand and just tossed the device on the carpet.

Ethan then moved to Mixy who was covered in strange crystal sticky stuff, this didn't look good Ethan thought and her body shape was all wrong, not round and fluffy. Being extra careful to move Mixy to the carpet, he used all his strength as she was heavy, he thought she had got bigger since she first arrived at Remiel House.

Yanni levitated the carpet and Ethan spread his huge silvery feathered wings, they took flight and they slowly flew back to Remiel House.

- Chapter 11 -

Phase Closed

Morack was in his throne room, Delvin do not need to sleep so he had no sleeping chamber, the throne room or main hall was where he was if not in his laboratory.

There was a new decoration behind Morack's throne, a pair of white feathered wings which were crudely nailed into the stone wall, blue fluid leaked from where they had been hacked off. Two grey Delvin stood guard at the entrance of Morack's throne room, he was now at war and now required security, he never knew when a Phase Walker may come in uninvited, the Lady of Light had rattled him.

Grimlock walked through the entrance, his black robes unnaturally flowing. Morack stood to face him, "What news do you bring?"

Grimlock smiled, "My Lord Morack, I have found the location of the Phase Walkers you seek."

Morack clapped his large clawed hands, "Fantastic! We will send an army in as soon as they are assembled, I will send word to bring my Delvin Phase Walkers home."

He signalled a grey guard standing by the entrance, "Go get my Phase Walkers."

The grey guard replied, "Yes Lord," and walked out of the hall.

Morack sat on his throne, "So where are they? Tell me now!"

Grimlock looked up at the white wings, "They're in the

Celestial plane."

Morack's army started to assemble in the throne room, within moments of the grey guard leaving. There were hooves, tails and large horns everywhere. Delvin of many colours, but mostly grey as they are the common species on Delvin.

Morack summoned Grimlock to the altar next to the throne by booming his voice, "Grimlock, come."

Morack then waved his muscled arms in the air and his black hair was not tired back, it flowed free to his waist, "Delvin, the time has come to avenge my clutch brother Zarack and to drain more Phase Walkers so I can experiment on them, then I, Morack, can make the Phase Walker ability among the Delvin permanent."

The Delvin all cheered and raised their weapons, some were materialised phase and some were Delvin design, snarls and growls were heard throughout the room then the stomping of hoofs echoed in the stone hall.

Morack continued, his voice was magically altered to be louder and boomed above the Delvin cheers and stomps, "Delvin of Nevid, Grimlock will lead the charge into the Celestial plane. Take his orders, try and first capture the Phase Walkers, only kill them if you have too. I need them to be alive to drain their essence and experiment."

"Grimlock, open the phase, then begin."

Grimlock reached for the phase as there was a phase point in Morack's throne room. The phase point was a burnt twisted clump of rock, the symbols burned with phase fire when activated. Grimlock began to use it but couldn't open the phase; he tried again, and again different symbols activating each time burning in shapes. Morack was watching and got frustrated and spoke, "Go now Grimlock!"

Grimlock reached for the phase to the Celestial plane again, the same set of symbols he used originally, he went over the symbols in his mind and they seemed correct. He pondered and then spoke, "My lord Morack, it appears I cannot open the phase."

Morack screamed in a rage filled voice, "What do you mean you cannot open the phase?"

Grimlock shifted the weight on his feet, "The opening to the Celestial plane is no longer there."

Morack screamed, "Fool, get out! Get out all of you!"

Grimlock spoke, shaking, "My Lord Morack, as soon as I find the opening again we will go to the Celestial plane and bring you the Phase Walkers."

Morack screamed again, "Get out!" then sat on his throne and began to tap his claws on it, thinking of his other problem, the Lady of Light.

The throne room took some time to clear as there was hundreds of Delvin gathered, even some still arriving.

Grimlock opened the phase to outside Morack's lair and stood trying to figure out what had happened.

Alastor was in his Anchor, it was warm and he was relaxed, something he could not achieve in the Nevid plane, the feeling was welcome. He started eating some of the strange green fruit that grew outside, it was sweet and nourishing, he was devising a plan of attack. His first concern was Keyness and her safety, he could only imagine she was very weak and in a bad way. He put the fruit down and cringed. His plan was to phase into Morack's throne room, go into the lab, free Keyness and phase back to Remiel House. Alastor flexed his muscled arms and then reached for the phase. He opened the phase and then was back in Nevid, in Morack's throne room.

Morack stood up from his throne and screamed, "Alastor you fool, you will regret your decision to free yourself. Guards, seize him!"

Alastor reached for the phase and materialised his weapon, it was a great long sword, it was silvery and ornate, then it glowed blue.

He ran down to the laboratory and used the phase to open the door, bursting in, he scanned the room, he could hear hoofed feet scraping down the tunnel. Morack and his guards were in pursuit. Alastor looked in the cage, Keyness was not there, it was empty, she was not in the laboratory, he could not think what Morack did with her because he kept all his test subjects in the laboratory.

Panic took hold and Alastor opened a phase point back into Morack's throne room. He stood still and studied the all too familiar surroundings. There was something that caught his eye above Morack's throne, he stared at it in shock and disbelief. It was Keyness's wings, bloody and dry, nailed to the wall. This can only mean that Morack took all her essence and killed her. Tears welled up in his eyes, the feeling was sheer pain and agony, the footsteps changed direction and they were coming back up the tunnel towards the throne room.

Alastor looked at the phase point in the throne room then reached for the phase back to Remiel House, the phase point burned its symbols glowing in fire but did not open, then Morack's screeching voice was getting louder and closer, "Alastor, I will flay you and hang your skin on the wall, such pretty, pretty skin."

Alastor's heart was pumping, he didn't understand why he couldn't open the phase to Remiel House and opened a phase to his Anchor. He walked through the phase and it snapped shut. He was alone outside his cottage again, his sanctuary of sadness. With heavy hooved steps he swayed his tail then walked inside the cottage and sat, remembering Keyness, her strength and courage. He vowed to avenge her and to kill Morack if it was the last thing he did, anger burned inside, torturing his very inner soul, he stood staring at the back of the cottage for some time.

Alastor, calming down a little, tried to think, he did not understand why he could not open the phase to Remiel House. He reached for the phase and opened another phase point to the Celestial plane, the only other one he knew. The Abbith market, a centre of trade within the Celestial plane. The Celestials were known for their making of fine goods, wielding light magic to create them. All Celestials have the ability to do so and some have refined things and became better than others, these were known as the Masters Workers of Abbith, they belonged to an exclusive guild. Alastor thought of his brother Ethan who was trying to get his skill up and become a member. Goods from the Abbith market were so well known that Phase Walkers were also known to frequent there.

On that particular day one particular coppery skinned Phase Walker was shopping in the Abbith market.

Alastor walked through the phase.

He arrived in the Abbith market, it was a large area and the centre of trade; the shops were all in small town houses, the fixtures were ornate and decant. Venders had their wares displayed in floating cabinets and glass cases. Magic was used everywhere, there was always the smell in the air of used light magic. Books were lined up on shelves and everything looked new and shiny almost perfect, nothing was old or dirty. The people that came from all over the Celestial plane had all oddities available for sale. Strange birds in cages, plants with large teeth, furniture with detailed designs and fresh food. People always wore their finest clothes, lace covered shirts for men and frilly loose dresses for women. The fashion for this year was to cover yourself in gold, so the trims on clothes were gold and many gold chains of jewellery hung around their necks. There was always background chatter in the market, people haggling a price and live animals making strange noises. Alastor was back in the Celestial plane, he didn't care that he couldn't reach Remiel Houses phase point because he knew it was less than a day's flight from the Abbith market and he could always intra-phase travel. Alastor started to look at the fresh food on the tables, rare berries that could only be conjujured once a month on a full moon tempted him.

Then a little girl with silvery wings and jet black hair screamed, "Sister, look, a monster!"

She pointed at Alastor. Alastor was genuinely surprised,

then realised the girl was pointing at him; his form must look truly shocking to the Celestial people. Alastor was used to his wingless changed self, it had been too long, he needed to be more aware of his appearance, he thought. Alastor was wearing a dirty ripped shirt and old short black trousers that revealed his black hoofed feet. His black small twisted horns were visible, poking out of his white blond hair. Alastor took a punnet of berries and started to run out of the market, his hooves clapping on the stone pebbled paths. He looked behind him and no one pursued him. Alastor tried to move more quietly and discretely hiding in shadows and moving along the walls of buildings, stopping only to put a handful of berries into his mouth. They were absolutely divine, he thought, he missed Celestial food so much.

He saw some washing hanging from a line in a back yard of a house that looked like it stored blue wheat or hay, as there were many bundles of it stacked all inside. Outside there was a scarecrow made of the same blue hay, it had a large blue rimed hat which had seen better days, ripped and discoloured. Alastor used the phase and opened a rift to the washing, he took a pair of blue long pants, a blue commoner's frilly shirt and a large blue long jacket. Alastor then went up to the scarecrow and took the hat and put it on his head. He knew he looked ridiculous but it hid his horns, one less thing to worry about, he wanted to blend in with the Celestials. He looked down at his feet which were black hooves, perhaps really, really, large boots could do it. Alastor opened the phase back to the side of the house and moved on.

Alastor was avoiding any Celestial he came into contact with, walking a different direction pretending to go into a house and almost climbing a tree until he finally came onto an open road, it was deserted and following it would take him to Remiel House. It had been two years since he had seen his family. Alastor could not help but feel joy and happiness at returning home and to feel the flow of light magic in the air, rather than the foul corrupted magic of chaos.

Alastor's feet were making a clapping noise on the road,

no matter how slow his steps the huge thick black nail at the base of his rounded foot made an impact noise. Alastor, frustrated, wanted to make shoes so he walked off into the trees and started to use light magic to create a pair of boots. He had not wielded light magic in quantity for some time as it was hard to access it on the Nevid plane, also light magic never really interested him and he usually made Yanni do such things; it was Ethan that enjoyed that type of thing. He reached out to the light magic, it was clean and felt like water but it was hard to grasp and kept dripping out of his hands as he tried to wield it.

Alastor was frustrated, something within him had changed, wielding light magic had always been easy and effortless to him. Fighting with the light magic Alastor managed to form a really crude pair of large black leather boots. They were not ornate or decorate but rough edged and the colour was uneven. Alastor was upset about it but he pulled the heavy boots on over his rounded hooved feet anyway. The boots did not look nice but the leather was soft and comfortable. Alastor felt magical afterburn from the simplest task of creating the boots; magical afterburn was what a small child would suffer from when learning light magic.

Returning to the path Alastor's feet made soft noises and almost looked normal, if large black platform boots were in fashion, also not to mention the fact he was walking and not flying.

Caitlin was in her room at Remiel House and was feeling better so she stood up from the bed, Wuzzle was at her bedside, her noble loyal friend watching and waiting.

Caitlin stretched, "Take me to the others, I can heal them."

Wuzzle smiled and spoke softly, "They're in their rooms, Ethan is watching over them."

Caitlin removed the Raznik, it glowed green and warm in

her hands.

She first entered Sarah's room, who lay peacefully on her bed and did not look hurt. Caitlin placed the Raznik on Sarah's stomach, it glowed and the green glow engulfed her body. Sarah started to stir and sat up.

"What happened, awe my head hurts," then lay back on the bed looking up at the ceiling.

Caitlin smile and spoke, "Welcome back, I have to attend the others. When you feel better go to the main room and get something to eat from Yanni."

Caitlin walked out of the room holding the triangle gemstone then slipped into another room. Sarah sat up again and headed to the main room. The large wooden dinner table was empty except Yanni hovering above it. Ethan, a permanent fixture to the room, was again sitting at the fireplace, Sarah wondered if he ever moved.

Mixy came into the main room, she looked bigger and more fluffy, there was a glimmer to her body it was like little rainbows of dust flecked all over.

Mixy saw Yanni and spoke, "Mixy hungry, so very hungry, lots of food please, you promised to take me home."

Sarah looked at Mixy and replied, "After breakfast we will take you home, I promise Mixy."

Sarah's iPhone beeped as she got an update, it was a message from William, 'change of plans how about just a romantic dinner for two tonight I know a great Thai restaurant at South Bank'. Sarah sent a message back, 'Sure sounds great, just let me know what time you're coming around to my house to pick me up'.

Shandra walked in, her hair was a mess but looked fine otherwise, Caitlin and Wuzzle followed behind her and she spoke "So did we close the phase point?"

Caitlin checked her pocket for the green Raznik, "I don't know, we have to go back and check."

Sarah looked at her watch, "What about Mixy, I thought we were taking her home back to her clutch?"

Little Caitlin in her cute pink dress spoke, "I think we

should check the phase point to Remiel House is closed, then take Mixy home. Mixy, where is the clutch? What phase are you from? How long have you been a Phase Walker?"

Everyone stopped what they were doing and looked at Mixy, even Ethan was watching intently.

Mixy spoke in a regal tone, "Well my clutch is where I was born, hatched from an egg, with my clutch brothers and sisters. I'm from under the big, big tree under the bark."

Caitlin sympathising, "Do you know your phase Mixy? You came through a phase point at Kelstone next to my house."

Mixy looking around with her huge eyes, "I didn't know I was a Phase Walker, I hatched from my egg, my clutch brothers and sisters were there, we were all hungry. So we left looking for food, I ate a lot but was still hungry so I ate a brown thing, it was tasty and squirmed a lot when I ate it. Then I felt this power it was like a tingling. I was not hungry for some time but I felt more powerful and had a greater understanding of things."

Caitlin looking puzzled, "Well it's a bit hard Mixy to take you back to your phase and clutch if we don't know where it is. Sorry Mixy, you're welcome to stay with us until we do find out where it is."

Mixy tilted her large fluffy white head to the side, a tear rolled down her face and she was still.

Sarah rushed forward and gave Mixy a hug and buried herself in her huge white fur.

Sarah spoke softly, "It's okay Mixy, stick with us we will find a way to get you home, we won't give up on you."

Mixy, with a quivering voice, "Ok I will stay with you until we find a way back to my home; I have no other friends or know where to go."

Caitlin was pondering thinking about the brown thing Mixy ate, that made her a Phase Walker, or perhaps it was random that she was eating at the time she noticed her powers emerging.

Caitlin spoke, "Mixy as soon as we find a way we will help

you get home. How long ago did you hatch from an egg?"

Mixy looked at Caitlin and pondered, "I hatched from my egg but a few days before I met you at in the forest near the funny tree with markings."

Shandra's eyes went wide with hearing that and she spoke quickly, "Mixy you are but a youngling of course we will help you. I do think we should go back and check the phase point now. "

Ethan stood up and walked to the table, "Ladies, are you not even remotely interested in how you got to Remiel House?"

Shandra turned to face her brother, "Good point. How did we get back here, and what happened?"

Ethan smiled and stretched out his wings, "Well Wuzzle came to Remiel House with Miss Caitlin unconscious and told me the rest, you all were unconscious at the Remiel phase point, so Yanni and I flew there. Yanni created a flying carpet and I lifted you all onto the carpet and flew you back home, then returned you to your rooms. Caitlin woke first and then healed you all with her pretty green stone."

Caitlin, hearing reference to the Raznik, protectively put her hand on her pocket.

Sarah laughed, "So you mean to tell me I rode a flying carpet and missed the whole thing!"

Shandra raised an eyebrow at Sarah. Mixy just stood silently, as did Wuzzle.

Caitlin was also shocked that Wuzzle spoke to someone other than herself, she did not mind but Wuzzle was honour bound to her and he usually spoke to no one, resulting in him using hand signals most times.

Ethan relaxed his wings and spoke again, "I guess you better go check that phase point then, you've been talking about it all morning."

Shandra was irritated at her brother's bragging, "Yes we are going now."

All of the Phase Walkers left Remiel House. Ethan followed behind, taking to the air.

Alastor was stepping heavily down the path to Remiel House, he saw something move in the corner or his eye but ignored it. He was feeling really paranoid about the locals; home was all he was thinking. A dark shadow cast over him for a second then went over his head, he looked up and saw flying, instinctively he jumped into the air as phantom wings spread and he landed with a thud as he hit his tail on his leg, a painful reminder that he was no longer fully Celestial. Alastor moved on and decided to cut through the forest in case he was seen heading in the direction of Remiel House. Visions of Morack and Keyness's wings kept seeping through his mind and spurred his step in anger.

Sarah, Caitlin and Shandra were walking toward the phase point near Remiel House, Ethan flew ahead off to the Abbith Market, something to do about a guild meeting.

Sarah, excited, spoke, "Guys, just so you know I need to go on a date tonight so I'll be leaving in the afternoon to pick out my clothes."

Caitlin, walking in almost a skip with Wuzzle trailing behind, replied, "Sarah, can't you see some things are more important?"

Sarah, a little agitated, spoke, "Well I only agreed to be a Phase Walker and help if it doesn't interfere with my life."

Shandra, annoyed, "Well this is my life, sorry you have a more important one."

Mixy followed, silently pondering ways to find her clutch, recalling details so she could find a clue. The thick sticky substance seemed to be getting thicker around her fur.

They arrive at the phase point and Caitlin tried to open the phase. Nothing happened, her little face twisted in her effort.

"It's closed," Caitlin said.

Sarah, happy, "Good! One less thing to worry about."

"Wow," Shandra said while she reached for the phase point and nothing was there.

"At least we know we can do it, now to wondering if we can create a phase point," Shandra said.

Caitlin smiled, "Well that would be fun to do."

- Chapter 12 -

Light Magic

Trigan was in the Abbith Market, there were wondrous berries in punnets before him, a little Celestial girl came out from underneath a cart and spoke in a loud voice, "Sister, come quickly, another monster."

A beautiful Celestial women with long shimmering jet black hair to her waist and a flowing white gown walked up to the small child that was pointing in Trigan's direction.

Trigan pointed back and poked out his blue tongue.

The little girl giggled.

Trigan picked up some berries in his hand and placed them in his mouth, the women looked up and smiled, "Trigan, the Master Workers are having a guild meeting soon."

Trigan was a Desnee, he had metallic coppery skin and looked humanoid, his eyes were purple and glowed but he had a friendly face. He wore very neatly tailored clothes that were ornate and stunning but they were obviously outworldly.

The beautiful Celestial with black hair smiled and the little girl ran back under a nearby cart. The women spoke, "They're in the guild hall, good to see you again."

Trigan smiled and poked his blue tongue out again at the little girl and replied, "Nice to see you again Lady Khan, I trust you are going to the meeting?"

Lady Khan replied, "Yes I will get mother to take over the shop and see you at the hall."

Lady Khan walked back into a shop that had levitating glass boxes of tiny strange bottles that contained many colourful liquids. A wooden sign floated overhead in the air, 'Emporium of Little Devices'.

Lady Khan was a Master Worker, she studied the art of magical object creation and was very good. She specialised in tiny detailed devices and was very good at working light magic in minute qualities to achieve tiny details of creation. She spoke to her mother in the back room and her sister came running from behind a tree directly through the doors out to the back of the shop, giggling.

Lady Khan waved at her mother and shouted back as she walked out, "I'll be back later, Guild meeting."

Her little sister ran out and followed her outside.

Once outside the shop Lady Khan waved her arms and spread her huge silvery wings, "Go inside my little sister, our father should be home soon."

The little girl ran inside the shop. Lady Khan stood still for a moment then took to the air and flew up into the sky, it was a lovely shade of blue, but it was unnatural like all on the Celestial plane, created from pure light magic. As she was ascending higher into the air with her silvery feathered wings, her long black hair danced in the wind, a large floating building emerged into sight.

At first glance she could only see under the building, shiny blue long crystal clumps reflected the sun as it hovered of its own accord, still and unmoving in the air. Rising even higher into the air Lady Khan could see the structure that was on top of the blue crystals, it was white and appeared not to have bricks or any joins, it looked like it was crafted out of one piece of huge white stone. The windows did not have glass and were open, they had arches and the top of the building had a landing platform.

Lady Khan flew to the landing platform, there was an open stairwell in the ground. Lady Khan stretched from the exercise and then put her wings down and a purple shimmer appeared. Trigan appeared after the shimmer, his fine clothes often impressed her as he created them himself using the light magic. He was in different clothes again, not the ones he wore in the market.

Smiling, Trigan spoke, "A pleasure Lady Khan, after you."

There was a loud flapping of wings, both Lady Khan and Trigan looked up. A handsome Celestial with silvery wings landed, he smiled and it caught Lady Khan's attention more than Trigan the outworlder.

Lady Khan picked up her long black hair from her shoulder, tossed in flight, and straightened it. Her skin was like white like snow and her eyes were green. She spoke, "Ethan, nice to see you coming to a guild meeting, I trust your apprenticeship is going well. Mammoth structures, I can't forget what you're learning because it's so opposite to what I specialise in."

Ethan smiled again and relaxed his wings; Trigan didn't enter the stairwell and just watched.

Ethan replied, "Yes, opposites, I'm attending the meeting to make sure I'm keeping on track to become a Master Worker, it's very important to me, makes me feel like I can do something, having two Phase Walkers in the family makes you want to achieve something more."

Trigan shuffled something in his pocket and spoke, "Don't worry Ethan, you will get there, it took me thirty years to become a Master Worker, as you know my speciality is clothing and cloth. I'm the finest tailor on the Celestial plane."

Ethan smiled, "Indeed, you're a wealth of talent, a Master Worker and a Phase Walker, so impressed," he grinned as it was a little jab, and he liked to get Trigan going.

Trigan spoke, "Of course I've got so much talent it makes everyone want to bow to me, I'm so great I've got tiger blood."

Lady Khan burst out laughing, "Oh really Trigan, so what if I don't bow?"

Trigan, half smiling, "It's okay, I will just make an

exception for you because you're pretty, plus you know I am winning."

Lady Khan blushed, embarrassed as she didn't expect that response. Lady Khan spoke, "My Trigan, looks I might have some tiger blood, if I knew what it was."

Trigan stretched, "Oh just this Earth creature, some actor called Charlie says tiger blood a lot."

Ethan spoke, "Aha, Phase Walker talk always hurts my ears, la la."

Trigan spoke, "Blah, big things hurt my eyes."

Lady Khan laughed, "Let's go in guys, the meeting will be soon or I will hurt both your ears and eyes."

Both Ethan and Trigan laughed, it was odd looking at Trigan's coppery expressions. Lady Khan went down the stairs, it descended sharply Trigan and Ethan followed. The room they entered was fresh and white, there were several windows around the walls, through the windows all that could be seen was blue sky, no wind blew through. There were fine chairs around a large rectangular white table which was made of stone. A ball of yellow light hovered above the table and several members of the Master Workers were standing around chatting.

Trigan entered and they all stopped talking. Trigan liked how he had that effect on the Celestials, there was only two outworlders that were Master Workers. Trigan was the only one that attended all the guild meetings, the other he had yet to meet and he was convinced it was made up so he could not brag about being the only one.

A few more guild members entered the hall, all the Celestials present had various winged feather shades from black to white, silver, gold and a mix in between.

The yellow light chimed three times and everyone stopped mingling and chatting then came to sit at the huge white table. There were thirty two seats in all, after everyone was seated there were several empty chairs.

The yellow glowing ball above the table spoke in a singing voice, "Greetings members of the Master Workers

Guild, we have received a big order from the Lady of Light from the plane of Lorvisa. I require you to take a break from your studies, except Jenith who has to continue with the specialisation of working light creation magic on Knoxcred stones. We will receive two bags full of the rare Knoxcred as payment to the Guild."

All the members looked at Jenith, he was a tall Celestial with jet black feathered wings and crystal blue eyes, his skin was dark brown which gave him a healthy glow. But looks can be deceiving because Jenith coughed and his hands shook, he was as weak as a kitten, working with the Knoxcred stones was not without danger as Jenith was learning the hard way. The guild members started chatting and the noise level rose.

The yellow glowing ball started to chime again and when there was silence it spoke, "All your talents will be required to make weapons of light magic for an army of the Lady of Light."

There was fast talking again and voices got louder.

The yellow glowing ball moved lower and chimed again.

Indigent faces looked at the ball but they all stopped talking.

The yellow glowing ball spoke again, "I have been working on a design for a magical light stunner and a magical light rod of death that will emit a death ray but I have put a failsafe into these magical devices that they will not work when targeted at a Celestial or one that emits the workings of light magic."

"We will meet again tomorrow, it is a large order, five hundred of each device have been ordered and, as always, our work is secret. I will be coming in person to start the production. I'm excited to be embarking on such a big consignment of work and to be receiving what we have been painfully been trying to source for such a long time, the Knoxcred stones."

"Once we acquire them we can start to build the project we have always wanted, to broaden our trade base. In service to the Master Workers, always."

All the members as the table spoke, "In service to the Master Workers, grandmaster."

Most guild members stood, but Ethan, Trigan and Lady Khan sat at the end of the table.

Trigan had to start with a smart jest, "So I hope that failsafe works because her magic creates tiny, tiny things, so tiny it might not detect it is light magic."

Lady Khan smiled, her green eyes sparkled with intelligence, "Oh really, well I didn't know tailoring used light magic."

Ethan interjected, "Well now, I make big things therefore I am the safest."

Lady Khan stood then wacked Ethan on the shoulder softly, "Come on, let's go."

The room was starting to clear.

Trigan spoke, "Yes, I have to see to my customers, see you tomorrow."

Trigan, Lady Khan and Ethan left for the stairwell. The yellow ball of light went out.

Alastor was on the last stretch of the way home to Remiel House, he was enjoying the walk, the familiar trees and even the same rocks stacked up neatly along the path. When Remiel House came into sight his heart beat faster and he couldn't wait to see his brother and sister. He thought up a few strategies to explain the period of time he had been gone and his appearance, he missed wings so much, being back on the Celestial plane made it so painful. He couldn't think of any way to tell them except the truth, he had been captured, tortured and experimented on by the Delvin leader, Morack.

Alastor, sad and scared, did not just walk on in; he knocked on the door like a visitor. Yanni opened the door and hovered in the doorway.

"Master Alastor, it is a pleasure to see you," Yanni intoned in a magical voice.

"Yanni!" Alastor spoke, happy to see his friend and that he was recognised straight away.

Staring at Yanni he could see chaos magic around its middle. It appeared to be binding Yanni somehow, Alastor reached for chaos magic, grimacing, and concentrated, trying to remove the band, and it slowly started to crack. Pushing harder, Alastor broke the band from Yanni. Yanni hummed and buzzed from side to side, happy to be free.

Alastor spoke to Yanni in his mind, "Where are my brother and sister? What happened to you?"

Yanni put a visual image into Alastor's mind and showed them leaving the house, then a close up of Shandra which was for a time, then little Caitlin, a large worm and a woman.

Alastor recognised little Caitlin but the strange white worm and pretty women he did not.

Disappointed, he went into the main room and sat on a chair by the fire opposite to the chair Ethan usually sat.

Alastor stared into the blue flames deep in thought. Yanni then offered Alastor a mug of tea, he accepted and sipped.

Pleased with themselves, Mixy, Caitlin, Sarah and Shandra started to walk back to Remiel House. Wuzzle trailed behind like always.

Caitlin, excited over a mini victory, "So we need to sit down and work out a plan. We need to investigate, the Delvin have crimes to pay for, the attack on the aquatics, the taking of Phase Walkers and perhaps Alastor was captured and taken there too."

Shandra was thinking of other things, the call of her purple stone was distracting her, making her want to use it. She desperately wanted to see what was happening with the Delvin. It was like an addiction, she needed to know, all this talk about the Delvin spurned on her need for it.

Sarah, breaking Shandra's concentration on the purple gem, spoke, "After we get back I will have lunch and head off, sorry guys but I did say I wanted to leave, I have a date."

Caitlin, getting annoyed with Sarah, "Okay, but after we have a talk?"

Sarah annoyed, "Okay."

After a short journey they returned to Remiel House, the front door was wide open.

Shandra was still, studying it, thinking how strange, Yanni doesn't leave doors open.

Shandra's reaction was to lift her hands, readying them with Celestial light magic, ready for an intruder, she also reached for her phase weapon, it materialised and the trident glowed.

Seeing her weapon, the others materialised their phase weapons. Caitlin's tattoo was glowing and her shiny silvery boomerang was on the ready. Sarah had out her sword and Mixy a lasso, all the Phase Walker's tattoo markings were glowing. Yanni came out of the open doorway and hovered, there was too much to say, so it showed Shandra a vision of her brother Alastor sitting by the fire and then Shandra released the magic and phase power, and ran into Remiel House.

Yanni then projected the image to Caitlin, Sarah, Mixy and Wuzzle, each having a different reaction. For Caitlin it was surprise and relief, she herself started to run into the house. Wuzzle faithfully walked behind her but had a smile on his fury long toothed face. Sarah thought, wow he's a cute guy, rather hot, she entered the house walking, not wanting to be outside. Mixy, well she just did not understand but knew there was another inside, she was hungry and followed Yanni inside.

Alastor stood from his chair near the fire when he heard fast footsteps coming closer, Shandra ran in and stood shocked, looking at Alastor she put her hands to her mouth and covered it, holding in a scream.

Little Caitlin came running in with the patter of tiny feet and almost hit the back of Shandra, she moved in front of her and stood before Alastor. Speaking without thinking, Caitlin said, "Alastor what happened to you, you look different?

Good to see you, we were all so worried. We were looking for you on the Delvin plane."

Alastor took a step back and spoke, "Sister are you ok? Do you not recognise me?"

Sarah walked in and smiled and looked at Alastor, he was tall, about six feet, very well-muscled and toned. He had whitish blond hair poking out from under a funny blue old hat. He wore a frilly blue shirt that was open, the material was very thin and you could see his tanned six pack underneath. He wore strange boots that make his feet look odd. Whoa, Sarah thought as a long tail with black hair on the end whipped around from behind, he doesn't look that much like Shandra's twin.

"I am fine, what happened to you Alastor? You have a tail," pointing to his long tail.

Alastor grabbed his tail; it had a life of its own unless Alastor concentrated on it.

"I have a long story to tell you sister, perhaps a meal and chat is at hand."

Shandra, demanding, "Why do you wear a funny hat?"

Mixy and Wuzzle were hanging back at this stage and Yanni came in, feeling the vibrations of many needing help and to be attended to.

Shandra gasped as she looked at Yanni, realising the holding band had been removed on Yanni, and it could now enter the phase.

Alastor spoke firmly, "Sister, it's part of the story, I would like to tell you in detail."

Alastor removed his old ratty hat, and two little black twisted horns poked out of his shiny white blond hair which fell down his back, tied in a warrior's tail with leather ties.

Shandra rushed forward and embraced her brother, while trying to work out in her mind who used chaos magic to release Yanni's bond.

Alastor smiled, relieved he had not been rejected, he had been really getting nervous with Shandra's reaction and he had had an audience. Shandra stepped back and looked at her brother again and smiled.

Alastor asked, "So where is our brother, Ethan?"

Shandra responded, "You just missed him, he went to a Master Workers meeting, like always."

Alastor smiled because he wanted his brother to keep up with his studies.

"So I guess some introductions are at hand?"

Shandra spoke, "Oh yes, well you know Caitlin."

Pointing to Sarah, Shandra intoned, "This is Sarah, she is from the plane of Earth, she is a new Phase Walker, Caitlin brought her here for training."

Alastor studied her intently and looked at her fine features, she looked Celestial for the most part except a little bronze colour in the skin, he thought.

Sarah felt off because she blushed at being the centre of attention. Alastor smiled, sensing her blush and spoke, "Pleased to meet you Sarah, I look forward to learning more about your plane."

Shandra pointed to Mixy, "This is Mixy, she is also a Phase Walker, don't let her size confuse you, she is also a youngling, so young she is merely a few weeks old."

Alastor was a little taken back that a worm creature could be a Phase Walker and that it was so young.

"Pleased to meet you also Mixy, Caitlin I hope you are well. I guess I better tell you where I have been and why I look different."

"It's not the best story to tell so I will be brief, please all sit at the table."

Everyone sat at the main table, it was wooden and empty but Yanni was changing that fast enough, materialising meals and putting them before the guests. Strangely Alastor was served first, which was against tradition of Remiel House, usually guests are always served first. He would have to talk to Yanni about a few things soon, Alastor thought.

Alastor, in a warm deep voice, spoke, his eyes calm, "Sister, friends and guests, first off, if I burst into rage please excuse my behaviour I'm finding it very hard to control my

Delvin side and keep it together."

"I was kidnapped, taken from right outside Remiel House by several Delvin, at first I thought they were Phase Walkers but they were just Morack's henchmen, more on this later. I was taken to the Delvin plane Nevid and kept in a cage where I could not use my phase walker ability along with another Celestial, Keyness, she was also a Phase Walker."

Alastor paused to compose himself as a sharp pain went through his body, talking about Keyness an image of bloody wings shot into his mind, then he continued, "Morack chose me for his change experiment, he wanted to make a slave race to do his bidding, he subjected me to weeks of pain and magical experimentation. Many days I would black out but each time I woke up I felt less like me and more like a Delvin."

"He warped my body, I lost my wings, literally they disappeared through Morack's use of chaos magic on me; I have a tail and hoofed feet and also these ghastly horns. I also lost all sense of the phase this is what devastated me more than the physical change," Alastor looked ashamed.

Shandra blurted out, "Oh dear brother, we will fix you, I promise."

Sarah also had a look of shock on her face and held her hands to her face; she wondered what Alastor looked like as a Celestial, she was trying to imagine it based on what Ethan looked like, the thought of that made her swoon. She was also shocked that his Delvin form she also found really attractive.

Alastor smiled and enjoyed his sister's concern, not so much for sympathy but to hear her voice and to be reminded that he was outside the hell of the Delvin plane.

Alastor continued, "There is more to the tale, the Celestial women kept in cage beside me, called Keyness."

"Well Morack had other plans for her, he used his vile chaos magic's to extract Keyness's phase essence, or life force, as they seemed to be linked. He strapped her to a machine and she screamed in pain as her very essence was drained from her body. Every time Morack did this process it was very hard to watch as Keyness became weaker each time, it gives me mental agony now even to speak of it but these injustices by him need to be exposed."

"Keyness's essence was collected in a jar, it was blue liquid and Morack would drink it or smear it on other Delvin's faces. It would make them Phase Walkers temporarily. The more they had of the essence the longer the effect. Eventually Keyness died when Morack used the machine to drain her, he extracted all of Keyness's essence and inducted his army into the phase by using it on all of his hunters and Delvin."

"I used the last of Keyness's essence to get here, I am ashamed to say. I stole it from Morack when I saw he had chopped of Keyness's wings as a barbaric trophy and hung them above his throne."

"I had lost my natural ability to phase in Morack's experiments and I saw it as a way to avenge Keyness for her torture and death and my torture and pain. I also want to stop Morack from ever taking another Phase Walker again, he needs to be stopped."

Shandra, stunned, "Yes brother I will help you stop Morack, we do know a way into the Delvin plane, in fact we were going there to search for you."

"At the very moment we opened a phase to the Delvin plane, a Delvin stepped through and saw us and stepped back in. We didn't want to risk them bringing more through so we sealed the phase point to Remiel House."

Caitlin spoke up with sadness in her voice, "I'm sorry for your friend Keyness and what has happened to you Alastor, it saddens me so much to hear this. Earlier when I was in Nevid with Sarah we overheard a Delvin conversation, they mentioned the name Alastor but I was not aware at the time you were missing and thought it a coincidence, I'm sorry we didn't look for you then, maybe we could of helped Keyness."

Alastor looked at Caitlin and gave a weak smile, "Don't be sorry Caitlin, you most likely would have been captured, I'm glad you didn't. I would be even more twisted inside if I learnt my friends were captured by Morack, he would of drained your essence, he is an evil vile being."

Caitlin sat forward on her chair, pushing forward her food on the table, "There is more Alastor, in my home plane of Kelstone I was attacked through my home phase point. A single Delvin was trying to capture and take me, it was very scary. Wuzzle and I fought for a long time with it."

My friend Martin, that you know also, jumped from the water of the nearby pond and tried to help, hurling water and stones at the evil Delvin. Then Sarah came through the phase point and helped me, she cut off the Delvin's head with her phase weapon."

"I told my elders and they brought up the veil to hide from any more Delvin that came looking for me. I thought Martin would be alright because his village was underwater in the pond and further out in the sea, but the Delvin must have tracked Martin down because at least half of his people were slaughtered in a Delvin attack. The village was destroyed, treasure was taken and Martin was killed."

"I'm so sad to tell you all this Alastor. I agree the Delvin are evil and they seem to be targeting Phase Walkers all over. I think its best we all stay together and try and find a way to permanently stop the Delvin and Morack. It pains me to hear what has happened to you Alastor."

Alastor, aghast, snarled like a Delvin at hearing this news, as Martin had been a friend.

"Caitlin, together we will plan and stop Morack and we will stop the hunting of the Phase Walkers if I have to kill every last Delvin myself."

Shandra watched all this talk and sat silently.

Sarah's phone beeped, she received a message, 'See you soon can't wait until tonight'.

Sarah looked at the time.

Sarah knew she had to go but didn't know the phase point from the Abbith Market, she wanted to ask but after everything that had been said she thought to wait a bit longer and miss her hair dresser appointment.

Yanni produced blue arms and put a bucket of food out in front of Mixy, who was growing larger, if that was possible.

Sarah's phone beeped again another message came up, it was William, 'Sarah can I swing by an hour earlier I have a surprise for you?'

Sarah read the message and started to feel really torn, she wanted to help and wanted to leave.

Sarah spoke, breaking the silence, "I'm sorry for all that has happened, I will help you but I have to go for a ... something on tonight, I will be back tomorrow I have a...," Sarah stumbled her words, she was going to say date but looking at Alastor somehow made it feel wrong.

Sarah continued, "I have an appointment, could someone please show me to the closest phase point now that the Remiel phase point is closed."

Alastor spoke, "I would be honoured to show you Sarah."

Sarah, a little embarrassed, "Okay thank you, but we need to leave now."

Shandra interjected, "No Alastor, we need to talk more, we only just got you back."

"Calm yourself sister, I will only be a few moments, I do not have to cross the phase, just open it. Sarah, link with me."

Sarah concentrated on ones, her tattoos around her finger glowed. Alastor thought that was strange. He thought of the Abbith market phase point and opened the phase, markings of swirls on his arms glowed blue lightly through his shirt.

Sarah smiled weakly, "Thank you Alastor, I will be back, see you all soon."

Sarah waved then walked through the phase, it snapped shut behind her.

Shandra asked after seeing Alastor use the phase, "How long will you be able to use the phase Alastor?"

Alastor pondered, "I don't know, I took all that was left of Keyness. I do know she would have wanted me to get out of there. I also used it so Morack could not. Let us eat our meals and we can talk more when our brother arrives home."

Shandra smiled, "Of course, brother."

"I really need a rest, I've had a long day," Alastor said, sighing.

Shandra spoke to Yanni, who was in the middle of clearing away some empty plates that Sarah left, "Can you please wake me when Ethan arrives."

Shandra smiled and waved, then walked to her room. Carefully closing the door behind her, in her bedroom Shandra took out her purple stone from her pouch and held it in her hands, it was vibrating and talking to her, "Shhhhandra, shhandra find out what's happening."

Shandra walked up to a bowl of wash water on her wooden drawers and placed the stone inside. The water glowed purple and went misty then cleared, she could see into Morack's throne room.

The large demonoid creature known as Morack stomped his hooves on the stone ground and he screeched his voice.

A grey Delvin was reporting to him, "My Lord the brood mother is almost dead, we need a cure now."

Morack's face contorted and steam came through his nostrils, "Must I do everything myself, form a group, we are going into Lorvisa to find the cure if I have to drag it out of the Lady of Light myself."

Morack walked back to his throne and sat down.

Shandra took the stone from the water, which cleared instantly, the stone spoke, "Shhhandra you must, you will rule the Delvin, you are destined to be a queen, but do as I say and get closer to Morack. First, offer your services again."

Shandra quickly put the purple stone back into her pocket and then climbed onto her bed, spread her wings and then closed her eyes.

- Chapter 13 -

Free Opera

Sarah was in a busy market, she wondered what she could buy but realising she was late it would have to wait for another time, she quickly opened the phase to Earth and walked through.

Sarah came out into the alley way to the Brisbane Chocolate Coffee House. She had to learn to use the phase point in her apartment she thought and will need to work on that. She was also running out of money, and, checking her watch, confirmed she had missed her hair dresser appointment. She took out her phone and responded to Williams's message, 'See you soon that is fine look forward to your surprise and Thai food', then hit send on her phone.

Sarah walked out of the alley to the nearest ATM, she was going to try to acquire money. She took a look at the ATM from a distance, walked around the corner and opened the phase to the back of the ATM, she put her hand into the phase and felt around, she felt nothing but wires and strange dials. Frightened of being discovered she closed the phase to the ATM, opened the intra-phase to her apartment and walked through.

"Bugger," Sarah said as she walked in to her bedroom. The bed had been moved to the other side of the room so Sarah stepped through and it was clear. Sarah quickly ran into the bathroom and started to get ready for her date.

Morack was in his throne room, his army had assembled yet again, this time there was a destination, this time he would be leading the charge. If you want to do something right you do it yourself, Morack thought. He also knew that his Phase Walkers had limited time before they lost their ability and he had no other Phase Walkers to drain bar one, which he kept in reserve and he was not going to use him unless he really had too.

That was a Delvin known as Knifegiver, he was a legend known to the Delvin for his adventures through the phase. Morack didn't know where Knifegiver was but he was a braggart and it was only a matter of time before he would show his face around Nevid again.

The Delvin gathered into the throne room, Morack's hunters were at the front of the massive crowd. Reednak and Nica, the blue Delvins, Canya, the purple holding a new weapon, a huge trident, stolen from the Persidion village, and of cause Grimlock, the red haired Delvin in his black robes. Morack opened the phase, he stood before an army of five hundred.

"We are going to find a cure for the brood mother, we cannot let our race die, without the brood mother our numbers will not grow. We do this for our kind, come brothers, for the brood mother!"

Horns and tails moved in the crowd and rough guttural voices cheered, "For the brood mother!"

Morack stepped through the phase first, into the plane of Lorvisa, so followed his hunters and his army. It was dark on Lorvisa, the forest was thick with vegetation and small animals moved through bushes. A huge crowd of Delvin emerged through the phase, taking up space in the forest. Morack stood at the phase point waiting for the remainder of his army, when he was certain all were through he closed the phase.

Morack sent out a few Delvin scouts and he used his foul

chaos magic to detect the location of the nearest village. Morack didn't know where the Lady of Light was but he was going to cleanse her population and collect Phase Walkers on the way.

The scouts returned and nothing was in either direction. Morack saw that as an all clear and the army started in the direction of the beings in the village he had detected. Morack decided to use more complex magic, a vision spell to see the village and plan ahead, but he could see nothing except forest even though he picked up many living beings. He used his chaos magic again and then asked Grimlock to confirm, he did.

Grimlock spoke, "My Lord it appears the beings are underneath, buried in the ground."

Morack screeched, "Well we will blast the ground and finish them."

The army moved to the village, it was not far from the phase point, little creatures and insects flew away from the collective fear the army was spreading. They arrived at what looked like a still serene forest with clumps of loose dirt in little patches scattered on the ground.

The Delvin started to use their chaos magic and their brute force to smash at the ground.

Dirt was projected everywhere and there was a layer of dust in the air. Humanoid brown spiderlike creatures scuttled from the ground and tried to escape, but the Delvin were cruel, they pulled and hacked their legs from their bodies, showing no mercy. The spider creatures had humanoid bodies and faces, they contorted their faces in pain. They did not fight back and fled if they could, some dug deeper into the earth but that was no escape as the chaos magic killed them underground. Morack's army met no resistance, it was a complete slaughter.

Morack used his chaos magic to ensure nothing else was living and felt nothing; he projected his magic to a wider distance and picked up another area of living creatures. Morack pushed his army forward toward the living creatures, he wanted to hurt things, not just because of the brood mother but because of his brother and the Lady of Light trying to pick a fight, he wanted to show that stupid winged bitch the Delvin might. Morack felt good.

The forest was flattened with the force of Morack's army moving forward; trees were knocked down and bushes squashed into the dirt, small creatures ran from the fear wave the army projected and fled into the night.

Morack came across a white structure, it looked Celestial made, it was large and contained many living creatures. Morack scanned it for an entrance, he couldn't detect one so he threw a lighting ball of energy into the side. Grimlock, in his dark robes, stepped forward and joined in, casting the same spell Morack did, in the same spot.

Black scorch marks outline the large hole that had been smashed in the side of the white building. The Delvin entered the structure through the blackened hole, stepping on white debris.

There were guards inside, winged creatures wearing tabards of blue with a golden triangle. There were also fat creatures that looked like worms, fluffy and white, lined on the walls in strange bays and being fed blue hay. Some sort of breeding area, good, Morack thought, they strike the Delvin's breeding, I strike back.

Morack was very happy, he started to blast the defenceless fat creatures that squirmed and wriggled in pain, twitching as they died – it was a terrible sight.

His army rushed in. The guards, less than ten in total, started to fight back. They had phase weapons, one flew to the sky and started to get away. Morack reached for chaos magic and started to fire bolts of flame at the flying creature.

He missed his mark and the winged creature got away. Morack was filled with anger and rage, knowing that it may come back with others, so Morack reached for raw chaos magic and a black ball of energy appeared. He shot it at the nearest winged guard, then he realised the winged guard was holding a phase weapon as it dematerialised before his eyes.

Morack was even angrier at himself for killing a Phase Walker. He looked up and noticed only four winged guards alive, his army surrounding them. He used his chaos magic's and boomed his voice above the noise of the battle.

"Delvin brothers, the guards are Phase Walkers, capture them and do not kill them, I need them, their essence."

The battle went for some time as the Delvin tried to capture the winged Phase Walkers, all four were captured and alive but badly beaten. Morack was good at tactics and he knew that winged guard that got away would be back with more, if not an army. Pleased with his prizes, the Phase Walkers, he decided to come back tomorrow for the brood mother's cure.

Morack opened the phase to the phase point, he will send his hunters back tomorrow to scout out the location of the Lady of Light, as much as he wanted to kill every living thing on the plane of Lorvisa, the brood mother didn't have that much time.

Arriving at the phase point, small animals and plants attacked him and the army. Even small bugs biting, he was sure it was the Lady of Light, it was such a pathetic attack. He opened the phase to Nevid and his army stepped through, hacking at the forest and splatting bugs while they waited their turn to walk through. The phase closed shut.

Ethan was flying home rather pleased with himself, Lady Khan always made him feel good. The air was charged with light magic, he felt the flows around him as Remiel House came into sight. Slowly he descended, thinking about the huge order he would have to help with tomorrow. This order was very important to the Master Workers Guild, free travel for all and phase trade would be a reality if the Guild was to receive the Knoxcred stones.

Ethan landed then walked to the front door, when Yanni did not open it, he opened it himself, thinking, how unusual. There was a murmur of chatter and he headed to the main room. He heard his brother's voice, hoping it wasn't a phantom voice he walked faster into the room. He stopped and took in the main room, stunned, his younger brother Alastor was there, he looked different, he had horns and a tail, his feet looked wrong, huge and strangely shaped, and he had no wings. Caitlin was laughing and Wuzzle was eating, Mixy was just snoozing on the floor. Sarah and Shandra were not in the room, Yanni left the room.

Ethan spoke, excited, "Alastor."

Alastor turned to Ethan and walked up to him and grabbed his hand, "Brother, miss me?"

Alastor stood back and grinned, releasing his grip, realising he had a clawed hand.

Ethan, shocked, spoke, "Where have you been? What happened to you, you look strange?"

"Brother, I'm very happy to see you again, I thought I would not see my family every again. Please sit by the fire and I'll tell you where I have been, unfortunately I have a story of sorrow to tell you."

Both Ethan and Alastor sat in front of the fire and were both in deep conversation, when Yanni entered the room again and Shandra walked in.

Shandra pulled up another chair to the fireplace and let Alastor tell his tale again.

The Lady of Light was in the chapter house, it was full of Lords and Ladies of Illumination.

A Lady of Illumination appeared before the Lady of Light, through the phase on the speaker's platform, she was singed from fire, her tabard burnt, but she looked uninjured. Her wings were green and pretty.

She spoke, "Lady of Light, I bring bad news, one of our clutches has been destroyed. It was one of your nobles, the Micon, not a wild peasant clutch. The Delvin blasted a hole in the wall and slaughtered the Micon larvae. The Illumination guards were fighting them, I got away to bring word to you, they fight as we speak, please they need help, they're outnumbered, the Delvin brought an army of Phase Walkers that also wield chaos magic."

The Lady of Light glowed brightly and spoke, "My Lady of Illumination, I will send help."

The Lady of Light tilted her head to the sky, looking up, her feelers on her head vibrating, she sent a vibration across the land, it was a message, "Please, inhabitants of Lorvisa, heed my call, the Micon clutch is under attack, please defend it and keep them safe, please attack the Delvin that invade our land."

Any fear that the Delvin projected was negated by the Lady of Lights devotion aura, every bit of life on Lorvisa responded, every bit of life looked and searched for the Delvin. Those that could not see Delvin eventually gave up, but those who could attacked with all their might. Unfortunately the living creatures that did see the Delvin were small and tiny, but still they tried their best, giving up their life force to hurt the Delvin, insects using their stingers, plants and trees lashing out with their branches. Small rodents jumping and biting as hard as they could. If the Delvin army were anywhere else they would have been destroyed.

The room smelt like curries and spice. The walls had pictures of elephants and flowers. There were spoons and forks on a perfectly set table.

Sarah was eating dinner at a Thai restaurant with William, it was divine. William kept trying to make her laugh by telling jokes and spoke a lot about himself. Sarah was distant, her thoughts elsewhere thinking about the Delvin and about Alastor of all things, a perfect Ken doll demon. Thinking about the horrors he went through and his strong body she wanted to leave William and comfort him, and then realised it was only her fantasy and stared into Williams face trying to be grounded.

A plate of chicken green curry was placed down on the table, it smelt wonderful, by a beautiful women who was dressed in a traditional Thai outfit. As the waitress walked off, Sarah smiled, looked up at William and spoke, "Thank you so much for taking me out, I have a lot on my mind and I really needed a break."

The Thai waitress arrived with a second plate that she placed down on the table, it was a beef red curry. William smiled, "Good, I was worried I was losing my touch."

Sarah laughed. They chatted about university but Sarah was bored, it all seemed so mundane. What was she doing she thought, relaxing when she should be helping Caitlin and poor Alastor. Sarah looked at William gazing into his eyes thinking that he had no fucking idea; William started to eat his food.

Sarah then watched an old couple sitting a table to her right, he was holding her hand and they were sharing a quiet moment. It was cute she thought and pondered. Another dish arrived at the table, spiced rice with cream.

William spoke to the waitress, "This isn't what I ordered, take it back and bring me plain rice."

Sarah cringed, then thought of Yanni, "So William, what was the surprise we had dinner early for?"

William smiled, "I was waiting for you to ask that."

He opened his wallet and pulled out two tickets to Phantom of the Opera.

Sarah loved that musical, so happy her mood changed, "Thank you William, I love Phantom! How did you guess?"

William laughed, "Well the Phantom of Opera sticker you have on your laptop kind of gave it away."

Sarah laughed also, "Oh yeah, that's a dead giveaway!"

William looked uncomfortable, "Trouble is I was wondering if you could pay for your ticket, they are rather pricey and dinner has wiped me."

Sarah, a little taken back she was paying for her own surprise, "Okay, how much?"

William smiled, "One hundred big ones."

Sarah panicked, not having the money, fuck she thought and how can he say that with a smile.

Sarah then spoke, "Oh well I need an ATM before we leave it seems."

William, who had started eating, paused and said, "Sure, there should be one along the way, let's finish our meal."

Truly no clue does he, Sarah thought.

Sarah and William finished their Thai food and headed to the theatre to watch Phantom of the Opera. On the way they came across an ATM.

"This one will be fine just wait here and I will be back," Sarah said.

William watched her cross the road. Sarah walked up to the ATM and studied it. Then walked to the side of the ATM looked over at William, waved, bent down and played with her shoe. She opened the phase, it was very small, just to allow her hand in, she reached in and felt around and took a wad of money from the ATM, played with her shoe some more and put the money in her handbag and walked back across the street.

"Ok let me see," Sarah reached into her handbag and gave William some money, more than he needed.

William blushed and took the money and shoved it into his wallet, "So did you have something wrong with your shoe."

Sarah was adjusting her handbag, the wad of cash was too much to fit so she discretely tossed half in the gutter, "Yes, I had a rock in my shoe, hate when that happens."

The theatre had bright white lights out the front and the smell of popcorn was in the air, they both went inside.

- Chapter 14 -

Visitors

The water was soft and warm, it lay still inside a wooden bowl, the purple stone sunk to the bottom and the reflection of a beautiful Celestial face reflected for a time before the water went murky. A voice boomed through the water, Shandra took a step back, she could feel Morack's hate projected through the vision bowl.

"Shandra, I know you watch me, I know what you seek, bring me back my pet and all will be forgiven."

The voice came from the stone in the water. Shandra picked it up and placed it in her pocket. She was unhappy that Morack knew she watched him; the purple stone did not speak to her. She walked to her bed, spread her wings and lay on it scheming.

The guild hall was clean and mostly white, the Guild Master was in, he had long flowing grey hair and deep blue eyes. His feathered wings were silvery white and he had a jump in his step as he walked to the members who had just arrived and greeted them, he had set up several work benches.

Some Master Workers were already creating rods, others mixing components to capture spells to put inside the rods.

Lady Khan was already at work, she was putting protective runes on the rods, carving intricate small symbols on their base using light magic.

Trigan was happy today working at another bench, a lovely blond haired Celestial was having a joke with him. They were creating magically bound bags to hold the rods; so that they would null the spells for shipment.

Ethan just arrived, he was late, he looked handsome, Lady Khan thought, flicking her black hair to the side to concentrate on what she was doing.

The Guild Master greeted Ethan, who looked rather too excited. Ethan spoke softly with the Guild Master and then walked to Lady Khan's bench.

Lady Khan blushed then looked up, "How are you Ethan, I think you're at the wrong bench."

Ethan grinned, almost identical to his brother's, he thought to himself, happy about Alastor's return, "Well the Guild Master thinks that I need some discipline, my speciality as you know is enormous large things but sometimes it's also good to practice my skills at making small things so he has charged this training to you, Lady Khan, for the day and I am to assist you."

Lady Khan had deep green eyes and soft features, she took a rod then demonstrated what she was doing, pausing and watching so Ethan understood.

Ethan picked up a rod and completed the same symbol he had been demonstrated, except he made the symbol so large it covered the entire rod.

Lady Khan laughed, "Well, maybe we need to practice more."

A silvery line appeared in the middle of the guild hall then a phase opened, a spideroid creature stepped through, it wore a blue tabard with a golden triangle. It had a human face that looked wise, deep warm brown eyes, a long brown beard and long brown hair down its back. It had six legs and each wore a black boot.

A few guild members stopped their work and stepped back watching. The Guild Master put his hands up and spoke, "Go back to work, this is our customer, all is well."

Not all members of the guild were accustomed to other races so they stared but slowly went back to work.

The spideroid creature made clicking noises those that were not Phase Walkers did not understand. The Guild Master was a Phase Walker and he replied, "Yes, we are on schedule, we cannot speed up production, I have all my Master Workers here working already, not just anyone can make what you require, only a Master Worker. I have even asked my apprentices to help, this is the best I can do. Please explain this to the Lady of Light."

The spideroid creature spoke, "Thank you, I will explain the situation but if you could please rush the order in any way please do."

The Guild Master replied, "We will try our best," and placed a finger on his chin in thought.

The spideroid opened the phase and left.

The Guild Master clapped his hands, "Sorry folks, it appears it's a rush order, if you can stay longer today please do."

There was a murmur in the guild hall but most Master Workers wanted to impress the Guild Master so the work on the rods would go through into the night.

Ethan laughed and spoke to Lady Khan, "So I get to have your company longer, all is good."

Lady Khan smiled, "Well I guess you do," and started to put a tiny symbol onto another rod.

Alastor was sitting up in his comfortable bed at Remiel House, his white blond hair was free and tossed over his face. He had a sleep, it was restless and many nightmares plagued his rest, waking him, they were fresh in his memory, he wished he couldn't recall them as pain went through his soul. When it came to sleep, being a half Delvin a cross breed had its advantages, he only required four hours at most to be refreshed, which also meant his nightmares only tormented him for four hours a night. He was awake, he had only slept two hours, he really needed another two. He lay down to sleep again, trying to get comfortable, he closed his eyes. Very quickly he went straight into slumber and another nightmare, the swirling tattoos on his arms glowed blue and he was surrounded by the phase.

Sarah was tired and at home from her date, she needed to sleep. She kicked of her shoes and wiped her makeup off then lay down fully dressed and went to sleep at eleven past one. Her tattoo around her finger glowed. The phase went around her body.

Both Alastor and Sarah were in the Delvin plane. Sarah woke up then sat, sleepily she saw a figure through the mist on the ground, she recognised where she was straight away, she had been here several times before. The rocks under her bare feet, the sulphur smell and the low lying mist. Below was a ravine that went to a platform.

She was in the Nevid plane, standing up she looked over to see Alastor, with no shirt on, lying on the ground in the mist. She stood studying his body, he had ripples of muscle on his toned flesh, Sarah had seen these types of guys with ripped chests in pin up magazines and pictures. She was a little taken back looking at the demon Ken doll, she walked closer to him and knelt down beside him, she placed her hand on his chest and tried to stir him to wake his slumber. His white blond long hair was untied and contrasted to the grey stone.

Frustrated, she pushed him from side to side, oh come on, she thought, then she lowered herself down close to his ear and spoke clearly, "Alastor, wake up, wake up!"

Alastor smiled with his eyes closed.

Sarah thought that was odd, so she spoke louder in his ear, "Wake up Alastor, we are in the Nevid plane."

Alastor sat upright with a start, Sarah startled and moved away at his reaction then she shuffled closer to him on her knees, leaning forward.

"Alastor, how did we get here? I was at home on the Earth plane, sleeping, then I was here."

Alastor pushed his long white blond hair from his face; he had a square jaw and a dimple in his chin. Sarah looked deep into his blue eyes as he spoke, his voice was deep for a Celestial but not a grinding guttural sound like a Delvin, "I was sleeping also, but in the Celestial plane in Remiel House, I don't know, lets phase back to Remiel House."

Sarah lent forward a little more and could sense Alastor's eyes on her bronze chest, she leaned back, "Okay, let's go, I want to get out of here."

Alastor stood and Sarah looked up at his tail, he put his hand down to her and she gave him her hand and stood, "Link with me and we will go."

Sarah had a lot of practice linking with Caitlin and thought of ones.

Alastor opened a phase to the Abbith market, he walked through holding Sarah's hand and she followed.

They were in Abbith market, it was night and still there were vendors selling cooked food and small delicate flowers, although most were closed, there was only a light murmur in the market not a loud chatter like the day. The ground was rough for a Celestial path even if the little stones did look perfectly lined up and Sarah had no shoes on.

Alastor was a good six foot something and Sarah a little under six foot high, she noticed this when they were standing together in the market. Alastor had dropped her hand making it harder for her to walk on the pebbled path. He walked a little ahead.

"Sarah, come over here and we will link again and open the phase to the entrance of Remiel House."

"Okay, ouch my feet," Sarah cried out, looking at her feet.

Alastor looked down at her cushy feet and wished his feet were not black and hoofed, "Jump on my back quickly then."

Sarah answered, "What!"

Alastor laughed, "Quickly let's get out of here, you have no shoes, I have no shirt or hat!"

Sarah gasped at realising his horns were visible, then jumped on Alastor's back. He held her tight with his hands behind his back and walked quickly behind a building and put her down. A purple shimmer appeared out of nowhere and a dark shadow was overhead. Alastor was confused, so was Sarah. There was a rushing of wind and a flapping of wings and two feet landed with a thud.

"Hello brother," Ethan spoke, then continued, "Why are you two in the market tonight?"

"Would you believe it if I told you, we were sleep walking," Alastor said.

Ethan glared at his brother and looked at Sarah's feet, "Phase Walker stuff? No shirt, nice look."

The purple haze shimmered thicker and Trigan materialised.

Ethan laughed as Sarah jumped, "This is Trigan, he's a Phase Walker too, like you guys, he is part of my guild, the Master Workers, we were working back tonight. We have a big order to fill so we have been very busy. I came to the market to get something to eat then fly home, I guess, and get some rest. I can't just blink around like all you Phase Walkers, anyways Trigan, my brother Alastor and Sarah, a friend."

Trigan had coppery coloured skin and it shimmered like the guy in Twilight, Edward, she thought, another outworlder, she was getting used to meeting beings or different races and it didn't seem to perturb her.

Trigan smirked, "Pleasure to meet you Alastor and Sarah. Do you think you would like a shirt Alastor and a pair of shoes Sarah, it doesn't look like you're dressed for night market shopping."

Alastor sighed, "Oh and a hat please, I want to cover these," pointing to his black horns.

Trigan smiled because he loved being useful, "Certainly, I have been practicing new hats actually."

Trigan moved his arms in circles then lots of hand waving and movement. It looked like the start of the Gangnam Style dance, Sarah thought and the song played in her head.

Trigan was working white creation magic, he was

drawing elements from the aether and constructing a shirt, shoes and hat all in one go, a difficult feat. He finished and the items appeared. The fine frilly shirt he handed to Alastor along with a lovely blue hat of fine material

"The latest fashion," Trigan said then winked.

Alastor took the items and pulled the shirt over himself. Sarah sighed inside, she had been enjoying the view. Then Alastor put the hat on, it covered his horns and he was happy.

Trigan offered Sarah a pair of soft boots which he somehow managed to make look dainty and ornate, they were black leather. Sarah sat on the ground, it wasn't lady like but how else was she supposed to put lace up boots on. She put them on and pulled the laces tight. She was amazed, they felt wonderful like she could go jogging in them. They had a slight platform and heel but she felt like she was standing at the right angle.

Ethan clapped his hands, "Great, Trigan and I are hungry, do you want to join us in the night market? I have barter chips and I'll look after you."

Alastor grinned at Ethan, "Well then if you have the barter chips, sure, I'm hungry myself, care to join us Sarah?"

Sarah was looking at her new shoes and looked up, "Sure, I'm actually getting the munchies too."

Alastor laughed, "Munchies?"

All four walked into the Abbith night market, Ethan saw lovely food platters at several vendor carts and Trigan pointed some out also, but they looked like they had weird tiny worms and strange fish on them.

Ethan turned to everyone and said, "Okay, I will find us a space and make us somewhere to eat."

Ethan walked over to a space away from the vendors, the night sky twinkled with stars and the trees smelt fresh, it was a little secluded from the market, that suited him. Trigan, Alastor and Sarah followed and watched Ethan.

Ethan first created a table, it was white and wooden with little ornate carvings on its legs. Then four white chairs at once, working his light magic. Sarah watched in wonder and surprise. Alastor, unimpressed, raised an eyebrow.

Trigan spoke while watching, "Show off."

"Well I'm not a Phase Walker, got to be good at something," Ethan replied.

"Please sit, enjoy," Ethan waved his hands in the direction of the chairs, "I'll go get us some food platters and drink."

Sarah sat on her chair and Alastor across from her, then Trigan sat next to her on her side of the table. Alastor looked up at the stars, "It's nice seeing them again."

Trigan poked fun, "So real a Master Worker could make one."

Sarah looked confused and asked, "What do you mean?"

Ethan answered from a distance, using light magic to carry many dishes to the table and placing them, "The stars are not natural, like everything on the Celestial plane, they were created from light magic by the Master Workers as a reminder of what once was."

Sarah taking it in, "That's really sad, the stars on Earth are real, maybe you all would like to visit one day."

Alastor responded in a warm deep voice, "Maybe one day I will."

Trigan put a bunch of little fish on his plate and looked up, "I think I have been there."

Trigan started to eat and Ethan replied, "Phase Walkers!"

Alastor and Sarah started to laugh then Trigan laughed just because it was infectious. Ethan laughed at Trigan because he was spitting food out with his weird reptilian laugh.

Back at Remiel House, Shandra was awake, she was standing in the doorway to Alastor's room, it was as she remembered, neat and clean thanks to Yanni. A plain bed, a chest of draws, a wooden lockable chest and a desk. Shandra walked up to the chest and opened it, nothing new, everything that was there before. She opened each one of his drawers, nothing of interest. She sat on his bed and held the purple stone it spoke to her, "Use your phase magic to bring him back through to the Nevid plane, lace his bed with an open phase again so he will fall through, maybe thicker this time as it did not appear to have worked before."

Shandra started to work her phase magic again on Alastor's bed thinking it didn't work last time because the stone would of told her if it did. Perhaps Alastor was somewhere else but she had to hurry before she got discovered.

Yanni was watching from a distance then flashed to another room.

Caitlin awoke in her room, she was sitting up on her bed a little upset she had a dream about her lifelong friend Martin and was trying to get her mind around accepting he was gone.

Wuzzle tried to console her and spoke "Miss Caitlin, you always have me, I will be forever at your side."

Caitlin was Wuzzle's life, he lived to be with her, that was the bond they shared.

Caitlin smiled, "Of course I have you."

She grabbed hold of Wuzzle's fur and buried her face, like a small child would with a teddy bear, except Wuzzle had glowing scary eyes that were bloodshot, huge fangs and large claws.

Caitlin had not forgotten Martin's son or that she had to get back the ianoid stones to return to the Persidion village. She wanted Morack and all the Delvin dead for their crimes, she wanted to hurt them. Plotting revenge she decided to speak about an attack, when it's dawn, she thought, and went back to bed to sleep. Wuzzle sat up against the wall and closed his eyes, looking like a giant teddy bear in a child's room.

Yanni looked into Mixy's room, she was asleep. Yanni studied her for a time, she looked uncomfortable in the room and couldn't stretch out, she was curled around. Today she had gotten bigger and probably would not fit through the door in the morning, so Yanni fixed the situation. The glowing blue energy ball, Yanni, used light magic to make the doorway bigger and moved the partition in the room out to extend it and make it bigger. Yanni put more hay in the bucket and some water in a wooden barrel then jetted off down the hall. Yanni enjoyed looking after the guests in Remiel House, it was all it wished for and to protect the family that lived there.

The Lady of Light was standing in the Chapter house and several members of the Illumination were adjusting silvery armour on her, it was ornate and complex, each piece radiated light magic, and it seemed the Lady of Light was preparing for war.

She got news reports of an undernest of spider folk just outside her court which had been slaughtered. It had happened in their sleep and she was mad with vengeance. She wanted all the Delvin dead, her only thought, it echoed in her mind. On a subconscious level she was projecting that vibration to Lorvisa but its habitants did not require much to be also thinking that way.

A phase opened on the speaking platform inside the Chapter house, good, the Lady of Light thought, she wanted news from the Master Workers Guild.

A Delvin stepped through the phase, it was grey and smaller than the ones she had seen in the past, it did not look surprised and held its hand up to signal a truce.

The Lady of Light demanded, "Why do you enter the Chapter house of Illumination?"

The Delvin firmly replied, "Morack sends his regards and wants the cure to the brood mother's poison; he will stop the attacks on Lorvisa in return."

The Delvin looked at the Lady of Light and was going to open a phase to leave as he did not get a reply.

The Lady of Light using her fast reflexes produced a pure ball of energy and released it at the grey Delvin, it turned to ashes.

The Lady of Light spoke calmly, "Post more Illumination

guards around the platform and put chaos detection magic on the platform also do this at the phase point in my court of Illumination."

Several members of the Chapter house ran to do her bidding.

- Chapter 15 -

Egg

In a huge cavern underground the only female Delvin on Nevid writhed in pain, her half naked body convulsed, she was huge and layers of fat rippled in her blue body as she coughed. She screamed in pain, a grey Delvin came and patted her on the shoulder, purple foam bubbled in her mouth then leaked down the side and she spoke her last words, "Take the egg, it's the new brood mother."

The grey Delvin was shocked and looked inside the dead brood mother's egg sack, which was sickly and festered. Usually fifty to one hundred eggs would be laid at once. He could not see anything so put his clawed hand inside and felt a large round egg. He removed it from the egg sack and held it up in his clawed hand, it was massive compared to a normal Delvin eggs, the hatchling squirmed inside the egg and was light blue and glowed. The grey Delvin placed the egg in a bag and headed to tell Morack of the brood mother's passing.

The grey Delvin who was at the brood mother's passing arrived with the bag in Morack's throne room, decaying Celestial wings were the main feature behind the throne, emanating a sweet sickening smell. Morack was seated on his throne, his red skin contrasted to all the stone and his twisted red horns where very long for a Delvin, he was in a bad mood, his messenger had not arrived back from the Lady of Light and he was beginning to suspect the messenger had been killed.

The grey Delvin knelt on one knee before him and spoke, "My Lord Morack, I bring news of the brood mother."

Morack stood from the throne, looking down at the Grey Delvin, his horns reaching up to the roof and his robes gathered around his waist, "What is it?"

The grey Delvin spoke with sadness, "The brood mother has passed away but—"

Morack screeched his voice, "What!"

The grey Delvin spoke, "My Lord Morack, the brood mother laid a female egg, this egg will be the new brood mother."

Morack looked at the grey Delvin, who took a large glowing egg from his bag.

Morack calmed himself, "This solves my problem then, I'll just keep attacking the Lady of Light till her race is dead, our race is safe thanks to the brood mother's egg. I take it the egg will hatch in 10 years?"

The grey Delvin smiled and spoke, "Female eggs hatch in one year."

Morack happy clapped his clawed hands together, "Well then let's keep it under guard, I shall build a special chamber for the new brood mother so the next clutch of Delvin will be guaranteed."

Morack summoned his guard, "Grey Delvin, what is your name?"

The grey Delvin replied, "ParPar, my Lord Morack."

Morack, staring into the ParPar's eyes, "Well ParPar, you have a new job you are now officially the keeper of the egg, stay with it at all costs. Go now, take the egg to my laboratory till the chamber is made. Guards, summon more, we will begin to create a new chamber, bring me my hunters."

Two guards standing at the entrance to the throne room walked off to get more, ParPar headed to the laboratory.

Morack was alone standing, he turned and stared at the wings on his wall for some time, deep in thought until the sound of hooves scraping the ground echoed in the throne room. Morack turned to see his four hunters.

Grimlock walked towards him, it looked like he was floating, his feet could not been seen under his black flowing robes, his red horns always striking. Canya looked more feral, he had many opened wounds on his body and carried a trident. Reednak somehow looked smaller then Nica, Morack hadn't noticed that before, the blues always looked the same to him.

"I have experiments to do but I want to continue the attacks on Lorvisa, take half my army and go to several areas and slay things. Try not to take to many casualties as I want to keep my army strong for the final attack, which will occur once I work out how to make the Phase Walker ability permanent."

Morack waved his hand and walked off to his laboratory the hunters argued who was the leader and walked out of Morack's throne room.

Morack's laboratory was bigger, he had been busy expanding it; he had four winged guards of Illumination strapped to the wall in chains. Morack had put a phase blocker on all of them, a device he created himself with chaos magic, he was very proud of its creation much better than the cage. It had since improved from the one he made for that stupid Celestial woman he thought. The device was a black spiked collar, his new improvement was voice activated pain, invoked by a single command for those that could wield chaos magic.

Morack spoke that very command word, "Light", the four guards of Illumination shivered in pain and their wings vibrated. Morack enjoyed the fact that the name of their leader now shot pain into their bodies and minds.

Morack played with machine parts and cast chaos magic on them, tinkering, his goal was to make the Phase Walker ability permanent.

Sarah and Alastor linked again, it felt natural to do so and Sarah did not even have to think of ones, the tingling sensation never occurred, or if it did she didn't notice. She was standing outside Remiel House with Alastor. Poor Ethan had to fly back, it must be annoying to have a brother and sister with the phase and watch them move around instantly knowing you are hours or days away, Sarah thought.

Alastor walked up to the door and Yanni opened it as he got closer. Yanni stood by the door hovering and glowing blue as always. Sarah followed with a skip in her step, she was having a good time.

They both walked into the main hall, Sarah smiled at Caitlin but she was scowling at her.

"Where have you been, we need to all get together and attack the Delvin."

"Indeed," Alastor spoke, feelings of joy gone and replaced by thoughts of Morack and revenge.

"My brother will be arriving soon, he needs sleep, I suggest in the morning we make a start," Alastor continued.

Caitlin smiled, "Yes, in the morning."

Shandra walked into the main room, "What's happening in the morning?"

Alastor took off his hat and put in on the table, "In the morning we strike at the Delvin."

Shandra stood silently and did not respond.

Sarah sleepily said, "Sorry, as much as I had a good time I need my sleep, it's late."

It was still a few hours till morning, Sarah felt like she had been on two dates, Phantom of the Opera and dinner with better company she thought.

Sarah walked into her room and went to sleep with her boots on because she thought she never knew where she may wake up and might need shoes.

Alastor sat by the fire and Yanni gave him a mug of warm tea. Shandra joined him, "I worry about you brother, you are changed physically and I feel your nature has changed also."

Alastor, unhappy about her pointing this out, "Of course it has changed me, I am now part Delvin, I fight with that part of me on a daily basis. The torture I was subjected to has made me twisted."

Shandra genuinely looked concerned, "Sorry this happened to you Alastor, if there is anything I can do for you please but ask."

Alastor smiled and sipped his tea, "Thank you my sister, in the morning I suggest we storm Morack's laboratory and trash it as well as him. I want to retrieve Keyness's wings from his throne room wall and perform the transition ceremony for Keyness, she needs to be put to rest."

Shandra replied, "I understand brother, I will sleep and in the morning we will leave."

Shandra put her hand on her twin brother's arm for a moment and then walked off to her room.

Alastor sat alone staring at the blue flames as his rage filled him.

Grimlock cast a command spell on the other hunters, their power struggle for leadership was getting annoying and he knew best. A small army assembled outside Morack's throne room in another large room that was used as a store room. Many Delvin responded to the call, probably too many, Grimlock thought, but he knew how the Delvin like to kill things, it was almost a sport to them.

This was Grimlock's time to shine as a leader, he spoke in a grinding guttural voice, "Delvin of Nevid this raid is for fun and sport. I do not wish for you to take unnecessary action to slay these beings, it's just a stroll and slaughter, not a full blown attack; a warm up for what is to come and to unnerve the Lady of Light. So who's in for some killing?"

The voices of hundred odd Delvin boomed in cheers and shouts, their guttural voices echoing in the room. Morack's hunters were the noisiest, Reednak and Nica howling, Cayna chanting in with the others, "Kill, kill, kill."

Grimlock opened the phase, it glowed purple before it opened to the only Lorvisa phase point he knew. He sent the army through first, he didn't want any surprises. The other hunters went through with the last stragglers. Grimlock went through last, after waiting some time for the army to pass. Walking through, Grimlock saw his army of Delvin, the ground was flat and trees ripped up from the ground, a reminder of the strange pitiful attack on the last visit.

Grimlock cast a location spell with his chaos magic sensing for living creatures, a group of beings were off in a north direction. Grimlock led the army off in that direction, he did not know what they were but he wanted to give his army something to kill, that was all he cared for.

The army moved at a steady pace, the forest thinned out and he stopped to look at the prey, a town of giant humanoid crickets, which moved around in a skittling manner. It looked like they were making structures, they also looked to be working together passing pieces of green leaves folded into green blocks and lining them up to make a structure. Their faces looked human, their hair green, short and cropped, their arms had hands and fingers, but they had long thick legs and bodies which were green and covered in a thick shell like texture. They looked identical, it was hard to tell any difference. At least one hundred could be seen, good odds, Grimlock thought, as he had about a hundred Delvin.

Grimlock was enjoying this, he was going to take them by surprise, and stood working his magic then cast a mirror image of himself. Two black demons with red horns wearing robes used chaos magic to boom their voices, "Attack my brothers, avenge the brood mother for the glory of Nevid!"

War drums filled the air as the Delvin used their chaos magic. The hunters and the army charged the cricket beings. The crickets seemed caught by surprise, but they worked light magic and hurled balls of bright light at the Delvin. The Delvin rushed forward and the crickets pushed forward, it seemed more of them came from a large mound, hundreds more of them. The crickets moved their wings fast, they did not fly but a high pitch noise emanated from their bodies, it was loud and the vibration interrupted the Delvin chaos magic, they could not wield it. The giant beings jumped very high when being attacked with chaos bolts and flame, the Delvin almost always missing their targets.

Grimlock was getting frustrated so he went into a wild frenzy and attacked a giant cricket with bolts of chaos magic, only burning the crickets shell. He materialised his phase weapon he had been practicing with, a pointed star staff emerged, it had a red stone that glowed. Grimlock projected the phase magic's at the cricket and it exploded, wings turning to shreds and green chunks flying in all directions. Grimlock cringed as he reached down and picked a chunk off his robes.

Grimlock used phase magic and boomed his voice, "Delvin do not use you chaos magic they appear to be blocking it, please use your phase power for attack, now go kill!"

The Delvin materialised their phase weapons, even though they had been given the phase power by Morack they had little practice and preferred to use their chaos magic or brute force.

Grimlock stood from a distance and exploded more crickets with his star staff, he giggled in joy to see the other hunters covered in muck, screaming at each other. This battle was fun.

Three giant crickets surrounded Grimlock, his army had pushed forward, he was alone. One reached forward with a huge hammer and smashed his mirror image. Grimlock panicked and used all his will on the star staff, the stone on top changed to green and three bolts of energy shot out at once and hit all three crickets. The three exploded at once, Grimlock was exhausted and buried in cricket guts and goo.

Grimlock had to dig his way out, unimpressed he called a retreat by giving the signal, a deep horn blew. Grimlock opened an intra-phase to the Nevid phase point and opened that to Nevid, last to enter first to leave he thought as he walked through the phase emerging outside Morack's lair. The army followed, Grimlock waited for them all to retreat, at first many came through, then waves of Delvin, he was mentally counting, he waited some more, then a handful, then a single Devin. Time passed and then none. A third of the army was missing, Grimlock felt dread of failure but he had a plan.

Sarah awoke in her bed at Remiel House; she looked at her iPhone, she had a missed call and a few messages. One such message was about a university assignment she had due tomorrow, shit, Sarah thought. She stretched her arms then planned to do the assignment later this afternoon, hoping killing Morack and raiding his laboratory would be quick, not sure how she could get out of this one.

Sarah left her bedroom and went into the main room, there was a lot of activity, Yanni was busy serving food, Ethan was sitting on the table waving his hands at Caitlin. Mixy looked sick, thick plates of hard rainbow material covered her body but she looked up when she saw Sarah. Alastor and Shandra were standing off to the side, talking in hushed tones.

Alastor smiled when he saw Sarah, "Eat and be ready for we have a lot to do today."

Sarah sat at the large wooden table; Yanni hovered over her and looked confused. Yanni's arms materialised and a plastic tray appeared. Sarah's food was in a brown paper bag and a drink in a container which had a straw. Sarah opened the bag and unwrapped a cheese burger and pulled out some fries, then she unwrapped a sauce container and dipped her chips.

Caitlin, the only one knowing what Sarah was eating, laughed, "Sarah, for breakfast!"

Sarah laughed too, "Ah, yes needed a hit of that good old Scottish food."

Sarah finished up, Alastor was watching her, hoping she would hurry but did not say anything yet.

The moment Sarah pushed the tray to the centre of the table Alastor said, "Okay let's go!"

"Ethan cannot come because, well, he's not a Phase Walker, so have a good time at the Master Workers Guild."

Ethan gave a weak grin, "Thanks for pointing that out brother, I would help if I could go but I also have made a commitment to the Master Workers Guild, I have to go work on an order."

"Indeed brother I am proud that you are pursuing your apprenticeship there, farewell," Alastor waved.

Ethan replied, "Good luck guys, kill a few Delvin for me."

Shandra chimed in, "Will do brother."

Caitlin waved and smiled, "Goodbye Ethan, have a good day."

Mixy was silent but when she moved her body crunched. Sarah stood by Alastor and waved at Ethan.

Ethan stood outside Remiel House and took to the sky, spreading his wings. He watched his brother, sister and friends walk out of the house, they looked tiny from the air except Mixy who looked big from any angle. Ethan was headed for the Abbith market also, but was sure they all would phase there and phase out before he even finished his journey flying there. Bah, Phase Walkers!

Alastor asked everyone to link with him and he opened a phase point to Abbith market. Alastor was wearing his shirt and hat from last night. Sarah was wearing her boots and had a backpack on her back, it contained her assignment because she didn't know if she had enough time to come back to Remiel House and get it, she wanted to leave straight away once it was done.

They all walked through the phase into Abbith market. It was a hive of activity, traders had their wares in floating glass everywhere and there was a murmur of chatter. Alastor looked at the phase point in the Abbith Market, it looked worn and old, it was white with greying cracks and the phase symbols were red. He opened the phase to the Nevid plane and walked through first, the others followed.

The Nevid plane was as before, grey rock and mist, no vegetation, barren and no wild life, not even bugs in the air.

The smell of sulphur was strong. Mixy was scared. Caitlin comforted Mixy by patting her, Caitlin had a calming effect. Wuzzle stood resolute.

Alastor spoke, "Okay this is the plan, we all link, I open a phase point to the laboratory, I know the lair's layout, then we kill Morack, destroy his lab and then take the wings from the throne room then we phase out, without a leader the Delvin will be thrown into chaos because they will all want to be leaders."

Shandra nodded.

Caitlin said, "Okay, sounds good."

Mixy spoke, "If it removes evil in this world I will try."

Sarah looked at Mixy, shocked she had spoken as she usually had little to say if it is not about her clutch.

Alastor looked at Sarah, "So you have the plan."

Sarah smiled she enjoyed looked into his eyes, "Yes, hopefully it's quick."

Everyone linked to Alastor and he opened the phase to the laboratory. They all walked through. They were all standing in a hallway outside Morack laboratory. There were two Delvin guards, they produced phase weapons. Alastor's eyes turned red and he went into a Delvin rage, he materialised his two handed great sword and beheaded a Delvin guard in one swoop. Caitlin materialised her weapon and a dainty boomerang landed in the other Delvin's eye. It screamed in pain. Alastor stepped forward and chopped its head off, the noise was irritating, he was thinking. Caitlin's boomerang returned to her hand.

Alastor smashed his body against the door, it was locked tight.

Mixy spoke, "Let me, I'm good at smashing things."

Mixy was covered in hard plates that had rainbows reflecting off them, she opened her mouth wide, it was scary, she had row upon row of teeth, in fact her entire mouth contained only teeth, she lunged forward at the door mouth first and took a big bite out of the wood. Splinters flew in all directions and, using her sheer body weight, the door snapped in half.

Sarah was a little taken back, she had no idea Mixy was capable of that or that Mixy could open her mouth so wide, oh and the teeth!

They all rushed inside the lab. Alastor was shocked because Morack was not there, even more shocked that the lab had been expanded. There were four creatures with black collars along the wall. They were Phase Walkers, Alastor was sure.

Alastor spoke, "Free them."

Caitlin and Sarah walked to the wall and started hacking the chains. The Phase Walkers on the wall looked really sick, they could barely hold their heads. They for the most part were human except they had antenna or feelers on their heads. They all wore tabards that were deep blue with a golden triangle.

One was freed, it spoke, "Please help us get away, Morack will be back, he's gone to his new egg chamber that he was building, he will return soon."

Another Phase Walker still hanging from chains spoke weakly, "The collars around our necks, we can't walk through the phase with them on, they stop us using our ability."

Alastor, frustrated, smashed the lab, then he came upon a jar of phase essence and, in his rage, he drunk the lot of it. He wanted the power to stop Morack, it was for the greater good he told himself, then continued his rage smashing equipment, it was making a large noise.

Shandra had an idea, I can use my light magic to remove them, let me try. She stepped forward and summoned light magic, it was hard and she struggled but she managed to start a crack down one of the collars. She concentrated and freed a collar, a small amount of chaos magic seeped into her light magic and it was all that was needed to release the entire collar. Then she continued and repeated the process, getting better with each collar. Alastor was making a lot of noise, not so much the noise of smashing but the primal noise that was coming from his rage, a guttural growl which sounded more so Delvin than anything else and he was totally unaware that his sister was using chaos magic.

Many footsteps were outside, Caitlin looked at Alastor in his rage, hmm okay, she thought, then she took over as leader and spoke, "We are going to make this a two part mission now, we didn't expect to rescue Phase Walkers, they're weak we need move them now, Alastor, stop yourself!"

Alastor did not stop, he seemed compelled to throw and smash things, his rage blinded his thoughts.

"Sarah, help!" Caitlin said.

Sarah panicked and opened a phase to the phase point outside in Nevid, turning to look at Alastor, frightened to see this side of him. His beautiful white blond hair was tossed all over his face, his hat was on the ground, his eyes filled with rage. All the majority of the laboratory instruments lay broken and tossed on the ground. Alastor had his phase weapon materialised, it was a great two handed long sword, Sarah studied it. Its gem was a little like hers, but was green; it flicked red, which seemed to happen in time when Alastor growled. The sword connected with a chair, shredding pieces of leather everywhere. Strange pipes connected to the chair and Alastor smashed each one.

Mixy walked through the phase, it was hard to tell how she was feeling. Shandra had what Sarah could only describe as a human butterfly draped over her shoulder. Studying it as Shandra walked closer to the phase, it had an attractive male face, its jaw square, it had antennae protruding from its head, its eyes were shiny mirrors and its wings shimmered a pattern of gold and light blue spots. Noticing they all wore uniforms, she wondered what the golden triangle meant. Caitlin was holding another butterfly human's hand, this Phase Walker did not look as bad and was female. The other two were male and clung onto each other as they approached the phase.

The phase was open for some time before the room was empty except Sarah and Alastor, who was slowing down his assault on the lab. Sarah picked up Alastor's hat and slowly stepped towards him. Alastor stopped then dematerialised his weapon and turned to Sarah, who held out his hat. He took the hat put it on his head roughly and grabbed Sarah's hand in a strange calm manner and led them through the phase. It snapped shut.

They were all standing at the Nevid phase point, all was still, there was no noise except Alastor's deep breathing. A thick mist lay around the ground, it smelt like sulphur. Sarah could see the familiar ravine. Sarah linked to everyone and opened a phase point, Alastor was still holding her hand. She stepped through taking Alastor with her, looked around and said in a loud voice "Shit!"

Everyone followed behind her.

They were all in an alley next to a garbage skip, it was daylight.

Caitlin looked around, "Um, Sarah, this isn't the Celestial plane."

Sarah let go of Alastor's warm hand, embarrassed, and flicked some hair out of her face, "Sorry I was thinking of uni, I have an assignment, the symbols got muddled in my mind, I do know the difference between them."

Caitlin started to open a phase point to the Celestial plane.

Sarah embarrassed, "You guys go back, since I am here I really should go to the library before class. I can catch up with you tomorrow."

Caitlin waved, annoyed, "That's fine, talk to you tomorrow."

Alastor looked around, never having felt this phase before, and was still fighting to calm down his Delvin side, he memorised the phase point. Caitlin urged him to walk again through the phase, he did, remembering the symbols to Earth as he passed through. The rest of the party walked through.

They were in a busy market on the Celestial plane. No one noticed the rag tag team's sudden appearance. Shandra led them to the side and opened another phase to Remiel House, they all followed, again Shandra spoke to the rescued Phase Walkers, "Last phase, then we are safe, sorry about that."

They all walked through and appeared before the entrance to Remiel House. It was daylight, the house looked huge and welcoming, small flowers grew at the entrance along each side of the door on the ground and each had perfect petals of many colours. The door opened then Yanni hovered outside the door way.

The group moved inside Remiel House, following Yanni into the main room.

Caitlin, leading the way, "We can all talk and rest inside."

A rescued Phase Walker replied, "Thank you, the Lady of Light also thanks you."

Mixy stared at the butterfly humanoid Phase Walkers in awe, feeling some sort of connection and spoke as Yanni hovered up to her, "Who is the Lady of Light?"

The companions occupied the main room's wooden table, Caitlin sat at the head of one end, so cute and tiny in pink, and Alastor the other. The four butterfly Phase Walkers looked tired but joined the table, pulling up chairs together on one side, folding their butterfly wings to sit. Mixy was stretched out along a wall in the room and she didn't seem to be getting any bigger so she fit, but she no longer had fur, she was covered in pearly white shell scales that reflected little rainbows. Shandra sat at the fireplace but turned her chair to face the main table.

The female butterfly stood and spoke in a singing voice, "Thank you again for rescuing us, we are Lords and Ladies of Illumination, we noticed that one of our kind joined you in freeing us."

"We look after noble larvae from the house Micon, they are our younglings. A Delvin army of Phase Walkers openly attacked our clutch and slaughtered our entire defenceless larvae. The Delvin creatures captured us because we were Phase Walkers and tortured us, we were taken from our home plane, Lorvisa."

Caitlin and Shandra spoke at once, but Caitlin's voice overpowered Shandra's, so Shandra sat back down, brooding.

Caitlin continued, "I'm very sorry for your loss. That is a

sad terrible tale, we are happy to save fellow Phase Walkers. Please have something to eat and rest here before you go back to your plane. Mixy is a Phase Walker and is looking for her clutch, can you help her?"

The female butterfly looking frail and regal walked to Mixy and reached for the phase, touching her shell scales. A psychic conversation occurred, a linking between beings.

'Hello I am Lady Rayne, oh your name is Mixy, larvae are usually not Phase Walkers, you are so young, your clutch is what you wish to know. You are from a wilder's clutch, it is under a large fallen tree, that explains why you have no clutch guardians to watch you. I am curious how does a wilder larvae become a Phase Walker?'

Mixy concentrated and projected her voice in response, 'I was hungry and left the clutch to eat, I ate a brown thing then felt different'; in Mixy's thoughts the brown thing was nothing more than a piece of fallen tree.

Lady Rayne was confused because eating something did not make you a Phase Walker, especially some bark from a tree, it was not unusual for larvae to even eat an entire tree. Deep in thought, she broke the connection, a little disappointed Mixy was not from a noble clutch.

Standing again, she realised how much she was drained then returned to the table and saw her favourite meal served up to a Lord, small colourful leaves and delicate flowers. The other Lords of Illumination were busy eating what looked like a traditional Lorvisa meal. She joined them and Yanni created a bowl and placed it in front of her and she began to eat her meal.

Mixy appeared to be happy, Caitlin, unaware of what took place, questioned, "So do you know her clutch?"

Lady Rayne did not look up and rudely continued to eat her meal. Caitlin looked indignant and cast her gaze over to Shandra, who just ignored her and stared into the fireplace watching the blue flames.

Alastor was not even taking in the conversation, he was sulking, feeling tortured, recalling what he had not had time to do. He had not had time to retrieve Keyness's wings, he so much wanted to perform the transition ceremony, it's what she deserved, to be finally at rest. Alastor's eyes turned misty red but he remained calm and bowed his head.

Caitlin, with her small height, was tiny compared to everyone in the room; she could feel this more so then ever before so decided to sit on top on the table, right in the middle. Yanni was hovering and she asked for pizza in her mind. Yanni materialised a pizza and she ate it, occasionally looking at the four butterfly Phase Walkers eating their meal. They did not seem to notice Caitlin sitting on the table.

Lady Rayne finished her meal, surprisingly she spoke in her singing voice, looking right at Caitlin on the table who had pizza all over her fingers, "Mixy is from my plane, she is from a wildling clutch, we would like to take her home and present her to the Lady of Light. Mixy needs to be with her kind as she is approaching the chrysalis phase."

Caitlin, caught off guard, asked, "Who is the Lady of Light? What is the chrysalis phase?"

Shandra stood and walked to the table and spoke slowly, "I know their plane, I have been there. I do know that they visit here on occasion to trade with the Master Workers Guild. In fact Ethan was talking about a large order they have with them. I suggest we let our guests return home and not keep them any longer."

"But, but, what is chrysalis? What's happening to Mixy?" Caitlin sounding very much like a small child.

Lady Rayne replied ceremoniously, "Thank you Phase Walkers for saving us again, and your hospitality. Mixy will become like us once the chrysalis has occurred. Yes, we must go back to the Lady of Light at once."

The other three Phase Walkers stood, still not looking healthy, the butterfly creatures linked arms and opened an intra-phase along the main room's wall.

Mixy was the first to move forward towards it and she spoke with emotion, "Thank you Caitlin, Wuzzle, Shandra and friend," looking at Alastor, "you found my clutch. Please say my goodbyes to Sarah, I hope to see you all again soon, come visit me for I call you all clutch brothers and sisters."

Mixy started to approach the phase, Caitlin rushed forward and gave Mixy a hug even though she no longer felt soft and fury. Mixy giggled then, feeling Caitlin release the hug, crawled into the phase. The four butterfly creatures walked into the phase and it snapped shut.

- Chapter 16 -

Fish

Bubbles surfaced from the pond, then hung in the air for a few moments and popped, many Persidion folk had been busy rebuilding their village, it was a hive of activity underwater. A lovely black Persidion boy with greens stripes and dark green eyes was not busy rebuilding, he was sitting outside a broken house going through a cycle of getting angry and then complete sadness.

Jas was only a small boy but he wanted to make a difference, he did not feel like he could rebuild, he did not want to stay, the memories were all too clear. His father Martin used to tell him tales of Persidion who walked as two legs, for bedtime stories. Jas wanted to be a two legs and seek the evil demons out. Jas, then full of emotion, swum into the ocean as far away from his village as he could, trying to get away.

Sarah was home on Earth, she left the alley way of the Chocolate Coffee House and wondered how mad Caitlin was at her leaving. It was just after lunch and she had an assignment due tonight and only had a few hours to complete it. Sarah hailed a taxi, with no fear remembering the last time she was in one, and arrived home to her apartment. She asked the taxi driver to wait outside while she rushed upstairs to retrieve her laptop and assignment.

She then asked the taxi to drive her to the Brisbane library. Sarah paid the driver a hundred dollar note and walked off not waiting for the change. The driver did not hang around to see if she wanted it either and drove off greedily away.

Sarah, wearing jeans and white shirt, carried her backpack and laptop into the library. The doors automatically opened and a soft murmur was heard from inside. She walked over to a spare desk and set up her laptop. She took out her assignment and read the title 'Making business decisions that matter, discuss', she figured she needed some reference books and went to look up some books on the library computer. There were a few titles available in the library, fantastic, Sarah thought and walked over to the book reference aisle. There, she heard some giggling in the far back corner, she turned to see Maddy smiling and giggling; that raven haired beauty always had some guy she was flirting with.

Interested just for gossip purposes Sarah tried to see without been seen who the guy was. So she walked around to the other side of the isle to look at his face and it was William, reaching over Maddy and kissing her lips. Sarah reached for the phase and realised what she was doing. She stopped and watched on, it was shameful flirting he reached over for another kiss. That's it, Sarah thought she could no longer contain herself, she walked over to them and confronted them. She stood watching for some time before Maddy realised she was there, Maddy wacked William's back, making him look confused and spoke, "Sarah what are you doing here?"

Sarah in a loud voice, "Researching my assignment for class, you know that's what libraries are used for. What are you using it for?"

William turned to Sarah studying her face and put his hands up realising what she must have seen, "I can explain?"

Sarah, angry at realising the things she gave up for this loser, "Go ahead, I would love to hear it."

Maddy raised an eyebrow, I guess she would love to hear

it too, Sarah thought.

William crossed his arms, not looking as attractive as Sarah remembered.

"We are just friends having some fun, and I was trying to cheer Maddy up because she hasn't been doing too well in a few subjects. In fact we came to study."

Sarah hand on hip, "Sooo let me get this straight, to cheer your friends up you kiss them, what are you studying, the art of the French kiss?"

Williams face dropped and turned red, "Oh, so you saw that."

Sarah replied, "Aha, well some hero you are. I can't believe I thought you cared, something should of gave off alarm bells when you asked me to buy my own surprise ticket to Phantom."

Angry, Sarah walked off, William followed her and spoke softly as it was a library, "Sorry Sarah, I guess it got out of hand, let me make it up to you, I can take you out tonight for dinner."

William gave a grin. Sarah once thought it was sexy but cheesy was a fair assessment now.

Sarah, considering the option pushed it aside, thinking to herself, you know what, I don't think I do care. Realising in that moment she had stronger feelings for someone else and that someone else was not even human.

Sarah returned to her desk and started to pack her laptop away, as William stood watching. She took William's card from her wallet and read it to herself, 'William Remiel, Entrepreneur'. The word Remiel never took her notice before, clicking in her mind thinking of Remiel House then she dismissed it as a sheer coincidence nothing more.

"Screw you, screw uni, I'm done, done!" she shouted at William, as she flicked his card in his direction.

William, knowing he had done bad, stood, taking in her words, and watched her leave the library.

Sarah stormed out of the library then hailed a taxi and caught it home, giving another taxi driver another hundred dollar note. She stepped out and arrived in the foyer of her apartment. The landlord was cleaning out some mail boxes and reminded Sarah of her rent. Sarah reached into her back pack and counted out fifty dollar notes for the next six month's rent and handed it to the wide eyed landlord.

"Inheritance," is what she muttered then she walked up to the lift.

Money didn't seem to have any meaning to Sarah anymore as she could just take as much as she wanted. She thought about this and decided being a Phase Walker and helping people is more important than university. What was the point of getting a good job and climbing the corporate ladder when she could already have anything she wanted? This convinced her that taking money was for the good of all. With that thought she opened her door and walked into her lounge room. She took out her laptop, relaxed on a chair and started to compose a withdrawal letter from university.

Sarah fell asleep in her chair, the laptop had fallen to the ground and run out of battery. Sarah was in a deep sleep, she was dreaming. In that dream Alastor was sitting outside Morack's closed laboratory door. He wore only a black pair of ragged pants, his chest was bare and ripped, any body builder would be pleased, a few tufts of his white blond hair were tossed over his face, his small black horns protruded through his hair, he was in pain and a tear trickled from his blue eyes. Screams of a female could be heard within the laboratory, Alastor rolled into a ball, his tail with a black tip wrapped around his hoofed feet.

The television in the lounge room flicked on and Caitlin changed it to the shopping channel. Wuzzle, looking bored, lounged on a couch.

Sarah rudely woke up, feeling Alastor's pain, it felt so real but she knew it was a dream. She frowned when she saw little pink shoes tossed on the floor and a big fluffy bear on her couch. Does she not get any privacy? She tried to compose her thoughts.

A strange limited edition bear was for sale on the

shopping channel, it had a little red hat and blue shoes and it was fluffy and brown much like Wuzzle's fur. Caitlin was watching it intently. Sarah picked up her laptop from the floor and looked at Caitlin, who was now holding the same limited edition bear.

Sarah sat on the edge of her seat, feeling her dream's sadness, it had not left her, "Caitlin what are you doing here? And should I ask how did you get that limited edition bear doll?"

Trying to be clear, she was not talking about Wuzzle.

Caitlin smiled, "I missed you, plus the butterfly Phase Walkers went home back to their plane. Oh, also some news for you. Mixy went with them she was from their plane Lorvisa. One of the butterfly kind knew of her clutch so yeah, she got home."

"I memorised their phase point symbols so we can visit later on if you want. But I think Alastor and a few others know them too, apparently the Celestial's trade with their kind from time to time. Ethan is working on some Master Worker stuff, it's supposed to be important, Shandra is well Shandra and Alastor is sulking away, which is understandable being half demon and all."

Caitlin put the toy bear to the side and sat forward in her chair, looking intently at Sarah.

"So how was your day? Did you get your super important thing done that you left us for?"

Sarah was glad that Mixy found her home and sad to hear about Alastor sulking, "I've been doing some thinking and have decided to leave university and take Phase Walker business more seriously. Also I broke up with my boyfriend William."

Sarah started to cry as it all became too much for her.

Caitlin did not know what to do because Sarah always seemed so brave, so she gave Sarah a hug.

"Do you think we should go back to Remiel House for a change of scenery, then you can think less of Earth type problems for a while? I'm also happy to stay here and do some shopping, it always works for me."

Sarah stopped crying because the thought of both these things made her happy.

A typical grey Delvin with long white horns, a little tubby around the middle but still very muscular, stretched his arms out. This Delvin could blend into a crowd of its own kind but a few things marked him as different; for one, he was very boisterous and for two, he was a Phase Walker. In fact he was Nevid's only known natural Phase Walker and that fact made him, Knifegiver, a braggart.

Knifegiver was jumping through phases before Morack's experiments started. He was careful not to get to close to Morack because he knew exactly what those experiments involved and wouldn't put it past Morack to use him as a test subject, being Delvin gave him no immunity, he was sure. With that information in mind, Knifegiver was almost never on his home plane. His only temptation in returning to Nevid was to tell of his adventures on other planes. Nothing made Knifegiver happier then to have a crowd of Delvin cheer him on and envy him.

Knifegiver was on the plane of Kelstone, having just been on a grand adventure. Knifegiver was sitting along the edge of a stream, there was a small waterfall and droplets of water sprayed into the air, it made him feel relaxed. The trees were huge and tall, it was usually populated with small insects and animals but Knifegiver was projecting fear like any other Delvin so there was none around his little sitting area.

His body ached and he was relaxing, stretching out his arms and legs. He was lucky to have come across a rare find and it was difficult to contain his excitement. His only thought was to return to Nevid and tell everyone about it. He opened up a small leather pouch and removed a strange yellow gem, he pondered thinking on how it made him feel last time, paused and stretched again as a reminder, then gave a jolly laugh to himself.

In the distance he could see several local villagers come to the stream with buckets, probably to fetch water as the stream was very fresh. He was sure the villagers did not feel his fear because he was too far away and he was unnoticed. Rubbing the yellow gem, Knifegiver smirked and got giddy, maybe one more time before I return to Nevid.

Knifegiver was excited and thought of a dangerous sea creature with spikes and jaws, imagining the faces of those villagers as he leaped from the water, perhaps he would even eat one. Knifegiver tried not to laugh loudly. He walked over to the stream and quickly jumped into the water, trying to be unseen submerging himself. He rubbed the yellow gem concentrating on a scary sea monster and slipped the gem into his pouch.

At first nothing happened then a yellow glow appeared around Knifegiver. Wanting to hide, as he knew it might attract attention, he dove under water deeper into the stream, a random thought went through his mind as two colourful tiny fish swum by, 'cute fishy'. With that, his last thought, he abruptly changed into a small colourful fish.

"Arrggh!" Knifegiver was mad, this was not the form he wanted, how did this go oh so wrong, he thought.

Teeny tiny bubbles came out of the colourful fishes little mouth which was now Knifegiver's mouth. At least he knew this was not permanent and within a day he would be his old self again. He didn't want to think about what aches his body would have when he changed back because this was his first water creature.

Making the most of it Knifegiver decided to keep this adventure to himself and enjoy it. He swam into the deep stream grass then floated inside an underwater air bubble that came from a suspicious looking clam. The stream for the most part was clear and the light shone through almost to the bottom. Knifegiver continued downstream, swimming at his own pace peeking at strange underwater things, it was fun to have a different prospective he thought.

He started to build momentum, swimming downstream,

it was more so from the currents pushing him along than his swimming skill. At first Knifegiver thought it was fun riding the currents but was quickly being propelled downstream too fast for his liking. He could hear murmurs above water briefly as he was quickly propelled past what he thought were the villagers collecting water. He remembered them being very far away and did not want to go far down stream so tried to swim upstream, he exhausted his strength in his efforts and was floating along the currents going out sea, totally out of control.

Sarah and Caitlin emerged from the shopping centre in Brisbane into Queen Street Mall. Sarah was wearing a red cocktail dress, fitting to go to the races, and a matching red feathered fascinator in her hair, she had just got it done in the hairdressers. Her pretty blond hair swirled in curls and was arranged in a formal manner. She had a matching red handbag and pretty red high heeled shoes. Today was Melbourne Cup and Sarah wanted to do something happy. Caitlin was carrying her limited edition bear, it wore a red hat and little blue boots, Caitlin was wearing her usual style but did have her hair in cute ringlets. It was getting close to three and the race would be on soon.

Sarah walked down the mall into a betting establishment and got in the queue to place some bets. Caitlin didn't really understand it but she went with it to make Sarah happy, she waited outside. Passers-by walked on, carrying shopping and talking on mobile phones. The mall was a busy place.

Sarah came out of the busy betting establishment holding tickets, "It won't be long now, I was told they are going to play the race over the PA system throughout the mall."

Caitlin held her bear tight, thinking about Wuzzle, Caitlin only left Wuzzle alone for short periods at a time because of her bond. She would feel physical pain if away from Wuzzle too long, but shopping was something Wuzzle could not do so she had left him at Sarah's apartment with a pile of pizzas.

Caitlin loved shopping.

An announcement was being made throughout the mall, Caitlin looked at everyone in the mall, people stopped talking and stood still, there was silence except the noise of the announcer talking fast about the race. Sarah looked excited, she held her tickets out proudly, people started to shout come on, go my horse, go, the winner was Green Ace. Sarah frowned, none of her horses got a place. A mother of four walked through the mall and complimented Caitlin to Sarah 'what a beautiful daughter you have' and kept walking. Sarah looked confused then looked down at Caitlin and grinned, "Come my daughter, I think we should go back to Remiel House, I've had my fun."

Caitlin played along because she wanted to lighten the mood, "Sure mummy."

Caitlin laughed loudly, they walked around the block to an alley, opened the phase and arrived back at Sarah's apartment. Wuzzle looked bored, staring at the commentary of the race, it was still going on the television. There were no empty pizza boxes or any sign of pizza but Caitlin knew he had had fifteen boxes because she had ordered it.

Sarah went into the bedroom and packed a small suitcase full of clothes and things she thought she would need and wheeled it into the lounge room.

Caitlin raised an eyebrow, "That's a lot Sarah."

Sarah struggled to push the suitcase out, its wheel squeaked, "Not really, this is my small bag."

Caitlin went into Sarah's bedroom and looked at the wall, "You know that phase point you have there should be able to go to other places than Nevid. Since closing a phase point I have a greater understanding, I think you may have made it Sarah and it's not complete. But with a few adjustments by adding symbols I can make it go to Abbith market."

Caitlin opened the phase to the Abbith market and all three went into the phase straight through Sarah's bedroom wall.

The Abbith market was in full swing, many vendors

shouted their wares, floating cases filled with treasure hovered around, there was a cart selling fresh flowers. It caught Sarah's eye, "Wait a minute Caitlin, before we walk off and phase to Remiel House can I buy some of these perfect flowers?"

Caitlin, happy, spoke, "Sure why not," and took some strange coins from her pocket.

Sarah could tell they were not there before, because she felt the phase around Caitlin and wondered what an ATM was around here, accepting the coins. Sarah purchased a bunch of perfect blue rose like flowers, they smelled lovely and each petal was perfect.

Sarah then followed Caitlin and Wuzzle to the side of the market, Caitlin then opened the phase and they all walked through to Remiel House.

It was coming on night and Remiel House looked friendly in the sunset hues, Yanni opened the door on seeing their arrival. Caitlin walked in talking softly to Sarah about horses and saw Alastor in the main room seated at the table with his hat. Alastor did not look happy and glanced up, he saw Sarah enter the room and stood looking at her odd clothes which he found strangely attractive.

Sarah felt his eye on her and felt the need to explain the fancy clothes, "We just got back from the Melbourne Cup celebration, it's traditional to dress up and wear a hat," she touched her red fascinator on her head.

Alastor smiled, it was cute Sarah thought and unexpected, "Oh well very lucky I am wearing mine today too," Alastor touched his hat in response.

"I'll just take this into my room," Sarah said, then placed the blue flowers on the table and wheeled her bag into her room, it squeaked a little which made her walk faster. Sarah decided she was staying a while and actually unpacked her clothes neatly into the draws.

Caitlin sat at the table and Alastor started to cast light magic, he seemed to be struggling but was crafting a pretty glass vase, the top was uneven but it was the best he could do, then he asked Yanni to fill it with water. He then arranged the dainty blue flowers with his clawed hands.

Caitlin, watching, almost laughed at the thought of a demonoid playing with flowers then got cross at herself, Alastor was no demon.

Sarah came in and saw the flowers on the table, she smiled, "Oh, they look wonderful."

"You're welcome," Alastor replied.

Sarah raised her eyebrow and tossed her blond hair, "So what have you been doing?"

Alastor took a ceramic brown jug from the table, "Thinking and drinking, this is mighty fine stuff?"

Caitlin looked up at the jug, "Oh that's Leeruff juice isn't it? If so give me some, I haven't had any in ages?"

Sarah puzzled wondered if it was alcohol and looking at small Caitlin felt it wrong for her to have.

Caitlin walked over to Alastor then looked at Sarah, "You should try this stuff, I should of given you some before, it changes moods and makes you happy ever so happy?"

"Caitlin, is that alcohol?" Sarah asked.

Caitlin smiled, "No, not at all, it's made from the bark of a common magical tree that soaks up light magic, very popular among the Celestials at feasts and gatherings."

Caitlin asked Yanni for glasses no words were spoken but two appeared on a tray and Caitlin took both. Wuzzle sat on the ground along the wall, forever waiting to be at Caitlin's service. Alastor poured three drinks, two into the glasses and one into his mug.

Caitlin sipped her drink then smiled, "Try it Sarah, it's a mixture of yum and fun."

Sarah took her frosted glass then raised it to her eye level and peered inside at the contents, it was a warm dark pink liquid, it looked thick like syrup, she swirled it in her glass then raised it to her lips and took a sip, "Wow, this tastes like a musk lolly on Earth and I feel great. I can see every detail in the flowers on the table, I didn't notice that before."

Caitlin laughed, "Did I mention it's kind of intense for

Phase Walkers to drink this stuff."

Sarah was going to frown then realised she couldn't, "What exactly does this stuff do?"

Caitlin spoke again, "It temporarily raises your emotions and you are happy, but stop drinking it and within an hour you are back to normal, for Phase Walkers you get an extra kick, it heightens the phase and your senses."

Alastor took his hat off and then took a swig of his mug and smiled radiantly.

Sarah was taken in by his attractiveness; she laughed again then spoke, "I guess this stuff is very moreish."

Caitlin poured herself and Sarah another glass, "Let's sit near the fire, these seats are not comfy."

There were three seats by the fire, they were bigger and had cushions designed for creatures with wings. Alastor stood from the table with mug and jug in hand then sat on his usual seat and Caitlin sat in the chair next to him. Sarah, in red high heels, tripped and landed in Alastor's lap.

Alastor laughed and gave Sarah a cuddle, not really thinking straight Sarah just laughed and continued to sit there.

"This seat is comfy for me," Sarah giggled again.

Caitlin just laughed and so did they all, including Wuzzle sitting down the end of the room along the wall, just another part of the bond with Caitlin.

- Chapter 17 -

Transformation

A silvery phase opened, the air was scented with pine and the forest was thick, two butterfly humanoids, Lords of Illumination, walked through the phase followed by another Lord and a Lady of Illumination, slowly behind them crawled a large white worm.

Mixy was overjoyed to be home, she could not wait to get home to her clutch. The phase snapped shut behind her. The Lords and Ladies of Illumination walked in the direction of the court, it was not far and the shiny glass dome could be seen in the distance. Mixy with her new phase abilities could now sense the location of her clutch, it was not in the direction which they were walking and she spoke to the Lady of Illumination, "Where are we going? This is not the way to my clutch."

The Lady of Illumination stopped and turned to Mixy then spoke in a regal tone, "I'm sorry youngling, I forget that your Phase Walker abilities give you a greater understanding for one of your age."

"We need to report to the Lady of Light of the attack and what happened to us. You are a special Phase Walker so we need to introduce you to the Lady of Light. All will happen in good time and you will be able to return to you clutch when we are done, I hope you understand."

Mixy wasn't sure how to take it as all she wanted to do was go back to her clutch, she had longed for it, for so long.

As the Lady of Illumination was turning to begin the walk back to the court a wave of love and devotion washed over Mixy and every living thing on Lorvisa. It was the Lady of Light, she was projecting, she was summoning nobles and those with business to court. Also reaffirming to every living creature and plant, to attack Delvin on sight for the safety of Lorvisa.

Mixy, feeling the Lady of Light, forgot about her clutch and followed onwards to the court of Illumination.

The Lady of Light was regal and sat on her throne of mirrors, it was unusual for her to be seated before the Lords, Ladies and nobles who had all arrived but she was angry. She wanted to talk to her people, the last Delvin attack was devastating not because many died but because they were a noble clutch from the house Micon.

The representatives of the populace of Lorvisa arrived, flying through the top of the dome, crawling or shuffling through the glass doors. The Lords and Ladies of Illumination were in full regal garb, not that they ever were not in the court of Illumination.

Mixy arrived through the side glass door to the court of Illumination, she followed the butterfly Phase Walkers inside, excitement thrilled through her and she was in awe of the Lady of Light even at this distance. Slowly she came closer to the Lady of Light and the throne, walking past rows of benches filled with nobles and people of Lorvisa. Mixy stopped and stared at all the humanoid creatures, cricket people, more butterflies, ladybugs, spiders and strange centipede creatures, all of which Mixy had not seen before. They made a strange murmur and clicking noises.

The Lady of Illumination urged Mixy onwards forward and asked Mixy to wait behind the speaker's platform, it was heart shaped and green. The four Lords and Ladies of Illumination stood on the speaker's platform. The Lady of Light waited a few more moments to allow late comers a chance to take a seat. Mixy looked around, innocent and childlike.

The Lady of Light stood, her blond hair fell to her waist. Those in the court went silent, all eyes watched. The Lady of Light spread her mirrored wings, they glimmered and shined. In a regal voice she intoned, "The court of Illumination is open, and I will hear those on the speaker's platform."

The Lady of Illumination spoke, as females held rank in Lorvisa, "My eminence, the Lady of Light, I wish to report to you an attack on our people, it happened some time ago so you may already be aware."

The Lady of Light nodded.

The Lady of illumination continued, "The noble Micon clutch was attacked by a small army of Delvin Phase Walkers, they slaughtered all our larvae and guards. The four you see before you were captured and taken to the Delvin plane, it shames us to acknowledge."

The crowd responded with a low murmur.

"We were tortured and our essence was drained by Morack himself. He was using it to create his Phase Walker army. We were lucky to be rescued by a group of outworlders. They gave us our freedom and sheltered us in the Celestial plane until we were strong enough to return to you. With the outworlders was Mixy, of our kind, a youngling larvae who is a Phase Walker."

The crowd on the benches cheered at acknowledgement of a new Phase Walker, it was tradition.

Mixy was happy and looked around at her people on the benches and smiled on the inside.

The Lady of Light raised an eyebrow and smiled, still standing, "Mixy, please present yourself to me, a larvae has never had the Phase Walker ability before, it's not present until after chrysalis, you are special and our first."

Mixy moved toward the beautiful Lady of Light and wondered what chrysalis was. The Lady of Light walked closer and put her hand on Mixy, she used light magic and the phase mixed together, Mixy's entire body glowed. Within that instant the Lady of Light knew everything and so did Mixy, Mixy also made a choice. The Lady of Light was sad, but understood it was a mistake.

The people on the benches cheered when Mixy glowed.

The Lady of Light spoke, "Rejoice, for Mixy is a Phase Walker and has accepted after her chrysalis that she will train to become a Lady of Illumination."

The crowd cheered and clicked and stamped their feet.

"Also rejoice that four of our Lords and Ladies of Illumination were returned to us."

The crowd cheered again.

Mixy was happy and returned to the front benches, but she had the full awareness of what she had done, eaten a young spideroid Phase Walker. She turned to look at the crowd and spotted a spideroid family. A small tear shed and she was so sorry.

The Lady of Light spoke, "Mixy has told me who the outworlders are that saved my people, I shall speak their names and may they be known throughout Lorvisa as friend to our people."

The Lady of Light began her devotion wave, it projected and bounced off every living creature and everything living.

"Those I shall name are friends of Lorvisa, remember their image," she projected, "Caitlin of the Kelstone plane, Wuzzle of the Kelstone plane, Shandra of the Celestial plane, Alastor of the Celestial plane, Sarah of the Earth plane."

"My people of Lorvisa, we will avenge the deaths of our kind and our younglings, a war is coming, prepare yourself, we will prevail and the evil Delvin that wield chaos magic will be cleansed," the devotion aura stopped.

The Lady of Light sat on her throne, waved those off the speaker platform and spoke, "Next order of business."

A ladybug humanoid started for the platform, she had the head and body of human except she had a red hard shell on her back and her skin was velvety black and she had long bright red flowing hair. She moved her black feelers and walked with a waddle.

It was dark and several icky sea leaves floated in the water. The currents were still and warm. Tiny white sea-creatures moved in calm ripples on the dark ocean floor. A green wavy stripe moved in the darkness, it shone brightly and slithered to higher water, getting closer to the surface and the light. The green was attached to black scales, as light reflected of it and it started to take the form of a child Persidion. The child looked unhappy, his human features in a frown of concentration, his jet black hair trailing behind as his black and green striped tail moved in a swaying rhythm closer to higher water.

Jas was getting hungry and wanted to get into mid ocean waters, this was where all the good food was and he wanted to feast. Jas swum past pretty coloured corals and came to a natural water rip, the ocean jetted through a small half tunnel of rock and shell in a pattern. A few small fish came through the last water rip and jetted past. Wonderful, Jas thought and approached the start of the tunnel waiting for the next incoming jet of water along the rip. Several chunks of water weeds and several large fish shot through the next rip. Jas grabbed for a large fish, it slipped through his hands and he looked disappointed as he was hungry.

Jas knew it was only a matter of time before he would eat so he waited patiently for the next jet through the tunnel. Then it did, several small colourful fish came rushing out of the rip skittling on the water Jas extended his hand and caught three, greedily eating each one, they were tasty. But that was not enough, he wanted more and waited again.

This time the rip jetted several small snail like creatures, Jas caught two and peeled their shells to bite into their pink flesh, still crawling. Jas remembered his mother liked these especially and swum up to the surface a little upset trying to get away from the memory.

Once Jas push through to the outside air, wind licked his face he could see a small island with rock pools on its border. Jas wanted to relax so swum to the rock pools knowing the water within would be warm and sometimes bubbly if he was lucky.

The rock pools were empty save a few crustaceans and the island was deserted. Jas leaped into the air and landed with a thud into a closed rock pool. He relaxed and stretched his green striped tail, the water was warm and refreshing. It was nice to be in the air, Persidion folk had a natural ability to adjust to breathing outside whenever surfaced but their skin and tails would dry out and eventually and turn to sores if out of the water for too long. His father did this once he recalled, it wasn't long ago either, he dashed that thought out of his mind before the memory of that day emerged as fresh as ever in his thoughts.

Staring up at the sky Jas saw several small blue birds, and thought of wings, that then led him to think of the birds legs for landing, he wished he had two legs. Jas then had a shock, a stomach pain occurred; it was so intense he curled his body over in agony. A yellow glow appeared around his body then nothing, the pain was gone. Jas straightened himself and moments after he felt his body change, his tail split into two dark coloured human legs that matched the skin tone of his arms and face. Shocked at what was happening and doing what any young boy would do, he stood.

He was amazed and overjoyed, then jumped on top of the rocks then walked, slowly steadying each step, to the beach. The sensation of the sand touching his feet was amazing, then he looked down and realised something, um well, he needed pants, he had human parts now. Happy at walking but embarrassed, he walked to a tree and took some large leaves to make himself a rough green skirt.

Possibilities were endless and a thousand thoughts shot through his mind. He sat cross legged on the beach breathing in the air and thought about his tail, wondering if the transformation was permanent. A yellow glow appeared at that thought of his tail, his legs started bonding together and forming a tail. No, Jas thought, this cannot be happening, not only did he lose his two legs but he was too far inland and it would be a massive struggle of flipping and rolling his body back into the water, panic set in as he realised he might be on the shore too long before he reached the water. His rough skirt broke and fell to the sand.

He started to roll down the sand, flipping his tail and using his arms to get closer to the water. Then he thought of two legs, oh how he wished they were back, and then it happened a yellow glow appeared around Jas his tail coming apart to form two legs.

Jas was confused, he tried to understand what was happening and came to the realisation he was causing the change and that his thoughts of legs and tails were activating it. He had no idea how he gained this ability but he was in control, panic left him and he lay naked on the beach deep in thought and occasionally touching a leg to ensure it was still there.

The guild hall was a hive of activity, the Master Workers and their apprentices had been refining the process to complete their order faster. The Guild Master had now made it a rush order. Considering it was a very large consignment, magical machines had been created to speed it up.

A large wooden machine woven in celestial light magic churned away, producing parts to make rods. Another magical machine tended by several apprentices wove cloth bags with a magical null spell, these were used to cover the rods for transportation, as safety of product delivery was very important when making magical devices.

Lady Khan was no longer casting single spells on the wooden rods, but merely casting a symbol that activated them thanks to the machine created with the help of the Guild Master. Ethan laid several rods on a wooden rack that spaced them apart, Lady Khan then would active them using the stun symbol. Then another two Master Workers would remove them from the rack and put them into a barrel that contained purple goo cast in light magic. This would deactivate the spells on rods for those targeted that wield light magic as a failsafe. Then more Master Workers would take them from the barrel and wrap them in individual null bags.

The bags that contained the rods were sorted to either the floating golden chest marked with a target symbol or the floating silver chest market with a lightning bolt. The order was for five hundred stunner rods that would stun a target for a period of time making them immobile and for five hundred death weapons, this is what Lady Khan called them. They were rods that would emit a death ray, instantly ending the life force of any organic creature. Lady Khan and Ethan did not work on the death rods, Lady Khan insisted, so the stun rods were what they worked on.

The chests were almost full and the order was nearing its end, there were only a few more to go.

Trigan, pleased with his effort in the weaving machine, just oversaw its operation while other Master Workers collected the bags it created, specialising in magical cloth and material was always useful he thought.

Trigan was always stylish, he wore outworldly fashions, today was no exception, he wore a purple wide brimmed hat that set off his eyes, slim fitted clothes that had a shine through them and boots that had layers of leather, very chunky, inspired by how Alastor's feet looked in the black boots Trigan had created earlier. Not many of the Master Workers took notice of his fashion because he was an outworlder, his metallic coppery skin, purple eyes and blue tongue, if you were lucky to see it, were very odd to celestials.

Trigan never spoke of what plane he was from even to Lady Khan, but he was from Telswan, where the sky was red, the seas green and the ground was nothing but a muddy swamp. Cities were underground metropolises of technology and magic, for the most part the people of Telswan, the Desnee, used summoning and creation magic. The summoning magic would pull elementals from the magical void to do their bidding, depending on how powerful the elemental was determined what they could do. Summoning magic comes in two streams, summoning light magic which calls forth elementals of wind, fire, earth and water. The other stream of summoning magic is rarely used but that is based on chaos magic; creatures called upon usually were devils, wraiths and various undead.

Trigan obviously was a light magic summoner and specialised in cloth, that is why he was invited to join the Master Workers Guild.

If one was a wielder of summoning magic and a Phase Walker they would have the ability to see exactly how Trigan's weaving machine was working. A small elemental was within, using its tiny hands to weave together the magic required to create magical cloth. It danced around the machine and was glowing red like a little flame; it was pulled from a magical fire void.

Lady Khan waved to another Master Worker who just entered the hall, "Samuel, greetings, how are you?"

Samuel bowed his head in respect and smiled at Lady Khan, "I am well Lady Khan, how goes the order."

Ethan came over and placed several rods on the wood rack. Lady Khan stopped and waved Ethan to her side then spoke, "We really need a break for something to eat, Samuel can you take over here."

Samuel looked at the rods, he knew exactly what she was doing because he did this last time he worked on the order, "Certainly Lady Khan, I am refreshed and ready to help, go rest a while, it looks like the order has progressed a lot."

Lady Khan backed away and missed a step then tripped, Ethan caught her by the arm, she looked up smiling at him, "I guess I am getting a little weary-headed and need something to eat, then I'll be fine, would you like to join me for a meal at my family's shop in the Abbith market?"

Ethan, very happy with the invitation, smiled and stretched his silvery feathered wings a little, "Sounds great Lady Khan."

This was the first time he had been invited to her shop.

Still holding Ethan's arm, Lady Khan fixed her dress that was not straight, "Ok let's get Trigan and go."

Ethan, a little disappointed that the coppery one was coming, sighed, "Okay, let's go."

Ethan escorted Lady Khan to Trigan, who was watching his machine, and she let go of Ethan's arm and said, "Trigan, ready for a break? Want to come for a meal with us at my family's shop?"

Trigan kind of bounced and the light reflected of his coppery scales, "Oh sure, I'm very hungry, I'm sure the machine will be ok without me for a while. Ethan, Ethan you're not as stylish as me."

Trigan moved his hands around and made a white floppy hat the same style as what he was wearing. Trigan offered it to Ethan, Ethan put his hand out to take the hat and Trigan placed it on Ethan's head, "There, guess we are all set now, I'm starving."

Ethan raised an eyebrow and snorted, Lady Khan laughed, "Well would the stylish gentleman like to join me?"

Lady Khan walked to the open window that was not far from the machine, spread her silver wings and floated in the air, hovering outside the window. Ethan followed and held his hat as he spread his silver wings and stepped out of the window then he moved closer to Lady Khan.

Trigan with a skip leaped out of the window and a small tiny carpet of blue weave appeared from nowhere under his feet. He stood upon it, hovering and smiling, and said, "Winning," he then winked.

The three of them flew overhead and then slowly down, they descended deep into the Abbith market. Landing, Trigan's carpet folded itself very small and flew into his waist coat pocket and he smiled. This is where Lady Khan had her shop and sold her wares as a Master Worker. Lady Khan's shop was shared with her family, her parents and a younger sister. It was the afternoon and still light, on foot they walked through the crowd to get to Lady Khan's shop.

Lady Khan's shop was called the Emporium of Little Devices and a wooden sign hung proudly hovering in the air. Several glass cabinets hovered from the ground at eye sight level, they showcased Lady Khan's wares, a tiny garden in a glass case with tiny trees, a little small neat blue box with "It's bigger on the inside" labelled clearly, tiny contraptions and pendants of all kinds with little labels like "Enchanted with water, break seal for a lake", "Enchanted with fire" and so forth.

Moving closer to the Emporium, the shop doors had intricate designs carved all over in the wood, Ethan recognised some of the designs to be light magic symbols of warding and protection from chaos magic.

Trigan walked behind because he took too long glaring into the floating display cases, "So what food you have planned for us Lady Khan?"

Lady Khan flicked her long black hair, opened the wooden doors and smiled "Surprise," she folded her wings completely, Ethan did the same as he was about to go inside. Trigan followed close behind, catching up.

Inside the shop was lit by a skylight, it was blue, round and covered the shops counter, which was made of rose wood and also had small carvings all over it. Lady Khan's mother was behind the counter, she looked ethereal just like her daughter, she had straight black hair to her waist which was braided in tiny silver clasps, a white flowing gown and darker green eyes. She had silver wings also and beamed a smile at her daughter, "Estel, how goes the Master Workers Guild? Trade was busy today."

Lady Khan flushed, a little embarrassed, "Mother, I'm known as Lady Khan in the guild and these are my Master Workers Guild friends."

Lady Khan's mother replied "Hush, I will not call you that, Estel Khan, and, please, guests, call me Morwen."

Trigan had a huge smile and took off his hat and put it under his arm, "Thank you Morwen, a pleasure to finally meet Estel's mother, we have worked together in the Guild for many years."

Trigan flashed Estel a cheeky smile.

Ethan, feeling out of place, not wanting to get Lady Khan

angry and not wanting to offend her mother, took off his white hat then responded, "Pleased to meet you Morwen."

Estel had her mouth open and a hand on her hip, "Okay, well I invited my friends to join us in a meal, I wanted them to try my new recipe I have been working on."

Morwen smiled, "Well come on in, your little sister is out shopping in the market with your father, they are looking for a new play toy for her because she has been so good lately."

Estel moved past her mother and lifted a light purple beaded curtain and waved Trigan and Ethan in to follow her, it led to a kitchen and then a cushioned room, to the side stairs led down to what looked like many more rooms. The cushioned room had blue sheer veils hanging from the walls and a small low lying table with a jug of water and empty glasses. Estel sat down on a cushion next to the floor table.

Trigan smiled, looking at all the material that decorated the room, "Oh what a lovely room, so much material," then sat at the other end of the table.

Ethan sat closer to Estel, his warm eyes staring into hers.

Trigan took a glass and poured water into it and noticed the jug did not empty and stayed full, no matter how much water he poured out. He took another glass filling it also, "Oh, a never ending supply of water, how handy, so what feast for us to taste do you have planned Lady um I mean Estel?"

Shuffling on her blue cushions, Estel responded, "Well I guess you can call me that in my own home, only back in the Guild I'm Lady Khan," her green eyes looked firm.

"As for our meal I actually had it on me, I just wanted a nice relaxing place to have it so brought you guys here."

Ethan raised an eyebrow, "You have it on you? I don't see any food."

Trigan also chimed in, "Oh yes, where is the food? I'm hungry."

Estel held out her hand and three tiny little red round balls were in her palm, no bigger than the size of her tiny fingernail.

Trigan looked at them "What is that, not some tiny jest?"

Estel looking at them both through her green eyes beamed a smile, proud of her creation, "Please have one, you will be very surprised."

Ethan took one and placed it in his mouth, "Oh wow this is not what I expected, my favourite meal, spiced meat and white vegetables mixed in seasoned flavours from the herb garden, oh and desert is honey toffee cake, wow and I taste my favourite mulled wine."

"How can this be from a tiny red ball? Is it possible to get happy drunk on this? It's started on the main course again."

Trigan looked amazed, "Give me one of those please Estel."

He reached over and took one from her hand eagerly and popped it into his reptilian coppery mouth, he poked out his blue tongue, "Mine tastes like silvery fish mixed with carnen juice and the delightful rosind berry from my home plane."

Estel laughed and put one in her mouth, she tasted her favourite dishes and smiled, "To answer your questions, Ethan, yes, yes you can get drunk. Also take care because you can also get fat."

"It's my secret recipe, something I have been working on most of my life to be honest, I can't give you my secrets. Keep it in your mouth until you are full then remove it from your mouth and keep the rest of the feast for another time, my gift to you. Oh and you never did mention what plane you were from Trigan?"

Trigan looked up in delight from being full from his meal, he took the tiny red ball out of his mouth, in surprise it didn't lose it size or shape, "So why do you want to know what plane I am from? Phase Walkers are usually only interested in it?"

Ethan took the red tiny ball from his mouth pulled out a white cloth and put the ball inside, wrapping it, then placing it in his pocket.

"I know what you should call it Estel. 'Tiny tasty feast'," feeling odd to call her first name, Ethan blushed.

Estel sat up and looked right at Ethan, a little shocked at hearing her name from him, but very happy about the name

Ethan chose for her creation, "What a great name, I will sell it as a 'Tiny tasty feast'."

"Trigan, I'm interested because you're an outworlder and my friend, I was just curious about your home plane and what food you were tasting when you ate the tiny tasty feast?'

Trigan put the red ball in his shirt chest pocket, "I guess I am with friends, I don't usually talk about my home plane."

Ethan sat forward and Estel looked very attentive.

Trigan continued, "My plane is known as Telswan, there are two races, the Desnee like me and the savage mindless lizards known as the Keevers. The Desnee live underground in cities, huge and vast, networked together using technology and magic, striving for a better society and having centres of great knowledge in our libraries. Centuries ago we were once like the Keevers but changed and evolved, we walked on two legs and our features became defined much like yours, then acquired skills, knowledge and summoner magic."

"Only Desnee are known to be Phase Walkers. It is a problem on my plane, the Keevers, many have tried to teach them but they are mindless creatures, they cannot walk only crawl, they cannot hold things in their claws and stumble around the surface living off the land, they cannot be domesticated nor taught, many have tried using all kinds of magic to communicate with them."

"Many offworlder Phase Walkers were also consulted to help with the problem to no avail. They only seem to have primal instincts to hunt, feed and breed. On the surface of my planet it is nothing more than a huge muddy swamp, this is where they live."

"So the two races live separate lives, the Keevers on the surface and the Desnee underground, over time we have pretty much lost interest in contact with them. This is why I don't spend too much time on my plane nor talk about it much to anyone."

Ethan closed his mouth and blinked his light blue eyes.

Estel looked sad and tossed her straight black raven hair off her shoulder, "I'm sorry for the Keevers problem in the

Telswan plane but glad you spend a lot of time on our plane."

"And in our company," Ethan said.

Trigan worried he revealed to much, stretched his arms out, "So Estel, I'm full up to the top, can't even think about eating or drinking another thing, that's some damn fine miniature light magic going on."

Ethan laughed, "Well yes, I even feel a bit giddy with the mulled wine I had tasted. If I was to do a feast I would make each piece of food gigantic and would serve it in a massive field so dinners could walk around and picnic."

Estel just smirked, "Bigger is not always better."

Ethan loved the banter and continued, "What about gigantic? That's much better then bigger."

Estel just laughed.

Trigan put his purple hat on, "Enough you polar opposites, don't we have an order to fill?"

Ethan smiled at Estel probably a bit too long, then stood and held out his hand to hers. She held it to stand and steady herself from the cushions she was sitting on, but once standing she still held his hand.

Trigan's purple eyes shone when he smirked, his coppery face enhancing the expression, he then stood up from the cushions as well. He noticed Ethan holding his white hat in his other hand. Trigan grabbed it from Ethan's hand and roughly put it on his head. The hat looked awkward and on an angle. Then Trigan jested, "On noes, someone save me, the two polar opposites are connecting, the plane may explode."

Everyone laughed and walked out of the Emporium of Little devices, waving at Morwen as they left. They all took to the air heading back to the guild hall but Ethan and Estel only let go of each other's hand moments before the guild hall was in sight.

- Chapter 18 -

Swimming and Flight

Jas was sitting on the beach, he could feel the sand pass between his toes, then stared down at his new humanoid feet and stretched them again. Pointing his toes he then noticed a strange pattern that looked like flowers drawn around his ankle. Looking at the marking, in darkish blue, he reached down and attempted to rub it off, but to no avail. Jas, knowing he could control the transformation, was trying to work out in his mind how exactly he was doing it, thinking more, he realised how simple it was, his mind controlled it, he controlled it.

There was a rustle in a large green bush behind him, where the sand meets the land, all the leaves in the bush moved, leading Jas to have a feeling something was in there. Jas stood quickly, strangely aware of his feet and crept quietly to the bush, it continued to rustle, leaves actually fell from the bush onto the ground and Jas could hear grunts. Stepping back from the bush onto the sand again Jas picked up a handful of sand, moved forward and threw it into the bush. A large boar like creature almost as big as Jas but much wider leapt forward from the bush, charging in his direction.

Jas stepped backwards fast, the movement foreign to him and to his surprise a dark green trident appeared in his hand, it felt powerful and a tingling sensation occurred in his body. A trident was the common warrior's weapon of his people. Urged on as a sign and blessing of his kind he raised the trident then held it forward and the stupid boar creature, charging, ran head on straight into the trident, running the three sharp pokers into its flesh through its grunting face. The boar stopped, heaved and passed out. Jas removed the trident from its fat grey flesh and watched as sickly blood trickled out.

Stepping away from the scene Jas studied the trident, he smoothed his hand up and down the handle then noticed a purple gem lodged in the base of the handle with small carvings of serpents. Jas walked into the water until it was knee deep, he felt safer in the sea, the land had many perils, he was but on land for no more than a few hours before he got attacked. The trident dematerialised, Jas realised it was gone then thought of his tail, a yellow glow appeared around him and he dove into the water, vowing to go back to his village, he wanted to let them know he had found the way to transform into two legs.

Lady Khan, Ethan and Trigan were back inside the guild hall, the floating structure that held the Master Workers of light magic. Each Master Worker had a light magic speciality and almost every Master Worker had an apprentice, Lady Khan and Ethan were still only apprentices, but senior ones, which became clear when a Master Worker called them back to work. Trigan smirked because he was a special case, the Guild Master invited him to participate as a Master Worker because of his fine weaving skills, and because he was an outworlder Phase Walker so no apprenticeship did he have to undertake, but he had been a member of the Guild for well over thirty years and was there before Ethan began his apprenticeship.

Trigan went back to his machine and to his surprise it had stopped and the two Master Worker apprentices were no longer around. Trigan walked up to the chests and peered inside them, they looked very full and was sure his machine stopped because they no longer required null bags.

He walked up to the yellow glowing light that hovered on top of the Guild's table and used some light magic to activate it, the glowing light intoned, "Yes, how may I help you?"

Trigan then replied, "Guild Master, my machine has stopped running, have you enough null bags."

The yellow glowing light intoned "Greetings Master Trigan, yes we have finished that part of the order and your machine is no longer required, can you please deactivate it and pack away, it won't be long until the final rods are finished and packed away, I will be back in the guild hall very soon, good work Trigan."

The yellow glowing light went dull but still hung in the air about the table.

Trigan sighed as he was very proud of his machine but understood it had to go as its usefulness was finished, so he walked to his machine, dispelled the little elemental hovering inside then thought of an idea.

Trigan walked up to Lady Khan and watched her for some time, she activated symbols on rods and Ethan refilled the rack again, they were getting near the end. On the final round of rods Lady Khan, Ethan and a few other apprentices cheered and clapped as the last stunner rods were being bagged and placed into the chest. The death rods were almost finished as well on the other side of the guild hall, cheers and claps also echoed from over there.

Trigan smiled and spoke to Lady Khan, Ethan moved forward to also listen, "My dear, good job, may I ask but a favour from my lovely friend?"

Lady Khan flicked her long straight jet black hair back and smiled, "Of course, Master Trigan."

Trigan continued, "Can you shrink my machine, make it tiny, tiny so I can fit it in my pocket. I want to keep it as a trophy, the magic within has been totally deactivated."

Lady Khan, happy that her speciality could be of use, replied, "Certainly, that's something I can do."

Ethan laughed, "But why don't you want it bigger, you could make it as huge as a mountain so people from all over the Celestial realm could admire your great design."

Trigan's coppery grin broke out to a laugh, "You know Ethan you really don't know how tempting that offer is."

Lady Khan snorted, "Ok let's go see."

Lady Khan raised her arms and started to chant, the weaving machine began to shrink slowly, it took a while before it even became small, it continued shrinking until it was tiny, well as big as the palm of Lady Khan's hand. She completed the task and walked over to the tiny machine then picked it up and gave it to Trigan, who was so happy he did a funny little dance, kicking his coppery feet up in those chunky black boots and swaying as if music played.

Ethan burst out laughing and so did Lady Khan. In fact many apprentices and Master Workers joined in the laughter and formed a little crowd around him.

Trigan didn't care, he thought the attention was great so continued until he noticed the crowd parted and the Guild Master walked towards him and clapped his hands. Trigan smiled and stopped, "Guild Master you are back, nice to see you, I didn't even feel the phase."

The Guild Master stretched his wings, "Trigan, I don't always use the phase to get around, glad the order is complete and some mirth is in the hall."

The Guild Master turned to the gathered crowd and magically lifted his voice, "Thank you Master Workers and apprentices, your skills in light magic are greatly appreciated."

"With this order we will acquire Knoxcred stones which will allow us to further our studies in phase travel and perhaps building permanent gates to different planes, allowing us to barter our trade everywhere. The Master Workers Guild will be a great place and the centre of trade throughout the planes."

There was much chatter among the Master Workers and apprentices. The Guild Master held his hands high and spoke again, "But first things first, we need to deliver this order tomorrow, go home and get a well-earned rest."

"See you tomorrow", Lady Khan smiled at Trigan who waved and made funny dancing steps to the window and jumped onto his flying blue carpet, then left the guild hall.

Ethan took Lady Khan's hand, she allowed it and they both walked to the window. Together they took flight and descended to the ground just outside Lady Khan's shop.

Ethan kissed her hand without asking and took to the air smiling, "See you tomorrow Estel."

Estel waved back and walked into her shop.

Ethan's long brown hair flapped in the wind along with his new hat, Ethan felt stylish even though it made it harder to fly, holding a hat. His white wings moving smoothly, riding the wind back home.

It was getting dark and the lights to Remiel House lit the windows, Ethan landed with a thud on the step and Yanni promptly opened the door, detecting his presence. Ethan could hear laughter within and wondered what was going on. Yanni hovered to the main room and Ethan followed, happy and content that everything was right in his world, after all he had kissed Lady Khan's hand.

Walking to the fireplace Ethan saw Alastor, his half-demonoid brother, laughing and drinking from a mug, then to his surprise he saw Sarah dressed up in red finery sitting in his lap. Caitlin was curled up in a little ball, half sleeping in the other chair and Wuzzle sat silently along the other wall.

Ethan took off his white hat, still happy, and spoke, "Brother how goes your day?"

Alastor's eyes thinned and he threw his mug into the fireplace, it hissed in the fire and then he pushed Sarah from his lap, realising his brother must not see he has feelings for her. Sarah stood and looked at him, hurt, then felt a twinge when seeing the gorgeous winged Ethan beam a surprised face at her, then she ran to her room. Caitlin sat up and saw Alastor almost in a rage, he looked mean, his fine features twisted and he spoke in a very deep voice, "My day went okay brother, we rescued fellow Phase Walkers but I did not retrieve Keyness's wings."

Caitlin, almost afraid to speak, did, "Alastor, that was rude of you to do that to Sarah. I will help you, we will return and get the wings, settle down."

Alastor stood and pushed the chair back with such force it hit the wall and he started to walk into his room. Ethan walked forward and blocked his path, "Wait brother, this behaviour is not necessary I need to talk to you, the order is complete and they need Phase Walkers to deliver it, will you come?"

Alastor looked in his brothers eyes and then walked off to his room. Caitlin, now standing on her chair to gain height, "I will Ethan, I will go to Lorvisa tomorrow, I want to see Mixy, I can help with your delivery. Come sit and we will talk more."

Ethan, very confused at Alastor's behaviour, took the chair that Alastor threw to the wall and righted it then moved it back into place next to the fire and sat down.

Ethan smiled at Caitlin, "Well I had a great day, are you interested in listening about it?"

Caitlin perked up, "Of course, I love good news."

Ethan started to tell Caitlin about Lady Khan.

Sarah was in her room, she felt funny really funny, not just because Alastor threw her off his lap, it was the drink, it did something strange to her, she could not concentrate on a single thought as they all fluttered through her mind while she lay on the bed.

Did she really have feelings for Alastor, she thought of his warmness and how he laughed at her stories sitting by the fire. Then she thought of Ethan and the strange zing feeling she felt when he had seen her on his brother's lap. Then she thought of William and trashed the thought, that was over. Then she wept at Alastor's rejection. She closed her eyes and tried to sleep.

Alastor was in his bedroom, his thoughts also drifting in all directions, he lay on his bed and thought of Keyness, he remembered her beautiful eyes and her jet black hair. He cried and moaned in pain waiting for tiredness to take him away from his thoughts.

Jas was swimming in the ocean, he was very close to its floor, he was trying to feel for his village, he could not be more than a day or two away from it. He swum deeper, there was a flash of grey and a ripple of water pushed past him, he looked up and saw a large creature swim by, he did not see its front but a huge grey body and a huge tail almost three times his size went by. The ocean was not without dangers and deep-sea gigantism was common. Jas waited some time for the creature to move on and tried to concentrate on his village, a tingling occurred over his body, Jas was confused and a silver line was in front of him, it shimmered and expanded.

The giant grey skinned creature swum over Jas it looked huge, its head was full of massive sharp pointed teeth. Jas moved into some long brown reeds of sea grass to hide and stared at the shimmering object in the water, he felt like he could pass through it. On instinct something made Jas look directly up, so he did, looking through the long brown sea grass. An open mouth of sharp large teeth was projecting downwards in his direction, Jas swum as fast as he could into the shimmering object, he passed through then fell to the ground. He looked at the shimmering object he just passed through and sharp teeth swum by then the silver shimmering closed so fast it snapped shut with a crackling of light and made a thumping sound.

Jas was alone, he was no longer in water, he was on land. There was a tree with magical symbols that glowed. The grass was green and all the trees around him ended with a green curl. This place felt familiar, but he did not know where he was, Jas thought of two legs as his tail was not suitable in a forest. A yellow glow covered his body and Jas was naked, he had two legs. Jas pondered, he didn't mind the change but this being naked thing was not fun. Jas gathered large leaves from the trees and tied them together to fashion a skirt, this was not the first time he had done this so he was getting better at making leaf fashion.

Jas then followed a well-used forest trail, looking around in wonder at the inland forest. He finally came to clearing and he could see a mound dwelling off to the distance and a pond. This was all familiar to him, then it clicked this was his pond that he used to surface with his father, that was Caitlin's house, he was home. Walking faster towards the pond Jas was happy to be home. He still did not understand how the shimmer got him here but he thought it was some kind of magic and just accepted it.

The pond was still and white water lilies floated on top, small insects flew around the edge of the pond. Jas ran and jumped into the water, he dove deep underwater then thought of his tail. The yellow glow appeared again and his tail returned, black with green stripes, the scales shiny, his tail gave him better movement and he projected himself to the village losing his leaf skirt.

Jas, wide eyed, looked at the village from a distance, there were almost no broken buildings around and it looked for the most part as he remembered it, untouched from the attack. Jas swum closer, there was a small market in the village but with only a handful of stalls and it looked more make shift. Jas could not believe this was all back together and rebuilt, he was only gone a day or two at the very least.

Two elder Persidion swum in Jas's direction, one was his neighbour, a blue scaled women who carried a reed basket filled with wild sea flowers, and the other a friend of his father, a golden scaled man with silvery spots, he had blue eyes and carried a shell covered backpack. Jas tried to recall their names, Pearl and Arod.

Pearl, excited, put her arms around Jas and stepped back to speak, "There you are, safe and well, we had been looking for you for weeks."

Jas a little taken back at this news, "I haven't been gone for more than a few days."

Arod took his backpack off, "Jas, you have been missing for two weeks three days, I should know because I have been out looking for you each day as have many of the villagers. There even had been an official message sent to the two other neighbouring villages of your disappearance."

Jas took this in and wondered how he lost so much time and replied, "I'm sorry to cause all this worry I really did not know I was gone that long. I am back now and I have news."

Arod and Pearl looked worried as to what Jas might have been doing while he was missing.

Jas continued, "I have found the lost secret, the secret of the two legs."

Arod looked perplexed and Jas continued, "I know how to change into two legs and walk on land."

Pearl quickly responded, "Silly boy we all know how to change into two legs, it's what happens when we mature, this ability happens when we are around thirty. I know you're still probably a bit young for that news, it's not usually revealed until you are much older."

Jas looked surprised "But I can do it now," and he concentrated on two legs, a yellow glow appeared around his body and his tail slowly split into two legs.

Arod didn't blink, just floated and put his backpack on his back, "Jas change back please, there are still a lot of younglings around, we don't tell the younglings because with two legs comes responsibility. Please, Jas and Pearl, let's go to my house then we can talk about this some more, it's what Martin would have wanted."

Jas's ego took a blow and he wondered about the shimmering light that took him above the water on the land, if that was another secret too. He changed back to his tail and looked at the ground, following Arod to his house, looking at the reconstruction of his village.

Arod's house looked new, the shell structure was very shiny, inside new sea furniture was planted as the roots did not seem well covered in the ground. Pearl sat on Arod's patch of fresh sea grass in his sitting room, Jas followed and sat next to her.

Arod took off his backpack and gave out clams to Pearl and Jas in hospitality. Arod looked weary but stood and did not sit, then he spoke, "Jas, I do not know where you have been, but it's clear that the stress of losing your parents has somehow triggered your two leg ability, so it's time you need to learn about it."

Arod sat on the ground so that he could face Jas and Pearl, whose face was relaxed then smiled at Arod.

Arod continued, "When a Persidion turns around thirty they come of age, when they seek a mate, some will choose another Persidion and some will leave the village and choose to live on the land. Those that choose a mate that are two legs surfacers will become a person from Kelstone and leave our people behind. Usually these land surfacers are fisher folk and people who live by the sea, it is very rare for one of our kind to choose this path but it does happen."

"Also for many male Persidion it is a rite of passage to adventure as a two legs before returning to their village to settle down and choose a mate, shocking to hear but this is our way. At any time we could leave the village and walk on two legs, but it's our way of life and tradition to live under the sea."

"The king and queen of the Persidion people have ruled that no matter what path you take you are always welcome back with open arms to the Persidion people if you have your tail. As you probably have been aware some of the elders go away for periods at a time but they always return, they are more than likely above ground as two legs."

Jas took this all in and considered, "Well I thought I discovered something, I had best intentions to share with all my people. I guess it wasn't news after all, I think I might leave the village and become a two legs for a while, I need to be away, it's painful for me to stay."

Pearl sadly spoke, "I understand it's something you should explore but you're younger than most so please take care."

Jas stood, "I am glad I returned here and this was explained to me now, I understand what is happening to me, thank you Pearl, thank you Arod. I now know what I have to do."

Pearl looked up to Jas and asked, "What is it you have to do?"

Jas started for the door and did not look back, "Revenge."

Jas then started to swim away from the village.

Arod swum faster catching up to Jas, "Wait please Jas!"

Jas stopped and turned around, "There is nothing you can say that will stop me."

Arod answered, "Damn you boy, I'm not here to stop you, I just was not finished."

Jas stopped cold and raised an eyebrow, "There's more?"

Arod continued "Yes, if you become a two legs and do no return to the sea every month on a high tide you will lose the ability to return to us and become a two legs permanently."

Jas gasped, "Okay, thank you again Arod, my father did well to call you friend."

Arod waved and returned to the village. Jas swam on until he surfaced in the small pond.

The small pond was peaceful and quiet except the buzzing of little flying bugs, Jas pushed past some lilies to the ponds edge then changed into his two legs. Stepping out of the water, Jas picked up some pond weeds and wrapped it around himself, not very elegant but it did the job in covering his humanoid flesh.

Jas walked over to Caitlin's dwelling, drips of water falling to the ground with his every step. Jas's only two legged friend was Caitlin so he was going to talk to her, perhaps she could help him with seeking out the demons. When Jas approached her dwelling he saw a mess, broken wooden chairs scattered around out the front of the dwelling. On closer inspection Caitlin's front door looked strange, he could feel it. Jas became fearful something happened to Caitlin as this was looking much like what happened to his village. Jas opened the door slowly and walked to the entrance of Caitlin's house, through the huge doorway, and saw things tossed everywhere although it looked like someone had attempted to clean a little. A wooden chest was obviously broken and dust was on the floor, meaning it happened some time ago. Jas was worried about Caitlin and started to pick up some of the mess, until he heard a noise.

"Squeak, Squeak!"

Jas jumped, something strange to do with two legs, and saw a little brown cute furry creature scuttle along, it had a long brown tail and blue eyes, Jas thought how simple it would be, to be as small as that and not have any worries. At that moment Jas glowed yellow and changed, his two legs became four his sense of smell was heightened and he had a tail, he became a furry creature then started to squeak.

Jas panicked and ran around in circles for several minutes before it sunk in what he had become. Jas forced his mind to think about his true form, nothing happened, he tried again. Jas didn't know what to do so he went under Caitlin's bed, it was dark and he felt safe, he began to think.

It was morning at Remiel House, everyone was home and awake. Sarah woke up a little stiff, she had slept in her clothes again, even her shoes. She was getting used to doing that on Earth, but the clothes she wore were fancy and not comfortable for the most part. Sarah stretched and got dressed into jeans and a white t-shirt, it just made her feel normal. She tied her long hair up in a ponytail, she felt cute.

She packed away her red racing clothes, folding the dress carefully as it was very expensive, so were the shoes. After she tidied her bedroom she put her joggers on and wondered for a moment how things will pan out when she saw Alastor and Ethan again. Bugger it, she thought and walked out to the main room.

Ethan and Shandra were at the fireplace, did that fire ever go out, Sarah thought, and what's these people's attraction to fire? It must be a Celestial thing, she thought. She walked to the huge main wooden table and sat along the side. Caitlin was sitting on the other side eating pizza of all things for breakfast and Wuzzle was eating the same behind on a new chair. The chair was made out of shiny white stone material and fitted with decorative cushions, it was huge and looked to be fashioned just for him, he looked very comfortable. Caitlin looked up from her food, "Sarah, good morning, I hope you had a good sleep."

Sarah stretched and looked about for Alastor, he was not there, "It was ok, the stuff we drunk last night was pretty strong, oh nice chair Wuzzle."

To Sarah's complete surprise Wuzzle spoke in a deep friendly noble voice, "Thank you, it's very comfortable," then Wuzzle started eating pizza again.

Both Ethan and Shandra turned from the fire looking at Wuzzle, also shocked to hear him speak. Then Ethan replied, "No problem Wuzzle, if you need anything else custom made I'm ready to be at your service."

Wuzzle did not reply but Caitlin did, "I'm sure we will think of something soon."

Ethan smirked, "Sure huge things are my speciality after all," and then returned to looking into the blue flames within the fire place.

Yanni appeared above Sarah and hovered a few moments; Yanni's blue glowing arms appeared then put bacon, eggs and a nice cup of coffee down on the table. Turning the coffee cup around the label read 'Chocolate Coffee House'.

Sarah started to eat very fast, she was surprised at how really hungry she was, it probably wasn't in a lady-like manner but she didn't care.

Alastor entered the room, he was smartly dressed, all his demon qualities were covered, shoes, hat and he somehow must of poked his tail down his pants Sarah thought, almost choking on a piece of bacon she was chewing. Sarah then picked up her coffee in an attempt to clear the bacon but snorted a sipfull through her nose.

Sarah was embarrassed and Caitlin didn't help by laughing. Alastor walked to Sarah then patted her on the back softly with his clawed hand, "Are you alright?"

Sarah, shocked, replied, "I'm fine," then looked at Caitlin, who said nothing.

Ethan also watched for a few seconds then stood up. Embarrassed still, Sarah went red in the face then started wiping up coffee spatters with a serviette.

Ethan moved to the front of the table, Alastor was still standing behind Sarah, and Ethan spoke, "Friends, family, I need your help, the Guild Master asked if any of my friend Phase Walkers would like to help deliver an order to the Lorvisa plane. I thought since you rescued Phase Walkers from Lorvisa and Mixy went there that maybe you might want to go, and helping is always a good thing."

"The Guild Master can't take the order in by himself and he's worried about a Delvin attack. He has Trigan to help, who is a friend, but just the two of them doesn't sound really safe. Did I mention you get to meet the Lady of Light? Damn, I wish I was a Phase Walker."

Shandra was the first to respond, "I know the Master Workers Guild is important to you brother, I would be honoured to assist the Guild Master deliver his order."

Shandra looked beautiful like a princess in a fairy tale, Sarah thought.

Ethan grinned, "Thank you sister."

Alastor's deep voice spoke from behind Sarah, who did not turn her head to face him but only listened, "I will come Ethan, if these people are prone to Delvin attacks it's my place to protect them."

Ethan nodded then Caitlin put her pizza slice down and licked her little fingers, "I'll go and help, that's what friends are for," she then beamed a cute smile.

All eyes were on Sarah who just finished spotting the serviette on the last splash of coffee, "Yes okay, I will come, I don't want to be left alone."

She looked up at Ethan, he had perfect light blue eyes, his brown hair flowed down his back. He looked to her like he came from a perfume commercial, too perfect, and he smiled back at her, she felt that zing again and it unnerved her.

Ethan, still smiling, put his hand on his hip, "Ok then, after breakfast leave for the guild hall. I'm going to head off now because you can get there faster than me, phase walking and all, I've just got the good ole fashioned way."

Ethan stretched his wings.

Caitlin giggled and Shandra responded. "See you soon brother."

Yanni started to clean, it took the plates and reached over to Sarah, Alastor was still standing behind her, he looked at Yanni, this time a black cord was around its waist. Alastor reached for chaos magic and fumbled using it, then broke the black cord, freeing Yanni.

Shandra watched on with dark eyes, feeling Yanni's release. Yanni buzzed happy and continued to clean the room. Alastor was deep in thought and caught Shandra's eye, who quickly looked away.

Caitlin stood and announced, "Let me tidy up and I'll be back, then we can go through the phase."

Sarah nodded and stood, her chair moved back touching Alastor, "Excuse me I want to take a small backpack, never know what might be handy."

Shandra stood by the fire place watching, "I'll be here".

Sarah tried to move out of the chair and Alastor, still standing behind her, didn't give her much room to get out, so she leaned into Alastor before she got behind the chair and moved it under the table. Strangely, Alastor just stood there, Sarah started to head to her room, Alastor followed, his footsteps heavy in his large leather boots. Sarah, half way to her door, turned to Alastor, she looked him in the eye, "Can I help you?"

Alastor breathed deeply, "Yes, yes you can, can you forgive me, I don't know why I do half the things I do, the Delvin part of me takes over sometimes and I am not strong enough to fight it, I am tortured by my Delvin half constantly."

Sarah smiled, "Okay, forgiven, but next time you push me like that you may be on the end of my sword, do not forget I am a Phase Walker."

Alastor just laughed, a cheerful laugh it echoed down the hall, "I'll let you get your things Phase Walker."

Sarah went to her room and filled her backpack with a nail file, another set of clothes, her makeup bag, a small bag of mints and her iPhone. Sarah read some messages on her phone, a party at friend's house, one from William "I'm sorry again Sarah", Sarah deleted it, and a new friend request. To Sarah's shock it was from Caitlin, she laughed then shoved the phone into her backpack and swung it on her back then headed to the door.

Back in the main room Caitlin had already opened a phase to the Guild Hall, they were gathered waiting for Sarah. Sarah smiled, "Thanks for the friend request Caitlin."

Caitlin responded "No problem, are you ready?"

"Yes," Sarah replied.

Shandra walked through first, followed by Caitlin and Wuzzle, Sarah then walked through, last was Alastor.

They were in the Master Workers Guild hall, it was very white and bright, the floors were clean and shiny, there was a huge table in the centre of the room, six times bigger than the main room's table at Remiel House, Sarah thought. There was many Celestials in the Guild Hall, they all watched, eyeing the Phase Walkers. Sarah thought she had died and went to heaven, literally it was so odd. Sarah pinched herself, ouch that hurt, she knew this was reality but sometimes it was hard to accept.

Trigan came towards the group, he had coppery skin and wore finely crafted fitted clothes, closely behind him was a beautiful Celestial women dressed in a fine white gown, she had long jet black hair, silvery white wings and green eyes. Alastor was a little taken back by her, she looked like Keyness except the wings were silvery. The likeness was eerie, the thought of Keyness pulled Alastor's heart, he wanted to attack Morack's throne room again, but knew he couldn't go alone, after this he would convince the other Phase Walkers to do so.

There was a sound like a flapping of wings and Ethan appeared in the window, he jumped down and looked red and sweaty, "Nothing like a quick flying sprint to get the energy going in the morning."

Lady Khan turned to Ethan and giggled, Ethan walked toward her and took her arm, Alastor paid very close attention to that, there was a lot of chatter for a time as Ethan introduced everyone to each other and went around in turn. Lady Khan just smiled, Trigan took off his hat with a flourish, Alastor muttered "hello" under his breath, Caitlin said "Hello", Sarah smiled deeply and waved to everyone, wondering if Lady Khan and Ethan had a thing, then wondered if that mattered to her, Shandra gave a typical Celestial response, she just said "Greetings".

The Guild Master entered the hall all the Master Workers went quiet and he approached the Phase Walkers.

"Wow, I have not seen this many of my kind before in one spot, the phase energy in this room is enough to blow a hole in the universe," he laughed.

Only Trigan, Ethan and Lady Khan laughed, the rest looked concerned.

The Guild Master continued, "Well let me extend my hand in friendship to each of you for helping the Celestial light magic Master Workers in delivering this order."

He shook everyone's hands then asked each their names. It was not apparent before but two floating chests were behind him, a silver with a lightning bolt symbol and a golden chest with a target symbol marked on it.

"Let's join and create a phase point to Lorvisa, there is one here at the Guild Hall," as he spoke and activated the phase point, the symbols glowed all over the shiny floor, only the Phase Walkers could see this.

All the Phase Walkers mentally joined him in opening the phase. The phase opened, it was huge and took up most of the room.

"Wow," the Guild Master said, then continued, "Are you ready?"

There were nods and yesses throughout the room. Several non-Phase Walkers who were Master Workers passed through the phase but they did not enter, they simply walked through, as if it wasn't there, to the other side of the room. Oh, Sarah thought, she had wondered what would happen if a non-Phase Walker would enter a phase, to her surprise, nothing.

The Guild Master entered the phase and pushed two chests in front of him though the phase. Alastor and Shandra walked through. Trigan followed closely behind then Caitlin, Wuzzle and Sarah walked through.

They were in a forest, Sarah thought. Lady Khan and Ethan decided to join in at an attempt to walk through the phase, watching everyone else, but to no avail, they just walked though nothing like strolling through the guild hall. The phase made a sound as it snapped shut.

"That was most eventful Lady Khan," Ethan said while holding on to Lady Khan's arm, I guess our work is done, would you care to come to lunch in the Abbith market, my treat. Ethan smirked because he had Lady Khan alone.

Lady Khan beamed a smile back, "Would love to."

With that said both Lady Khan and Ethan headed for a window and flew out into the market.

- Chapter 19 -

Golden Phase Point

Shuffling along was difficult as Mixy's outer skin was so hard she felt she could barely move, little rainbows reflected off her outer scales but she was determined, she was going back to her clutch, she followed the advice given to her on its location and she followed her instincts and she started to recognise things, a fallen tree, a mound of grass, a cool breeze. The she came to the entrance of a huge rotted tree, this was her wilders clutch. Slowly Mixy entered and to her surprise there were some of her clutch brothers and sisters there, she snuggled up to them, they were also in her same state, scaled and hard, unmoving like worms do. She tried to communicate to them and there was nothing, no response, so she spent the night just snuggling close for comfort.

Mixy was in her clutch she felt warm and safe until a Lady of Illumination walked in with a Lord of Illumination, Mixy sighed, "Already?"

The Lady of Illumination responded "Yes, I'm sorry Phase Walker we need to move you for your own protection, and your clutch brothers and sisters. Being a Phase Walker will attract attention, as you have been made aware."

Mixy responded slowly because she was so sleepy and finding everything so hard to take in, "I know I promised the Lady of Light, I will be sad to leave but know I must."

Mixy started to crawl ever so slowly out of the clutch, sadness as she was leaving but knowing it was the right thing to do as it might attract Delvin and she did not want to put her clutch brothers and sisters in danger.

The Lady of Illumination tenderly spoke, as a mother to a child, "I think we should phase back to the noble Ander clutch, you look so tired Mixy."

Mixy responded slowly, "Yes, so, tired."

The Lady and Lord of Illumination opened a phase to the Ander clutch, Mixy linked and the phase opened, they all walked through the phase then it closed, leaving behind Mixy's clutch.

Mixy was in a room, it was still and quiet, there were several shelves lined with royal blue cushions, they had intricate designs, the room was domed with a large skylight, the natural light shone through. Guards were posted in the room, several at each exit it seemed, a little excessive but this was the noble clutch of Anders. Only two larvae lay on the shelves, it was almost empty. Mixy climbed to a middle tier shelf, it was very comfortable, even more so then her clutch, Mixy was ashamed to think. She closed her weary eyes and went to sleep. Within hours her skin was hardening up, almost as hard as a rock, then a layer of hard shell started to form.

The guards did not move, they were not worried, they had seen this before many times.

It was dark and the air was scented with rose and dust, Jas's sense of smell was very strong, he could single out lesser scents as well but they were not as strong as the rose scent, Jas was relieved. For about the hundredth time Jas tried to concentrate on changing himself back to his form but he couldn't, he cried, he was only a boy after all. A single tear slid down his furry brown face, then he saw a shadow, it ran by quickly. Jas emerged from under the bed to have a look, another furry like himself was running around.

Jas called out to it, "Hey, over here."

To Jas's surprise it did, it headed straight to Jas, then

from a distance stared at him. Jas desperately tried to communicate and he did, "Hello, who are you?"

The brown fluffy responded, "You look like me, you smell wrong, this is my place and you are an intruder."

Jas tried to speak calmly, "I came here by mistake, what is your name?"

The brown fluffy was angry, "You leave my place, leave, not your place."

Jas held up a tiny paw, the brown fluffy attacked, he launched forward and took a bite on Jas's head. Jas was so taken back he yelped in pain and stood on two legs. Jas's instincts kicked in, he saw the brown fluffy wiggle its bottom ready to launch another leap and bite, so he reached for the phase and a trident materialised, it was small and the right size to be in Jas's paw, it had a purple gem in its hilt and serpents were carved in its handle everything was the same as before except small.

The brown fluffy leaped into the air ready to launch another attack and Jas held the trident and pitchforked the brown fluffy. Jas was then overcome with sadness, he really enjoyed talking to the brown fluffy even though it was mean. Jas pulled the trident out of its brown fluffy belly and closed his eyes.

Jas felt a tingling sensation and glowed yellow, he started to grow huge and then realised he was turning back into himself, Jas two legs. Jas was relieved, he was scared and he was naked. He was inside Caitlin's dwelling, sitting on the floor and he had a tiny trident tooth pick in his hands, it quickly disappeared. Jas was tired, oh so tired, all his muscle's felt like they were on fire, he also had a tiny bite mark on his head. Jas touched it, he was not impressed. Jas rested.

After a time Jas picked himself up and took the brown fluffy outside and dug a little grave, said a few words then buried him. Jas was feeling exposed so went inside and took some of Caitlin's pink blankets and wrapped them around his waist. Jas needed a plan and all that came to mind at the moment was wait and see if Caitlin came home. He sat on Caitlin's broken bed looking around at the mess then decided to clean up. So up he got and started to clean.

The room was still until pearly white scales broke the silence with a crunching sound, several scales fell to the floor, they were hard and very thick. The scales fell from a large cocooned creature that laid upon royal blue pillows, moving and wiggling. A hole was starting to form in the middle of the cocoon and a hand shot out. Two of the clutch guards came forward to watch for a time, they wore blue tabards with a golden triangle proudly displayed in the centre. One moved forward and pulled some of the white scales off and threw them down on the floor, another hand emerged, it was long and elegant, it was also light purple. Soon the hole was large enough for a figure to sit up, the guard held out his hand and a creature covered in sticky goo emerge from within the cocoon, stepping out onto the ground.

Another clutch guard came forward and threw water over the creature and more details could be seen. It was smiling, its body was light lilac and it had wings still stuck together, it also had antenna, four arms and two legs. It was a butterfly humanoid, it spread its wings for the very first time, they were purple with silvery mirrored dots. The guard spoke "Are you ok Mixy, how do you feel?"

Mixy replied, "I feel great although a little sticky."

The guard ushered Mixy into another part of the clutch chamber, there was a pool of clear liquid and royal blue robes hung on the walls, small flames lit the room and it smelled of pine. Very elegant, Mixy thought.

Mixy lowered herself into the clear pool and a Lady of Illumination came in, she didn't seem to be a clutch guard. Oh, Mixy realised, it was the same Lady that brought her to Lorvisa.

The Lady spoke, "My friend, glad to see you made it through the change and how beautiful you are."

The Lady of Illumination began to wash Mixy's white silvery hair and the sticky stuff from her wings. She raised an eyebrow, questioning, as she looked at Mixy's wings, she had mirrored spots, only high born and nobles had these markings and she knew that Mixy came from a wilder's clutch. She could not help but think that the Lady of Light somehow had something to do with this but knew it was not her place to ask. Once Mixy was clean she emerged from the water, she had beautifully rounded breasts, a slim waist and long legs, her four arms looked elegant.

The Lady of Illumination helped Mixy get into some silky navy blue robes, intricate patterns were in the material, those fitting for any noble. Mixy stretched her wings, "I can't believe this is me, I am so dainty and I can move so freely."

The Lady of Illumination spoke softly, "Congratulations on a successful chrysalis, I will take you to the Illumination chamber, there you can seek audience with the Lady of Light then you will be inducted into the order of Illumination, Phase Walker."

Mixy beamed a smile remembering her promise and choice she made with the Lady of Light, "I am so happy to be able to serve Lorvisa and the Lady of Light."

The Lady of Illumination smiled and led Mixy away outside the clutch chamber and to another building.

This building was much more ornate then the clutch chamber, it had patterns and swirls all along the outside wooden frame to the entrance and silvery threads hug from the roof. They both moved inside, there was a small chamber, a single bench and a throne. The throne was silvery and had many carvings, they actually looked like phase symbols Mixy thought. Behind the throne was a large banner, it had the golden triangle displayed. There was a golden triangle on the floor in front of the throne and the ceiling had sparkling stars that even twinkled during the day.

Mixy was motioned to sit on the bench and the Lady of Illumination left the room. Mixy sat in her new form, still getting used to four arms and running her fingers along the silky dress, feeling its texture, this sensation was all too new for her. She stilled herself then studied the room in more detail. Silvery sheer material hung in what looked like a curtain along the back wall. Thinking this is where the Lady might emerge, she held he hands all tightly together, not knowing what to expect next.

After what felt like only moments the roof opened up from above the chamber, Mixy did not expect that, and the Lady of Light fluttered her silvery mirrored wings and descended to the ground right in front of her throne.

The Lady of Light beamed a smile at Mixy; she was beautiful, the Lady of Light thought, but she expected nothing less of a Phase Walker. The Lady of Light sat on her throne looking at Mixy, who was wide eyed. The ceiling slowly closed and all was still within the chamber.

The Lady of Light held a golden triangle and raised it above her head, a glimmer of light magic was woven around it, followed by nature magic and then some phase power, it bounced around the triangle, going from one corner to the next in a motion.

The Lady of Light smiled, "This is the symbol of Illumination, it is the oldest and most influential symbol in the areas of mind and knowledge, it is the soul of our people, it brings strength, courage, hope, light and unity. Today is the day you accept it and become one with Illumination. I asked that you place all four hands onto the symbol of Illumination, come forward, with its touch you will be enlightened."

Mixy stood royally and proudly, then moved forward to the Lady of Light standing on the golden triangle symbol on the floor. She then placed all four of her elegant lilac hands on the golden triangle held by the Lady of Light, and felt its power.

It surged through Mixy's body, a mixtures of phase, light and nature magic, she could see the entire population of Lorvisa, she felt it, the plants, the insects, the creatures, everything, even the warmness of the sun. Mixy felt love and saw flashes of scary things, demon monsters hurting her people, slaughtering the innocent and felt her role in saving them, healing them and protecting them.

The Lady of Light carefully lifted the Symbol away from Mixy and held her four hands in her own, "With this symbol of Illumination you are now a Lady, you know your role, you have been shown, I joyously welcome you into the Light."

Mixy was happy and ecstatic, feeling the euphoria, "Your Eminence the Lady of Light, I will not let you down, I vow to ever be at your service."

The Lady of Light smiled and stood then waved. A Lord of Illumination entered the room then gave Mixy a navy tabard and golden net. Mixy accepted both the items and placed the tabard on over her head.

"Go now, Lady of Illumination."

The ceiling of stars parted again and the Lady of Light took flight up, up into the sky she went, the open ceiling then closed again, Mixy was happy and alone. She picked up the golden net, knowing it was for those on the Illumination guard, warriors of the Lady of Light. Mixy then realised the net complemented her phase weapon, the lasso.

A Lord of Illumination was at the entrance and spoke to Mixy, "Please report briefly to the Warrior's barracks then head to the Chapter house of Illumination, there is a gathering of Lords and Ladies to discuss our war plans."

Mixy knew that war was coming and she knew that she wanted to be part of it, her hatred for the Delvin intensified after becoming a Lady, she could feel it. Mixy walked long strides, very proudly wearing her new tabard and silk dress. She tucked the golden net under her belt and headed to the barracks.

The guards of Illumination were in a burrow, an elaborate display of flowers grew around the entranceway in a circlet which led downward into a sloping tunnel large enough for Mixy to walk down. Mixy reached the bottom of the tunnel and to her surprise a vast room was underground, it lead off to several other rooms.

A ladybug humanoid with velvety black skin wore a blue

tabard with the golden triangle symbol which marked her as a Lady of Illumination, she sat at a huge desk, its legs made out of woven green grass, it was planted in the earth and the top of the desk appeared to be a shiny solid oak wood; she had what looked like a paper map and was bent over studying it in intense detail. She did not look up until Mixy approached.

She beamed a smile, "Greetings Lady of Illumination and welcome to the Guards of Illumination, the Lady told us of your coming, we are readying for a war meeting in the Chapter house within the hour."

She stood and looked over at a group of guards standing around a huge stone table, it had miniature buildings, trees, terrain and tiny miniature groups of Lorvisa people, also she could see circles placed on phase points. A Lord of Illumination came toward the desk and stood, he was a spideroid, brown and furry with a humanoid head.

The Lady of Illumination spoke, he paid complete attention, "Please take the new Lady of Illumination to settle her in to new quarters, then both report back and we head off to the Chapter house."

The Lord of Illumination waved at Mixy. Mixy walked behind him, he walked through a doorway that went past a room of weapons and then past a room with long tables, there was a smell of food in the air, he then kept walking to another room that was filled with colourful cushions, it had twenty if not more doors leading from it, the doors all had different markings.

He walked to a wooden door marked with a blue square and surprisingly spoke in a deep voice, "This is your room, make yourself comfortable and familiarise yourself for a small time, then come out to the break out room, I will be waiting outside when you are ready."

Mixy looked at the blue square on the door, the door had a round wooden handle and she opened it, looking inside there was a large room, it was dug underground but the walls were painted in blue and even had little white flowers evenly spaced growing out of the walls and roof. There was a large green bed, it had a soft mattress, and there was a mushroom chair next to a desk with a mirror. A wooden cupboard had two extra tabards of Illumination hung on hooks. A very small water hole had been dug and filled with sparkly fresh blue water. Mixy took it all in, so this is home, she thought and then lay down on her bed and closed her eyes for a few moments.

The brown spideroid Lord of Illumination was seated on the cushions in the break out room, some time had passed and he was getting nervous, so he stood and knocked on Mixy's half open door and walked in. Mixy was sound asleep, it must have been a big day, the Lord thought. He scratched his head with one of his brown fury arms, thought for a while, then shook Mixy to wake her up.

Mixy awoke smiling, realising where she was, then sat up and stood, "Sorry, I must of fallen asleep, the bed is very restful."

The spideroid Lord of Illumination laughed, "It's okay, it's not every day one becomes a Lord or Lady of Illumination, we must go and attend the Chapter house for the war meeting, please follow."

He started to scuttle very fast, all six of his legs moving in motion, back through the barracks to the main room, which was empty, and up the tunnel. Mixy took large steps to keep up with the spideroid and once she reached the tunnel did something that surprised herself, she started to move her wings very fast, so fast her feet lifted from the ground and she hovered up the tunnel with ease, keeping up with the Lord, once out of the tunnel she shot up a little distance into the air. The Lord looked up at her and smiled then continued on the path to the Chapter house.

Mixy only a short distance from the ground, just above the spideroid Lord's head, spoke, "My name's Mixy, what's yours?"

The Lord, still keeping his pace, "Its Henry, from the Recluse clan, pleasure to meet you Mixy."

"Thank you Henry," Mixy replied.

"Almost there," Henry slowed down a little.

Mixy landed next to him on the ground, she looked at the Chapter house, it was above ground and huge. Both Henry and Mixy walked in together, another Lady of Illumination came up behind them, the room was a murmur and almost full. Inside was a totally organic living building. Many plants entwined around each other to form a large hall. There were live flowers around the doorway and a thick rectangle of grass formed hallway carpet. Inside, large mushrooms formed seats which were all occupied by Lords and Ladies of Illumination.

There were many standing and still more coming inside. Mixy gave up trying to count but she was sure all of them were Phase Walkers and that she remembered what Caitlin and Shandra said, Phase Walkers were rare, like no more than a few per plane. There had to be hundreds in the Chapter house.

Mixy looked at the throne, it was at the back of the room, smaller than the Illumination court throne but still decant, ornate and shiny. More seemed to come through the open doors. The Lords and Ladies of Illumination wore their blue tabards with the symbol of a golden triangle. The murmur stopped when the Lady of Light materialised in front of the throne. Those standing sat on the ground.

The Lady of Light was beautiful, her wings shined. There was complete silence as the Lady of Light was going to speak and her words were joy, "Greetings my Lords and Ladies of Illumination, I gather you all here as a pre-meeting before court, our order from the Master Workers Guild in the Celestial plane is complete and they will be here in a few hours. The order will arrive at the phase point in the Illumination court. I need three bags of Knoxcred stones."

There was a murmur amongst the Lords and Ladies, the Lady of Illumination frowned and all was silent.

"Our order consists of two types of weapons, five hundred magical stunners and five hundred rods of death. I want the magical stunners to go to non-Phase Walkers, workers of the field, workers of the sun, and workers of the builders. The five hundred rods of death will go to Phase Walkers and royalty, noble dukes, duchesses and their guards even if not Phase Walkers."

"Those with the stunner weapons are those that will stay to guard Lorvisa, while nobles without Phase ability will also stay. All other Phase Walkers with death rods will go to the Nevid plane. I will now let the Illumination war leader continue with instructions on the attack plan. I must ready myself for our visitors from the Celestial plane, please attend court once you are done here."

With that the Lady of Light simply disappeared.

A Lady of Illumination pushed forward, she was the same ladybug who was studying a map in the barracks, Mixy thought, she stood on the step "My Lords and Ladies of Illumination, the Phase Walkers are already sorted into their groups the mining workers, the guards and the guardians of Sky Shade."

There was a murmur again as everyone broke out talking, the Lady of Illumination clearly did not have the crowd under control like the Lady of Light did. It was some time before she could get silence again. The war leader continued flourishing her velvety black hands, "We will enter the phase simultaneously, the Lady of Light will signal us all with her joy into three known phase points. The mining workers will head to the southern phase point near the new mining excavation, so this will be easy for them to get to, and will attack those in the underground brood mother's complex. The guards, which will be the frontal attack and will use the court of Illuminations phase point, they will descend underground to Morack's lair and slaughter all the Delvin within including Morack, there is also reports of Phase Walker prisoners which should be released and set free."

"Guardians of the Sky Shade are rarely seen within the court of Illumination, as their task is tradition and sacred to our people, but they will attack those small conclaves of Delvin scattered around Nevid from the sky. The Lady of

Light has sent their orders as they are not here now, there is a phase point unknown to me but close to them, they will use it."

"I suggest you all go to court, the Lady awaits us and the order will arrive shortly."

The Lords and Ladies calmly stood then exited the Chapter house, there was no rush as the door bottled-necked with the crowd. There was a soft murmur, nothing more, the war leader rubbed her hands together looking nervous and paced the stairs to the throne. Mixy stood and instead of going to the exit with the other Lords and Ladies, she approached the war leader.

"Greetings war leader, I wanted to make a suggestion, I could ask my friends to help, they are Phase Walkers and are known to our people, they would gladly help our cause."

The war leader looked at Mixy and studied her face, took the end of her blue tabard and pulled it down, "Yes the Lady of Light has let the heroes who saved our kind in Nevid be known to the populous, Caitlin of the Kelstone plane, Wuzzle of the Kelstone plane, Shandra of the Celestial plane, Alastor of the Celestial plane, Sarah of the Earth plane."

Mixy smiled proudly at hearing her friend's names being spoken, "They could help us if you let me find them."

The war leader calculated in her head then spoke, "We don't have the time, I am sorry Mixy, the order will be received within the hour and then the Lady of Light will call the attack."

Mixy, clearly upset, understood and accepted it, she spoke softly, "I understand, I will head to the court of Illumination."

Mixy followed the last group of Lords and Ladies leaving the Chapter house, she used her wings for the second time today and took to the air, she looked radiant, her wondrous wings of shimmering silvery spots reflecting like mirrors, she headed to the island of Illuminoid. There were many Lords and Ladies in the air, she could see in the distance, and they were easy to catch up with, which surprised Mixy because it was effortless to her. Looking down she could see the land with her kind, all humanoid variations of centipedes, spideroids, ladybugs, crickets and other unknown insectoid half-breeds, all wearing the tabard of Illumination, crawling, walking and moving towards the island of Illuminoid.

Looking down and ahead she could see a bridge made from vines and flowers entwined around themselves, it was a long and very impressive structure, nature magic held it upright, Mixy could tell. This was something new to Mixy because she never really was in tune with nature magic. She thought further while flying toward the island and realised she probably was never really exposed to it.

The bridge from the main colony led straight to the court of Illumination's glass entrance way, many of her kind were using the bridge, not all had tabards, on closer inspection some nobles and their house guards were also walking inside. Mixy could see a few different coloured tabards, this was the first time she had actually seen nobles. Mixy was going to fly to the top of the glass dome, there was a small opening that many of the flying of her kind were using.

Mixy, reaching the opening to the dome, hovered for a time and looked around, a few Lords and Ladies passed her and went inside, she could make out small red creatures wearing red tabards as first she saw only a few but more appeared as she waited. Mixy then flew down, inside the glass dome she descended to the ground.

There were a lot of voices, the phase power within the dome was amazing, Mixy had never felt anything like it. She was used to the feeling of some phase power around her, as she had spent time at Remiel House with Phase Walkers, but that had been nothing compared to what she was feeling at the dome. It was over whelming and her entire body tingled.

Strangely, one symbols hovered in the air, but everyone seemed to be ignoring them. Mixy saw a spot on one of the very full benches, then realised why it was free, it was near the phase point within the court of Illumination. It was not a favoured spot because she could barely see the throne. The phase point in the court of Illumination was a large piece of living wood, it could not be described as a tree because it had no leaves and had a flat oval piece free standing in the ground. Unnaturally formed, it had symbols carved around it in a dark green, it also appeared to be planted firmly in the ground by roots which kept it alive.

More entered the Court of Illumination, it was a huge and vast outside space that could hold more than what had already arrive, but it seemed almost everyone was here. Elders from the mining workers arrived by the phase just outside the glass dome entrance, making the influx of people on the bridge stop for a time while they entered. The mining workers were all black ant humanoid creatures, only fifty entered but what took Mixy by surprise was that they were all male and looked identical. A few workers of the Sun could be seen up front, they wore yellow tabards with a sun symbol, Mixy did not know what they did. There were no workers of the builders, but the builders themselves were here, elder cricket humanoid creatures, the torso, arms and head were human-like but all green, their legs and lower body were of a cricket, long and green. The builders had hammers around their necks and they looked old, all had greying hair and long grey beards behind their green faces with many wrinkles. About ten were seated on a bench not far from the front.

The Lady of Light appeared in front of her throne, the most beautiful creature on the planet made its entrance, she was regal and her beautiful mirrored wings were blinding, shining the light into the crowd, her blond hair braided in a complex pattern glowed with radiance as did her brown coppery eyes. She wore a different gown, it was red and velvety, it had golden patches embroidered throughout, Mixy moving her head way over to the side to see around the phase point could make out the symbols, a triangle, a hammer, a sun, a tear, strange shield designs and stars. Mixy could only think that the regal outfit was meant to represent all on Lorvisa.

A huge group of field workers arrived by the back entrance, the entire court turned to watch them enter as they made so much noise, they seemed a ragtag bunch, all different races of Lorvisa were represented amongst them, no finery was worn by them, some even wearing rags.

The Lady of Light smiled and raised her arms, her devotion aura was being projected to the populous of Lorvisa.

There was complete silence as the Lady of Light was going to speak and her words were joy, "Greetings my Lords and Ladies of Illumination, workers of the Sun, elders of the builders, workers of the field, elders from the mining workers, noble dukes and duchesses of the ten colonies and guardians of Sky Shade."

Her voiced echoed around the plane of Lorvisa like sonar, except on a grand scale, each living creature felt her voice vibrate them, each living creature on Lorvisa obeyed the will of the Lady of Light.

There was silence and a sense of awe above the glass dome, Mixy did know what it was because she was hypnotised by the Lady of Light's devotion aura, watching her every word even though her neck was getting sore at looking at her at this angle around the wooden phase point.

The Lady of Light continued, "Our way of life has been threatened, as you are all aware one third of our population are Phase Walkers, the highest concentration of Phase Walkers of the entirety of known planes. This has attracted those that want power and wish to take it from us through our very people. This evil is the Delvin army led by Morack the leader of their kind on the plane of Nevid. We have gently tried to tell them to stop taking our Phase Walkers, we have sent a small warning for them to stop the attacks on our people and still they come."

"This is the time that there appearance on Lorvisa will end, not one more of our kind will be taken. We the people of Lorvisa will not let this happen. The weapons we need to make this happen will be arriving soon and the attack from three phase points will occur, you know your instructions, the various war leaders have informed you, be ready for it will begin soon."

The Lady of Light turned off her devotion aura, her mirrored wings stopped vibrating, she sat on her large mirrored throne. There was a small murmur within the huge crowd. Mixy then had the sudden urge to look up, hundreds, if not thousands, of bee humanoid creatures flew overhead, each had stripes and wings but they were many colours; greens, yellows, oranges and reds, a spectacular sight. Mixy could not believe how much she had learnt of her people in just a few short days and the adjustment to becoming a butterfly humanoid, it was a lot to take in. Mixy smiled and studied the bee creatures, the guardians of Sky Shade she assumed.

A cute young female brown spideroid with dainty coloured flowers around her feet and in her hair, carrying a book, came to Mixy's side. She was a Phase Walker, Mixy could feel it, she also felt a strange feeling like she knew this spideroid that she had not met.

The pretty spideroid smiled and spoke with a happy voice, "Greetings Lady of Illumination, I can't help but be drawn to your smile. I am a Phase Walker, my name is Anita, but I chose the path of adventure and freedom, I am writing a book of my travel and the events of our people, today is a big day in Lorvisa history and I am lucky to be able to record and witness it all."

Mixy pondered and it came to her this was the sister of the twin she consumed, she felt sad and a bond with little Anita at the same time. It was obvious that Anita did not know the dark truth and Mixy was nowhere near ready to reveal it to her, if ever.

Mixy smiled and spoke, "My name is Mixy. I'm happy to meet you Anita, it sounds great that you are recording the events of today. I look forward to reading your book one day."

The Lady of Illumination who was a butterfly humanoid sitting next to Mixy stood and moved to the back of the court. Mixy motioned Anita to sit next to her, so she did.

A golden shimmer occurred around the phase point in the court of Illumination, the Lady of Light stood from her throne and watched a phase open, it was blurry. Mixy could only see from behind she stood to get a closer look.

The Lady of Light watched on as two huge chests came through, one a silver and the other a gold, then a frail old man in white robes, a grey beard and white wings, he had a glimmer in his eye. The Lady of Light sat back on her throne of mirrors and relaxed, and then more Phase Walkers came through as a group. A reptilian, a giant bear with a little girl, a woman with blond hair, a female Celestial, and a strange half-Delvin-Celestial creature. The alarm that detected chaos magic went off but she silenced it and watched on.

The Lady of Light smiled and spoke, her tone was musical and clear, "Thank you Guild Master for personally delivering the order to us, welcome friends of Lorvisa, saviour of our Phase Walkers, Caitlin of the Kelstone plane, Wuzzle of the Kelstone plane, Shandra of the Celestial plane, Alastor of the Celestial plane and Sarah of the Earth plane."

Trigan could not contain himself and felt it was proper protocol to introduce himself, "Greetings Lady of Light, I wish to make myself know to you as you seem to know everyone else."

The Lady of Light, amused, beamed a smile.

"I am Trigan of the Telswan plane, I am also an accomplished Master Worker and I am part of the Master Workers Guild."

The Lady of Light smiled, "Welcome to Lorvisa, I am glad to meet you and that you are part of the Master Workers Guild outworlder, I know little of your plane."

The Guild Master felt a little awkward, Trigan was always the centre of attention, he stepped forward to the chests and clapped his hands using a little phase magic wrapped in light, the chests both opened.

He pointed to the golden chest with a target symbol, then

he spoke, "The order is complete, before you is five hundred stunner rods each wrapped in a null bag for safety and transport."

The Guild Master then moved over to the other opened chest, silver with a lightning bolt symbol, he picked up a null bag carefully untying the string and took out a rod. The rod was black with silver tiny symbols.

"This is the death rod, focus and whatever living thing you want destroyed will turn to ash. There are five hundred of these also," the Guild Master then slipped the rod carefully back into its null bag.

The Lady of Light spoke, "I trust these all have been made correctly Guild Master."

The Guild Master, proud of his guild's work, replied, "Yes indeed, the reputation of the Master Workers Guild is impeccable."

The Lady of Light smiled because she knew this to be true and the Celestial people were good and honest by nature. She motioned her hand and several Lords and Ladies of Illumination took the chests off to the side.

Mixy found herself standing from the bench, little Anita pulled at her dress for her to sit but Mixy moved forward to the chests and the Phase Walkers standing before the Lady of Light.

The Lady of Light spoke in a musical tone, "There is someone here that would really like to meet you," seeing Mixy move forward and smiling like a parent does of a child.

All eyes were on Mixy, there was no recognition on the Phase Walker's faces, she moved to the front of them and smiled, "Hi, I'm your friend Mixy," then waited for a reaction.

Caitlin ran forward and hugged Mixy, Sarah and Shandra smiled and moved forward. Sarah gave Mixy a hug.

Alastor smiled and said, "You're looking lovely Mixy."

Wuzzle waved, missing Mixy, she was his eating buddy, looking at her new form.

The Guild Master, not trying to be rude, spoke, "This is touching even though I don't know Mixy, but a Guild Master's work is never done, I need to get back to the guild hall, do you have my payment?"

The Lady of Light, understanding, motioned a group of Lords of Illumination and they came forward with three brown bags of Knoxcred stones.

The Guild Master spoke, "Thank you Lady of Light, a pleasure doing business, should you require any more of our services do not hesitate to contact me."

The Guild Master turned to look at Trigan, who was looking at Mixy, and spoke, "Can you create some levitation carpets for these, they looked heavy?"

Trigan flashed a grin.

Trigan, happy to be showing off his speciality to such a huge crowd used light magic to summon a small elemental that quickly crafted a magical flying carpet. He motioned the Lords to place the bags of Knoxcred stones on it and stepped back. Levitating the carpet, he then guided it through the phase, with himself following.

At that exact moment another phase opened at the phase point, it had a purple hue.

The Guild Master did not see this and spoke to the Lady of Light, "I will keep you no longer, thank you for your business," and walked into the phase back to the Celestial plane.

At that very moment several Delvin stepped through the purple hued phase, it was growing exponentially fast, bigger than the Celestial phase, almost double its size. At least fifty Delvin stepped through with phase weapons drawn.

The crowd burst into chaos, Lords and Ladies rushed to defend the Lady of Light.

The Lady of Light boomed her voice and it echoed "Kill the Delvin intruders, use the rods," her devotion aurora woke every living creature, every living plant, the message was clear, kill all Delvin.

The guardians of Sky Shade entered the dome their wings making a loud buzzing noise, rushing forward with strange phase weapons, poles with spike and floating pods that burst into fire. The Delvin kept coming through the court of Illumination, which was crowded, the sounds of battle and screams filled the air.

Caitlin let go of Mixy and leaped up to Wuzzle who caught her with a clawed furry hand and placed her on his shoulder. Mixy ran to the Lady of Light to protect her. Shandra spread her wings and took to the air, confused for a time, holding a strange leather bag, then quickly flew into the Celestial phase that was still open and she snapped it shut behind her.

Alastor was annoyed that she did that, he of course could open a new one but that took time. Sarah looked around confused, standing alone, six grey Delvin came towards her with phase weapons raised, they had twisted horns and snarls, Sarah materialised her phase weapon, a Delvin rushed forward about to strike Sarah. Alastor caught eye of this and rushed toward Sarah, picking her up in his strong arms and instinctively called the phase, he went through and so did Sarah, she was in Alastor's Anchor.

Caitlin touched the Raznik in her pocket and knew this was the time to use its other ability. She concentrated and activated it, she felt a zing and so did Wuzzle. They were moving outside time, faster than all around.

Caitlin materialised her phase weapon, the small silvery boomerang and ordered Wuzzle to attack the Delvin, she was moving fast and could easily kill them without any retaliation, it was kind of like a game.

Caitlin slaughtered many Delvin, thinning their numbers as they passed through the purple phase into the Illumination court, a giant blue Delvin was giving her trouble, he was much larger than the rest and was proving problematic to hit with her boomerang, another blue appear at its side, he seemed to be working in unison with it, so she went off to easier targets, as she knew she had to get their numbers down fast to save the Lorvisa people.

Caitlin was not alone, the entire army of Lorvisa was battling the Delvin, a handful had rods of death, a group of giant grasshopper people had a purple Delvin surrounded, he had a bow and arrow and was doing too well shooting several giant grasshoppers to the ground. Caitlin and Wuzzle came forward, then Caitlin threw her boomerang at the purple demonoid, it hit him a few times on the face and he escaped. Annoyed, Caitlin continued her attacks on several other Delvin.

An hour passed and it was still going, you would think that they would retreat, the amount of dead Delvin on the ground was getting ridiculous, there were some dead from Lorvisa but she did not want to see that. Caitlin was relentless, she went into a kill trance; almost every fighting member of Lorvisa had a rod, the waves of Delvin were still coming.

A powerful Delvin in black was causing trouble, he hovered within the court and cast chaos magic mixed with phase power, silvery lightening hit several Lords and Ladies of Illumination. The Lady of Light had left the court many hours ago. Caitlin was getting tired, another wave of Delvin with only three came through, then to her surprise the purple phase snapped shut. The Delvin were slaughtered.

Caitlin activated the Raznik to stop the speeding up of time, she fell off Wuzzle's shoulders and Wuzzle also fell to the ground, they were both unconscious. A few Lords and Ladies came to their side and took their bodies to the Chapter house.

One thing that the people of Lorvisa were good at was using nature magic to heal. The Lady of Light came herself to heal them, their bodies were laid out on plush cushions in a breakout room in the Chapter house. The Lady of Light knelt down to Caitlin and concentrated, placing all four hands on her, a green glow appeared around her body and she healed. The Lady of Light then moved her hands onto Wuzzle, who was warm and furry, she concentrated hard to heal him, she tried her best but there was something she could not fix no matter how she tried, it was a soul string going to Caitlin it was torn and fraying, the Lady of Light was actually worried.

Caitlin sat up from the cushions and looked around, she started to cry out loud, she was in pain, not physical but mental soul pain, her bond to Wuzzle was hanging by a thread, it was close to breaking. She knew she had to go home back to Kelstone, she needed the elders, they would know what to do. Wuzzle stirred and opened his eyes, he seemed confused but Caitlin knew he was perfectly aware of what had happened to him. Wuzzle held out his paw, reaching toward Caitlin and Caitlin put her tiny hand in his. The Lady of Light looked on and offered to help take them to a secluded phase point away from the death and bodies that lay in her Chapter house.

Caitlin accept and the Lady of Light opened an intra-plane phase to a private phase point on Lorvisa. She helped Caitlin stand. Caitlin reluctantly let go of Wuzzles paw, then several Lords and Ladies of Light helped Wuzzle stand. The Lady of Light walked through the phase, Caitlin and Wuzzle followed. Wuzzle walked with a heavy step and Caitlin walked like she was in physical pain.

They were in a well-lit cave, the room was golden and full of treasure, a phase point was there, it was made from a solid piece of gold and could easily be mistaken as treasure, but the symbols that marked it as a phase point were engraved in silver for those who knew its purpose.

Caitlin started to open the phase to Kelstone, the Lady of Light linked to help. A silvery line started to emerge and then the familiar furry blur that was Caitlin's home plane followed. Caitlin held Wuzzle's hand, they waved and walked through the phase. The Lady of Light actually shed a tear as she knew their bond would probably not last to their destination. She felt the raw soul pain and she saw the damage. The phase snapped shut and the Lady of Light returned to the Chapter house.

- Chapter 20 -

Cease Fire

Alastor landed in his Anchor on the edge of his familiar island, Sarah was in his arms, she hid her head under his shoulder and peered around. Alastor let Sarah down from his hold and she stood up then felt awkward. Alastor was tall, Sarah really felt that height walking behind him headed towards a picture perfect cottage, like those Sarah saw in picture magazines or painted on plate collector's plates. Alastor opened the door, walked inside and sat in front of a blue flamed roaring fire, he motioned Sarah to sit beside him, he pulled up a chair to the fire.

Sarah sat on the ornately carved wooden chair and raised an eyebrow at Alastor in an effort to break the silence.

Alastor spoke, looking into the fire, "I don't know why you are here Sarah, and not even my own twin sister can come here."

Sarah looked directly at Alastor, "Well you brought me here, you saved me from the Delvin, opened a phase and we both went through."

Alastor was puzzled and didn't answer for some time.

Sarah spoke again, "Where exactly are we?"

Alastor looked at Sarah, "You are in my Anchor."

"Shandra tried to teach me about my Anchor but we didn't have enough time to go through that, something about each Phase Walker has their own personal plane…"

Alastor finished off Sarah's sentence, "Yes that is correct, personal plane, and I wonder how you got through to mine."

Shandra blushed a little watching the blue flames, "Well maybe there is a reason I can come into your Anchor, and I don't even know how to get to mine."

Alastor, really blinded to any reason, spoke, "Well welcome to my Anchor anyways, this is my cottage, there are fresh fruit trees outside and we are on our own personal island, there is a comfortable bed over there."

Alastor, in shock, stared at the bed, it had changed, it had gone from a single bed to a much bigger one, he didn't recall changing it.

Alastor continued and pointed, "There is a small kitchen and the cupboards are usually filled with food I buy from the Abbith Market, not sure why I am telling you all this, you may not be able to come in here again, perhaps because it was a life and death situation the phase let you in or something weird like that, there are still so many unknown things about Phase Walkers."

Sarah beamed a smile, "Perhaps you could teach me how to go into my Anchor?"

Alastor looked at Sarah, "Perhaps, but I am no teacher, I fight even now with my demon side to even talk to you."

Sarah stood up and moved over to Alastor, she took off his hat, it fell to the floor, and put both her hands on his face, he had a warmness to his blue eyes, then a terrifying stare, he grabbed hold of Sarah's hands and tossed them roughly to the side. Sarah stood back, indignant at what had just happened.

Alastor stood, "I told you what I fight inside, I cannot help these impulses, the Celestial inside fights every minute to be on top of my decisions."

Sarah's mind was racing with thought, she had seen a lot and been through a lot, bugger it I'm going to let the cards fall and see where they land, life is too short.

There has always got to be one to do this if anything was going to advance, she thought, then spoke, "Alastor, I really admire what you have overcome and I'm very attracted to you, if you have not picked that up yet, I'm trying to sort out my feelings for you, they are very strong."

Alastor's eyes looked cold and uncaring, "Sarah I have no such feelings for you, in fact the state I am in, I do not think I will have any feelings for anyone. How can you even say such things, look at me, I am a monster."

Alastor pointed at his horns and swung his tail, "I will not love, I am incapable of it. So any ideas you have need to end. At the best the only thing you can expect from me is to protect you from the Delvin like I protect all Phase Walkers."

Sarah crossed her arms more angry than any other emotion, "Fine then, whatever."

Alastor was happy with her reaction. He picked up his hat and put it back on his head firmly and sat by the fire again, staring at the blue flames.

Sarah stood looking at him, "So how do I get to my Anchor, it's very crowded in here."

Alastor, not looking away from the fire, "Think of a safe haven, then open a phase and walk through, it's that simple. I am surprised my sister mentioned the Anchor and did not tell you the simple details of how to use it."

Sarah, wanting to get away from this man thing before her, thought of a safe haven, she concentrated on the feeling of being safe, even closing her eyes a phase opened very fast, she felt it and opened her eyes. Sarah looked over at Alastor, who was not paying any attention to her and looked deep in concentration staring into the fire. Sarah thought, what's with those damn blue fires and Celestials, it's just weird.

Sarah standing before an open phase spoke, "After I spend some time in my Anchor, I'll go home I guess."

Sarah waited for a reaction for a few moments then walked through the phase, it snapped shut. Alastor, feeling the phase close, turned to see if she was gone. Alastor felt really confused about Sarah, he had only known her for a few moments in time and was sure he felt something for her, and was even more sure that he had to suppress it for the good of all.

There was a loud voice in the distance, "Fuck!"

It was a woman's and sounded familiar and angry. Alastor stood, horrified that someone else was in his Anchor, he walked to the door and looked out, he could see a figure at the edge of his island. Alastor continued out of the cottage then down a path, he could see Sarah.

At the same time Sarah could see Alastor coming down the path, oh he has a smug face she thought, but a cute one, damn why does he have to be so attractive, I can't even stay mad, it's like being mad at superman or something.

Alastor asked, "How did you get here?"

Sarah responded, "Well you asked me to imagine feeling safe and wanting to go to a safe haven, I was thinking about a tropical rainforest actually. Then I walked through the phase and landed here again. I'm so tired I just want to go home to sleep now."

Alastor was a little taken back, Sarah's Anchor was his. This cannot be. Alastor, showing some empathy using all his strength, "Sarah, I know you're tired, please come back inside, I don't know how to explain that you cannot find your own Anchor, rest in the bed then I will show you how to go back to your own plane from here. I do not need to sleep."

Sarah felt she didn't want to rest here and wanted to go now but decided to spend some time with Alastor the demon Ken doll, even if she was sleeping.

Sarah followed Alastor back inside the cottage and even though she was very tired she had to contain herself from bursting out laughing, Alastor had his tail poking out from under his coat it moved like it had a life of its own, funny and weird, Sarah thought and wondered what exactly the tail's purpose was and tried to hold in another laugh.

Alastor went to the cupboard in his kitchen and got out a mug and turned to Sarah, "Do you want a tea before you sleep?"

Sarah replied, "Sure", and went and sat by the fire again.

She was watching Alastor out of the corner of her eye, trying not to let him see. Alastor used light magic to boil water inside a brown jug, well she assumed it was water, then started to use light magic to make another mug, it was huge and did not look as nice as the other mug. He put the newly created one on the table next to other, then sprinkled herbs from a box in the cupboard into the mugs, then poured the steaming contents of the jug into the mugs. He put the jug down on the kitchen table and took both mugs. He passed the funny looking one to Sarah. Sarah looked at her mug, it was not smooth and had a rough feel to it. Alastor sat in his seat holding the other, well-crafted, mug full of tea.

Sarah, feeling indignant, stood from her chair by the fire and walked over to Alastor who raised an eyebrow thinking, oh not this again. Sarah took Alastor's mug from his clawed hand easily and replaced it with her own and sat back down to her chair. Alastor ignored what just happened and sipped from the rough edged mug.

Sarah, satisfied, sipped her large mug of tea, it was actually divine, better than anything she had had at the Chocolate Coffee House and she had pretty much sampled all their herbal teas, nothing tasted like this. A strong herbal infusion with what tasted like sweet caramel honey mixed with a little whisky. Sarah was feeling sleepy with every sip; she wasn't sure if it was the tea or just her body saying you have done too much. She greedily kept sipping almost falling asleep with her last sip. She looked at the fire she was so tired, she dropped the mug, it fell to the ground with a thud.

Alastor was surprised when he looked at Sarah she was in a deep sleep in the chair. He picked up the mug and put it on the kitchen table with his own, went back to Sarah in the chair and studied her for some time, looking at her fine features. She did not wake so he lifted her in his arms and placed her on his cushioned bed, walked back to the kitchen table, filled the smooth mug up to the brim from the jug and sat back by the fire sipping from it and smiling.

The court of Illumination was scattered with bodies of the

fallen, there was a horrible smell in the air from used magic, chaos, nature and light, the death rods also made their targets burn, mixing the smell in with ash and sickly sweet burnt flesh. The Lady of Light was exhausted but it was very important that she was there to oversee the clean up and be a symbol to her people, she sat on her throne with five guards on either side, each wearing a blue tabard and the symbol of Illumination, some had muck spattered on them mixed with blood, others were clean, each Lord and Lady unmoving, intent on guarding the Lady.

A small group of ragtag insectoid creatures came forward, they were of all different races, these were members from the workers of the field, they came before the Lady of Light, bowed and then started to pick up bodies of the fallen Delvin, and then carried them out of the court using the back doors. There were many small groups doing the same. Only the Ladies and Lords of Illumination picked up the fallen of Lorvisa, it was an unspoken honour the people of Lorvisa expected. Their bodies were carried to a burial chamber, it was very full and another was being built, the workers were many, of all different races and houses joining in as a hive.

There was smoke further away as a pile of fallen Delvin were being burnt with nature magic, turning instantly to dust so another pile could begin.

It was some time before the Court of Illumination was looking back to its old self. Guardians of the Sky Shade cleaned the windowed large glass dome from splatterings of blood. Workers of the sun and field used nature magic to grow back patches of the grass and clean patches where the fallen had laid.

All the bodies were removed and the Lady of Light stood, she used her devotion aura and projected a message to the populace, "Greetings all of Lorvisa, I would like to extend my love to you all. A great wrongdoing has occurred today, an evil act, a Delvin army of Phase Walkers entered in the middle of my court and attacked my people. We fought bravely even though it was unexpected, we killed all the Delvin that came through the phase. I did not see any escape but it came at a cost, many of our kind have fallen. I am very said and mourn them."

"Rest, my people, for tomorrow is a new day, we will recover from this and we will avenge our kind and put a stop to these Delvin ever coming into our plane again. Those that have rods place them in their keeping bags. There are still some here in the court, please come and collect them as I do not want any of my people to be injured by accident. Rest a few days and those that require healing please go to the chapter house."

"After a few days another court of Illumination will be in session, this time we will be ready, this time we will go to their plane, bring your weapons."

The Lady of Light collapsed exhausted, the guards rushed forward to her and she slowly disappeared.

The throne room was empty and Morack was looking through his vision pool, he saw the battle, every detail, and the slaughter of his kind, he was not happy but he did see many of the Lorvisa people fall, watching the last wave die.

Morack return to his throne. A phase opened in to throne room, Morack was not alarmed because there was a purple glow, he had since learned that his people made that colour when a phase was opening. What could be described as a ragtag group of adventurers came through the phase, four Delvin, and the phase snapped shut. Grimlock, in a black flowing robe, took a deep breath, his red hair a wild mess, Reednak, a blue with his sword still drawn, cracked his neck to one side, Cayna, with small cuts on his purple skinned arms carrying his bow, tilted his head in a bow and Nica, the large blue that over shadowed them all, stood silently.

Morack looked at them and spoke, "So this is all that remains of the army that was sent through, my hunters."

Grimlock who positioned himself as the leader of the hunters spoke, "My Lord Morack, we have dealt the Lady of

Light a massive blow, I know the cost was high but we only took three quarters of our army."

Morack was indifferent, he was not pleased or that upset, so the outcome was what he was expecting, satisfied he felt a ping of happiness. That would have to do before his new brood mother hatched and he had more numbers, the other quarter of his army would stay on as guards till then.

Morack spoke harshly to Grimlock, "How many Phase Walkers did you capture?"

Proudly Grimlock replied, "We filled all the cages in your new holding cell, each Phase Walker has been fitted with the null bands, they cannot activate the phase. We did it pretty much unnoticed, it was easy to work out which ones were Phase Walkers because they all wore blue tabards. We have some really weird looking ones too this time."

Morack smiled, "Good I don't think I've had this many Phase Walkers before, I'm going to be busy, very busy indeed."

Caitlin and Wuzzle arrived at the Kelstone phase point, Caitlin quickly opened an intra-phase point to the veil, she was in so much pain. Both Wuzzle and herself stepped through. In a panic she started to rip the veil quickly, not a nice cut, she didn't bother to close it behind herself and she ran staggering into her village, "Help me," she cried.

This caused a ruckus, several Kelstone villagers come running and some bonded animals. Heading to the Elders hall, she spoke to those that started to follow her, "Get the druids, my bond to my Arktos is almost broken, I am in pain."

A few villagers, wide eyed, went running to fetch druids; a bonded animal ran to the village Chief. Caitlin ran into the village hall, she stood in the room, she could still feel Wuzzle she stared at him and spoke, "It's going to be alright, they will help us."

Two druids walked into the hall with a few villagers that had fetched them. They walked to Caitlin, one started to cast an investigative look at her bond with nature magic. His eyes went wide and he asked the villager behind him to fetch the other druids, he had kind eyes and wore a brown robe, he smelt like lavender and spoke, "I can hold your bond until the others get here Caitlin, it will require several druids to repair."

Wuzzle looked comforted, he could feel the bond with Caitlin, it was faint but it did not feel like it was shredded, it did not feel like tiny fibres of it were coming loose as before., it just felt distant like when Caitlin left him to go shopping. Caitlin hugged Wuzzle and buried her face in his fur. The Chief entered with two other druids, there were five in the hall now.

The village Chief of Fas spoke, "Caitlin what goes on here?" he looked at the other druid who was in concentration holding the bond.

"I'll explain later but my bond with my Arktos is almost broken, can you fix it, please?"

The Chief, not looking pleased, took the hand of the druid concentrating and motioned the others to join in, several more druids arrived and they all linked hands, linking their nature magic. The bond was thickening and growing stronger with every moment, Caitlin in every moment was feeling more aware of Wuzzle, she could hear his breathing and felt he was at ease.

Wuzzle in turn could feel Caitlin stronger, he knew she was worried and that she was not looking forward to talking to the village Chief.

There was a glow around them both, it was the feeling she knew when she was bonded as a child, excitement and euphoria went through her body. Then sleep, she slowly fell to the ground, Wuzzle slowly sat on the ground and curled over. The druid circle unlinked and the village Chief asked them to take Caitlin and Wuzzle into the spare room in the hall. In the room off the hall there was a small bed which they placed Caitlin on and a rug on the floor Wuzzle was placed on. Just as the Chief closed the door an elder druid came up to the Chief and spoke in a whisper, "Caitlin cut some of the veil, we are exposed."

"By the stones," the Chief responded and walked with a few druids back to the veil and then started to close it and thought, little good it will do anyway because it does not hide Phase Walkers.

The elders were summoned to a meeting while Caitlin slept. The table was full inside the Village hall and decisions were made, it was clear once Caitlin wakes in a few hours they would ask her to leave the village. An elder druid with kind eyes and a brown robe asked that she stay to recover a few days to ensure the bond had healed but it was overturned. The elders left the hall and the Chief sat on his chair thinking, waiting for her to wake, what have you been up to Caitlin?

Hours passed and Caitlin woke up in a straw bed, she felt for her bond to Wuzzle straight away and it was there, stronger than ever, she was so happy. Wuzzle was at her feet still sleeping, she did not recognise the room but knew she was in her village, she felt her pocket for the Raznik, it was still there. She got out of bed and stretched, she had a kink in her back and looked back at the bed, ugh it was straw, she thought, then realised she should bring back a mattress from Earth, they are by far more the most comfortable in the known planes, ah pillow tops, she thought.

Caitlin smiled when looking at Wuzzle and walked quietly out of the room so she didn't wake him. Wuzzle opened one eye, grinned and closed it again, he did not want to hear what the Chief was going to say.

Caitlin was in the main hall, the Chief was sitting at the elders table alone, Caitlin walked up to the table and sat joining him, she smiled.

The Chief played with his many chains around his neck and glared through his wise blue eyes, "Caitlin what are you smiling about, you put us at risk today, you do realise you cannot stay?"

Caitlin looked sad, "I know, but it was an emergency, your only Phase Walker was going to suffer the unbonding, and you know what torture that would be and even worse for a Phase Walker."

The Chief responded, "I'm not without compassion, I do understand, but I need to know how this happened?"

Caitlin put her hand in her pink pocket and took out a green triangle gem and placed it on the table, "The Raznik, I used it in battle on the Lorvisa plane to speed up time and fight the Delvin that attacked its kind people."

The Chief picked up the Raznik and stared at it, "Losing your bond to your Arktos should not have happened, perhaps being a Phase Walker as well interfered. Do not use it that way again."

The Chief placed the gem back on the table and pushed it toward Caitlin.

"I trust that its healing properties are working well for you?"

"Oh yes I have used it many times," Caitlin replied and placed the Raznik back in her pocket.

The Chief smiled, "I'm sorry to rush you but you know you have to leave. I suggest you go back to your house and spend a night or two before you enter the phase again."

Caitlin sighed, "Yes Chief."

Wuzzle was at the door, he had overheard the end of the conversation and walked towards Caitlin. The Chief stood and followed Caitlin outside. Many elders were on the street, they stood and waved, some cheered, and a few villagers gave Caitlin and Wuzzle flowers. Caitlin waved and moved towards to veil and started the nature magic to split it.

The Chief interrupted and said, "Oh perhaps I should do that, I just want a neat cut, easier to repair."

Caitlin looked confused and let him take over, the veil was spilt and she walked though, so did Wuzzle who was carrying a bunch of fresh Earth flowers. Roses and Baby's Breath, Caitlin recognised them because she had planted them.

She turned to look at the veil the Chief waved, "I'll summon you when we will lift the veil, please look after yourself," then closed the veil neatly.

Caitlin's village was gone.

Even though the veil closed Caitlin was happy because her bond with Wuzzle was there. She dared not use the phase even for intra-phase travel until she rested, she didn't want to risk anything happening to her refreshed bond with Wuzzle, so she walked through the forest looking at the trees with their green curly loop at the top of each and curly loops in the bushes, a hall mark that she was on her home plane, Kelstone. She headed towards her dwelling by the pond. She remembered the mess outside her house, perhaps she would do some nesting. It took quite a while before she came to the pond, getting nearer she could see her mound and then could see her yard had been cleaned up.

Her broken chairs were crudely repaired with vine and lined up under the table that had a new wooden top. The fire pit was remade and pretty shiny stones circled it, they looked like they had been shaped that way from the sea. There were fresh flowers planted either side of her front door, that was not what she remembered. There was a nice smell coming from inside though she did not recognise what it was.

Caitlin slowly opened the door it swung outwards, Wuzzle was behind her. The room was different and neat. A strange black boy stopped stirring a pot on the fireplace and came running forward. To Caitlin's shock he wore a pink skirt!

The boy spoke, "Hello Caitlin, I have been waiting here for you, hoping you would return soon."

Caitlin gasped, recognising who the boy was, "Jas, is that you?"

Jas nodded, "Yes, I have two legs now and I wanted to talk to you about the Delvin."

Caitlin, taking this all in, scanned the room. Her IKEA bed had a straw mattress, she poked out her bottom lip. Her pink blankets had been crudely sewn together with green thread. Her collection of cards was neatly presented and everything was neat and tidy. There was a strange collection of shells on the side table.

Caitlin put a bunch of flowers down on the table, so did Wuzzle who sat down against the wall.

Jas looked at the flowers, "Oh let me do something with these," he studied them, "these land flowers I have not seen before, I have been learning them in my spare time."

Jas then placed the huge bunch in a strange glass bubble of water and moved them off to the side bench.

Caitlin spoke, "They're actually from Earth, so not of this plane, well they were grown on this plane but I got the seeds from Earth."

Jas grabbed his dark hair and put it back over his shoulders, even though he was just a boy he was still taller than Caitlin, "Would you like something to eat, I have been boiling clams?"

Caitlin sniffed, "Can't say I have eaten clams before but willing to give it a try, Wuzzle is hungry too, then we really need to rest and sleep. We can have a big talk afterwards."

Jas, happy, started to serve his clams.

Shandra was not feeling herself, the purple stone was all that she could think of. She congratulated the Guild Master on a successful trade and did not mention the Delvin phase point but she mentioned that the others were more than likely enjoying the Lady of Light's hospitality.

The Guild Master was so happy about the Knoxcred stones he just waved her goodbye. A handful of Master Workers surrounded him and the stones, there was a lot of excitement in the air because the Guild Master could start setting plans in motion.

Shandra, paid no attention and unnoticed, walked up the stairs to the landing platform. She was not going to be rude and leap into the air from a window, not very dignified, landing platforms were built for a reason. She stood for a few moments feeling the air above the floating guild hall, stretched her golden feathered wings and took to the air for a time then started to descend to the Abbith market, she needed to talk to a certain vendor about the purple stone.

Jenith entered the guild hall, he had not been in a while but the Guild Master had summoned him. He looked very sickly, but it was unnoticed as cheers were heard and he was also mobbed by other Master Workers like some sort of hero. Jenith thought it was over the top but his eyes sharpened when he saw the stones.

Landing in the Abbith market away from the crowds, Shandra sidestepped vendors and buyers carrying baskets and hovering their goods in the air. She went deep into the market and walked for some time until she came to a silvery brown building, it did not have any sign that marked its entrance and there was a strong smell of herbs coming from within. Shandra walked up a few stairs and entered.

The herbal smell was overpowering, a Celestial with silvery grey wings walked up and smiled, "May I interest you in herbs, spices?"

"Where is Jenith?" Shandra asked.

The grey winged Celestial hushed her and walked her to the back room and spoke, "He's not here, he's been summoned to the Master Workers Guild hall."

Shandra's eyes went wide she had been just there, and then thought it was probably for the best he did not acknowledge her. Shandra, holding the pouch that contained the purple stone, spoke, "Tell him I will be by here tomorrow, we need to talk."

The grey winged Celestial replied, "Okay, I hope all is well."

With that Shandra left the building and opened an intra-phase to Remiel House.

Walking into Remiel House, Yanni greeted her, she was mad and confronted Yanni, "You! Why must you follow me, I do not require your protection."

Yanni glowed blue and was currently free from any bonds of chaos magic, "Shandra, I will stop you, you cannot do these things, you need to stop communicating with the stone, I will not allow you to bind me again or send Alastor back to the Delvin."

Shandra's eyes went wide, she was unaware that Yanni knew this much and she realised that Yanni must be destroyed.

Yanni in that moment knew that she was in danger so she did what she hadn't done in a long, long time, she phased out and phased back into a safe spot a place where she knew she could work out what to do. Yanni spoke but one final word, "Daughter."

- Chapter 21 -

Knoxcred

Caitlin awoke from a very deep sleep, she really needed it, and she felt as fresh as ever, until she sat up.

"Ouch," she touched a kink in her back, "oh how I dislike straw beds."

Jas was awake and was cooking up some kind of grain for breakfast, it smelt divine, Caitlin thought. Wuzzle was already eating a bowl, she wondered how many he had had. Jas looked over and saw Caitlin, "Morning to you."

Caitlin smiled, "Morning to you Jas, that smells so nice, what is it?"

Jas happily replied, "Sea grain, I bought a sack from my village market this morning."

Caitlin replied, "Oh how we need to talk Jas, put a bowl of that nice sea grain over here, that would be lovely."

Caitlin felt a spark of phase come from Jas, sitting at the table she turned and watched him and felt for the phase to confirm. Oh, he's a Phase Walker, oh, how we need to talk.

Jas was still wearing a strange pink skirt that he fashioned from Caitlin blankets, Caitlin made a mental list, we have to fix that too. Jas put a full bowl in front of Caitlin and passed her a teddy bear spoon.

Caitlin picked up the spoon, "I really love these spoons, they remind me of Wuzzle, an Earth thing, ever been there?"

Jas looked at Caitlin confused, "No, why would you say that?"

Caitlin took a lovely mouthful, "Well things have changed for you Jas, how about you sit down and tell me how you have two legs and why you're here?"

Jas knew this conversation was going to happen, he anticipated it for a while now he didn't feel like it, he sat at the table never-the-less.

"A few of the elder villagers and my family's friends think that the shock of losing my family triggered my coming of age ability early. It's natural once a Persidion comes of age around thirty to seek a mate and we get the ability to transform into a two legs, also it's a rite of passage for males to explore being on land before settling down with a family in an underwater village."

"It's not without responsibility, I must return to the sea every month on a high tide or I will lose the ability and become a two legs permanently. I must admit that part really scares me, I am only twelve years old, so I have been returning to the water almost daily to visit the village. I have been a bit worried to go too far on land and decided to come here and wait for you, as you were father's only land friend."

Jas paused and studied Caitlin's reaction. Caitlin who just listened and ate from the bowl didn't act surprised. Caitlin wiped her mouth and looked over at Wuzzle who put down an empty bowl.

"Wow Jas, I had no idea your people could do that. Could you please give Wuzzle another bowl, he's still a little hungry."

Jas, a little taken back by the reaction, took the bowl, filled it and gave it to Wuzzle, then sat at the table again.

Caitlin smiled, "Thank you so much Jas, but I know there is more to this story."

Jas looked up, thinking she might know of his revenge on the demons, and spoke, "Well I wanted you to help me in avenging my family's death and to slay the demons that did this. I also want to recover artefacts from the village, Ianoid stones, the elders in the village are missing them, I was told I would know them if I saw them."

Caitlin finished her bowl and stretched, "I know there is still more Jas?"

Jas looked confused, "What do you mean Caitlin?"

Caitlin smiled, "You're a Phase Walker."

Jas was puzzled, "What do you mean?"

"I feel the phase all around you Jas. Concentrate on ones, this symbol—," she licked her finger and made a one in salvia down a part of the wooden table.

Jas closed his eyes and concentrated, really not knowing what to expect.

Caitlin reached out and he joined her phase energy. Caitlin released it and spoke, "Oh, you're so a Phase Walker."

"Well Jas two legs you're in luck because I happen to be helping my friends kill Delvin, they are the creatures that attacked your village. I just returned from a huge battle with them. We also rescued people from their attacks. I'm sure they would be happy to have another Phase Walker join. But you will need to train in the phase, you also need to keep returning here every few weeks to go in the water to keep your tail. That's going to require extra thought because sometimes, time is different in some of the planes. I have an Earth friend Sarah that uses her watch and phone to keep track of her home plane time. Earth is a very scheduled place all running on time. I was actually thinking of going on a shopping run to Earth, I should buy you some things before you start phase walking, don't want you to lose track of time, Jas two legs forever sounds scary."

Jas in that moment knew all the weeks of waiting had been worth it. Caitlin was going to help him with everything, he was so relieved.

"Thank you Caitlin, I knew father had you as a friend for a reason."

Caitlin smiled, "Your father was a very good friend, don't worry I will look after you, oh, and you need some two leg clothes as well. I can get them for you when I go to Earth, oh, and shoes. I want you to stay here, I shouldn't be too long but if there are any signs of trouble run, ok, do not fight, you haven't been shown your cool Phase Walker abilities yet."

Jas quickly spoke, "Shouldn't you show me before you go?"

Caitlin looked over at the straw mattress on her IKEA bed frame, "Did you make that bed Jas?"

Jas smiled, "Yes I mended it, it was broken."

"Oh, I don't think I could stand another night's sleep on straw, it's okay, I will be back soon, I should probably be leaving. I feel refreshed and my old self."

Wuzzle stood and Caitlin had a skip in her step, she loved to shop. Caitlin opened a phase point right in her house, it was silvery then expanded to a blurry patch in the room, it hung freestanding. Caitlin turned and waved, then walked through the phase, Wuzzle followed along, then it snapped shut.

Jas was amazed, he ran to the spot the phase had opened in and walked around it, feeling it with his hands, but it was gone. His body had stopped feeling tingly. Jas tidied up the bowls and started to pack away the breakfast mess, he was so happy.

Jenith was tired, they had moved and set up his entire lab in the Guild hall. All his equipment was spread out on benches and labelled. He had been the centre of attention all day, at first it felt great to be looked upon by your peers as a knowledge base for everything Knoxcred, but all the questions were draining. He was excited that the Guild Master assigned him five apprentices and two of them senior, also several Master Workers who had specialities that can help him with his research stepped forward as volunteers. His research was now under the spotlight and he knew if he needed any support the Guild Master would give it.

Looking around the Guild hall, Jenith waved at the Guild Master who started for his direction, leaving a deep conversation he was having with a few Master Workers. The Guild Master looked up and smiled, "I trust everything you need is here Jenith."

Jenith's crystal blue eyes looked tired and he replied, "Guild Master, I have had enough for the day, I will return in the morning."

The Guild Master smiled and touched Jenith's shoulder, "Get some rest," then walked back to the Master Workers he had been talking to previously.

Jenith walked the stairs to the landing platform on the roof of the Guild hall, he painfully spread his jet black feathered wings and took flight, descending into the Abbith Market.

Jenith was a gemmologist, it was his Master Worker speciality, he used his light magic to identify and use properties in magical gemstones. He would acquire many findings from other planes through Phase Walker traders in the Abbith market. Jenith had a small laboratory under a herb shop, he rarely sold any of his gemstones unless they were useless, he prided himself on his collection of magical and rare stones.

A silvery brown building came into sight, Jenith started to cough, a little blood trickled down his mouth, he licked it and walked up the stairs, there was a strong smell of herbs coming from within.

A Celestial with silvery grey wings walked up and smiled, "You had a visitor, a beautiful Celestial woman wanting to see you, she said she will come back today."

Amused that someone wanted to see him, because every Master Worker in the guild today did, he sighed and replied, "Really? Me, a visitor, I don't know why, but what's left of my lab is a mess and I really need to get some sleep. Wake me if the visitor comes back, okay Topaz?"

A female Celestial with a small male child walked in. Topaz smiled and waved at Jenith, "I will, excuse me, I have a customer."

Jenith walked tiredly down the stairs to his laboratory which was also his dwelling. Most of his equipment had been moved into the guild hall, there were many people in here today helping with the move. He did not so much mind his stuff moved to the hall, but it really taxed him of his energy. He noticed a notebook of his findings was just laid out on the floor, he picked it up then sat on his plush white cushioned bed, it was made of the finest materials and was so soft, there were veils of soft whisper material hanging from the ceiling. The notebook he held out and flicked through the pages, this notebook was old and written some time ago.

There was a knock on his door, what now, he thought and opened the door using light magic. Shandra was at the door, she looked ethereal, her long golden hair and blue eyes, the same as her twin's eyes. She walked forward to Jenith seductively.

Jenith put his hands up, "Shandra, this is a surprise visit, what brings you here?"

Shandra spoke in a musical voice, "Jenith, do I need an excuse?"

Jenith smiled, his dark tanned features made him very attractive, "I guess you don't, but I have had a very long day."

Shandra sat down next to Jenith on his bed and lent over to stroke his face, "I missed you."

Jenith was puzzled at her seduction, he was always here and she knew that, if he remembered rightly a few weeks back Shandra saw him in the Abbith market and walked right past him without any acknowledgment. Jenith went cold and spoke, "What do you want Shandra?"

Shandra sat up straight and looked at him, "I need your help," she unwrapped a leather pouch and a revealed a purple gem.

Jenith stood up, "What are you doing with that, you stole it from me, it has a captured soul inside, I never did work out whose. You must have taken it out of my glass containment case."

Shandra smiled, "I would like to say borrowed, but I don't want it anymore, it takes over sometimes, I want you to help me be free of it."

Jenith had another coughing fit and his body shook.

Shandra really was not a bad person; she really wanted to get rid of the stone. In a panic she held the stone to Jenith face, "Who is in the stone, whose soul is inside?"

Jenith put his hand up to push Shandra away and blood trickled down his mouth in a big gush. Shandra was getting frustrated he didn't answer, then the stone answered, 'Shandra, my you're curious, if you wanted to know who I was you had only to ask, I am Zuel, king of the Delvin people, now that black winged Celestial knows too much, you have exposed me, finish him and leave here, we have a lot of work to do.'

Shandra did not know if the voice spoke out loud or in her head, but she looked at Jenith and he was already on the ground covered in blood, she did not know how he got that way so she fled as swiftly as she could, almost knocking the grey winged celestial over. She took to the streets and opened a phase to Remiel House.

Jas was outside Caitlin's house, he wanted to show gratitude and the only thing a twelve year old boy could do was to help around the house, so he did. He made a little pearly white fence around her new front garden, it was made out of sea materials, it looked like the inside of shells. Her new little front garden had flowers all lined up in pretty colours. Jas was just planting some more when he heard a big crash inside the house, his body started to tingle. He dropped a flowering plant and ran into to the house. A phase was open, he could see things being thrown into the room and an occasional glimpse of a fuzzy clawed brown hand, a few more items then Caitlin stepped through followed by Wuzzle, the phase snapped shut. Jas's first thought after the tingling left his body was, what a mess.

Caitlin smiled and waved, "Hi Jas, as you can see we went shopping, let's get this big thing out of the way first. Don't take offense but this is a pillow top, ah, a pillow top. I will show you, Wuzzle take this outside please."

Caitlin pointed to the roughly put together straw mattress, Wuzzle picked it up over his shoulder, tiny pieces of straw fell from it and floated to the ground, Jas gasped.

Caitlin spoke, "Jas help me with this, you will like it, it's called a pillow top."

Both Jas and Caitlin put Caitlin's new mattress on her IKEA bed.

Jas then lay on the bed, "Oh I see what you mean, nice."

Caitlin laughed and passed Jas a few things and he sat up, "This is a diver's watch, you can wear it underwater too, I'll show you later how to track the days, this is two legs clothes, um, what you are wearing isn't really high fashion," Caitlin pointed to Jas's pink skirt.

Jas just looked blankly at Caitlin, not really understanding all that was said, Caitlin started to put the watch on his wrist and play with settings, smiled, then continued, "Well go on over there and get into that two leg outfit, I bought designer too, and these, they go on your feet."

Caitlin relaxed on her pillow top, oh how I missed you, she thought and rested a moment.

Jas tapped Caitlin on the shoulder, "Like this?"

Jas had put the clothes on perfectly and looked really cute for a kid, she was happy he even put his socks and shoes on correctly.

"Great! You look perfect, ready to go to Remiel House I would say. Are you ready? I don't really want to hang around here long, Phase Walkers emit a phase energy which can give our location away. Much safer on the Celestial plane at the moment."

Jas looking down at his shoes then tossed his black jet hair, "Okay, I guess I want to be safe and want to fight the Delvin with you Caitlin."

Caitlin responded, "Yes fighting Delvin and such, probably some introductions and eating first when we arrive, link with me."

A phase opened in Caitlin's house, Wuzzle walked back with straw through his fur. Caitlin sighed, and picked a few pieces out, "Let's go!"

Caitlin walked through the phase, Wuzzle followed and Jas without hesitation walked right through, they were at the phase point in Kelstone, at a tree with symbols. Caitlin naturally linked with Jas, she wondered if it was because they were from the same plane that it was so easy to link with him. She opened the phase to the Celestial plane in the Abbith Market. They all walked through, Jas was very wide eyed.

The market was a bustle of people, there seemed to be more than normal and the vendors seemed to be loud, trying to get the crowd's attention as they called their wares on the street. Caitlin told Wuzzle she wanted to walk because Jas was short too, only a hand or two taller. Caitlin took the long route through the market because Jas was enjoying the carts and stores, he gasped at floating glass display boxes, ate a sample of some berries offered to him and was in awe at the perfectness to detail everything was, he even studied the pebbled path for a few moments, looking at the stones line up.

Caitlin smiled and said, "Okay, just over here is a good spot to open an intra-phase to Remiel House, I like to aim for the front door, link with me."

Caitlin opened a phase naturally linking with Jas, it opened and they both walked through with Wuzzle trailing behind.

Jas could not believe how big the house was, he still was excited seeing the wonders of Abbith market. The door to Remiel House opened and Yanni glowed blue brightly, Jas was a little taken back, he watched for a time and Caitlin spoke, "Jas, this is Yanni, if you need anything don't be afraid to ask Yanni for it in your time here, Yanni, Jas needs a room please."

Yanni spoke, "I will ready a room for Jas, please come in, only Shandra is home, I will let her know you are here."

Yanni buzzed down the hall. Caitlin and Jas headed for the main room.

Shandra was in her bedroom, thinking, when she heard

the knock on her door, she opened it and Yanni was there, Shandra growled, "Go away, what do you want?"

Yanni spoke calmly, "We have visitors. Caitlin, Wuzzle and Jas."

Who, Shandra thought, and then composed herself and walked into the main room.

Caitlin was settled at the wooden main table and she had a little friend, a very dark skinned boy, he was jet black including his hair, his eyes had a green shine in them. He was smiling.

Shandra spoke in a regal tone, "Good afternoon Caitlin, I trust you are well," waiting to be introduced.

Caitlin happily replied, "This is my friend Martin's son I told you about, he is also a Phase Walker, we just found out."

Shandra gasped, "Another youngling, how do you find all these Phase Walkers Caitlin?"

This was the first time it really was pointed out to her, she thought for a few moments, "I don't know, just lucky I guess. Can you teach him Shandra, he wants to help fight the Delvin?"

Shandra, a little drained of her new role as teacher of the phase children put on a smile, "I guess, but we start tomorrow, I wish to rest."

Shandra left the room, Yanni hovered over the table. Jas, watching Shandra walk away, thought she looked beautiful, her lovely blue eyes and golden wings, he wished so much that he could have wings. A yellow glow surrounded Jas and he started to change, his eyes turned a lighter green and he grew wings, bright fluffy white wings. Caitlin couldn't believe her eyes, she stood back from Jas, away from the table.

"Jas, what's happening?" Caitlin was concerned, could this have to do with his two leg ability.

Jas was confused and stretched his white wings, flexing them, "Is this the phase Caitlin?"

Caitlin looked at Wuzzle, who was not reacting, "No this is not the phase, I don't know what to tell you Jas."

Jas responded, "I know I did this, but I do not know how

to change back."

Jas certainly looked stunning and sharp, the bright white wings contrasted to his pitch black body and hair Caitlin thought.

Yanni glowed brightly and announced, "Your room is next to Caitlin's and is ready whenever you need it, are you hungry?"

Jas nodded, "Yes, I am very hungry."

Yanni materialised a feast of seafood served on a shell plate and placed it in font of Jas, who folded in his outstretched wings then started to eat the meal before him, he was very impressed. Yanni materialised a pizza with pepperoni and cheese for Caitlin, she started to eat it and think.

Ethan was at Estel's dwelling, he was offered a real meal this time with her family, he ate up big and followed Estel into the cushioned room. Estel was carrying two glasses and a bottle of honey mead. She sat next to the low lying table and poured two glasses and offered one to Ethan. Ethan took one and took a sip, he was really happy, he hadn't felt this way ever!

His brother's return, the Master Workers' order filled and the excitement of the Knoxcred stones, and best of all the attentions of Estel. At first he had Trigan as a rival, but soon realised that he was just her friend, it was him she wanted. Strangely Ethan, in a fleeting moment, thought of Sarah, her long blond hair and tanned skin. Estel spoke, breaking his thoughts, and he smiled, happy at this moment in time. Estel took out a small glass dome and put it on the table, a little eco system was inside the dome, a small deer creature came out from behind a bush and leaped into a puddle of water, it splashed itself then jumped back to the bush again.

Ethan laughed, Estel spoke, "Cute, isn't it, but it was kind of a mistake, perhaps it's something you can fix Ethan. I was not aware it was in the forest, it was captured by mistake. I have not made living creatures small before, I do not know how to fix it or even if the deer was created with light magic."

Ethan smiled because he was confident that he could fix this problem, "Estel this is why we are good for one another, we complement each other. Let us fix this problem tomorrow when I am less drunk."

Estel laughed, "Yes, of course," and passed out, sleeping on the cushions.

Well this is awkward, Ethan thought and put his glass down, stood, kissed Estel on the cheek and left the room. On the way out he waved to Morwen and spoke, "Estel is taking a sleep, too much honey mead."

Morwen frowned, "Okay, well I hope you had a good time Ethan," and waved.

Ethan was a little tipsy and left the shop, he took to the air and headed to Remiel House, it was mid-afternoon and the sun was setting. It was a nice flight, he couldn't wait to come back tomorrow and show Estel how great he was using his light magic to fix her problem.

Ethan could see Remiel House and descended lower to arrive at its front step. Yanni did not open the door so Ethan did and within he heard laughter of children inside. Walking down the hall into the main room he saw a strange Celestial child, perhaps that honey mead was too strong, he thought, trying to clear his head, nope he's still there, and Caitlin laughed. Caitlin turned and waved to Ethan, Jas looked in his direction and smiled.

Caitlin spoke, "Good afternoon Ethan, this is Jas, he's Martin's son, my friend I have told you about."

Ethan smirked, "I'm confused, I thought Martin was a Persidion, he looks Celestial."

Jas flexed his white wings.

Caitlin continued, "Oh he is but he also has a few abilities of his own, did I mention he's also a Phase Walker."

Ethan, astounded, "What! Why is everyone a Phase Walker except me? Anyway welcome to Remiel House, I need my sleep."

Ethan headed for his room looked around for Yanni and didn't see it.

- Chapter 22 -

Wings

Sarah awoke inside Alastor's Anchor, she sat up from a great sleep and saw him sitting by the fire drinking from her mug, the smooth one. She wondered how long she had slept for.

"Hello Alastor," Sarah said from the bed.

Alastor stood with his mug and came and sat on the end of the bed, "I was worried, you had a long sleep, eight hours I think."

Sarah shrugged, "That's normal."

Alastor offered the mug to Sarah, who accepted it and took a sip. Alastor spoke, "I think we should both go back to Remiel House and see if everyone is okay."

Sarah looked deep into his eyes, sensing how close he was to her, "You are right, sorry I sleep so much, it's a human thing."

Alastor raised an eyebrow, "I need to remember that."

Sarah asked, "And why's that?"

Alastor sat back a little on the bed, "Well, we do share an Anchor, I don't know how else to explain it."

Sarah took another sip and looked into the mug, "Do you figure there is a reason for that?"

Alastor, sitting straight backed, his black horns poking through his hair, answered, "No."

Sarah looked up at him and he was intensely looking at her with his light blue eyes, "Alastor, there is something you need to know, when I first manifested my Phase Walker ability I went into the Nevid plane, it was the first time I had phase walked. You were in that plane, don't you find that strange."

Alastor, knowing what she was trying to say, warmed his face and smiled, "Sarah I cannot reject that we have some sort of bond, sharing an anchor has pointed that out, I am not sure why you were drawn to the Nevid plane but I cannot possibly have feelings for you, I am part demon, but there is something more I can give you–"

He paused for a while, staring into her eyes.

Sarah asked, "What is that, Alastor?"

Alastor rubbed his hand through his white blond hair, "I can give you this, a promise that I am yours to command. But nothing more, it's the best I can do, I am a demon Sarah."

Sarah replied, "I accept that promise."

She smiled and the light reflected in her green eyes, Alastor could not deny a warmness went to his heart at that moment, he then stood from the bed and held out his arm to Sarah.

"We should get back to Remiel House."

Sarah took his arm and stood. She shook out her blond hair and Alastor took the mug from her hand and placed it on his kitchen bench like it was made of gold.

Sarah asked, "So how do we open a phase from here without a physical phase point, oh and is that mug important for some reason?"

Alastor replied with a sad smile, "It was my mother's, she crafted it herself."

Sarah, wide eyed, replied "Oh, it was very nice to hold."

Alastor took Sarah through an exercise in her mind, imagining the symbols, explained that it will only work in her anchor, nowhere else, you need a physical phase point to go from plane to plane. They linked together and opened a phase to Abbith market, they both walked though.

The Abbith market was busy for this time of the afternoon, Sarah grabbed Alastor's clawed hand and she guided him through the crowd to a side street. Alastor tried to let go, feeling the intensity of her gasp. Sarah turned, noticing, and said, "I command you to hold my hand."

Alastor laughed, "This is not what I meant."

They both opened a phase to Remiel House and they both stepped through.

Sarah released Alastor's hand and they both walked through the front door that Yanni did not open, that was unusual, Alastor thought, and worried, thinking of the chaos band around Yanni he found a few times. He still had not gotten to the bottom of it, but he suspected his sister, though he had no proof.

They walked into the main hall, Caitlin and a strange celestial boy sat at the table.

Caitlin smiled, "Hello Sarah and Alastor, this is Jas."

Sarah knew who Jas was but it didn't register, "Have we met before?"

Caitlin had almost forgotten Jas's transformation, "Yes you have, this is Jas, Martin's son, he has an ability to transform himself, he's also a Phase Walker, he wants to help us with the Delvin."

Alastor spoke up, "I'm pleased that you are here to help, I did not know your father but Caitlin spoke well of him."

Sarah spoke softly, "Jas, I knew your father for a short time, I am very sorry what had happened to him and your family, I gladly welcome your company. If I can help you in any way just ask."

Sarah smiled kindly.

Caitlin continued, "Glad you two made it out of the battle okay, I did see you go through a phase so I wasn't worried. Where did you go?"

Sarah looked at the ground and that left Alastor to answer, "Into a safe phase, did you get out okay Caitlin?"

Caitlin smiled, proud of herself, "Hmm, I take it you're not going to tell me what plane, fine. Well I am a hero among the Lorvisa people, I stayed to the end, until I could fight no longer. I destroyed many Delvin until I was mortally wounded then I had to return to my village to get healed, that's when I found Jas in my house waiting for me. I found out he was a Phase Walker and brought him here. The Lady of Light is going to strike again, she will send word if she needs us, I assume."

Sarah's mouth was wide open, "But wait, you stayed? The rest of us left, oh I feel bad, you got hurt? You look fine Caitlin."

Wuzzle snorted loudly, everyone looked in his direction, he spoke in a deep regal voice, "We got very lucky, I don't think we will push ourselves again like that, will we Caitlin?"

Caitlin, surprised Wuzzle spoke, continued, "Yes I am sorry Wuzzle, it will not happen again, what happened to us was bad, you may not see the wound but it was deep on the inside. My bond to Wuzzle was almost destroyed in battle but we were saved thanks to the Lady of Light and my elders from Kelstone."

Jas was also wide eyed because he did not know the full story, this was the first time it was explained.

Alastor walked over to the fire and sat down. Sarah walked over to the fire and joined him, Alastor raised an eyebrow, then stared into the flame, then asked loudly, "Where is everyone else?"

Caitlin frowned, "Hey you two, it's rude to turn your back on someone you want to talk to."

Alastor turned his chair, "I'm sorry Caitlin, indeed it is, the fire calms my inner demon."

Sarah got up and walked back to the table and sat next to Caitlin. Sarah whispered to Caitlin, "Company is better with you anyways."

Caitlin spoke, "Well, let me see, your sister is cranky and in her room, I don't know why because she went into the phase after the Guild Master and Trigan entered, I'm pretty sure those two were unaware of the Delvin attack because the phase opened after they left but Shandra knew. I'm sure Shandra closed that phase too, leaving us to our own defences. Maybe you can talk to her Alastor she is your twin,

I just expected her to help that's all. Something's different with her, not the Shandra I remember."

Alastor, feeling a little defensive, spoke, "Maybe she panicked because I sure did when I saw Sarah surrounded by a handful of demons, that's why we both went fast into a phase."

Shandra, almost on key, entered the room, "Did I hear my name?"

Caitlin spoke, a little agitated, "Yes you did actually, I was wondering why you closed the phase behind you, blocking us, and didn't stay to help."

Shandra crossed her arms, "I'm sorry, I wasn't thinking at the time, not much else to it, next time I will do better."

Caitlin interjected, "Well we were asked to help guard from a Delvin attack by the Guild Master, the entire reason we went, anyways Ethan is home and a little tipsy, he said a few funny things and went to his bedroom."

Alastor laughed.

Shandra called for Yanni, Yanni did not come. Alastor was worried and spoke, "Shandra you didn't do anything to Yanni, did you?"

Shandra, indignant, arms still crossed, "What Alastor, no, why would say such a thing? Yanni has gone missing before."

Alastor spoke softly, "Sorry, my demon half does not have patience, I hope Yanni returns soon. It also means we have to go to the Abbith market to eat."

Jas, a little shaky in his voice, "Yanni welcomed me to Remiel House and set up a room for me, that was a few hours ago."

Caitlin smiled, "I'm sure Yanni will return, the place is not the same otherwise."

A silvery line appeared in the main room, everyone stopped chatting. Alastor stood then Caitlin, Sarah and Jas stood from the table, Shandra was already standing. The phase got bigger and blurry. A beautiful butterfly humanoid stepped through.

Caitlin spoke first "Mixy!"

Mixy smiled, she was a vision, she had lilac skin, four lovely slender arms, beautiful butterfly like wings with mirrored spots, and long white silvery hair to her waist; she had lilac antenna on her head and wore a lovely navy gown finished with a tabard of Illumination.

Mixy spoke with an air of importance in her voice, "Hello my friends, I bring an official message from the Lady of Light. In two days' time we will go to war on the Nevid plane and finish the evil of the Delvin race. We seek to destroy Morack and his army, his lair and free any of his captives. Once we have cleansed his plane, Phase Walkers and the people of Lorvisa will be free to live in harmony. Would the brave Phase Walker companions who saved our people before aid us in the war?"

Everyone spoke at once, Jas agreeing straight away, Wuzzle mumbled something, Raznik, no, Caitlin excited said yes. Alastor mentioned something about getting wings and Sarah agreed with a nod while Shandra stood listening and took it all in.

Mixy was a little confused, "I'm sorry can one person talk at a time please, Caitlin first?"

Caitlin gave a cheeky grin and looked at Jas, "Wuzzle, Jas and I would gladly help."

Mixy smiled, "Thank you, Sarah?"

Sarah, who was silent before, spoke up, "Yes Mixy, I will help."

Mixy looked at Alastor, "Will you help?"

Alastor, trying his patience, responded, "Yes I will help, I also want to retrieve a fallen Celestial's wings from Morack's throne room, can that be arranged?"

Mixy responded graciously, "Yes of course Alastor, all those captured by Morack will also be freed."

Mixy smiled at Shandra, who didn't look keen, her arms were crossed, "I will help the Lady of Light, Mixy."

Alastor was not close to his twin anymore, the close bond he once felt with her was gone, but he wasn't entirely sure if it was because of his change, or more so something to do with

Shandra, he didn't recognise his own twin any more. The way she spoke and carried herself was all so different.

Mixy spoke, "Thank you all for accepting the Lady of Light's invitation to go to war with the Delvin. Might I suggest you come into the Lorvisa plane tomorrow so we can talk tactics, we go to war the following day."

Caitlin spoke, "Will do," then rushed forward and cuddled Mixy, who smiled and placed all her four hands on Caitlin, who looked like a tiny child because Mixy was so tall.

Mixy spread her silverly mirrored wings and opened a phase back to Abbith Market, Caitlin could tell because she used it so often the blurry image was becoming recognisable. Mixy turned and waved then walked through the phase.

Caitlin turned to Shandra, "I think Jas and Sarah need a Phase Walker lesson."

Shandra uncrossed her arms, "I guess so, it seems tomorrow we go to Lorvisa, let's go, follow me."

Yanni glowed blue, she was inside a cave where there was a pool of green water, it was still, Yanni felt safe, she was underground and this place was familiar to her. Yanni floated above the green water of the pool, hovered for a time, then dove straight in. The cave was silent and the water was still.

There was more coughing, Jenith lay on the ground. A splatter of blood was on his bed and a pool of blood on the floor. The price of working with the Knoxcred stones was taking its toll. Jenith stared up at the ceiling, wondering if this coughing fit will pass like the others, then wondered about Shandra, annoyed she took something that was his, but sad that he scared her away. Jenith lifted his weak hand to his mouth and wiped more blood away, his vision began to blur and he could make out a grey moving blur, at first he thought it was wings, but he could see it was hair and a flash of white wings.

It was the Guild Master, he must of come to check on his progress, "Jenith, I did not realise you have been unwell, I apologise I did not notice earlier, you will be ok, just rest."

Jenith relaxed and closed his eyes.

The Lady of Light was standing in the Chapter house and several members of the Illumination were adjusting silvery armour she wore, it was ornate and complex, each piece radiated light magic, and it seemed the Lady of Light was preparing for war.

There were several personal guards of the Lady of Light in the Chapter house, each was wearing ornate armour, each was from a different house. Two spideroids, grasshopperoids, centipedoids, along with a handful of Lords and Ladies of Illumination, it was a great honour to be on her personal guard. Only leaders and elders were in the Chapter house.

The court of Illumination on the Island of Illuminoid was almost empty, several guards were placed around on minimum watch and there was a bad smell in the air.

A phase opened, it was silvery and slowly widened, several guards came forward ready and watched. Another guard went to summon more.

A little girl stepped through, she winked at the guards of Illumination, smiled and said "Hey there."

The guards stood back, a few went back to their posts, and a huge brown bear walked through on his hind legs and came to the little girl's side. Several moments later the little girl turned to watch the phase she just walked through, putting her small finger to her face she started wondering what's taking so long. A little boy came through the phase, he was jet black with large white feathered wings, he looked striking then walked with purpose and held his head high, he tried not to open his mouth at the strange things his saw, the high glass dome and strange smell.

The little girl smiled, "Hi Jas, over here," then gave a small wave.

Jas replied, "Hi Caitlin, we had to clean up a mess before we came through."

An angelic blond haired Celestial with huge golden feathered wings out spread stepped through the silvery phase, she wore a white gown and blue symbols glowed on it.

She looked at the two small children and spoke, "Yes there was a mess, it's been very hard with no Yanni."

Shandra walked closer to Caitlin and turned to watch the phase, with the others.

The guards watched on, so did the small gathering of Phase Walkers, a cross breed walked through the phase, it wore a hat, coat and large boots. At first the guards looked tense then they just watched on as a pretty human with blond hair, wearing blue skinny jeans and a white shirt, walked through. Looking closer there was a tiny food stain on the front of her shirt. The phase snapped shut.

The guards returned to their posts and a high ranking Lady of Illumination smiled and flew towards them from the sky "Greetings Phase Walkers, the Lady of Light is in the Chapter house, please join her there, rooms will be made available to you for rest, tomorrow is a big day, preparations have been ongoing."

The Lady of Illumination landed completely her wings stopped flapping, "This way please, follow to the Chapter house."

The Phase Walkers followed the Lady of Illumination over a bridge, off the island of Illuminoid, past several structures, until they reached the Chapter house. Jas was a wide eyed child the entire journey, it was not that long ago that he spent his entire existence underwater, the other Phase Walkers, even Sarah, getting used to seeing different things on other planes merely just took it all in.

They arrived at the Chapter house, which was huge with many rooms. It was totally organic, a living building. Many plants entwined around each other to form a large hall which the Phase Walkers walked down. There were live flowers around the doorway and a thick rectangle of grass formed hallway carpet. Inside large mushrooms formed seats and a throne was at the back of the room, smaller than the Illumination court but still decadent, ornate and shiny. A few Lords and Ladies of Illumination were seated in the hall chatting softly. More seemed to come through the open doors as if a gathering was taking place. The Lords and Ladies of Illumination wore their blue tabards with a golden triangle. The whispering stopped when the Lady of Light materialised in front of the throne.

The Lady of Light was beautiful, her wings shined. Her long hair moved as she walked down the stairs from the throne to the mushrooms. There was complete silence as the Lady of Light was going to speak and her words were joy, "Greetings my Lords and Ladies of Illumination, greetings Phase Walkers," the Lady of Light Smiled.

The Lords and Ladies turned to see the entrance of the Phase Walkers. A Lady of Illumination showed them to mushroom seats which had promptly became unoccupied. Caitlin looked strange, this small tiny pink dressed creature sitting on a mushroom, even stranger a large brown bear called Wuzzle stood behind her. Sarah and Alastor shared a mushroom, both sitting at the very edge away from each other. Jas and Shandra also shared a single mushroom seat, Jas was in awe of everything and stared at a butterfly humanoid Lord.

The Lady of Light waited and then continued, "Tomorrow our people and trusted friends will go through to the Delvin plane. There we will attack not only the Delvin but Morack himself. We will set wrongs and make them right, freeing any hostages Morack has taken in his lair and slaying any Delvin that are in sight."

"It is unfortunate that we have to cleanse Nevid of the Delvin but the Lorvisa people cannot live in fear of the next attack. We simply cannot lose any more of our populace and cannot give any more power to Morack. The plan of attack was as before, we will enter the phase simultaneously, I will signal all three known phase points."

Jas squirmed in his mushroom seat, he could feel a transformation coming on, trying to stop it he tensed. He tried to control it, straining, but once in motion he gave up and relaxed, and raised an eyebrow to Shandra who was looking at him.

The Lady of Light did not notice and spoke on, "The mining workers will head to the southern phase point near the new mining excavation, so this will be easy for them to get to, and will attack those in the underground brood mother's complex."

"The guards, which will be the frontal attack and will use the court of Illuminations phase point, they will descend underground to Morack's lair and slaughter all the Delvin within including Morack. There are also reports of Phase Walker prisoners, which should be released and set free."

"Guardians of the Sky Shade will attack those small conclaves of Delvin shattered around Nevid from the Sky."

"Phase Walker friends, which group would you join?"

Alastor stood and spoke, "I will join the guards and go to Morack's lair."

Sarah also stood and spoke, "And I."

Caitlin stood on tippy toes on top of her mushroom, "We will all go to Morack's lair, it's best we stay together."

Jas and Shandra stood silent. Caitlin looked over to Jas and he had changed form, he was a Lord of Illumination, a nice shiny black one with mirrored wings. She ignored his change and sat down, no one else seemed to have noticed Jas's change.

A Lady of Illumination motioned with her hands to follow and the group of Phase Walkers were led down a hall to another room that was filled with cushions and then branched off into what looked like many bedrooms.

Once out of the main chapter house the Lady of Illumination spoke, "Please relax here or take a rest in a bedroom. Early before dawn you will be awoken to prepare for the attack on Nevid. Food will be brought soon."

The Lady of Illumination bowed and then left the room. It was quite.

Everyone sat on cushions in the room, even Wuzzle who usually stood.

Caitlin looked up, "I'm actually tired, I need a rest, I know what needs to be done in the morning."

Caitlin walked off to a bedroom and Wuzzle faithfully followed behind her.

Caitlin came into a little room, it had flowers growing out the walls in little patterns. A bunch of straw material was piled in the corner, Caitlin sighed, "Pillow top, I need you," then walked up to the straw and tried to curl up and sleep. Wuzzle sat on the ground not far and lent up against a wall and closed his eyes.

Shandra sat next to her twin brother Alastor and Sarah sat a little away, where Jas was. Sarah questioned, "Is that you Jas?"

Everyone looked his way, awaiting a response, "Yes, sorry, I changed form again."

Sarah looked at him, a short Lord of the Illumination, the only thing he was missing was the tabard – he wore the same clothes that he had before as a celestial boy. The texture of his wings and addition of antenna were his only change of shape, he was still the same size of a boy.

A little embarrassed, Jas shrugged being left with the adults, he stood and said, "I think I need to sleep for a while myself, see you in the morning." Jas headed into another bedroom.

Sarah smiled and replied, "Have a good sleep Jas."

Shandra tried to hide a laugh and put her hands to her mouth.

Sarah shifted closer to Alastor and Shandra.

Shandra spoke when Sarah looked at her, "This time I will battle, I am ready and I also feel the cause just," she gave a strange smile and flexed her wings almost as if smiling about something totally different.

"I usually don't require much sleep but I need to clear my head by myself," Shandra clutched a pouch hung from around a belt and walked into another bedroom then shut the door loudly.

Sarah smiled at Alastor, "I guess that leaves you and me."

Alastor looked distant and deep in thought, he looked at her like it was the first time and responded, "I need to rest for a few hours myself."

"As do I," Sarah said and stood at the same time as Alastor. They both walked off to a bedroom and realised there was only one unoccupied. Alastor stood at the bedroom door, "I will sleep in the common."

Sarah raised an eyebrow, "Don't be silly, we share an anchor, can't see why we can't share a room."

Alastor, a little taken back by what was said out loud, looked around to see if anyone heard.

Sarah saw that he was hesitating, "I command it."

Alastor walked into the room, Sarah followed and closed the door.

Sarah looked around expecting a bed, then realised she would have to sleep on straw, not something she had ever done before, and with a giant demonic angel in her room that she commanded.

She pondered for a while and sat down on the straw piling it around herself, Alastor stood watching, unsure what to do.

Sarah patted the straw next to her and said, "Come on I don't bite."

Alastor took off his hat and pushed white hair from his face, then placed his hat on the floor. He sat awkwardly next to Sarah and spoke, "I only require a few hours sleep and then I will await you in the common room."

"Fine," Sarah replied, then rolled on to her side to take a closer look at him.

Alastor lay on his back in the straw and looked up at the ceiling, his tailed poked to the side.

Surely he could feel her eyes on him, Sarah thought. Alastor did not move his head but shifted his eyes to glance at Sarah, smirked, then closed both his eyes, having demon thoughts.

Sarah watched him for some time until she realised his eyes were not opening again, then went to sleep, a deep sleep.

Alastor had a dream of sheer torment, a vision appeared, Morack's face was snarling, his red flesh flashed past Alastor. Morack turned to fill a glass vial with liquid, his black braid flicked past Alastor who was strapped into a chair, holding him down. Alastor flexed his arms again to try and get free, he knew this was a memory of one of Morack experiments. Morack's demonic face was close to his while he injected him with Chaos tainted magic through a large needle. It was burning Alastor from the inside; pain was all through his body. Alastor awoke in a sweat and sat upright. He looked over to see Sarah asleep in straw, some poked through her hair. Alastor reached over and pulled a few bits of straw out with his large clawed fingers. Sarah did not move and Alastor picked up his hat and walked out to the common room, closing the door softly behind him.

The common was empty except a few navy blue pillows that scatter the floor, all the doors to bedrooms were closed. Alastor stood silently for a time until he heard words whispered within a bedroom. He slowly crept to the door and listened, he recognised it to be a female voice, that of Shandra, he wondered who would be in there with her.

"I will do it, you can count on me, no, I am not backing out of this, that is correct."

Alastor's hoofed feet were in his black leather boots, sometimes he lost his balance in them and tonight was no exception, Alastor slipped and caught his step, roughly stamping his foot down. The bedroom door opened and

Shandra looked out.

Alastor, caught in his own surprise, smiled at Shandra, who was putting something into a leather pouch around her waist. Alastor spoke, "Sister, do you want company, I came to see if you were awake?"

Shandra straightened her dress and came out, closing the bedroom door behind her, "Yes Alastor, I always have time for my twin brother, let's sit," she motioned to the cushions on the ground.

Alastor and Shandra sat together and spoke in whispers, occasionally Alastor laughed softly.

It was morning and the Phase Walkers were starting to awake, Wuzzle was hungry and he was the first to enter the common room, Shandra and Alastor stopped talking and Wuzzle shrugged. Caitlin followed in her girly pink dress and stood behind Wuzzle, hand on hip, and Wuzzle moved to the side.

Caitlin yawned, "So where is the food?"

Shandra looked up and responded, "I do not know, perhaps we should go look."

Shandra began to stand and in that moment Sarah opened her door and walked into the common room. Sarah walked towards Shandra, standing next to her. Caitlin looked at the only door still closed, "Someone needs to wake Jas."

Caitlin walked up to the door and started to knock when it opened, a mini black Lord of Illumination walked out, he was also wearing a tabard of Illumination with the golden triangle in the centre.

Caitlin giggled, "Well what do we have here?"

Jas smiled, "I found it in the cupboard, if I'm going to look like one of them I might as well wear their fashion."

Shandra broke into the conversation a little rudely, "Let's look for breakfast before we go to war," then started to head out of the common room.

A Lady of Illumination came toward them as they were

walking through the Chapter house hall, "Do you require anything before you go to the phase point as planed?"

Shandra spoke coolly, "Yes, we all require breakfast."

As if on cue, Wuzzles stomach gave a low growl.

The Lady of Illumination motioned with her hand and walked on, going through several halls and open rooms until she came to a well set up eating hall.

She motioned them to sit at a wooden log fashioned into a table and small grass mounds which could only be described as the chairs.

Everyone sat on the grass mounds except Wuzzle, who was too big; he sat at the end of the table. Several servers came toward the table and placed bowls of food on the table, Wuzzle was indeed hungry. A bowl contained flowers and leaves, another had strange smelling liquid and a third had grainy porridge of sorts which looked cold and the most inviting. Shandra began to heat the porridge using light magic and dished it out into several smaller bowls, then placed a pretty blue flower onto of hers. Caitlin copied and the rest followed and ate in silence.

The room was warm and much more ornate than Morack would of liked, a large stone alter with a rounded blue egg glowed through straw. A small fire was to the side, a source of the warmth, and two grey Delvin bowed then stood along the wall. The room smelt like sulphur and ash.

Morack touched the egg, the creature inside squirmed at his touch. He looked over at the grey Delvin and spoke, "Any changes report to me immediately, our new brood mother will bring glory to our kind."

Without waiting for a response Morack walked out of the egg chamber and scraped his hooves on the stone floors leading upwards. He passed outside a large wooden door and stopped, loud guttural voices came from within. There were many scratches from claws on the wood of the door and a small hunter's spiral symbol was deeply carved.

Morack pushed open the door. There were four large wooden beds along the wall and a large fire pit was at the very far end, four shadows danced along the walls. His hunters, Morack thought, then clapped his clawed hands together and walked to the fire pit.

- Chapter 23 -

Keyness

Sarah was standing in the Court of Illumination, the glass dome shined and, strangely, a calm breeze brought a sweet smell to the air. Alastor stood at her side, he looked worried but determined. His sister Shandra stood with her arms crossed and Jas and Caitlin looked like strange action figures standing before a large army of butterfly humanoid creatures. Sarah had to rub her tattoo a few times to try and snap her thoughts back to the situation.

A feeling of joy came over Sarah, it felt intense, and then she heard the voice of the Lady of Light, "My people, today is the day that we no longer will we live in fear of Delvin attacks, no longer will our kind be taken and captured by those demon creatures. You have been briefed and know your roles, go forward now and cleanse Nevid of the Delvin."

The joy left Sarah's body and she looked over to Alastor, who smirked at her. Sarah then began to tingle, the phase point within the Court of Illumination began to glow, it was intense, so much phase energy was active, many Lords and Ladies of Illumination were activating the phase. It grew and was silvery and misty, but features were starting to fine up, she could see what was on the other side of the phase, her mind filled with ones, she could do nothing but link with them as the pull to open this phase was strong, the phase grew larger then she had ever seen. Morack's throne room was clear and every detail was to be seen, down to the stone textures on the floor, it was empty of Delvin from what she could make out. A group of Lords and Ladies of Illumination charged into the phase, some using their wings and flying into the phase, it was that huge.

Alastor started for the phase at a brisk pace, Sarah had to almost run to catch up to him, watching him step through the phase, and then she followed.

Morack's throne room was empty, the Lords and Ladies of Illumination ran down the many halls, guttural loud roars were heard and the clash of phase weapons. Alastor knew exactly where he was and ran down the hall, Sarah followed, dead Delvin littered their path, Alastor walked over them and arrived at a locked door. A lord of Illumination conjured a strange axe phase weapon and smashed the door open, the room was vast and not like Alastor remembered. Cages of Phase Walkers lined the walls, they cheered upon seeing the Lords and Ladies come through the door, Sarah looked around and followed Alastor like a shadow. Alastor saw his prize, Morack, who was standing at the end of the room, he was drinking from a cup which he dropped when Alastor looked at him. Morack opened a phase and walked through, snapping it shut, but not before a Lord of Illumination used light magic to strike his arm.

Alastor ran to where Morack was standing and looked around as if Morack may come back. The Lords and Ladies started to free the phase prisoners, carefully removing their collars.

Caitlin, Wuzzle, Jas and Shandra moved though the Phase into Morack's throne room, the smell of sulphur lingered in the air as it caught their senses. The cries of battle echoed down the hall, but the noise did not distract from the horrendous sight before Caitlin's childlike eyes, what she saw was the wings, dried blood marked white feathers and crude rusted nails poked out, attaching them to the wall. She knew these were what haunted Alastor and pointed them out to Shandra, who took flight up to the wings mounted on the wall and started to take out the nails using light magic. Caitlin and

Jas stood watching, Shandra brought them down and placed the bloodied huge wings at Caitlin's feet. Shandra was silent and merely nodded.

Shandra looked sickened and twisted in disgust, an expression Caitlin had never seen on Shandra's face, she took a step backward to Wuzzle. Shandra stared at the wings for some time then was very angry at the trophy winged display of one of her kind. She put her hand to her leather pouch and spoke coldly, "Jas, come with me, Caitlin, you stay with the wings and block any Delvin that attempt to escape."

Caitlin agreed with a nod and Jas silently followed Shandra who was heading down the hall. Jas was wide eyed and saw many fallen Delvin and a few Lords and Ladies of Light running through the halls, some with wounds that looked fatal. A group of Lords and Ladies of Illumination walked by, they looked weak and frail, their eyes gaunt and haunted. Shandra pushed through it all and walked for some time, the echoes of screams and battle become distant, Jas still following behind. Heavy footsteps were behind them and Shandra and Jas turned around with phase weapons drawn, Alastor and Sarah were running toward them.

Alastor spoke when almost upon them, "Things have changed from when I was here, like that door," Alastor pointed at a large wooden door with a deep spiral etched into the wood.

Listening to the door using the phase, Alastor could hear guttural Delvin voices. Alastor spoke in a whisper, "More in here."

Shandra snapped her fingers, "Allow me brother," she wove a spell that contained light magic mixed with chaos, Alastor could feel it but at that very moment did not care, he wanted the door open, he could not contain his building demonic rage.

The door swung open and four Delvin stopped packing large bags and looked in the direction of the open door. Alastor knew these were Morack's prized hunters and did something he thought was beyond him, a strong light magic flowed from his fingers it was raw and untainted and struck all four Delvin. Nothing happened, Alastor was angry and charged them. A black Delvin raised his hand and blinked away, Alastor felt phase power. Two blue Delvin dropped a large grey sack to the ground and also blinked away, followed by the purple that grinned and also blinked away. Alastor knew exactly where they went, their Anchor, and then began to scream in frustration, almost a howl. Sarah was scared and had not seen this side of Alastor before, she stepped back until the cold wall touched her back.

Jas stepped forward and looked inside the sack then grinned. He reached inside and picked up a handful of Ianoid stones holding then up, "These are from my village, they were stolen when my village was raided."

Shandra's eyes gleamed at the gems, she touched her pouch again, her movement looked odd, and then folded her arms "Take them to Caitlin, we will meet you in the throne room."

Jas started to drag the sack of stones as they were heavy, he still was only a child and the butterfly humanoid form did not give him any extra strength. He looked down at his diver's watch he was still wearing, three more days, he thought to himself, and left the room dragging the sack.

Shandra watched Jas's struggle and then walked to him and held the other side of the grey sack, "I will help you."

Alastor glanced at Sarah, seeing her standing back away from him and became ashamed he could not control his demon within, rage still filled him but he willed himself to contain it.

They were in a large cave, it was warm and everything felt right in the universe. The sound of hooves scraping stone echoed inside the cave which contained large Delvin sized chairs and a table. Grimlock was at the end of the table, he was wielding chaos creation magic but there was something more, a strange feeling but it wasn't bad. Grimlock smiled upon seeing three Delvin faces approach. He tossed his deep red hair back and raised his arms, then smirked and clapped his hands. A Delvin feast appeared, chunks of meat and cups of ale. A strange arrangement of pretty flowers was oddly in the centre of the table. Grimlock reached over grabbed the flowers, puzzled, and then tossed them under the table.

"Brothers, glad you made it, please sit."

Reednak, the smaller blue skinned Delvin with a scar, sat at the table and began to eat. Grimlock raised a red eyebrow, which was very noticeable on his black skin, "So where are the Ianiods?"

Reednak just shrugged and Nica emerged and replied, "We dropped the sack before we came here?"

The purple Delvin, Cayna, approached the table with caution and stood holding a bag filled with weapons.

Grimlock snarled and pointed to Reednak, "Go get it."

Reednak stood up and opened the phase, it felt strange, and then stepped through.

Grimlock strangely smiled, "Well that is solved, please eat."

Cayna and Nica both sat at the table and started to eat, time passed and more ale flowed. There was loud guttural laughter and lots of loud talking.

Grimlock drunk more ale and looked up, "So now Morack's in trouble I say we stay it out in here and do our own thing, go to other phases and take what we want, we can be kings."

"Kings, and have what we want," Nica, the large blue oversized Delvin, responded in a deep cheerful voice.

Cayna gave a grin then sipped his cup, "We can be anything we like, without Morack we have the power."

Cayna reached for the phase and waved his hand around, "Look what I can do,"

Cayna opened a phase, not like any other because you could clearly see everything on the other side, gold and treasure, strange glowing balls hovered over the top. Then he snapped the phase shut.

Grimlock smiled, "I'll be in that."
Nica responded, "And I."

Alastor moved toward Sarah and gave a faint smile, Sarah pointed behind him with her delicate index finger. Alastor turned to see a blue Delvin with a scar on his face, its phase weapon, a sword, was drawn. Alastor raised his fist and started to run toward the Delvin, it laughed as it smacked Alastor to the ground with the hilt of its sword, "Morack's pet is weak."

The blue Delvin started toward Sarah and she reached for the phase, her sword materialised and she rushed forward and started to hit out at the Delvin as Alastor laid at her feet. The blue Delvin stopped and looked at the doorway, perplexed. Sarah used this time of its indecision to strike and a small cut slashed the blue's arm.

The blue Delvin screamed in pain and looked in the doorway again, then he blinked out of the room.

Sarah released her phase weapon, her long sword, and went to Alastor's side, a huge bruise was appearing above his forehead, she sat for a time and studied him, unsure what to do or how to help. She peered down at his features, all so human, she thought, then stroked his white hair from his face, revealing his black horns, and waited until Alastor moved. Alastor did slowly, he put his hand to his head and sat up.

Sarah helped him stand and was feeling a moment. She stood closer to Alastor on tippy toes and kissed him softly on the lips. Alastor pushed her firmly away and took a step back. Sarah studied his face and ran out of the room.

Alastor was dizzy and sat on the ground.

Sarah was not thinking, she ran through the halls not recalling which way she came in, she cried and slowed her pace as she passed a room that was warm. There were footsteps behind her, she did not care she only imagined it was Alastor. It was dark and the only thing she could think of was to get out of here, she walked further into the darkness and opened a phase to Earth.

Sarah stepped through, she was in an alley, the bins smelled, she covered her nose with her hand as she opened another phase to her apartment then promptly walked through, it snapped shut behind her.

Another studied the phase to Earth for a time, one that had seen many phases and this destination was new. It was a figure that held a large blue egg, its contents squirmed and in the dark the figure stepped through the phase it snapped shut.

Morack was in an alley, it was daylight, there were large bins to the side, it smelt bad, his large horns reached for the blue sky and red skin shined from the sun. His hooves scraped on an asphalt ground and his tail swayed in the wind. Unsure of where he was, he followed the road to the main street clutching the egg. A passer-by stared, then walked on and several cars were on the road.

Sarah stepped out of a warm shower, she looked down at a bruise on her leg, wiped it softly, then reached for her white fluffy dressing gown, rugged up, and then took her bathroom towel and towelled her hair dry, finishing off wrapping her hair in the towel. She sniffed and could still smell sulphur in her nose, she sprayed soft rose perfume to mask its smell.

Sarah walked out of the bathroom went to the cupboard and looked for chocolate, none. She walked into her lounge room, sat on the lounge put her feet up then turned the TV on. A romance movie, pass, she flipped to music videos and then concentrated, she opened a tiny phase put her hand in and pulled out several large chocolate bars, she closed the phase, sniffed and started to unwrap them. Her phone beeped with a message, then again.

She put the chocolate down and read the message on her phone 'Sarah, are you ok where are you? Caitlin'.

Sarah sent a message back 'I'm back home on Earth resting I had to leave sorry –Sarah'.

The moment she hit send another message arrived on her

phone, 'I'm sorry, I miss you – William'. Seriously, Sarah thought to herself then picked up another chocolate bar.

Alastor was dizzy, he had a massive blue bump on his head that looked painful, he was alone in the hunter's room. He stood slowly and could hear nothing, so he walked back to the throne room, several bodies of dead Delvin were in the hall, he stepped over them, the throne room was a hive of activity, several Lords and Ladies of Illumination were carrying their dead and walking through the large open phase.

Caitlin put her mobile in her pink pocket and was softly talking to Shandra, Wuzzle was holding what looked like a celestial body, but getting closer Alastor could tell it was Keyness's wings. He walked quicker and came to his sister. Shandra stood with her hand on her hip and was about to speak when Caitlin interrupted, "You are awake and you had a small hit to the head, we thought it best to let you rest a bit, the throne room is clear and we have gone through all the rooms. We were actually about to come get you so we can go back to the Lady of Light, she is very happy with the outcome here and wishes to thank us personally."

Alastor walked closer to Wuzzle, "But Keyness needs to be at rest," bowing his head.

Shandra took his arm, "Brother the Lady of Light will not keep us long, we have come this far."

Alastor nodded, then a fleeting set of thoughts raced through his mind, Sarah running and the look of shock on her face, he dismissed his thoughts and let Shandra hold his arm and walked through the phase back to Lorvisa.

The phase power was strong, stepping through and arriving in the environment of Lovisa, Alastor was tired and felt fleeting thoughts go through his mind, once again of Sarah, he suppressed them. They walked on until he was standing in the court of the Lady Light, it was bright daylight and the sun reflected off the glass domed roof. There was a large gathering and many flying creatures hovered overhead. The Lady of Light beamed with radiance, her armoured wings reflected the light.

She used her devotion aura, all on the planet Lorvisa felt it, all paid attention to her words, "Thank you people of Lorvisa, today is the first day of sheer Light, today is the day we are truly free to not live in fear, today is the day all the evil Delvin have fallen. Rest my people for today and tomorrow we rejoice."

The devotion aura got weak, then could no longer be felt.

The Lady of Light fell to a knee and several Lords and Ladies of Illumination rushed to support her and rest her on her throne. She sat for a time and looked at the Phase Walkers, she motioned one of her hands forward and gave a weak smile.

The Phase Walkers moved forward, closer to the stairs that led up to the throne and stood, Alastor was being supported by his sister's arm. There was an awkward silence as three Lords of Illumination stood to one side of the throne in their regal tabards, unmarked and clean, while three Ladies of Illumination stood on the other side of the Lady of Light, wearing tabards battle marked, ripped and bloodied.

The Lady of Light spoke, "It saddens me to see there is one of you missing."

Alastor spoke quickly and deeply, "Sarah is hurt?"

Caitlin looked cross at Alastor for speaking, "Sarah, the other Phase Walker, returned to her home phase."

The Lady of Light smiled and spoke, "That is good to hear, I would like to thank you all for what you have done for my people, and you will always be welcome on Lorvisa. If there is anything you need our people will always be at your service."

Shandra bowed awkwardly, as she was holding Alastor in one arm and had the other hand on her pouch, then spoke, "Alastor is in need of healing, if you could help?"

The Lady looked over at Alastor, "Indeed he is, please come forward Alastor of the Celestial plane."

The Lady of Light stood and walked down the steps, her armour made a metallic rustling as she moved. Light reflected off her wings in many directions. Shandra moved forward with Alastor, his head was bruised and he was very weak, so not himself. The Lady of Light put two hands on either side of his bruised head and two hands on his hips, supporting him with all four arms as Shandra stepped back. The antenna on the Lady of Light vibrated and Caitlin recognised nature magic at a strength she had not felt before, even stronger then when the circle of elders healed Wuzzle and herself.

Alastor stood silently as waves of nature magic went through him, he was relieved as he felt the pain of the bruise leave his body. He was no longer feeling tired and was alert. Surprise then was on Alastor face as he felt a euphoria surge through his body, then he felt dark chaos magic leaking through his skin, leaving him, a strong connection to light magic was forming.

Shandra put her hand over her mouth in shock, Caitlin was excited and happy, Jas watched silently with Wuzzle as Alastor's body was changing before their eyes.

His black ebony horns were shrinking through his white hair and his hooves became feet, his tail disappeared and buds of white feathers grew at a rapid rate on his back forming giant wings. The transformation was finished and Alastor was healed, well so he thought, a tiny pang of chaos magic remained surely just an echo of what once was. The Lady of Light let go of Alastor and fell to the ground. The Lords and Ladies rushed to her side, she stood weakly then walked up the small stairs to her throne and sat.

Alastor spread his wings and took flight, hovering over the Lady of Light, "I am restored, you have saved me, I am forever thankful." He felt for chaos magic and he felt a tiny slither he ignored it and rejoiced in his change, feeling every feather in his wings.

The Lady of Light's eyes looked glazed and she motion her hand, "I need to rest, we will talk again, go now," then she collapsed, there where gasps from a small crowd of watchers and the Lady of Light disappeared.

Alastor landed facing Caitlin and Wuzzle, he was feeling good, so good, a small trickle of tears marked his cheek, he turned to see Keyness's wings, his compassion to her plight was strong.

Shandra walked to the centre of the court of Illumination and opened a phase to the Celestial plane. Wuzzle, Caitlin and Jas walked towards her and then through the phase, Alastor walked slower to the phase point, following, and realised not only were the tears for Keyness but for the strong overpowering emotion to another, he felt love.

The ceremony was put together quickly but there still was a dignified elegance to it, the room was open and stood on top of a large tower, the smell of incense was in the air it was silent and an elder of light magic landed through the open arch into the room. The elder's wings were silvery and his robes lined with white magic symbols that glowed silver blue. He walked up to an altar, a white sheet was covering what was left of Keyness. Many flowers were placed at the bottom of the altar and small silvery gems where placed around the white sheet.

Many were in the room, Ethan was comforting Lady Khan by holding her arm, her long black hair covered her face, for that day she said goodbye to her sister. Keyness's mother stood behind her daughter and a younger sibling peeked from behind her legs with tears in her eyes. An elder Celestial held a glass ball.

Jas was back in celestial form, he blended into the crowd. Caitin and Wuzzle were not as lucky, many cast eyes on them as guests landed from flight into the room. Alastor stood furthest from the altar, with his back against the wall, with his sister Shandra. Casting his eyes into the corner of the room he could see Trigan watching on.

A time passed and the light magic elder began to cast magic, everyone was silent. The shiny gems surrounding

Keyness's body glowed with magic and then a wraith-like Keyness appeared, an apparition, a ghost created with light magic, she gave a sad smile and reached for her parents and sisters. There was a soft murmur, words were spoken and not heard. The glass ball glowed with energy as a small part of Keyness allowed herself to remain, as is the tradition of the celestials. Alastor watched and was moved, then Keyness's spirit in turn went to all the guest's, communication was going on but none except those communicating knew what was said.

Keyness came to Alastor's side she placed both of her ghost hands on Alastor and rubbed where his horns used to be, she spoke something to Alastor that Shandra did not hear, hovered to a few more remaining relatives then back to the altar. The elder light magic celestial clapped his hands loudly, releasing strong light magic, all the crystals on Keyness's remains glowed and vibrated, then everything on the altar cleared, no longer was there a white sheet no longer were there flowers.

A bell rung to mark her spirit passing into the light and, as with tradition, everyone left the room taking flight into the air.

Remiel House was full, Ethan was sitting at the fire with Lady Khan, who had a sweet smile that contained her sadness. Shandra was in her room and Wuzzle, Caitlin and Jas sat talking in the common room. Yanni had returned, it was not known why she left but Alastor suspected foul play and chaos magic and still could not shake it was all Shandra's doing.

Trigan's metallic coppery skin glowed off the flames of the fire as he stood behind Ethan, a good friend he was to his brother, Alastor thought.

Trigan moved to Alastor and smiled, licking his lips with a blue tongue, "Ethan told me you need some help with your appearance?"

Trigan popped the collar on his stylish shirt and beamed

through glowing purple eyes.

Alastor motioned his hand over to his bedroom, "I prefer privacy."

Trigan followed into his room, Alastor closed the door and stretched his white feathered wings, "I need help hiding these – but, but! I don't want to lose them again, okay. I want to enter another plane where wings do not exist."

Trigan laughed, "Oh that plane doesn't happen to have that pretty Earth girl on it, anyways it's pretty simple, watch this."

Trigan twitched his face holding in a laugh and started to move his fingers in light magic, creating what looked like a silver net, then handed it to Alastor.

Alastor held it out, "How's that to help?"

Trigan, looking at his coppery nails, "It's covered in what I call deflectors, whatever it covers is concealed, let me help you."

Trigan took the silvery net and placed it over Alastor's wings, it tingled for a few moments then the wings were gone, Alastor, a little overwhelmed, started to flap his wings faster.

Trigan held his hands up, "Stop doing that or you will break the net and I'll have to make another."

Alastor smiled, knowing his wings where simply just hidden, "Actually could you do that, I probably will need a spare."

Trigan started with light magic, using creation magic, then produced a second, handed it to Alastor and said, "May the luck of the Silver Snake of Igloo be in your favour," winked and tipped his hat.

Alastor packed a small bag and headed to the common room, in a loud voice he spoke, "I've got some business to finish off."

Everyone in the common room stopped talking and looked in his direction, Alastor turned to Lady Khan and bowed, then left through the front door and took flight.

Alastor was wearing blue ripped jeans and a white shirt that Caitlin selected for him, he still did not understand why the jeans had to be damaged, he carried a bag and looked around, he had been here before, if only briefly. It was afternoon, there was a large garbage bin, it smelt bad, he was in an alley. He had Caitlin's memory that she shared to intraphase jump to Sarah's apartment, so he used it, reaching for the phase.

Alastor was in a hallway, there were several doors but he knew which Sarah's was. He walked up to the door and politely knocked. There was movement within and he could hear clicks of locks opening and then Sarah's face peered through a small gap. She opened the door, she was wearing pink pyjamas with bunny rabbits, Sarah's face was surprised, "What are you doing here, please come in."

Alastor entered Sarah small apartment. Sarah looked down at her PJs realising only now what she was wearing and told Alastor to "please sit," motioning to the lounge room.

"I'll just get changed from my sleeping clothes," Sarah walked into her bedroom and slammed the door shut she began to fanatically pull clothes out of her wardrobe and found some jeans and a nice shirt.

After getting dressed she stopped suddenly still and thought, did he have horns and hooved feet, I don't recall horns. She ran to her bedroom door and flung it opened and stared at Alastor.

"You look human," she blurted out, "Why are you here, I haven't heard from anyone in days since the Delvin battle and, um, well your bad reaction to me."

Alastor was sitting on the lounge, he was flicking animal hair off its arm. Sarah looked down at him and spoke, "Oh, that's from Wuzzle, I need to vacuum."

Alastor stood, moved to Sarah, and spoke, "I apologise for my behaviour, I was tainted with demon blood, but now I am free, I have been freed of chaos magic, it is no longer part of me." He felt the tiny glimpse of chaos magic within and shunned the feeling.

He pushed his fingers through his white blond fringe, where his black horns used to be.

Sarah leaned over and put her fingers through his hair then smiled, "So you're human?"

"Not quite," Alastor reached behind himself and pulled the silver net off his wings, "Merely concealed."

He stretched his white feathered wings to full height as they were getting cramped in the net.

Sarah took a step back, taking in Alastor's new form.

Alastor spoke in a warm voice, "Sarah, I came back to you to tell you something."

Sarah raised an eyebrow, recalling why she hadn't spoken to any Phase Walkers lately.

Alastor moved forward and kissed Sarah, who received the kiss in full. They both blinked out into the phase.

Alastor and Sarah, still kissing, were in their Anchor, a small room with an IKEA bed to the side, fresh strawberries and earth cola was in glasses.

They stopped kissing and Sarah laughed, "You don't have to tell me, I know, so does the phase."

Alastor gave a hearty laugh, then with a serious face spoke, "It has to be said, I have feelings for you Sarah."

Sarah hugged Alastor and smiled, "We should have some of the strawberries and coke, I guess we have catching up to do."

Morack attempted to cross the busy road and a car honked their horn, Morack ran across, not knowing what to think of the strange metal creatures that contained creatures. His black hooved feet were loud and clipped and clapped like a horse. He ran until he was in another back alley, there were backdoors and bared windows in the alley. A car turned into that very alley behind Morack, who snorted in a panic and cast chaos magic to dig a hole down, creating an escape, he fell into the hole and sealed it shut above his head. He was in a round tunnel underground, bad smelling water ran under his feet, a smallish dead thing floated down the water, Morack stood to the side and watched it for a time.

The tunnel structure looked made, there were cables on the roof and what looked like a small ladder with sun beams shining through shadows. The cables on the roof glowed red and made a static noise. Morack was curious and wanted to see what it was, after all he was in a new plane he placed the large blue egg down and reached up to touch the cables, because of his height it was very easy for him to reach, he was standing in the smelly water.

Electricity surged through his clawed hand and into his red muscled body right down to his demonoid tail and through his horns. Morack could not let go and could not reach for chaos magic, his huge body shook and pain seared through. The blue egg rolled on its side as Morack's hooved foot kicked it in his spasmodic dance. A larger gush of water came through the tunnel, just enough to catch the egg and push it down stream slowly. Morack finally let go of the cable and fell to the side, his eyes open staring at the cables on the roof of the tunnel, lifeless. A small furry brown rat ran to Morack's lifeless body and a gush of dirty water trickled over his hooved foot.

THE END

Made in the USA
Charleston, SC
31 August 2014